The creation of this work was made possible by the generous support of my patrons. It was originally published on the Archive Of Our Own under the alias *duckbunny*. Additional works can be found through www.patreon.com/duckbunny.

Benedict von Kein is a pseudonym of Benjamin Cain.

THE CHALICE INVERTED

A NOVEL
BY
BENEDICT VON KEIN

For Isobel, Penny and Roz

PART ONE:
THE DISTANT THRONE

CHAPTER ONE – SUMMER 196

The Senate of the Empire meets in a building of wood and canvas, raised bare inches above the Anvil soil. The room is plain and almost featureless, with only a little nook at the entrance where the scribe prepares the motions, and the silent presence of the Throne upon the dais, a seat of smooth bare wood carved with Imperial horses. The banners of the nations hang upon the Senate walls, and beneath the Throne, on the Senate floor, the business of ruling is done.

The public gallery on this hot summer evening is almost empty. The Emperor is not present, leaving the harassed Speaker to pace the dais and keep the Senate in order. She is a lanky Dawnish yeowoman named Marianne, whose purple sash of office clashes badly with her yellow-gold livery, and she looks to Isaella's eyes as though she would like a drink, or failing that, a large stick with which to corral the Senators.

Isaella found her way to Anvil almost by accident. Her second tour with the Black Thorns in newly won Segura is up, and she is undecided on whether to sign for a third; her chitty of service is enough to purchase a grove of ambergelt in her native Miaren, and her saved wages enough to pay someone else to manage it.

Her feet are drawn to walk the Trods again. And so she has been walking, with no particular goal in mind, and fetched up here at the solstice, almost the breadth of the Empire away from the western border. She has been to Anvil before, but only during the quiet of the seasons, when there is nothing to be seen but the empty Senate and the ancient stones of the monuments. This tent city is new to her.

The Senate is as fabled in legend as the dusty fields of Anvil that surround it, but just now Isaella cannot see why. The Senators are reputedly the finest political minds of the Empire. At least two of them are drinking already and most of the rest more concerned with greeting old friends than the business set before them. Perhaps they are more solemn when the Emperor sits among them, but Isaella wonders. She watches comfortably from the viewing gallery, leaning over the railing to eavesdrop on the polite disagreements over military funding and keep an eye on her own Senator, who is apparently up for re-election tomorrow.

Footsteps ring loud on the suspended floorboards of the Senate. Isaella turns to see who's joined her in the public gallery, and her hand leaps to her knife.

He is young, unmarked by age or care. His skin is winter-sallow, in defiance of the season, and made paler by his ivory robes, the sash of burgundy silk around his waist. He is half-smiling, the expression lingering on his face from the moment before their eyes met. His right hand is lifted, cocked over the magician's rod at his belt.

For a breathless moment, neither of them moves. The thread between them draws tight.

Then he raises his hand, with his weapon still undrawn. His eyes flicker towards the Senators, oblivious in their chamber, as if to say *we can't fight here*. Isaella's knife hums eagerly under her fingers.

She releases it. She spreads her hand, to show that it is empty, and lets it drop to her side. The heat fades from the air, the pounding beat of danger.

He is beautiful.

The stranger steps closer, though still out of arm's reach, and bows. "Nicovar," he says.

Isaella ducks her head in answer, aware of how inelegantly she bows, and knowing better than to think he will shake her hand. The people of the mountains do not touch strangers. "Isaella Thornborn."

Nicovar half-turns, to lean against the railing and give at least the appearance of watching the Senate business. Isaella echoes him, keeping her hands pointedly relaxed. "This is interesting," she says, almost daring him to name what just happened.

"Yes. You're important, clearly. I don't understand why yet. But you felt it too; what would the Navarri call it?"

Isaella's heart leaps. Clever, as well as beautiful, and all the more dangerous for it. "The Great Dance," she says, "the meeting of souls that know each other."

"What kind of knowledge is this, then?" Nicovar looks at her sidelong, from under his dark eyelashes, his gaze flickering down to her shoulders, her hands, a breach in his Urizeni reserve. She shrugs, letting her muscles flex more than is strictly necessary.

"That remains to be seen," she says, while the Senate divides down the middle, voting nay on her side, aye on his. "But I look forward to finding out."

He is the loveliest viper she's ever seen.

Nicovar had plans for this evening, but he has forgotten them. There is a creature of deadly grace standing next to him, casually resting her arms upon the railing as though her whole posture did not shout her readiness to fight. He can see it in the line of her back, the bend of her knees, as she can no doubt see it in him.

She is glorious. He is no stranger to the charms of warriors, knows his weakness for the physical arts. But though he has bedded soldiers, he has never seen anyone like this. She is not dressed in robes and sashes; she is barely dressed, by conservative standards. Her dark arms are bare to the shoulders, her tunic belted in at the waist, and her trousers are distractingly tight. A deep red tattoo, the colour of fresh blood, loops down her brow and onto the curve of her high cheekbone, framing her eye in a coiling twist of vines. A long knife is sheathed at her back, where her hand snapped when he came in, when their eyes met.

She's dangerous.

The scholarly description of – *this* – might be a spontaneous manifestation of the Web. Things are connected. Something has flamed into existence between them, and if Nicovar thinks she might kill him if he touched her – if he might kill her, if she tried – whatever the shape of it, the shock of recognition cannot be denied. Isaella is important.

The Senate is not so interesting, but now is not the time to lose himself in mysteries of the soul. He understands the apparatus of the Empire, on paper; if he is to achieve anything, he must see how to pull their strings, and here before him is a lesson. He tries to pay attention.

Isaella is a flame beside him, blazing in the corner of his eye.

She leaves first, when the Senate have moved on to wrangling over the precise funding of a new fortification in Spiral. Nicovar finds himself turning as she goes past, guarding his back from her knife. Isaella half-smiles, but she does the same, stepping backwards away from him. "I'll see you around," she says, and it's not a question. He can think of nothing more eloquent to do than bow.

The Imperial Conclave does not meet until even the late summer sunset has faded from the sky. It's almost full dark before Nicovar steps up to the black stones of the regio and invokes the Lock and Key.

The air ripples around him as he steps forward. There are snatches of voices, his fellow magicians, around him on this path through a place that may only theoretically exist, flashes of colour and light. Then there is a steady golden glow, and the chatter of a crowd so dense he stops in his tracks.

He knew, of course he knew, that the Hall of Worlds would contain many magicians when the Conclave met. He did not expect it to be empty.

He only expected it to be larger.

There must be a hundred magicians here. At least. And the room is large enough for a fifth of them. There's no way to move around without brushing into someone. He can hear more people pressing in behind him, voices energetically loud, and Nicovar thinks *lowlanders* in a vicious wave of disgust, before he catches himself. The lowlanders may be comfortable in this crowd, but they are not responsible for the size of the room, and there is a space in that corner where he may be able to breathe.

He is not the only Urizeni retreating to the back. They fold their arms carefully, tuck their hands into their sleeves, trying to take up less of the limited room and avoid unintentional contact with what must be near-strangers. Nicovar finds his hand drifting towards his weapon, and forces himself to stop. To draw wand or blade in this room would trigger a bloodbath. Instead he takes himself to the very edge of the space and sets his back to the gently glowing wall.

He wishes he'd come into the Hall of Worlds before. But he wanted to see it like this first, being used for its proper purpose – antechamber to the Realms it may be, but that is only nature. Humanity has made it more than that. It's a shame humanity could not furnish it with better acoustics, or a floor not carpeted in grass, or more space. The Orders are all intermingled, until Ruth of Necropolis, the Conclave's chief civil servant, rings a piercingly loud bell and demands that the Grandmasters present her with their head-counts, now, please. Then there is a moving chaos, as the magicians try to finish their conversations and find their Orders and divide into groups in a space much too small for them. Nicovar discovers his place by the simple expedient of waiting until he can pick out someone shouting "Arch! Celestial Arch, over here," and then taking a steadying breath and pushing his way through the massed bodies.

The Grandmaster of the Celestial Arch is a tall woman with tightly curled horns, grandmotherly in her red Varushkan wool. She sighs at Nicovar when he raises his hand to be counted. "You're new. Are you in the Arch? Have you got the arcane mark?"

"Yes," he say, truthfully, "I got the mark from Demeter – she hasn't attended recently-"

"Fine. Nice to meet you, glad you could make it, try not to speak out of turn. Anyone else new?"

When the numbers are called, the Celestial Arch is the smallest order present, at seven members, and positioned towards the back. It seems a sad situation for the party of ambition to be in. The Grandmaster threads her way to the front, at the edge of the clear circle around the sand-timers, and without fanfare, the Conclave begins.

The rules of the Conclave are strict, for all they are enforced only by common consent. Nicovar cannot speak on any matter unless he is nominated by a Grandmaster, and it quickly becomes evident that the Celestial Arch is accustomed to letting themselves be spoken for. It chafes. He wants to take up the loose threads of arguments and worry at them until the whole thing falls apart – interrupt the posturing of the Unfettered Mind grandmaster who declaims on the importance of creating rituals to enhance the new Imperial fleet, and receives a profound lack of enthusiasm from her own order. But he isn't given the chance to unravel her arguments with polite interest in why she can't enthuse an order of research magicians enough to have some actual rituals to present, because his Grandmaster barely glances back at the order. Most of them aren't paying attention anyway.

The Warmage stands with an unfolding of long limbs and a broad smile. "Good evenin', boys an' girls," he says, and the Conclave laughs and waves at him, more than ready to be entertained. "I'll keep this short, we've all got more exciting things to be doing. Would you like to know how the wars are going? We've taken back Segura." He waves away the muttering with one hand. "Yes, yes, I know, we took it two seasons ago. Now we've finished the job. That leaves us with four armies that need resupply and a nasty little Thule problem up in Skarsind. We'll be needing a Summer coven with the courage to disturb Cathan Canea's rest and get us a fortress up there, and I know there's at least two of them so don't you give me that look, Anton, it doesn't have to be you. I'll be fighting there tomorrow and I'll let you know how it goes when we get back – any questions? Yes, Bill?"

"Us and who else in Skarsind tomorrow, James?"

The Warmage pulls an exaggerated face of dismay, as if he'd been caught out not knowing. "Marchers, Varushka, Wintermark and Urizen tomorrow. That leaves Dawn, Highguard, Navarr, the League and the Brass Coast going to Spiral to kick some Grendel in the face, they're getting a bit antsy again. Grendel have got a resupply caravan we want to knock over, Thule tomorrow is just a good honest ruck-"

"One minute!"

He spreads his hands and shrugs. Ruth is trying to manage the sand-timers as well as the agenda, and has probably let him run a bit over, but the one-minute rule is as sacred as the majority vote. "Any comments from the orders?" Ruth asks, and adds "for mana," when half a dozen hands go up. They all drop again, except for one man who beckons to James instead and starts picking his way around the room to speak privately.

Conclave, Nicovar concludes, needs shaking up. It's complacent, in danger of becoming a grandmasters' circle-jerk. It needs to be reminded that it constitutes the magical might of an Empire, and should take pride in it.

He's going to rule this chamber, and they won't even see it coming.

Isaella finds an Imperial summit to be strangely slow.

There's bustle all around her, but she has very little to do with it. The bodies of the Empire meet in their separate chambers, but the only one she can enter is the Senate, and then only to watch in silence. She does anyway, to get an idea of her senator Rhonwen's style, which is direct and short. She's clearly an intelligent woman, but she seems to grasp the problems better than the diplomacy needed to solve them; the Senate listens, but doesn't like her. Still, by election time, Isaella is content to keep her.

Besides that one vote, she has nothing to do. It's almost a relief to learn around the campfire, between drunken and increasingly filthy songs, that Navarr will be fighting tomorrow. She has to ask around to be sure what that actually means.

It means that an hour before noon on a blazing midsummer morning, Isaella and sixty of her compatriots are armed and armoured, standing before the Sentinel Gate.

The Gate is a huge stone arch, far older than the Empire, brought down from the mountains when there were still horses to lend their image to the stones. It is wide enough for six to march abreast, thick enough to shelter beneath it from the rain. No moss grows on the rough granite, no rust on the heavy chains that brace it upright. Isaella watches the Egregores open it, the spirits of five nations working their will in turn, and with every opening the air around it grows stranger. The Gate fills with roiling white smoke, reaching out to entangle the waiting troops, until at last the portal gapes wide and through it they can see the high slopes of the mountains, with snow still clinging to their peaks.

The Gate tingles against her skin as she passes like a thousand tiny sparks, and then she is in Spiral and there is a battle to fight.

She catches a glimpse, on her return, of a figure in pale robes and a deep red sash, waiting to see the fighters return, and she smiles.

CHAPTER TWO – AUTUMN 196

The orcs of the Lasambrian hills are not entirely resigned to losing Segura. After a season of wasp-sting raiding across the new border, the Imperial generals have had enough. They can't – or won't – spare the armies to reopen the western front, not with the Grendel and the Thule both gearing up for war. They need breathing space, time to replace their fallen soldiers and train the new recruits. Armies moving to the west is out of the question.

But the heroes of Anvil are not an army. The heroes of Anvil are a chaotic, joyous rabble, and they relish the chance to spend a morning in Segura's warm spring and give the Lasambrians a bruising. Isaella's spear is glossy with blood.

The Sentinel Gate opened with magnificent precision, fifty feet from a loose column of orcs. The Dawnish led the charge, hammering into the side of the enemy hard enough to break the column in two, making space for the Marcher bill-blocks to press in and lever the orcs apart. The Highborn are holding the Gate and the Navarr are freed to fight at their flanks and keep the Imperial forces from being separated.

The Lasambrians are reforming around the solid knot of the Marchers, trying to surround them and push them back towards the Gate, when the Dawnish succumb to the excitement. Dawnish soldiers are more disciplined, trained to stick to the plans they are given, but this is a mob of knights and they are out for glory. They hurl themselves out into the orcs, bloodied shields smashing into them again, but they have been fighting for an hour and the surprise that carried them through their first charge has long faded. The Lasambrians are ready; the Dawnish are swallowed, carried along by their own momentum, exposed to the blades suddenly stabbing at their backs.

Isaella grabs the nearest body and shoves her forward, pointing her towards the mounting disaster. She does the same with the next and the next and then she's running herself amongst two dozen Navarri, trying to pierce that mass of orcs and drag the Dawnish back to the line. The Marchers are doing the same, a wedge of their more mobile fighters pushing out while the bill blocks hold and hold and hold. Isaella sinks her spear into the back of a thigh, drags it out and stabs over a shield into the throat behind. There is a Marcher threatening to trip her, rolling underfoot to avoid a Lasambrian sword and she reaches down and heaves on his wrist. "Get up, you lanky git."

He bounces to his feet, using her to keep his balance. "Thanks, love."

That's about it for the pleasantries; half the Dawnish are on the ground bleeding and there's work to be done. They step forward together.

The battle is, broadly speaking, a success, but they carry back through the Gate two Navarri, a Highborn, four Dawnish knights and the bloodied circlet of Earl Perivell, clutched by her weeping sister.

Isaella's new Marcher friend has taken a nasty wound to the gut, from a Grendel who made it past his applewood staff. She has to half-carry him from the battle, letting him sling an arm around her shoulders and stagger along that way. They crowd through the Gate, trusting to the Highborn to hold the rear, the shout of

"Step! Step! Step!" keeping the shield-wall together as they retreat. Isaella feels exhaustion set in the moment the Gate passes overhead. She almost buckles under the weight before someone rushes in to prop the Marcher up from the other side and they all three stumble across the grass. Isaella concentrates on keeping them upright and out of the way of the retreat, until she can lower her burden to a low bench for a physick to cluck over. She drops to the ground next to him.

"That was quite a fight," she starts, and only then notices the figure who helped them here, the pale gold robes splashed with mud. The dark red sash. Her hands flex around her spear.

Isaella doesn't make it all the way to her feet before dark fingers close around her wrist. "Stay put, darling, they can look you over after they've sewn me up."

"I'm fine," she says automatically, "cuts and bruises, nothing serious," but he doesn't let go.

"I'd do as the Warmage suggests," Nicovar says, and she stares. "You mean you didn't know?"

He looks amused, his mouth curving into a smirk, perfect eyebrows arching in feigned surprise, until a lump of mud hits him in the chest. It leaves a smudge on his elegant embroidery. His eyes narrow, just a little. Reserved. Careful.

"Be polite, boy-o," the Warmage says, "I didn't see you out there saving my life today. At least three times as I remember. Now this Thorn and I – you are a Thorn, love? – we're going to stay here and let the physicks do their thing and you are going to bugger off and if you like you can make yourself useful at the Gate, I'm sure."

Nicovar's jaw tenses, but he goes. Isaella yields to the tug on her wrist and sits on the floor, puts her back to the bench and rests her spear across her legs. The Warmage's hand settles on her shoulder. "I'm James," he says warmly. "Was a pleasure fighting beside you today."

"Isaella."

"What's that youngster to you, then?"

"I don't know," she says, and James' hand tightens on her shoulder.

"Don't moon after him. You can do better."

Conclave does not become shorter, or less crowded. It drags endlessly, while Nicovar feels every body in the place like sandpaper against his skin. There is not enough air in the room. Their breathing runs together to make a noise as vast as the sea.

The question at hand is a declaration that the Conclave regards a particular variety of innovative magic as potentially sorcerous. They've been around all of the orders for comment twice already, wrangling over the precise details of what sorcery is and whether they'd better interdict the thing and it seems half the speakers do not in fact know the powers of the Conclave, and Nicovar has had enough. He steels himself to the physical contact and picks his way through the massed magicians, to tap Grandmaster Vesna on the shoulder and whisper, "May I speak?" before she can nominate herself again and say nothing of substance – again.

Mercifully, she waves him forward.

"Honourable colleagues, the question of what this declaration should be is a distraction. We can address only what is on the agenda before us and that is a declaration of Concord. We cannot alter the wording. It relates to research magic, spontaneous magic, and we cannot Interdict something that has never been formalised. I remind the Conclave that we are free to declare any magician a sorcerer for any reason, and that a Declaration of Concord cannot bind future Conclaves. This Declaration can only be advisory, it has no legal force, and it is futile to spend our time discussing what else we should do instead. We must consider the declaration as it has been presented."

There's a flurry of whispers around the room. Nicovar feels obscurely proud of himself; evidently the Conclave did not know these simple legal facts. He holds back a grin. He feels giddy, his first speech before Conclave and he did it without notes or planning, but this is not the time to exhibit delight. Instead he steps back, clearing the floor for the next speaker, and keeps his posture straight. Vesna looks almost embarrassed by him, but the Warmage is watching him with interest. Perhaps he's made up for his blunder of this afternoon. Nicovar stands a little taller, and waits for the voting to finally be called.

CHAPTER THREE – WINTER 196

The Hall of Worlds follows the seasons of Anvil. It's a little more pleasant – it never seems to actually rain, and the grass underfoot doesn't get worse than soggy – but it's cold. Nicovar's fingers are stiff with it, even tucked into his sleeves. He's wearing three layers of robes, but the hems are soaked to the knees with mud. This is one of the warmest places he could be. It's still bad.

The Conclave is filled with bad tempers and Nicovar's is one of them. He doesn't care about the complex negotiations the Archmage of Autumn is conducting with Estavus. He'll grant that the Autumn realm is important, and a ritual to trade unwanted magical items for mana is potentially useful, but it seems that just agreeing to a trade is far too simple. Someone in the Golden Pyramid is angling to be the next Archmage. Someone in the Unfettered Mind is angling to stop them. All of them need to stop posturing and close the deal before Estavus gets bored.

On reflection, Autumn eternals probably don't get bored of mortals using negotiations with them to enact conflict amongst themselves. They're a tiresome breed.

The Navarri who heads up the Rod and Shield has been nominating the Archmage – a kindness to allow her to keep speaking, though at her own expense – but after four rounds of petty bickering the Grandmaster has had enough. She pointedly turns her back. Her Order snigger; someone shouts "Vote!" and half the Conclave loudly agrees. The other Grandmasters share a look and refuse to nominate their argumentative colleagues.

Ruth wearily recites the substance of the declaration – an agreement to hold Estavus in neutrality, reiterating the legal position that already exists, pointless except as some arcane favour. The voting is perilously close. Ruth buries her face in her hands. "We'll have to count."

The Conclave groans, those who were enduring the wet ground dragging themselves to their feet. The Autumn-mage cringes. Her position must be feeling very shaky, Nicovar thinks to himself, and serve her right for failing to manage her underlings.

Her declaration fails to pass by three votes.

The Navarr camp is raucous tonight. They've lit the biggest fire-pit, six feet across, in the clear space beside the road, letting the smoke spiral up into the sky. It's a bitterly cold night, even close to the fire. The mud froze when the sun went down, which only made it easier to walk on. Under the trees the grass is growing frosted lace.

Isaella knows why they're celebrating. The battle this morning was hard, and they did well, and no Navarri died. The Thule incursion into Karsk has been definitively repulsed. But the other nations did not come off so lightly. The Marchers lost several, from a household already hit hard last summit, and their camp is quiet with sorrow. Isaella has been by, to pull James down into a hug and tell him how sorry she is. "They were good friends," he'd said, "solid folk, we'll miss 'em." The Highborn and the Leaguers are both celebrating their death festivals. It makes for a melancholy evening.

When the drunken singing starts up, Isaella retreats to the darkness between the sparse trees. She watches the gathering with a soldier's eye, picking out the threads of tension. The Senator for Hercynia is beleaguered by – now isn't that interesting – two Navarri Guides and a Highborn with his hood up. Something religious, perhaps, or some interest the Synod is taking in his activities. She'll have to look over the Senate motions tomorrow and see if he's doing anything interesting. Bryn Fastfade is flitting busily about, trying to amass the funds for his latest benevolent project, but he doesn't seem to be getting many takers. There's a group of merry Dawnish applauding the songs, who might turn boisterous but aren't looking for trouble. Picking his way through, looking searchingly at the crowd, is – ah.

Isaella steps eighteen inches to the left and lets the firelight fall on her.

Nicovar's winter overrobe is the same deep burgundy as his sash. It sets off the ivory of his sleeves, the delicate gold embroidery at his cuffs. Shadowed eyes meet hers for a moment. He turns on his heel.

He turns back.

She lets him come to her, weaving his way between the crowded bodies, careful never to brush against them. His face is calm, but he keeps glancing towards her, keeping track of her position. Isaella steps back into the shadows as he approaches. He doesn't hesitate to follow.

Nicovar stops just outside arm's reach – comfortable conversational distance, for an Urizeni. He's not carrying his magician's rod, no more than Isaella has her spear to hand, but no doubt he has a knife somewhere. That's fine. So does she. They're within earshot of the fire, in view of anyone who troubles to peer between the trees. It's not a good place for a murder.

"How was Conclave?"

Nicovar's lips twitch into a slight smile. "Tiresome. If the Archmage of Autumn loses her staff, she will deserve it. She ought to have had the grandmasters on board before she started. How was the Senate?"

She stands a little straighter at that. At the casual assumption that she was there, that she will know.

"Brief. The Emperor was there, to see the funding for the fleet go through. I think he's worried. There's not enough weirwood to go around."

"Did they fund it?"

"They did – but all four Leaguers stood aside."

His eyes widen, lovely deep brown eyes. "Interesting."

"I thought so." Isaella steps closer to him, closer than Navarri stand to talk. He's almost exactly of a height with her. She watches his lips part. His hand comes up to pluck uncertainly at her sleeve.

He kisses hard and sudden, the way she thinks he would fight. Isaella kisses back and keeps kissing, even as she shoves him backwards, pins him against the nearest tree. He wraps his arms around her and presses his mouth to her neck, hurried and hungry, until he bites at her skin and she tangles a hand in his loose hair and yanks his head away. She wants to feel the warmth of him under her hands, but through his winter layers all she feels is cloth.

Her voice is steady. "This is a bad idea."

Nicovar bares his teeth. He tries to kiss her again, but she's still got a hand in his hair. He fights it. "Which is of course why you've stopped," he says fiercely, and she lets him kiss her then, lets him turn them both and push her back against the tree, shoves him off again to fist her hands in his robes. It's unwise. It's good.

There is a beast on the battlefield, a hulking monstrosity built of frost and claws. It mows through the front line before the Imperials realise what they're dealing with. They stave it off with pole-arms and magic but the damage is already done; Nicovar finds himself staggering back through the Sentinel Gate before the battle is half over, with a semi-conscious General leaning heavily on him. Her right arm is ruined.

The Anvil side of the Gate is almost deserted. The fighters aren't expected back for an hour yet. But there are always some physicks nearby, always some priests, someone who thinks it worth their time to be ready for those who come back injured. Nicovar hands off his burden into the arms of a pair of identically dressed Leaguers and turns to go back to the field before he remembers – the gate doesn't stay open. He can't go back out.

"Don't worry about it," one of the Leaguers says, "you did your best. Let the rest of them do the mopping up. Have you met my sister Cressida?" She gestures at the woman kneeling over the General, poking with professional interest at the deep slashes in her muscles, and Nicovar notices for the first time that they're twins. They have slender, ridged horns curving back from their temples, ending just above their ears, holding wispy dark hair out of their eyes. The one speaking to him is wearing a mask, or he would have noticed the resemblance sooner.

"This one's for you, Lucy," the bare-faced twin says calmly, and wipes her bloody hands on the grass. "Hush, General, you'll be fine, you just need magical healing for that limb. Hello, darling, I see you've met my sister Lucrezia?"

She holds out her hand, and Nicovar hesitates. Cressida notices and sets it flat on her chest instead, tutting at herself as she bows.

"Oh, of course, Urizeni. Silly of me, really. We're the d'Holberg twins, I'd tell you what we do but you wouldn't believe me. Did I see you at the Celestial Arch election yesterday?"

Nicovar smiles. "I don't know whether you saw me. I was there."

"Not much of an election, really. Uncontested. Seems odd, for the Arch – You should have run."

"Why me?"

"People will always vote for a pretty face."

Nicovar doesn't have any illusions about his appearance. He's nicely formed, his figure is well suited to robes, and his features are unremarkable. He would be rather more attractive if not for his lineage – Draughir sallowness does not appeal to most people. At this precise moment, he has a disgusting combination of blood and sticky clay in his hair and smeared all down his sleeve.

"I might do that one day," he says anyway.

CHAPTER FOUR – SPRING 197

Isaella has known General Gwyneth for years, but never seen her before. In her time in the Black Thorns she grew used to receiving announcements from the General at least once a season, keeping the army briefed on the progress of the war and the objectives they were pursuing. Her handwriting is large and spiky and she has a particularly straightforward way of phrasing things, which now makes perfect sense – somehow Isaella had never picked up that Gwyneth was a merrow, but the pale blue scales striping her neck extend well above the scarf protecting her gills from the bitter wind. She stands with a stiffness in her left hip that says marching can't be easy for her, and speaks as plainly as she writes.

"Senators, you called me here to be your expert witness on the funding requirements for the northern campaign. If you choose not to grant the General's Council what we have requested that is your right. But the Black Thorns and the Hounds of Glory are both in dire need of resupply and we are unanimously agreed that they will be resupplied this season. You may either give us the coin to do it quickly, or we will return to our home nations for as long as it takes. There is no third option where we move to the northern front without resupply. If you give us everything we've asked for, both Highborn armies will be able to recruit from the religious wave in Casinea. Or you may give us nothing, and watch the Empire crumble. It is your call to make, Senators. Select an outcome and work for it!"

It's interesting, Isaella thinks, to watch how the Senators react to that. Most are somewhere between bored and irritated – they understand what Gwyneth is saying and they're not pleased about being lectured on it – but two of the Leaguers and one Marcher are standing very near the door and looking as though they'd rather escape through it than vote.

Footsteps shake the wooden floor of the gallery as Segura raises her hand to speak, and James the Warmage says, "Hello, love."

Isaella looks up over her shoulder to smile in greeting.

"What's happening?"

"Funding vote for the Generals."

James breathes in sharply through his nose, his gaze snapping out across the Senate floor.

"What?"

"I'll tell you later," he says softly. "You think they'll pass it?"

Isaella considers it. "The whole ask? It's a big ask."

"I know. It had to be, because – Later."

It's not like James to be so conspiratorial. She'll let him keep his peace for now, but – "Later had better come soon, friend," she tells him, and James nods, his attention already fixed on the Senate.

The funding passes with enough to resupply the armies they'd otherwise have to rotate out, but narrowly fails on the extra for the Highborn recruitment. James doesn't let go of the balcony railing until the last count is in, leaving dents where his nails pressed into the wood.

Isaella turns away from the senators still milling before the next motion gets underway, and rests her elbows on the railing behind her. "So, what was that about?"

James runs a hand through his springy black curls. "Politics."

"Yes, obviously, but details?"

"Let's walk and talk."

The spring sun is fiercely bright, but the air is still cold, and the wet wind rakes Isaella's bare arms like pushing through thorns. She widens her stride to keep up with James, glad for the warmth of movement. "So, talk."

"What did you see?"

"No, I'm not a pupil, don't give me the runaround."

"Power play between the generals and the Emperor."

Isaella looks up to see his frown. "The Emperor wasn't there."

"No, and it might not have made much difference – The point is, the level of funding they've just approved doesn't leave enough in the kitty for the navy this season."

She whistles. "That's deliberate? That's exciting. They'll have to put the shipbuilding on hold, and by their own argument that it's about military strength they can't object to restoring the strength of the actual military – Why don't the Generals' Council want the navy to be finished?"

"They don't want an admiral commanding it without being required to cooperate with them. The theory right now is that the admiral will be independent of the generals because she won't be fighting on the same fronts."

"That's a terrible theory. Who came up with that? Did they just forget about the Grendel? That the Jotun raid Wintermark from the sea?"

"Well, exactly. So they're pushing for the Admiral to be counted as a General, and when they get that promise they'll start considering the needs of the navy as if it was another army and miraculously the funding will all work out."

"Sneaky," Isaella says, approvingly. "And much tidier than having a public fight about it. Though of course it will delay the construction, unless some private citizens have very deep pockets, and those willing have already pitched in to buy the weirwood. It worries you, though."

James grimaces. "I don't like how they're going about it. The Navy's not of strategic importance yet, but if we do open another front against the Grendel, I don't want our harbours being destroyed because we played politics with the shipbuilding. It's already been approved by the Senate. We should let them build it."

"Nobody forced them to vote. If they can't do sums enough to know what they're sacrificing perhaps they shouldn't be senators."

"Perhaps."

They've reached the looming black stones of the regio, their carvings slick with mist. James blows out his cheeks. "I have to get back to work."

"Go," Isaella says cheerfully, and watches his hands dance in the air, and his body ripple into invisible elsewhere.

Nicovar is starting to think that the field marshal did not entirely think this plan through. Worse, he's starting to wonder whether the field marshal had a plan at all. The gate opened on a steep grassy slope, the edge of an almost-circular valley with a lake nestled in the basin and a fortress of slate and magic perched malignantly on the far slopes. The Thule had not been expecting them, not in the specific, but – the Empire has had the Sentinel Gate for a very long time, and their enemies are familiar with the chance that Imperial warriors will pop out of the air on the solstice. They go armed. They keep close to their walls.

The Highborn general leading the battle gambled on reaching the fortress before the Thule could seal the entrance. But the distance was further than she'd hoped, and the slope much steeper. Climbing up to the fort was slow even for those not in heavy armour. By the time they got around the lake the Thule had swung the gate shut and were shooting at them from the walls.

They tried to regroup, but there were not enough shields between them to keep the arrows off, and then the Thule came out again.

They pinned the bulk of the Imperial forces against the lake, and cut them off from the last banners coming through and the safe haven of the portal back to Anvil. The archers on the walls kept shooting, whittling down the Highborn lines and the mostly shieldless Varushkans. The last and largest Marcher bill block is still trying to push forward to join them, but the Thule have the run of the valley and it's a slow hedgehog-creep, billhooks grinding against rough steel on all sides.

Nicovar is holding the portal. He wishes that were not necessary – knows that ordinarily it isn't – but while the barbarians can't get through it to Anvil they can put their bodies in the way and make the Imperials bleed trying to retreat. They have to hold this beachhead or everything is lost.

Someone taps him on the shoulder. Even braced for combat, he flinches at the touch. The Warmage pulls him back from his post between two swordswomen. "New plan. We're taking down the fortress. I need your mana."

Nicovar stares for a moment, his mind spinning like wheels in the mud, useless. Then he digs into his pouches even as James repeats himself, "Mana, everything you've got. I'll pay you back if we survive."

"Don't be ridiculous," Nicovar says, and holds out a handful of crystal. "Eight, I have eight. How much more do you need?"

"That might be – Hang on."

He spins away, fitting himself between the crowded bodies and for a moment Nicovar has a lurching sense of dislocation, the way James moves as if he's in Conclave and this is just one more piece of politics, and then it all snaps back and Nicovar takes a deeper breath than he's managed since he came through the portal and saw the state of things.

This is a game board. This is a puzzle. He can do puzzles. The Warmage needs mana to take the fortress down and that means his coven is here and they'll be casting – Winter, he's heard that somewhere, that the Warmage is in a Winter coven – and they won't need to cast near the gate but they do need to get to it before the ritual unravels and the backlash goes straight through their doomsayer. They'll never get to it in time going across the valley.

Nicovar turns to stare at the ridge above them. They're going to go around.

When the coven have finished, the cold thrum of Winter magic shaped by cadences he can't follow, drawn from traditions Nicovar doesn't share, they clap each other on the shoulders and start inching back towards the portal. "We'll hold here," a woman says, her dark hair plaited tightly to her head. "Keep it open for you. Just get it done, Jimmy, and get your arse back over here."

James kisses her forehead and turns away. Some of the Marchers – those not bracing pikes and billhooks – break off to follow him, and Nicovar makes a lightning decision to join the Urizeni doing the same. He speaks to the sentinels in the line around him, quick and low, "The Warmage needs an escort to bring the walls down," and they glance at each other and come to wordless agreement over who will go and who stay. They assemble in a ragged knot a little above the portal.

James rolls his staff between his palms. "Nine minutes. Get me to the walls, alive and talking. Anything else is gravy. Questions? Short ones?"

"Round the top?" a Marcher with a crossbow asks, fitting a bolt in punctuation, and James nods grimly.

"You got it. Eight and forty. Let's get moving."

They take off at a run, one man tripping on a jagged rock on the steep slope and rolling down several feet before he can scramble up. He sprints flat out to catch up with them, his stride uneven. Nicovar presses in close to the back and concentrates on his breathing. The board is shifting down in the valley, the Thule pushing until the Imperials are ankle-deep in the lake, but none of them have realised yet that the queen is moving. They're halfway around before the archers on the walls notice them.

Nicovar hears the arrows zip past them with a detached interest – *ah, so we're in range now*. They're committed to the strategy. They're shifting too far down the slope, gravity betraying them, and Nicovar summons enough air to shout "Keep left! Keep level!" and feels the group reorient with him, his legs burning as he tries to run up that deadly hill. If they stop they'll die. A sentinel drops under his feet and Nicovar skins his palms on the ground and staggers forward again. The Thule coming the other way collide and break around James's staff, the crossbow taking one straight through the neck, the sentinel with the shield in front. Nicovar frantically blocks their swords, strikes at their heads where he can, their elbows, their fingers. How much time do they have left? How much?

James doesn't stop running. He hits the black slate wall with a howl of grief. The woman with the crossbow is spitted on a Thule spear behind him. "I call doom upon you!" he shrieks to the stone, "Fall, you fucking arsepit of shitweasels! Get down here!"

Nicovar sees the first spiderweb cracks spreading out from where James landed. This was as far as the plan went. Time for a new one.

When they finally stagger back through the gate, exhausted from battle and the final grinding push uphill to retrear, they leave far too many dead Imperials behind. Most of the Thule will survive. They brought the fortress down so the armies can move past it. Nothing else. No Thule generals slain, no secrets captured. Just blood and ruined stone.

Nicovar can't make himself go to the Marcher camp.

He writes James a letter instead.

CHAPTER FIVE – SUMMER 197

The hardened clay drums under Nicovar's heels, dust scuffing up in his wake. Anvil ruins his clothes whatever the weather, powdered soil clinging to the cloth as stubbornly as the mud. He is beginning to understand why the Navarri wear mainly earth tones.

The Highborn camp is even more crowded than usual, squeezed into the space between the Dawnish and the hedge. Nicovar tries three different gaps between the tents before he finds a path not blocked off by guy ropes. He's here looking for Ruth, while he still has a chance of finding her in daylight. Grandmaster Vesna's family are here, but when he went to the Varushkan camp to find her, she was missing. She's dealing with an emergency. He couldn't get a clear answer about what kind of emergency, except that it involved ghosts. Vesna won't be here until tomorrow, if she arrives at all, and Nicovar needs to know exactly how inconvenient that's going to be.

He finds Ruth sitting on a bench with her papers spread out on the peeling wood. Kneeling beside her, so tall that he's barely below her eye level, is the Warmage, and the sight brings a shivery tension into Nicovar's chest. He has a sudden vivid memory of James's fingers splayed on fortress stone, and the measured nod of approval he once gave Nicovar in Conclave, and lets himself smile for a moment. So. That's something he hadn't noticed before.

James sees him coming and murmurs his thanks to Ruth, passing her a mana crystal as he stands. He claps her on the shoulder in friendly goodbye and Nicovar can see the exact moment he remembers Nicovar is Urizeni and stops, with his hand already raised to greet him the same way.

"Good to see you," Nicovar says, and looks up through his eyelashes, and touches James very briefly on the arm.

James rubs the back of his own head, blinking. "Hi."

"Thanks for the advice in your letter. It clarified some things."

"Any time," James says, still looking off balance. "I – have to get back to my camp, but I'll see you at Conclave?"

"Of course."

James smiles shyly as he steps away. He was very warm through his thin summer shirt. Nicovar's heart thumps pleasantly.

"She hasn't nominated a proxy," Ruth says loudly, pulling his attention away from James's long legs.

"Sorry? Oh, Vesna, yes, I was going to ask – she hasn't named one. Right. Where does that leave us?"

Ruth shuffles her papers theatrically. "It means you're fucked. You can't get into your vaults and you can't speak unless the other orders help you. Two people have asked so far and I'm giving you the same answer I gave them: you can't elect a proxy and since Vesna is still alive, she still holds the title and you can't replace her until election time."

A spark of anger lights him up at how stupid that is, but Nicovar just bows his head a fraction. "I understand. While I'm here, I'd like to raise a declaration, please."

"What kind? And I'll need one mana," Ruth says, and Nicovar digs in his pouches for a crystal.

Conclave is poorly attended. There are no elections tonight, nothing to encourage the gossipers out of their camps. Ruth glares at Nicovar when he comes to offer the attendance numbers for the Celestial Arch.

"You're not the proxy," she says irritably.

"No, and I haven't claimed to be."

"This is the Grandmaster's job."

"Ruth, the Grandmaster isn't here. We don't have a proxy. That's bad enough without losing our share of the mana. Will you please note down our attendance? There are four of us, you can count us yourself if you like. Please?"

Ruth stares at him for a moment. "Alright. Four. I'll record it for splitting the font, but that's as much as I can do. No Grandmaster, no gambits, no nominations."

"Alright. That's fair. Thank you."

He threads his way back through the press to his tiny Order, Tom Pollard the Marcher and Artemia of Canterspire, her hands folded into her robes and her slitted eyes already half-lidded. She hisses out her question, "Did she say yes?" and Nicovar nods.

"Reluctantly, but she did."

"Sorry about that," Lucrezia says brightly. "I annoyed her earlier and she hasn't forgiven us yet."

"What did you do?"

"I told her I was proxy."

"Are you?"

"No, of course not. I don't have a letter. But we'd be much better off now if she'd believed me, wouldn't we? I took a gamble."

"Alright," Nicovar says, surprising himself. "Alright, be proxy. Ruth won't accept it but I'll vote for you. Artemia? Thomas?"

Artemia tilts her head. "Impress us."

Tom looks between them and shrugs.

"Okay then," Lucrezia says, and her smile is wicked. "We can't do much without a legal appointment. That doesn't mean we can't do anything. We need to stay visible, look like we still matter, even if there's only four of us. So what I'm saying – as your *proxy* Grandmaster – is that we need to vote as a block. That will make them take notice. And we need to stand at the *front*."

Lucrezia, elegant in her doublet and mask, may not have any legal authority, but she looks the part. She stands right behind Ruth, her arms folded, chin raised, and before every vote she turns to the little cluster of Arch members gathered behind her and whispers her vote for their agreement. The fourth declaration is another complicated Autumn deal, and Lucrezia wants to vote for, but when her three order-mates all disagree she narrows her eyes and mutters, "Fine," and raises her hand against with the rest of them.

By the time Nicovar steps forward to make his proposal, the Conclave is paying more attention to the Celestial Arch than they have in a year. Ruth is unwittingly helping, pointing out with every call for comments that the Arch have no Grandmaster and can't nominate speakers, and by now the Grandmaster of the Unfettered Mind is openly offering Lucrezia the chance to choose before she uses her nomination.

Nicovar's declaration is a nothing motion, almost a private matter. He steps out into the centre and raises his voice to be heard above the general muttering. "My spire have asked me to bring this. We have a contract with the Great Library that we purchased last season at auction. It allows one ritual text to be retrieved from the library but the choice of ritual has to be approved by Conclave. The ritual we're proposing is Focus of the Stars, which we believe allows a location to be temporarily added to the Heliopticon. That would be helpful for battlefields, among other things. There is no cost to the Conclave, you'd just be ratifying our choice of ritual."

"Questions," Ruth says. "The Celestial Arch cannot nominate. Unfettered Mind?"

"Lucrezia, anything to say? Right. Question for the proposer – how is this ritual different to Winged Messenger, which we already have?"

"Winged Messenger is one message in one direction. A Heliopticon node allows two-way conversation. We're not sure of the exact cost of Focus of the Stars but it will probably be more expensive to cast."

"Which Realm?"

"Autumn."

Someone at the back says, "Can Ankarien even cast Autumn?" and Ruth is already shushing them – "no nomination, no questions, please" – but Nicovar says "Some of us," anyway and that seems to be it for questions. There's some muttering in the Golden Pyramid ranks about whether it's the best ritual to choose, but the Grandmaster says "They own the contract" and doesn't nominate the complainer to speak. Nicovar stays where he is until the vote passes.

The Celestial Arch vote in favour as a block.

When Saturday evening rolls around, after the Senate elections and a brutally straightforward battle in which three hundred

Grendel and two Imperials died, Isaella goes looking for a good time. She starts off in Navarr, but she's heard all these songs before. The night is warm and the stars too beautiful to spend it under the trees. Anvil is calling to her.

She has some idea of going around all the nation camps, but in the end she doesn't get further than the League, a little way down the hill. Cressida is holding court outside a trade house, her dark eyes flashing in the firelight, and Cressida feels like a fast friend already, having patched Isaella back together twice after battles. Isaella could probably squeeze onto the benches, but the ground is dry; she drops to the grass instead and stretches her feet out toward the fire, enjoying the chance to take the weight off them.

Cressida's hand lands on her shoulder once she's finished her story. "Hello, darling."

Isaella tilts her head back. "Hi. You seemed to be having fun so I thought I'd come and join in." She fumbles in her thigh pouch and for a moment thinks she's lost it, but then smooth glass meets her fingertips. She brandishes her prize. "I brought rum!"

"Ah-*ha*." Cress claims the bottle at once. "*You* can stay. Marcella has been drinking my cherry wine all evening and she didn't even bring a song to pay for it."

"I sing like a dying crow," Isaella says.

"Really? We should find a crow and check. That's an interesting anatomical problem."

"I know a song about a dying crow!"

"Sing it then, Marcella!"

Marcella opens her mouth. She takes a breath, and closes it again. "No, no, I actually don't, but give me ten minutes, I'll think of something."

"Looks like it's on you, Isaella. You don't get your rum back unless you sing."

"I can't, I told you. Will a story do?"

"Hmm. Because you are a friend, I will accept that variation. Under protest."

"I need cherry wine to wet my throat."

"You sneaky cheat!" Cressida complains, and while the gathering laughs and shouts, "Navarr!" at her she passes down an almost empty bottle. Isaella shifts position to free up her hands for drinking and talking, and ends up with her back braced against Cressida's legs. Cress strokes her hair.

"Alright," Isaella says. "Have you heard the one about the ox, the boat and the waterfall?"

CHAPTER SIX – AUTUMN 197

The Navarri are the news-bringers of the Empire. They are the messengers, the couriers, the rumour-mongers and gossip-sharers. Very little happens within the borders that some Navarri, somewhere, does not know.

As the golden summer of 197 turns to a windblown autumn, the news runs striding-swift through the Empire: Jotun in Western Scout. After forty years of almost-peace, the barbarians have come back in force. The Mourn was too difficult for them a generation ago, the Marchers driving them back into mutual raiding, daggers striking across an uneasy border. Now the enemy is marching again.

The people of Western Scout are a fierce breed, toughened by constant skirmishing and the looming Vallorn at their backs. Those who settle there keep their spears close. But there is no army standing guard in Liathaven to support them and when the nation gather at Anvil, in the swift dusk under the trees, they already know the score. The border has been breached in Liathaven. The Jotun have come back to make war.

General Gwyneth stands on a bench, her feet spread wide to brace herself. The crowd around her is hot with fury.

"Liathaven is under attack," she says bluntly. "The Black Thorns have been resupplying in Miaren. We're marching to the border now. If anyone has a personal force that can reach them faster, First Light steading needs help getting their research out of harm's way, speak to Bren about that. I don't have a casualty report on the civilians but I know we lost less than we could have if some of you hadn't stepped in. One person you know we did lose. Si Greenfall died at Stonecamp three weeks ago. He is gone, but we will see him again. That's all."

Gwyneth steps down, ignoring the shouted questions and chatter around her. The Senators stand forward to keep the Standing going – there are newcomers to be welcomed, elections to be announced, all the work of Anvil that goes on whatever the wars may do. Isaella threads her way through the crowd to Gwyneth's side.

"General," she says, under the noise of the Standing, and waits for Gwyneth's pale eyes to flick to her. "Isaella Thornborn. I knew Si. He was a good soldier."

Gwyneth nods. "He was. We'll miss him."

The polite apology for bluntness is on the tip of her tongue, but Isaella looks at the General she almost knows and swallows the words back. They're not wanted here. "He was your Adjunct. Have you chosen a new one yet?"

"Not yet." Gwyneth turns towards her, reading her face. "You have someone in mind?"

"Me."

Old habit makes Isaella straighten up under the General's scrutiny, and square her weight a little better over her feet. Gwyneth's lips quirk in amusement. "Military experience?"

"Four years in the Black Thorns. I retired a year ago. I've a good head for figures and maps and I know how to hold my tongue in a meeting."

"Where did you learn that?"

"Senate public gallery."

Gwyneth laughs. "Expanding your portfolio? Alright. No, I'm sure loyalty is in there too. I appreciate someone who knows her way around Anvil. Yes, for now – it's not an official position and I can change my mind any time I want, but you can come to the Military Council and we'll see how it goes. Don't be late."

The silence hangs expectantly between them, but Isaella knows a trap when she hears it and she knows what time the meeting starts and where. "I'll be there," is all she says, and waits for Gwyneth's nod before she turns away.

The Senate rejoices in the luxury of a building for its meetings, a real building with windproof walls and a solid floor. The Military Council has no such pleasure. The tent over Isaella's head is sagging alarmingly under the weight of evening rain.

In the dim lantern light even the eerie precision of ushabti-script is difficult to read. Isaella squints over Gwyneth's shoulder at her briefing papers. Three choices, and two chances for a battle this summit; something will fall by the wayside. The map table is seven foot wide, painstakingly inscribed with details of territories, boundaries, terrain, and littered with the coloured markers of armies.

Laid out like this, the problem is obvious. Three Jotun armies sit at the edge of Liathaven, crowded into Western Scout in a tight little point, and the border north and south is only lightly defended. The soldiers will have to be brought across the Empire if they are not to invite attack elsewhere. The Black Thorns are marching west from Miaren, but that is four hundred miles away, and they are only one army. They will need help.

The two conversations flow at once. Which battles will be fought tomorrow, and which armies will be moved in the coming season. The questions interlock like gears. Weaken an army here to send a defending army there; provoke retaliation here to keep the enemy in close. Gwyneth seem to be able to keep a dozen possible strategies clear in her mind at once. Isaella watches her work and keeps silent.

One battle, a rescue mission for some Liathaven stridings caught up in the attack, is finally set aside. Isaella feels certainty coil frozen in her stomach. Those people will die. The generals have left them to die. But for that price, a supply caravan in distant Skarsind can be taken out along with the mithril the Thule desperately need to resupply their faltering troops, and thus keep the pressure off the northern front and therefore the Fire of the South can march for Liathaven.

The line fighters and skirmishers will go north through the Gate. The more mobile heavy troops will go east to the eternal struggle over the Barrens, to winkle a Druj general out of her stronghold before she can prepare to invade.

"The Marchers can bring the fortress down, of course," someone says, and the whole room goes quiet for a moment. They look at the Warmage. James rubs his hand against his beard.

"We have the magical strength," he says at last. "We don't have the heart."

"That tower has to come down," insists the first speaker, a Highborn Isaella doesn't recognise with a flaming sword embroidered on her tunic. "Are you saying you won't do it?"

Jenny of the Bounders pushes herself up to standing. She speaks slowly, picking each word like steps over uncertain ground. "James is right. The Marchers are heartsick. Right or wrong they feel they have sacrificed more than most. The Warmage isn't saying it, but the only reason they can hit a fortress is two fifteen-year-old girls who wouldn't be citizens yet if we didn't need magicians so badly. We need another way."

"Then we'll do it," says the Towerjack general who led the charge against the Grendel, in the summer. Isaella liked him then as she likes him now.

Jenny says "How?"

"Well, I don't mean to step on Marcher toes, but we've got enough Spring magicians in Holberg to raise the dead. I'll knock their heads together and get them under a mercenary banner for tomorrow."

"Will they want paying?"

"We'll cover it. Or if my carta won't, I'll pay for it myself. We've got the mana. Leave it with me, I'll kick their anthill over. You just bring along some billhooks for the ants."

James nods at him across the map table, "Thanks, Giuseppe," and gets a careless salute in reply.

Nicovar is hungover.

He's not badly hungover. He didn't drink that much last night, or stay up that late. He's stayed up until dawn discussing theory before, and he's pretty sure he had at least four hours sleep. But all the same, he is slightly hungover, and grateful for the misty breeze cooling his face.

The Urizen, as a matter of national pride, always pitch their camp closest to the regio, which makes it easy to sit under the Ankarien awning picking at a bowl of raisins until the general they're meant to enchant shows up. His morning coffee is down to the dregs and he's considering another, for all he'll probably regret it later, when a little cluster of Navarri moves towards the stones and his spire-mates start picking up their staves. It's

General Gwyneth, again, and there was some concern about her spending too much time under the Master Strategist effect, but she's had half a year without it and doesn't seem to be losing her grip, so they agreed to put it on her again. Nicovar thinks it's overcautious – people stay under enchantments for years on end and it's not like this one is experimental – but there's a conservative faction in the spire who like to worry.

He doesn't notice Isaella until they've started the ritual. Perhaps he's more hungover than he'd thought. She's standing beside one of the regio stones, carefully not leaning against it, with that odd squeamishness so many Navarri have about magic. Her biceps swell against her tunic. Nicovar can't afford to think about that, or her, while he's working, and he turns his thoughts back to the ritual with all the strength he can find. Clarity, clarity, pure rational thought. The General's grey eyes, and not Isaella's brown ones.

He steps over to her when they're done. "Come to watch the rituals?"

"I'm with the General," Isaella says, turning a little towards him, wary. "She lost her adjunct in Liathaven."

"My sympathies," Nicovar says automatically. "So you've stepped up? Congratulations. I look forward to watching your career advance."

"Oh, really? And how is yours doing? Shall we race?"

That stings. Nicovar keeps his face pleasantly neutral. "My career in the Conclave is doing quite well, thank you. It takes time to build a reputation. You know that. And last I checked, adjunct was still an informal position."

Isaella smiles. There are knives in it. "So we *are* racing. Won't that be interesting?" Gwyneth has finished her conversation with the spire and Isaella takes half a step back, preparing to follow her. She hesitates for a moment. "If you're friendly with the

Warmage, will you write to him? He's lost people every summit this year. I think he could use a distraction."

"I have been," Nicovar says. "I will again. Thank you."

She nods at him, and strides away into the mist. Nicovar tucks his hands into his sash and allows himself a very private grin.

CHAPTER SEVEN – WINTER 197

Isaella's fingers are numb around her spear. The grey sky presses down on the world, sullenly bleeding snow. Everyone has cold feet. The Marchers are singing their most rousing war song – *you're going home in a Marcher grow-bag, make the crops grow higher* – to keep the shivers away. It's rare for it to be this cold in Anvil even at midwinter. The soothsayers grumble about bad omens and keep their eyes on the stars.

They are going to Liathaven, to embattled Western Scout, to hunt a Jotun general. She's been a formidable opponent, her skills honed in border skirmishes with the Faraden, outside of the Empire's watchful control. The beachhead in Liathaven is solidly established. Western Scout is lost – the Navarri cling on to hope, to the few scattered Steadings still defending their homes, but the Military Council were all in agreement last night. There is no way to drive those armies away except by re-conquering their own land. They could have tried to hit the forward edge of the invasion force today, to take out the scouting bands and raiding parties before they disperse into the Liathaven woods and become useful to the enemy, but the generals prefer to strike at the head.

Giuseppe of the Towerjacks is playing with the field marshal's rod, tossing it up in the air and nearly always catching it again. Isaella shifts her weight between her feet, trying to keep herself limber despite the cold. This waiting must be over soon.

When at last the Egregores have all opened the gate and the four nations assigned to this battle can pass through, the weather in Liathaven is almost a relief. The wind is up, shaking the treetops to rain dead leaves onto their heads, but the low grey cloud of Anvil gives way to bright white skies, a knife-edge border over the Sentinel Gate, changing around them like the turning of a page. The expedition force pours through into the forest.

Liathaven is densely wooded even in its tamer parts. Here, on the isolated western edge cut off from Imperial territory by the ravenous Vallorn, the ground is carved up by sharp ridges overgrown with trees. From their knife-edge tops you can see the gullies to either side, but no further.

Isaella stalks warily through the trees. There's no hope of silence here, with two hundred Imperials mostly unused to woodland, and dry twigs underfoot to announce their presence. The League and the Marchers try to keep their heavy blocks together but the terrain forces them into columns, spreading out amongst the ridges. So it is that when the expedition force reaches the Trod, they are already scattered wide.

The trees give way suddenly, and the ridges beneath them, to a wide bare road. The earth has been flattened by thousands of passing feet, but not recently. The clouds make a white ribbon above their heads. Looking along the Trod Isaella can see General Giuseppe, the light gleaming off his bald head as he confers with the scouts. They have all straggled to a halt, waiting for directions, here on the welcoming road.

There is a moment, before any trap springs, when the prey knows it has been caught. Isaella knows in the split second before the arrow strikes Giuseppe in the chest, leaping out from the trees like a scarlet bird. The volley that follows is caught by shields and plate armour and undefended flesh, and then the orcs come out from the trees.

The Imperials have spread out along the Trod, little clusters of fighters fractured along the open ground. The orcs come at them in three solid points to split them further apart. Isaella loses sight of the command group almost at once behind the swarming enemy. Her hands move without prompting, to stop a rust-streaked hammer from swinging into her head. The freezing shock breaks.

Isaella backs up towards the treeline. The Trod whispers underfoot, tempting her to stay on the clear earth, telling her that safety is here and danger in the trees, but that is part of the trap. She shouts "Get off the road! Get off the road!" over and over until it sinks in to the fighters around her and their stumbling band, cut off from the rest of the force and losing ground fast, turns its retreat towards the shadowed trees.

The orcs are cautious. On the road, spread out, they have the advantage of greater numbers and a solid line. They follow into the forest only slowly, keeping together. Isaella is surrounded by panic, by wide-eyed fighters and a tiny Navarri briar with a longbow slung across his body, bandaging wounds and bullying the injured into chewing packets of herbs. Isaella keeps her eyes and her spear on the enemy in front and lets the physick do his work behind her.

They move awkwardly backwards along the narrow gully. There's a stream down the bottom, threatening to trip them and soaking their ankles when they break through the thin ice. The orcs have decided to treat the little valley as a road, as if its walls could not be climbed, and formed themselves into a five-strong shield line. The Navarri take out three or four with their bows, climbing the steep slopes to get over the blocking shields, but when the trees thicken they are forced down to the valley bottom again. They're vulnerable enough without getting further separated.

There's a crashing through the trees on their left like a herd of charging elks. Isaella and half her companions turn to guard their flank, arrows trained toward the ridge. Her heart sinks at the scale of the noise. They don't have the numbers to defend on two fronts.

The figures pushing through the undergrowth wear long pale robes, some blue, some cream, stained to the knees with mud and grass.

Isaella grins. She shouts "Enemy down the valley!" to get the Urizeni back on their guards. Lightly armoured they may be, but a phalanx of magicians was never unwelcome in close fighting.

The newcomers trickle down into the group. Isaella finds herself next to Nicovar, his beautiful red overrobe stained black from a roll in the mud. He says grimly, "We need to push on to the gate."

Isaella doesn't turn to stare at him, but only because she needs her eyes for the orcs. "The gate is back behind you."

"No, it isn't."

"It is. We bore right across the ridges when we came through and down towards the Trod. That's the direction you came from."

"There's a Trod?"

She stabs her spear towards the neck of an advancing orc, who catches it on her shield and keeps plodding stubbornly forwards. "The road. The big road, in the middle of a forest, what the hell else would it be? Didn't you feel it?"

Nicovar's voice is very calm. "Evidently I need to become more familiar with Trods. I will work on that. Later. We reached the road but the main force had already been driven off it. We were looking for them when we found you."

"There's no chance of finding them now, not in this terrain. We wouldn't know if they were in the next valley over. We have to get home."

For more than an hour, thirty Navarr and Urizeni argue over the points of the compass, tell each other not to panic, and stumble through undergrowth that rises sometimes higher than their heads. Isaella kills two orcs who try to put steel into Nicovar; he paralyses one on the point of skewering her. Their physick with the longbow runs out of arrows, and then out of herbs. Isaella concentrates on defence and tries to ignore the creeping dread along her spine.

In the end, they come at the gate from behind. They are spread out along a ridge too narrow for a crowd, with two orc scouts in the valley at their feet, trying to shoot them down before they can bring more forces to bear. They can't take another battering from the heavy troops, and Isaella knows they're too widely spaced on this ridge, but she can't bunch them back up without raising her voice and alerting the enemy. She is searching for a clear path down the slope when she finally sees the Sentinel Gate, standing proud on a ridge, dark grey against the dull winter trees. They came past it in the confusion and need to almost retrace their steps, but they've found it. She grabs Nicovar's arm to point the way.

Her stomach heaves when she passes back under the Gate's stone archway. Her vision blurs. Gateshock, they call it, the backlash of magic against those who stay too long on the other side. Anvil wraps around her like a grey blanket, snow folding down amongst the tents. She staggers wearily away from the gate. It's habit, to get herself out of the way of the massed troops behind her, even when a loose band of twenty-six is all she has brought home. Nicovar is still at her side.

They are swept apart by a flurry of physicks. Cressida takes Isaella's spear and sighs at her. "Really, Sal? The collar-bone again? You're going to be aching for weeks. At least break the other one for a change." Isaella tries to shrug and immediately regrets it; she sits down on the bench she's pointed at and lets Cress work.

"Where's Lucrezia?" she asks, when her stomach has calmed down enough for conversation. "She's usually here, isn't she?"

"She's doing politics, darling."

"Really? Conclave?"

"Mm. She's going to be Grandmaster by tonight. Don't shout it around too loudly, it's not strictly definite yet, but your friend Nicovar is on her side and the whole order only has about eight voters present, so it's a sure thing."

Isaella looks at her smiling face suspiciously. She can't prove anything, but Cressida carries on her belt an identical mask to the one Lucrezia is never seen without, and sometimes they hide in dark shadows together, and Cressida's memory is oddly patchy – "Congratulations. I haven't heard they've done much recently. Lucrezia can shake them up a bit. And anyway, he's not my friend."

"Isn't he? I'm going to lift this arm up so I can get your armour off. Brace yourself."

Isaella takes a deep breath, and watches the silent gate for survivors.

CHAPTER EIGHT – SPRING 198

By the spring equinox, Liathaven is well and truly lost. The Vallorn holds the centre, a monster centuries old, as dark and hungry as ever. The Jotun have overrun the rest. The fighting still grinds on in Liath's Ring and the Glen, but there is no real hope there. The Imperial armies will have to dig in their heels and wait for reinforcements.

Isaella is bitterly familiar with the state of the war. She spent her season on the front, carrying General Gwyneth's messages from one barely-held point to another. The Black Thorns were her own army, not two years ago, and too many of the dead are her friends. They lay the bodies in the corpse glades, reclaim their armour, and march on.

She sits with James on the edge of the Senate dais, after a grim Military Council meeting that dragged on into the night. The generals will make no advance in Liathaven. The Jotun offer a compromise, a peaceful border on the north provided the Imperials move no armies there, make no preparations to defend themselves. There is no decision yet on whether to step into that trap. The Marchers of Bregasland are sharpening their pikes.

James passes her a flask. She sips from it, incautious, expecting apple brandy; the taste of strong ginger shocks her upright. The burn in her throat owes nothing to alcohol.

"What is this?"

"Ginger cordial." James takes the flask back and drinks slowly, letting it linger on his tongue. "Bess makes it. With, I think it's turmeric root, and common vervain. Good for the aches."

"You know common vervain doesn't work like the real stuff, don't you?"

James shrugs, handing her the flask again. "Then it tastes like it's good for the aches, which is close enough." He leans back on his hands, face tilting up to the canvas ceiling, and sighs heavily. "Where are you from, Sal?"

"The Black Thorns, mainly. I grew up in Miaren, got a bit of forest there now, but I pay a forester to manage it. I did two tours with the army, and now I'm back again. What about you, you're a Mournwold boy, aren't you?"

"Mm. Far west, we've got family in Bregasland, but it's the Mourn for me. Too close to the Jotun, nowadays."

"Aren't we all?" Isaella looks at him sideways, the line of his body and his long legs stretched out, and leans backwards to match him. Their shoulders bump together.

James glances at her, his lips quirking. "Thought you were carrying a flame for young Nicovar?"

"Him?" Isaella shakes her head. "He's very pretty. And rude. And a little up himself, if we're being honest."

James laughs out loud, his eyes crinkling up. "He's ambitious."

"Why are we talking about Nicovar?" Isaella nudges James with her knee and takes another sip of his ginger cordial. "You know, this stuff is growing on me. You don't drink?"

"I don't drink at summits," James corrects her. "Too much else to do."

"Very wise."

James raises a finger. "Prudent. Cautious, even. But wisdom lies in action, and should never be confused with... sensible restraint." His eyes are very dark in the lantern light, before he leans over and kisses her.

His kiss is gentle, undemanding, inviting her to respond, and Isaella answers it willingly. His beard prickles against her skin. She is shifting her weight to reach for him when James ducks his head and dissolves into laughter.

"What?" Isaella sits up to stare at him.

"I'm sorry, I can't." James shakes his head, laughter making him breathless. "I feel like the throne is watching me."

Isaella cackles. "Should we invite Barabbas? An Imperial witness? Maybe he'd want to join in."

"Could you really? With an Emperor?"

"Well," Isaella says, pretending to consider it, "maybe not with Barabbas."

James runs his hands through his hair. It springs back wilder than before. "Definitely not with Barabbas."

"And not here."

"Not here."

Isaella rolls onto her feet, her tired back twinging in complaint. James sprawls on his back. He looks very foreign in his Marcher shirt with his face unmarked by ink. She smiles. "There's always a fire in Navarr, this time of night. Singing. It's a nice way to spend the evening."

"There's not much evening left." James looks up at her, considering, and reaches for her outstretched hand. "But I'll spend some time in Navarr."

His hands are very warm in the cool spring night, and he tastes of ginger.

The Ankarien tent is filled with refugees.

Nicovar sits outside it, in the sunshine, basking. It was a bitter winter among the lofty spires of Urizen and the naga in the delegation are all outside with him, moving as the light moves and pretending they have good business to keep them out here in the sunbeams. Yesterday Archimedes brought out his huge cushion and lay on it reading stories to the children and tanning the back of his neck. He had no shame at all, and so neither will Nicovar.

At least, he has no shame in enjoying the sun. The tent full of refugees gives him a sour feeling in the pit of his stomach. It's foolish to feel guilty. He has spent his life on the far side of the Empire from Liathaven and its sudden wretched collapse. Urizen has done its share of fighting, is fighting now, twenty sentinels gone through the gate to shore up the defence of the Barrens, and unlikely to bring all twenty back again. Why should Nicovar feel ashamed that he is not hurt?

He does, all the same.

Archimedes has not been their Arbiter for long, but he did not earn the position by being stupid. He cracks one slitted eye and says "Do something about it, if it upsets you."

"It doesn't upset me," Nicovar says, "it offends my sense of justice."

Archimedes hisses out a laugh. "Yes, you're still young enough to have one of those. Who told you there was justice in war? It wasn't me. I taught you that when you can't win, you find a different weapon. So far you've tried moping – how's that strategy working for you?"

"Lend me a mana crystal," Nicovar says.

Archimedes opens the other eye. He glares at Nicovar for a moment, then digs in the folds of his sash, serene again. He tosses a sharp-cornered crystal over, flashing glassy-bright in the sun. "Don't spend it all at once."

The Ankarien spire has several awnings, but the Liathaven refugees are gathered in the big meeting tent. It has nice clear boundaries, smooth white canvas drawn right down to the floor, with only the rolled-up flap of the doorway breaking the perimeter, and Nicovar can walk all the way around it with his stave touching the cloth. Perfect, in other words, for an enchantment.

The ritual isn't strictly one he knows. He's read scripts for it, of course, and he understands enough magical theory to know how it's put together, but he hasn't memorised the invisible mechanics. He's juggling pieces in his mind as he walks and hums, twisting the stars into place as he goes. Archimedes listened with his head cocked and nods approvingly, lifting his feet out of the way with his eyes still comfortably closed. Nicovar can feel how inefficiently he's using the crystals, his own and what he borrowed, but it's doing the trick. The magic coils into place around the tent.

The voices inside drop lower. The edge of panic eases away from them, fraying tempers soothed by the balm of magic, cool dawn light overtaking the fires. A simple ritual, practically a spell, and Nicovar's own nerves are so much easier with the hubbub inside the tent gentling down that he might learn it properly, to cast more easily the next time.

Nicovar looks in through the open flap. He meets the eyes of an exhausted refugee, her toddler sleeping on her lap and an ugly brand of leadership on her cheekbone, the burn still fresh. He nods to her respectfully. It must have taken courage, to step up in the face of disaster. Lucia sits among them like a dove among sparrows, serene and upright in her fine ivory robes, unmarked by road dirt or grass.

The Brand glances at someone beside the door, half her attention still on the difficult conversation about resettling them near the Spire's timber plantation, and the someone turns out to be a young woman barely out of her teens. She carries a wicked knife at her hip. Nicovar moves back a little to make room for her as she steps across the threshold and back inside, her head raised as if listening while she passes into enchantment and out again. Old stories may speak of magicians with silver marks on their skin, but this is the clearest sign of a practitioner Nicovar can think of.

"Solace of Chimes?"

Nicovar nods. "Yes. I thought it might help."

"It won't make anyone feel better," the young woman says bluntly. "Magic never does."

"Perhaps not, but I personally prefer to be unhappy and calm, if I can manage it. Wouldn't you rather have the choice?"

She sniffs. "Urizeni. We're not like you, magician. We don't shame people for having hearts."

Nicovar is still searching for a response when she scowls and ducks back into the shaded tent, to rejoin her people.

CHAPTER NINE – SUMMER 198

Kimus is a creature of crystal and blinding light. Its chambers are filled with eyes, some hollow as glass and shimmering like soap bubbles, some polished quartz, or flickering balls of bluish fire. They spin about an invisible centre, their orbits unfathomable to any mortal mind.

There is a figure, in amongst the dancing eyes, but it does not move. It is draped in yellow veils, their ends waving in a breeze no other being feels, and its eye sockets are bare empty skin. The light comes from behind it, painfully white, no matter where you stand to look from. It does not move or speak.

Nicovar thinks it isn't alive.

Alive is a slippery concept in the realms of magic. Even in the mortal world it blurs around the edges, the not-yet-living and the almost-dead. Here it is worse, for not everything that moves has a spark of its own. Magic can move a body as easily as it calls a storm, and this body with no sight that stands amongst the Thousand Eyes, although it breathes, although it smiles, seems only a statue that magic built.

The Eternal herself – itself – is scattered amongst the floating eyes, and they are always watching.

The hairs on Nicovar's neck began prickling the moment he walked into this chamber, and they have not stopped yet. One of the smaller globes came to inspect him, flying around his head and exploring the openings of his sleeves, before a voice from everywhere said "I have come. The Archmage has not come to greet me. That is impolite."

It *was* impolite. It was completely contrary to protocol. But, as many Eternals did, Kimus had at some time left a minor magical artefact in the world, as a way of attracting interesting conversationalists. Lucrezia had won the black marble ball (perfectly round, of course) in a wager on a Dawnish tourney, from a shipbuilder who knew what it was but had no real use for it. It did only two things – it could be burned like mana to power a particular scrying ritual or, much more usefully, sent back to the Eternal in exchange for an audience.

They ought to have invited the Archmage along, but they hadn't.

The eyes spin around them, uncomfortably chaotic in their movements. "You have names," Kimus says, serene.

"Yes, we do," Lucrezia agrees. "Would you like to know what they are?"

A globe of solid crystal floats in front of her face. "Masks are for concealment. The League use them to assume roles and, by choosing how they are observed, shape themselves. The Urizen control their expressions for the same purpose." Nicovar tries not to flinch as the globe flies over to him, staring into one eye and then the other. "I would like to know your names."

"I am Nicovar, of the great Library of Ankarien," he answers, keeping his tone level. "This is Lucrezia d'Holberg, Grandmaster of the Celestial Arch, my friend and head of my Order."

"It is a long time since any dignitary of the Empire sought audience with Kimus."

"Well," Lucrezia says, grinning beneath her mask, "that's why we thought we'd pay a visit."

The presence of the Emperor in the Military Council should in principle, make no difference. Barabbas might not have been a General before he was appointed to the throne, but he has attended many times since then and should have known how the meetings went.

Isaella, watching silently from her place behind Gwyneth's shoulder, thinks that perhaps he doesn't care.

"I understand about Liathaven," the Emperor says impatiently. "I understand about the threat to the Marches. I also understand that the Jotun have granted us a ceasefire and they always honour their treaties. All you have to do to protect the Marches is keep the raiding from getting out of hand. New armies and fortifications – you can't move the army into Bregasland even if you could equip it."

"Do not be so light about Liathaven, Barabbas."

"I am not light about it, Giselle. If you have a plan to retake it with the Jotun as strong as they are, please, tell me! But I don't believe you do. I don't believe any of you do. I know how the Military Council feels about the Navy. I also know that the treaty with the Jotun forbids us from moving our armies into place. But it says nothing about naval forces and we must weaken them somehow or the Marches will be lost and who knows how much more? I am not here to give orders. Virtues guide me, I've learned my lesson about that." Some of the assembled Generals only wince at his levity, but there's a scattering of honest laughter. "I've come to suggest a compromise. Will you hear it?"

The generals glance at each other, wary. Isaella can almost hear the thought forming: what harm could it do to listen? Papers are set down on the map table, a pointed reminder that while they are listening they are not doing the work they came here for, and finally Miriam of the Silent Tide hands over the field-marshal's rod, surrendering her authority to Barabbas.

He sets his hands on the map table, framing himself in the lantern light. "Thank you. My council, my generals, I know we have not agreed on how the Empire's navy should be run. I know what you have done to slow it down and I have not fought with you on that. I have not taken the money, as the Throne can, to build what my generals wish I should not. But the time is over for politics. Liathaven lies under the yoke. The Marches are threatened. We must let them play on our borders, or else be forsworn. And so I ask you this: dig deep. Find your courage. Let me finish the fleet, and I give you my word, not as your Emperor, but as an Imperial, that until we agree how the admiral is to be governed, I will not let an admiral be appointed. I will take the fleet myself. I will submit to the guidance of this council on where that fleet should sail and what it should do there, until we are ready to return it to the nations. I can't force you to do this – I *won't* force you to do this. If you refuse to fund the fleet, it will not be built. But if it is not, then Bregasland will fall, and Liathaven will be lost for a generation. We have not always been friends. But we are all Imperials, and if we cannot work together, we will fall apart."

Barabbas lets the moment stretch. He straightens slowly, fixing the generals in turn with his stare. The lantern flickers in the silence, until at last he offers Miriam her rod again, and sweeps out into the dusk.

Saturday's Conclave is always a mess. Nicovar has learned this since he first came to Anvil. Friday may pass quickly, as people give their speeches and make their bids for mana supplies, but Saturday is both the first session since they have had a chance to do something and the last session at which they can do anything, and the combination makes for chaos. The agenda fluctuates through the day, as people raise their motions and remove them again, trying to push private deals through with the threat of public attention. Nicovar just put his on the list when he came out of his audience with Kimus, and went to find his dinner.

His spire don't exactly welcome him as a hero when Conclave is over. Half of them were at the session anyway, and not all of them voted in his favour. Archimedes rose from his cushion to stand pointedly with the abstentions. Nicovar endures the quiet disapproval from his spire-mates while they discuss the other business of the day, the scrying they'll need to do tomorrow for the Warmage and the complex arrangements being made with the Thrice-Cursed Court to keep them at each other's throats and inclined to give boons to the Empire for helping them quarrel.

"I suppose you're not sorry?" Archimedes says at last, looking at him, and Nicovar sits up a little straighter.

"I'm not at all sorry," he says. "I was within my rights to meet with Kimus and within my rights to propose amity with it. The Conclave approved the declaration. I have nothing to be ashamed of."

"It was rude," Lucia says, very calm. "Julia is an ally. You should not have used it to ambush her. You could have had all the credit you deserve without embarrassing the Daymage."

"The Celestial Arch has found its ambition again. I hope that Ankarien will do likewise."

Archimedes sighs. "So, you're going for the Archmageship. As you so eloquently put it, you're within your rights. But it's a rough hand you're using. You should have told us, Nicovar, your spire, and we would have supported you. We know you have potential. We would be delighted to bring the Archmageship home again. But you have to trust us. You went off to this audience alone, with only a Leaguer for company, and she's an autumn mage – do you really think she won't turn on you?"

"Lucrezia is a sound ally," Nicovar says, stung.

"At the moment." Lucia folds her hands over her sash. "We won't stop you from standing. But if you want us to campaign for you, you will need to give us some trust in return. We are your spire-mates, and you are young. You cannot do everything on your own."

"If nothing else, you'll need our help for rituals," Archimedes says, and Nicovar has to smile at that. Archimedes can't sound mercenary even when he's trying. He's been bargained with more effectively by toddlers.

"Very well," he says, leaning back in his chair. "I apologise for keeping you in the dark. Where would you like to start?"

CHAPTER TEN – AUTUMN 198

Isaella wakes early by long habit. Years in the army, and then with the army she's no longer part of, have ground a rhythm into her bones. Here in the gathering autumn she wakes almost exactly with the sun's rise, and curls a little deeper into her blankets, watching the grey light creep under the canvas. There is a breeze coming through along with it, promising a bright day and hands reddened by the cold. She needn't get up yet, not at a summit, not with a breathing warmth against her back, and Isaella closes her eyes again and sleeps.

She is woken the second time by a pathetic groaning. She rolls over in her cocoon of bedding to see James lying on his back, his hair springing wide as a halo, with his hand over his eyes.

"Good morning," she says brightly.

"No," James says. "No. I disagree."

"You can't possibly be hung over. You barely drank anything."

"Make the light go away," James says plaintively. "It's bad. Why is it so bright?"

"You're in a tent, lover." Isaella eases herself out of her blankets, leaving them ready to creep into again tonight. "Light comes into tents. Do Marcher houses not have windows?"

James rubs his face. "I live in a cave. I have a burrow. I'm a potato that got up and walked around."

"Very long-legged potato. Sit up, dear, you can't have breakfast until you put your trousers on."

He peeps at her through his fingers. "Coffee? Coffee, Sal?"

"Trousers first."

"You drive a hard bargain."

James doesn't have the trick of slipping snake-like out of his blankets without tangling them. He pushes the layers off himself and lies there a moment, apparently dazed by the exertion. He raises his head when Isaella straddles his thighs, but she's only climbing over him to find herself a clean tunic. "If we all go home and sleep instead, do you think the Empire will notice?"

"We need to fund the armies first. They will definitely notice if they stop getting paid. And we should probably let Barabbas have his fleet to play with. But that's just budgets. First Senate session is at eight, they can pass the funding and we can all go home by what, ten o'clock this evening?"

"Sounds good. I can poke the Conclave with my poking-stick to adjourn until winter."

"Ah yes, the official Warmage poking-stick for recalcitrant magicians."

"It's not official," James says mournfully. "I have to supply my own poking-stick. These are hard times, Sal, hard hungry times."

"Would porridge make them easier?"

"Significantly."

"Good. There's a Striding in the woods that does porridge and coffee for a ring. You can get me some as well."

James makes a show of how creaky his back is trying to get his trousers on whilst lying down, and goes to fetch breakfast.

Nicovar is not used to being nervous when he goes to Conclave. This should all be routine by now, the agenda as familiar as the banners on the walls, a tamed and docile thing. He should not be tempted to tuck his hands into his sash to hide the sweat of his palms. He should not feel his heart pressing against the cage of his ribs. He should be calm.

He feels unready. That's the difference here, against his other speeches and declarations. He knows what he's going to say, he knows his arguments, but it doesn't feel like enough. The Conclave does not like time-wasters, or arrogant upstarts who lose elections – if he doesn't take the prize this time it will be years before he can sensibly try again.

Julia rolls over to him, looking very stern in her belt and chain of office, the staff strapped to the back of her chair like a flag. "Good evening, Nicovar."

"Good evening, Archmage."

"I thought you might try this, after that little victory with Kimus."

Nicovar bows politely. "The Empire is well served by friendship with Kimus. I was honoured by your support."

"Once you raised the declaration, I could hardly speak against it. I'm saddened that we can't work together, Nicovar. You're a very bright young man. Your ambition does you credit. But have you considered the effect on the Conclave?"

"I hope it will be enlivened by the change."

"It will be fractured by the debate." Julia turns to sit beside him, looking out over the Conclave together. "They are factional. Small grudges become magnified in this chamber. A major disagreement now will damage our ability to act for seasons to come. We are too slow to respond to crisis now. Are you willing to hinder us further?"

Nicovar admires the strategy even as he counters it. "Stagnation will not help us. If we are factional, perhaps we need someone new to unite behind."

Julia looks at him sideways, and shakes her head.

"You know me," Nicovar says to the assembled Conclave. "You know that I brokered an alliance with Kimus the All-Seeing, after decades of silence that profited our enemies. You know that I have negotiated with Phaleron and played chess with the heralds of Zakalwe. I will not speak against Archmage Julia. I respect her wisdom. Even more than that, I respect her expertise. But change must come. A new Archmage forces our Eternal allies to reconsider how much they give us. It shakes them out of complacency. We have been well served by Julia's leadership but this Conclave has stood still for too long. We are fossilising. We must change."

Julia, as the incumbent, has the right of defence. Nicovar would normally step back to let the Archmage speak – he takes a small pleasure in holding his position as an equal. "You know Nicovar," she starts. "You also know me. I have served as your Archmage for four years. I have overseen the scrying of our borders, every battlefield, every season. Nicovar speaks of change but change is not good in itself. I have given you stability. When this election is over, I will continue that work. Amity with Kimus is a valuable thing and I do not deny Nicovar's achievement. But it is not enough to build an Archmageship upon. I will take questions."

The factions form just as Julia said they would. They reveal themselves by their questions, who they ask, what they imply. One calls Julia "Archmage" and pointedly asks her to expand on her achievements; one asks Nicovar if he won his chess match; Daniel of Rachel's Guard is very polite to the honourable Archmage, has nothing but respect for her leadership, but has been doing most of the scrying coordination for two years and would be happy to continue doing it for whoever carries the staff. Lucrezia throws Nicovar a bone, asking about the most flattering details of the Kimus meeting. Archimedes speaks up from his cushion to suggest that Nicovar's spire is bigger, more able to cast major rituals on short notice. Julia's spiremates jump in to make some counterpoint about practice and only manage to reinforce the point.

The show of hands is very tight. Ruth nods and says "We'll count. Julia, move to the left, please, Nicovar to the right. All Imperial magicians present have the right to vote. If you're part of the Faraden delegation, please stand at the back, and any abstentions can join them there. Everyone who is voting, form up on the side of your chosen candidate in lines of five. Thank you."

It comes close. It comes unbearably close. The Conclave takes a long time to settle, shuffling between one side of the Hall of Worlds and the other, lining themselves up, speaking with their allies to make their choices together. Nicovar counts the lines as they form and feels the knot tightening in his chest. Julia was right. Factions. Fractures forming under their hands.

Julia turns to face him.

"I concede."

The Conclave, still shuffling into place, does not hear her. She raises her voice. "I concede to the challenger. I support Nicovar for Archmage. Please do not vote for me. I concede."

Nicovar stands stunned, while the magicians crossing the hall break around him, a flowing tide. He can almost taste the salt in the waves.

There ought to be a moment to breathe. There ought to be stillness, between the battle and the weary onward march, a silence after the great tree comes down. Nicovar holds himself stiff, keeping his composure while magicians shake his hand or pause to bow in congratulation. The agenda picks up again, the river rolling onward, before he can thread his way through the back of the crowd to find Julia.

She raises her chin. Nicovar bows.

"I am humbled by your character, Archmage."

"No longer Archmage." Julia reaches over her shoulder to snap the buckle holding her staff in place. She draws it into her lap, seven foot of wood and craft.

"Legally speaking, the honour is yours until the Conclave adjourns tonight."

Julia's eyes narrow. "Do not presume to teach me. Under the circumstances, you'll understand if I prefer to return to my camp. I have been suddenly struck by weariness."

"Quite understandable," Nicovar agrees. "I meant what I said, about valuing your-"

"Don't. Have some manners, Nicovar. Give me a season before you start fishing for my pearls."

She slips an ornate chain of silver and white enamel over her head. "The Chain of Aesh, and the Belt of Stars. The chain has been used, the belt has not."

Nicovar puts on the chain, takes the wide belt that looks so much like armour, stiff pale leather inscribed with the symbols of his Realm. He looks at the staff resting on Julia's knees.

She sighs and holds it up, balanced in her strong hands. "This is not my staff. It belongs to the Empire."

Nicovar reaches for it and stops at her glare.

"This is not your staff. It belongs to the Empire. Use it well – and give it up, when the time comes."

He bows low, accepting the lesson, before he takes the symbol of his new office and turns to the business of his Conclave.

CHAPTER ELEVEN – WINTER 198

The first sign of something wrong was when the messages stopped.

The news flashed around the Heliopticon in frantic shards of light: the Winged Messengers will not fly, we have no word, the Emperor's fleet does not respond. Barabbas is silent. Barabbas is lost.

There is a peculiar delicacy around the word "dead". The scholars of Ankarien, good citizens of the Empire, talk around the Emperor's death as they might step around a crack in the floor. They say "If he is truly gone," as if they could not read the signs. Messages from outside Urizen are always slower to travel, but not by much, with the Navarri messengers running every hour of the day. They know there has been no word, that along the coast the merchants have fled home on the breath of a storm, and the whole Empire waits. And waits, three more weeks, until the keel of a warship washes up in Madruga, a wooden breastbone snapped clean of every rib.

Even before the summit begins, magicians are gathering around the regio. Tomorrow is the solstice, and neither sunset nor the Emperor's shade will wait for them. By the time Nicovar has strapped on his regalia and made his way to the stones, they are already glowing red with power. The circle is filled with Marchers, the Warmage's coven, their faces eerie in the magelight. The centre is held by twin girls barely old enough to work, their staves braced against each other and perpetually pushing apart. The duality of life and death, from which they will bring out the fallen soul; Nicovar admires the metaphor even as the mist coils in to hide the working. This is one of the great rituals, the kind magicians dream of performing, and like all such magic it is dangerous. They have set their lure for Barabbas. Other things may still take the bait.

There is a noise like thunder, or cracking stone – Nicovar dodges away from the nearest pillar before he realises it isn't falling. The circle is half-filled with mist, with smoke from the torches, with moving bodies, but in snatched glimpses he sees the feet of the girls are sliding over the grass, their staves pushed apart by a darkness blacker than the dusky sky, and moving. It holds his gaze. The darkness twists and contracts, building itself a body, and for a moment every hand is tensed upon a weapon, until it speaks.

"Where am I?"

The teenagers look panicked, but they keep their hands on their staves. One of them turns her head, her mouth opening to speak, before the coven leader raises one hand and steps forward. "Do you know my voice?" she demands, and the shadow figure flinches.

"I don't know you. Who are you? Where are we?"

She steps forward, the torchlight gleaming on her braided hair. The shadow is taller and yet she looms over it. "Do you know my face, spirit?"

Somewhere in the darkness, eyes focus on her.

"I do not know you," it says at last, in the voice of the dead Emperor. "I have forgotten. It has been so long."

"Do you know your name?"

"I have forgotten. There have been so many. I forget them all. Who are you asking me to be?"

Annie looks down for a moment, fumbling to fit her wand back into its sheath. She looks weary, her eyes tired – Nicovar realises with a start that she has been weeping. "Were you once the Emperor Barabbas, who was my friend?"

"I do not know," the shadow says earnestly. "I might have been once. I will try to be, if you like."

"Barabbas was last heard of aboard the Basilisk's Daughter at the head of the First Fleet. Do you remember what happened to the fleet?"

The figure looks from side to side, perhaps trying to think. There are hints of a face under its shifting cowl. "I don't recall. Are you sure it's happened? Might it still be to come?"

Annie's shoulders sag.

She keeps questioning the figure as long as it stays, through the whole span the ritual can give her, but the shadow never gives her anything of worth.

Driven by habit, Isaella heads for the Senate when the summit begins, but she doesn't make it down the slope. Anvil looks like a kicked anthill, everyone out and mingling regardless of the deepening mud. She can almost see the gossip flowing along the road.

"Senator," someone calls from behind her, "Senator! A moment, please?"

She squints through the dusk at a pair of Navarri brokers. "I'm not the Senator – I was her proxy, last time, though. What do you need?"

"Is it true about Barabbas?"

"That depends what you've heard. It's true he's missing. The whole fleet is missing, we've had no word for seven weeks. What else are they saying?"

"That the Grendel ambushed him and wiped them out."

"I hope that part's not true," Isaella says honestly, "but I can't know for sure until there's been some scrying done. We should know more by tomorrow. Tonight, if the Warmage moves fast."

"I heard the Warmage was trying to bring him back."

Isaella recognises the fascinated horror of a Navarr faced with high magic. She wore the same expression this morning when James explained what his coven was planning.

"It's called Whispers through the Black Gate. It's not meant to bring anyone back. It's just meant to let them talk to him. I know it's – uncomfortable – but we definitely won't have Barabbas wandering around when he should be dead. Apparently they might bleed from the eyes if he's not actually dead yet. They're magicians and the risk is to themselves."

"But they're not *vates*," a new voice mutters, and Isaella turns to re-affirm that while Navarri magicians should be vates, Marcher magicians are beholden to other rules, and pushes down the instinctive twist in her own stomach at the thought of meddling with magic unprotected.

The conversation draws others, and more rumours to dispel, until Isaella shouts for someone to bring her a box and starts over with what she knows. She is finally interrupted by a Highborn racing past them, her boots threatening to slide out from under her, shouting "Barabbas is dead! The Emperor is dead!"

The crowd turns in stages, trying to find the Highborn in the dark. Isaella stops trying to speak over her and points instead. "You, in the white hood! What have you heard?"

"The Marchers talked to him! At the regio!" The Highborn skids to a halt and leans on her knees to cough. She waves away the flask hastily offered from the crowd. "I'm a scholar. I know that ritual. He's gone. The whole fleet's gone."

The summit passes like a dream. Isaella keeps waiting for the world to shatter, like a bowl dropped from wet hands, frozen in the moment before it falls. The Throne is dead, unexpectedly and before his time. The fleet is missing. The sailors may all be lost. And yet – and yet – the summit goes on. The Senate holds its votes. The generals meet in council. Nothing has changed at all.

She finds Nicovar without meaning to, digging mechanically into his lunch of mushy rice, stained yellow with turmeric and dry smoked fish. Isaella sets her plate down and sits beside him.

"Bean stew?"

"It looked better than the rice."

He huffs out something almost a laugh. "I've eaten worse, though not willingly. Next time I'll stick to beans. How's your summit been?"

Isaella pokes at her stew, trying to decide if that's swede or just a very yellow potato. "Long. And short. And strange."

"The Throne is dead."

"Yes, he is. I was not expecting that, this time in autumn."

"And yet here we are."

The stew is still uncomfortably hot. Isaella nibbles at her spoonful, watching Nicovar's careful way of eating, keeping his wide sleeves out of his bowl."How has your summit been?"

"In two halves," he says, considering it. "One, here, in Anvil, where Barabbas is dead, and we mourn a great disaster. And one in the Hall of Worlds, where it is – a change in the tides. They watch, but they do not care."

"Do you mean the Conclave or the Eternals?"

Nicovar frowns at his rice.

"So now what? Do we – I know what we do, I've read the Constitution, I understand how this works – but do we just go on? Pretend nothing will change?"

"Of course we've changed." Nicovar turns towards her, his bowl abandoned. "The stars are moving above us. Everything will change. But you see it yourself, the shape of the Empire holds back the chaos. We don't have to drown here. We can harness the tide."

Isaella looks at him, eye to eye, and for a moment her fingers itch for the dagger at her belt. "To take us where, Nicovar? You have one title. Are we still racing for another?"

"The Throne cannot stand empty forever," Nicovar says, and his smile is fierce and secretive, like the fire in his eyes.

CHAPTER TWELVE – SPRING 199

The Sentinel Gate spits them out into a blaze of morning light, glittering across the ocean's face.

The Imperials stream through the Gate in their separate sections; the Highborn first, spreading out into a solid mass of shields, to hold against the enemy, and behind them the roaring mass of Wintermark. Navarr and Urizen take the rear and the flanks, to pick off stragglers. They have the wide empty hills of Urizen on their left, and the sea on their right beats against the crumbling cliffs. The narrow cliff-side path pokes bare rock through the grass and guides them, onwards and down, towards the harbour and the Grendel ships.

There are five ships sheltering in the little bay, leaning over as their bottoms sink into the mud, stranded by the tide. Navarri and Highborn archers, all in brown leather with only tattoos to tell them apart, cluster behind the shield-wall, waiting for their moment. A leggy changeling youngster carries the keg of fire tar, its wood swollen from soaking in water all night, and two full quivers of arrows on her hips. Isaella watches the archery group from her place on the cliff edge. Not yet, not yet. Not time to light that barrel of tar. Not close enough to the ships.

A shrill whistle sounds from the path ahead and a Grendel pops out from the rocks, the deep shadows hiding her until she was almost underfoot. She races away from them unencumbered by shield or comrades. A Navarri arrow takes her in the thigh, its fletching dyed in red stripes, and a sober black Highborn bolt follows it into her side. The orc howls. She vanishes under the boots of the army. But ahead, orcs are appearing on the decks of the five ships, and pulling on their armour.

The army bunches together as the cliff-top narrows, pinched between the sea and a steep dip on the inland side, the bones of an old quarry softened in the spring grass. They do not see the orc encampment in the green hollow until the enemy is already flanking them, far too late to swing around and meet them head on. The orcs hammer into the side of their line.

Order vanishes. This is the warfare Isaella is used to, friend and foe wildly intermingled, choosing her targets based on how their swords swing towards her, the glimpse of a sharp grey eartip. She drives her spear into the mass and keeps her eyes open for a charge from the harbour. Here would be the perfect place to pin them down, if the shipboard orcs can climb the hill in time.

A clump of Urizen breaks in front of her, giving way before the spiked clubs of the Grendel. Isaella fits her dance to theirs, stepping alongside them to let the orcs spend their strength on empty air, until one elegant rolling dodge takes a fighter straight over the cliff.

She recognises Nicovar in the instant that he falls.

The Grendel have to be dealt with first, or the club swinging at her head will bury iron in her skull. Isaella takes a deep breath and knocks his feet from under him with the butt of her spear. The Urizen are on him like wasps. Another orc, another stab to the stomach and block to save her knees, and she can let the new line close ahead of her and take the three steps to the place where the grass ends.

She drops to her knees and crawls to the edge, her spear clutched in one hand. The sea is not quite beneath her, hissing around the rocks under a slope of crumbled stone. Nicovar is halfway down, lying on his stomach on a broken corner of rock. His sash flutters beneath him like a ribbon of blood.

Isaella travels light, especially in battle. A wandering Thorn may fight with her whole life strapped on her back, but a soldier has the luxury of pack-oxen. She reaches into her shirt for the only tool she has for this moment, and blows an alarm on her army whistle.

Three Winterfolk are the first to answer. They drop to the grass beside her.

"He's dead."

"Might be. I still want him back. Are you carrying rope?"

"Why would we carry rope?"

"Move it, girls." A Navarri scout braces herself on Isaella's back to look over. "Yeah, I can handle his weight if you can climb for yourself."

"Oh," says the Wintermark woman who doesn't carry rope, "well, I can help lift you both if you're going down for him," so Isaella turns on her knees and lets herself down over the cliff.

The slope is vertical for the first ten feet. She clings on with her fingertips, digging the toes of her boots into crevices in the soft rock. Sand crumbles away under her hands.

Nicovar is a pale bundle of cloth in the corner of her eye. Isaella can't spare him a glance, even when she hears him start to groan. She moves carefully sideways, avoiding a place where rainwater has eaten the stone away to crumbs, a miniature valley of treacherous ground. A crevice between two large boulders gives her something like a path, another few feet down the slope, closer to where Nicovar is struggling to his knees. If he rolls, he will fall, and perhaps take the whole cliff-side with him. The

Winterfolk are shouting from above. Isaella ignores them and waves at the Navarri woman, who sits up on her heels and throws down the end of the rope, knotted around a stone for the weight.

Isaella wraps it around her wrist and takes a deep breath. She looks up, once, to check that the Wintermarker has caught up with events and is bracing her from above, and then she shimmies backward on her stomach until the boulder curves away and lets her drop to the next precarious perch.

Two more boulders, and the climb back is looking very high when Nicovar's hand closes on her ankle. He pulls too hard, throwing her off balance, but her foot lands on a solid notch and the rocks hold firm. Isaella lets him guide her to the next foothold, and the next, and then she is standing beside him on a fragile ledge of sandstone, thirty foot from the cliff's edge, and forty more from the waves.

"I can't go up," Nicovar says. He is on his knees, one arm crooked across his body. His voice doesn't shake.

"That's what the rope is for," Isaella tells him, "and if you argue I will push you off this cliff and then *I* will be Archmage of Day."

"That's – not how it works."

"Are you sure?"

"I think my elbow is broken."

Isaella gnaws her lip. "Do your legs work?"

He shrugs, with only the undamaged side. "I think so. Breathing hurts a lot."

She eyes him up. The wide Archmage belt is probably bracing his ribs enough to be worth making him stiff – she favours climbing unarmoured whenever possible, but needs must – "Take off your sash."

Nicovar is calm, but evidently in too much pain to be rude. He only squints at her for a moment and says "I'll flap in the wind."

"You need it for a sling – no, okay, you're right. Can you move that arm at all?"

"If I take it slowly. I can't grip anything."

"Brace yourself, then."

Balanced on the rock, she helps him pull his overrobe off his shoulders, first the easy side and then the careful, painful second. It hangs down over the sash, fine cream wool, flecked with beads of red glass. Nicovar pulls his arm back against his stomach, blankly stoic. Isaella lifts the Archmage's chain over his head.

He opens his mouth as she wraps it loosely around his bad wrist. "Isaella. What...?"

"If that flaps into the rocks you'll choke yourself," she says briskly. One problem at a time. She can think about the drop under her feet later. "Hold still, I'm going to get this shoulder back into the robe, and then you can put your arm through the other side."

It's a poor sling, even held snug by his sash. Isaella feeds the rope under his armpit and around his chest. Three loops and she ties it off to the main length, watching her fingers intently, thinking about the knot instead of who will fall if it gives way.

"Don't kill yourself climbing," Nicovar says suddenly. "We can throw the rope back down to you."

"Why, Nicky, darling, I didn't know you cared."

"Yes, you did."

She meets his dark eyes. "Yes, I did. You're going to have to do some of the work to get back up, but there are physicks at the top for your arm."

"And my ribs," Nicovar reminds her. "My breathing's getting worse. Has the fighting moved downhill?"

For a moment Isaella's instincts tell her to lean out, to get a better look along the cliff. She stops herself in time and listens instead. "I think so."

"Then we'd better start climbing."

Nicovar is putting a brave face on it, but he isn't capable of much. His feet slip on the rocks, threatening to tip Isaella into the sea, if he falls while she's steadying him. His good arm can keep him balanced but there's too much damage to his ribs to pull himself up. Isaella steels herself and pushes him up little by little, sacrificing her own hand-holds to keep Nicovar moving. The Navarri holding the rope keeps reeling it in, until finally it pulls clear and taut between them, freed from the sloping boulders.

Isaella puts a hand over Nicovar's. "Let go of the rock."

"That seems – No," he says, shivering with shock and fear, dark veins peeping through the pale skin on his cheeks. "No, that's a bad idea."

"You have to hold the rope," Isaella tells him gently, "I'm right here, you won't fall. You have to hold the rope instead. See, it's safe, it can take your weight, but you have to hold it and not let go. That's it. Like that, that's it. Hold on tight and don't let go. They're going to pull you up. Just hold on tight."

Where one Navarr could have braced him, three Wintermark helpers can lift him bodily. He kicks at the rock, loose grit showering down into Isaella's face. She presses herself against the cliff and spits out sand. The way is easier without Nicovar to lift as well, but she's bleeding under her fingernails by the time she reaches that last sheer wall of rock. Her Wintermark friends lean over the edge to pull her up.

The battle has moved down the hill, towards the sea. Dead orcs lie around them, outnumbering the few Imperial corpses. Isaella rolls onto her back just as one of the burning ships collapses in on itself.

She grins at the sky.

CHAPTER THIRTEEN – SUMMER 199

Nicovar pokes his head into the Military Council's tent and finally finds James, squinting down at the map, with his scribbled scrying notes spread out across the countryside. He glances up at Nicovar. "Be with you in a minute."

His eyes take a moment to adjust to the gloom of the tent. James must have been in here for a while, or Nicovar would have found him in his determined circuits of the camp. It's so pleasant to be out of the dust and wind that Nicovar can perfectly understand why. He thinks he might move in permanently.

James gathers up his notes and sighs heavily. "If you had three more scrying covens in your back pocket, you'd tell me, wouldn't you?"

"I wish I did. Ankarien can step in, if you're desperate -"

James snorts. "And lose my strategic rituals? We're counting on that Clarity to get into Liathaven without kicking over the wasp's nest. I hope I'm never that desperate." He moves one of the tokens on the board, little carved figures like playing-pieces. "Look at this. Three Jotun armies in Liathaven and another nosing around the borders of Bregasland, but we can't get a lens on it. We know it's there. The folk on the boundary are seeing the scouts come through. Meanwhile we're massed in the Mourn but we can't get a step closer until tomorrow or we'll be buried in Jotun shit. So, you're right. This is a bad time to have an empty Throne."

Nicovar hides his surprise. He inclines his head and smiles a little.

"Sal told me." James fiddles with the Jotun pieces. "She – It's not that she doesn't trust you. It's that she doesn't think she ought to. You're a hard man to read."

"I'm Urizeni," Nicovar agrees. "You'll do better by asking."

"Alright, then. I'll ask. What are you trying to achieve? And don't give me the good-of-the-Empire sales pitch."

"I'm still working on that pitch," Nicovar admits. "No. It's not just that. I want the Empire's good, yes. But so do a ten thousand citizens who never come to Anvil. You did, and I did, because we want something more. I look at the Empire and I see an unfinished sculpture. When the First Empress took up her chisel, she knew she would not finish. I know I will not finish. But I want to be a part of the work. I want to make the Empire greater and more beautiful. I want to look at it and say, I myself had a hand in this, and be proud of what I have done."

James clicks his jaw, considering. "Ambition is a virtue."

"It is. But you and I both know that the most virtue does not always mean the best outcome."

"We do know that."

Nicovar steps forward, too close for an Urizeni, comfortable for a Marcher listener. "The Senate can give the Throne to any citizen they choose. Do you think they will, if no-one steps forward? Do you think anyone who steps forward will lack ambition?"

The answer takes a while in coming. It's an uncomfortable sort of honour, to be weighed up so intently by someone so dedicated to his own path. James sets down the last map token before he speaks again. "I wouldn't trust myself to make this decision alone. But if you can persuade two-thirds of the Senate, I won't be making it alone. You're right that we need a Throne. And the qualifications for that..." He meets Nicovar's eyes. "I'm not pledging eternal loyalty to you. If I change my mind, I'll say so, publicly. You need to keep persuading me, because I'm not quite convinced you're the man for the job. But I'll help you try."

The Ankarien camp has been rearranged. For as long as Nicovar has been coming to Anvil, the Spire's delegation has had a single communal tent for all their meals and meetings, along with its awning in good weather, and the smaller tents were all private. Now the long table with its benches is under a new canvas with open sides, open to the breeze, and the main tent has been split in half: this side of the curtain for Spire life, that side for politics. The Arbiter's cushion dominates the new meeting room.

Ever the mediator, he had insisted that above all the room should be pleasant. Nicovar wouldn't have thought of it himself, but now he understands the strategy. They are holding court, as much as any Eternal sitting in state. They need to appear capable of the task they have set themselves. And besides that, there's the emotional effect, playing under the surface: here is a good place, you are welcome here, stay and be part of this. For the same reason, there's no enchantment on the room to clear the mind or refresh the spirit. Electing an Empress is an emotional business.

When Nicovar comes home to his spire after the first Conclave session, the meeting room is warm with lantern-light. Archimedes is sprawled on his cushion with a palmful of almonds to snack on as he talks. Isaella is already here, with a Leaguer Nicovar recognises as a general – Giuseppe, who took an arrow the day they were ambushed on the road. Nicovar slips into his place at the back, in the centre of things. Cressida hops down from the bench to sit beside him.

"This is very exciting," she whispers loudly. "Are we sure it's legal?"

"Not in the least. This is absolutely illegal and we're all going to be arrested at any moment."

"Oh good. That always brightens my evening. Ah, here's Lucrezia. Lucy, darling, come sit with us. We're plotting against the magistrates."

"I will turn you both in," Archimedes grumbles. "Come in, Grandmaster, have a seat, have a drink. Warmage, you too. Is this everyone?"

"For now," Nicovar says.

"Then you'd better introduce us."

Nicovar sits up, letting Cressida steal his second cushion. "We all know James the Warmage, I think. Isaella is the customary proxy for Miaren and adjunct to General Gwyneth, Giuseppe is the general for – sorry, Giuseppe, remind me?"

"Towerjacks."

"Thank you. I am Nicovar, Archmage of Day, and this is Cressida and her sister Lucrezia of the Celestial Arch, and Archimedes, the Arbiter of my spire. We all know by now what happened to Barabbas, and we all see that for stability's sake, we need to fill his shoes. We are here to elect a Throne."

"Ooh," says Cressida, "are we a shadowy cabal? I love shadowy cabals."

Giuseppe looks around. "We don't have any senators."

"We do," Archimedes says.

"Who?"

Archimedes inclines his head.

"Ah. Congratulations, Senator. Well, that's one vote. It is Nicovar we're electing, I assume?"

"Of course it is," says Lucrezia. "Unless you want the job, General?"

Giuseppe huffs out a laugh. "No, I don't want it. You should know, though. Miriam does. General of the Silent Tide, one of our field-marshals. There's a lot of Highborn who'd like to see her elected. They think she'd bring – stability, as you said."

"But you don't support her?"

"She wants to fix the borders, as the Peacemaker did. I don't agree with that. I think taking Segura was the best thing the Empire has done in a generation and we shouldn't stop there."

James sets his staff behind him, settling in. "You want to conquer Faraden?"

"Not as much as I want to conquer the Barrens. And that will help you get the Dawnish on side – Miriam would abandon the Barrens, the Dawnish won't like that. But Nicovar – Isaella tells me you threw yourself off a cliff last season. Are you planning on doing the same with the Empire? What's your intention?"

Nicovar smiles. "I want to build, Giuseppe. More than that, I want to polish. The Empire is the greatest civilisation in the world but we all know it could be more. We know we have roads, schools, harbours that need upkeep. All those resources, diverted to build the Barabbine Fleet, we can use them here at home. I don't think we should stop expanding and I don't think we need to. We need to let the armies do their jobs, strengthen our infrastructure here at home, and give you the support you need to keep pushing forward. Miriam would fix the borders? Say we're done, this is enough now, we're not capable of better? Then she would abandon every human outside to a life without Virtue, with no hope of transcendence. I won't accept that."

Giuseppe nods approvingly. "I can appreciate that philosophy. What will you do when they say you have no military experience?"

"That's why you're here, Giuseppe," Cressida says, leaning around Nicovar to be seen. "Barabbas thought he could learn it all himself and look how that went. Nobody can do it all. Nicovar is surrounding himself with good advisors from the beginning."

"What are you here to advise on?"

Cress throws her hands joyously into the air. "Jollity and mirth! And finances. Nicovar can't calculate anything more complicated than mana costs."

"Which is what you're here for," Nicovar agrees. "Isaella is military and pays more attention to the Senate than anyone I know."

"More than some Senators," Isaella says. "I can tell you they're not comfortable having an empty Throne. Barabbas ruled for a long time and they got used to having him there. They're willing to be wooed."

Archimedes clucks thoughtfully. "From what I've seen of my colleagues so far, I agree. None of them seems willing to step up and I think I can persuade them that they shouldn't. They're feeling isolated. I think there's obvious merit in looking for a Throne with closer ties to the other parts of our government."

"That'll be good for you, Nic."

"But also for Miriam. It reduces rivals, puts us in a stronger position – I agree. It's a sound argument."

Lucrezia lifts her mask a moment to scratch the bridge of her nose. Cressida looks unaccountably tense until she puts it back on. "I'm not sure the Conclave can do much here."

"Not directly," Nicovar says, "but you have influence. The Celestial Arch attracts people with connections and you're their Grandmaster. It helps to extend our Net. We have Archimedes, that's one vote, and my Spire stands with me, that will help get Urizen on board. There are four Freeborn senators who will need to be bought, not necessarily with money. What does the Brass Coast want?"

"To keep Segura," Giuseppe says. "It's not really secure yet. The Lasambrians still want it back. Promising to aggressively defend it might be a start."

"What about Navarr?"

Isaella looks stung. "We're not for sale. We gave our loyalty to the Empire a long time ago. But that doesn't mean we've abandoned –" She shakes her head. "Broceliande isn't part of the Empire. It should be. It *will* be. It's part of Navarr. But it's mostly held by the Vallorn and it has no Senator, so it's technically outside Imperial borders. Broceliande was our greatest city once. No Navarr will vote for anyone who wants to abandon it."

The conference goes on long into the night. Cressida stretches across the tent with her feet propped up on Archimedes' cushion, pretending to be asleep between bouts of mathematics. Lucrezia somehow ends up with her head in Giuseppe's lap. He looks mildly alarmed whenever she shakes her head, her horns poking him in tender places. James passes around something stingingly ginger that Nicovar can't bear after the first cautious sip, though everyone else seems happy to partake. The delegation's oldest child pokes her head into the tent three times to listen before her father finally takes her off to bed.

Nicovar can almost hear the bricks of his foundation dropping into place.

CHAPTER FOURTEEN – AUTUMN 199

They say that the weather in Anvil reflects the constellations. When the Sentinel Gate is aligned to the north, Anvil freezes; when the stars turn it south, Anvil bakes. Today the dry leaves skirl across dry ground, hollow-drum solid underfoot from its summer baking, but the breeze is wet with oncoming rains. Autumn in Liathaven comes late and sudden.

The Jotun were ready for them. That was always a given. They have been fighting the Empire for generations and know how it goes. If the Empire keeps its word at all, it will not stretch an inch further than it must. Attack was inevitable the moment the ceasefire ended.

Isaella has a suspicion they don't really want to hold Liathaven. The land on a map seems good, rich timber forests with a sound climate, hills but no impassable mountains. But the Vallorn squatting over the ruined city makes navigation impossible unless you take the long winding road around the edge, and devours what comes into its reach. Half the territory is unusable for any mortal purpose. The Jotun forests to its west are far more forgiving. Perhaps the orcs only wanted it as a beachhead for Bregasland.

And Bregasland has suffered this season. As inevitably as the Empire reaching for Liathaven, the Jotun have invaded there. The Marchers have dug in over the seasons of waiting, refusing to abandon an inch of their land. When the Jotun came past the boundary stones, the Marcher yeofolk fought them, and died. There would be no evacuation of Bregasland. The Marchers would not leave.

In the face of all that, Anvil summits are the simplest times in Isaella's life. She force-marched to get here, eight hundred miles in two weeks along the grass-rivers of the Trods, their currents of magic impossibly quickening her steps. The night before the summit she pitches her tent under the eaves of the oak trees and goes hunting through the darkness for Marcher accents, to find James and twine their bodies in companionable sleep. Tomorrow will be soon enough to start work.

The summit won't officially start until sunset. Isaella takes advantage of the extra time to have her first leisurely breakfast in months, dark bread and butter and stewed Marcher apples, sweet with the new crop. James drags a bench into a sunbeam and sprawls on it, his long legs overhanging the end. Isaella makes him sit up to take his bowl and sets herself down before he can reclaim his space. He glares at her over his breakfast. She smiles very innocently and hands him a spoon.

"What's on the plan for today, Sal?"

Isaella finishes her mouthful of bread-and-apple before she answers, "Move my registration to Liathaven, I think."

James looks startled. "I thought you'd done that already? You've hardly been anywhere else all year."

"Exactly. So I should put that on the books. And there are plenty of displaced Navarri who'd rather form a fighting band than resettle. But I have a forest in Miaren I haven't sold back yet, and – well. Liathaven is going to need a Senator very soon and the candidates will have to be registered there ahead of time. There's more than one reason to do it."

James taps their bowls together, a makeshift toast. "Here's to good planning. You'll be raiding for real, of course."

"Obviously."

The Military Council is more in agreement than Isaella has ever seen them. They argue about trade-offs and practical concerns, which armies should hold and which advance, but the priorities are all the same. The western front is the only place of interest. They leave two armies in Spiral to hold the border, they keep a scattering around elsewhere, but the Empire's focus is on Liathaven and the Mourn.

Isaella watches Miriam's attempts to direct the conversation. She's subtle, but the effort is there. Giuseppe and James do their part to undercut her leadership, and the field-marshal's rod for Saturday goes unexpectedly to the Bounders general, on the theory that she knows the terrain best. Miriam's chance to command this summit has just been lost; Highguard will go to Bregasland tomorrow, with Dawn and the Marchers to help them make a wall, and Navarr to shoot over their heads. The Urizeni will go too, but everyone knows they only have thirty fighters present. It's a question of numbers. Urizen tomorrow, the Brass Coast on Sunday, to avoid weakening either force by putting the smallest nations together, and Wintermark will lead Varushka and the League to make a more mobile group and chase a Jotun general through Liathaven woods.

It's a point of national pride to Isaella that the Marchers can't be asked to fight away from their own threatened lands, and Navarr is trusted to understand. Not that there isn't some anger, back at the fire-pit in the woods, but they all show up in the morning dressed for battle.

The Sentinel Gate opens in a shimmer like heat-haze. In Anvil it hasn't rained for days, the tents bone-dry and browning with kicked-up dust. Isaella knows when she's passed through by the splashing underfoot. Southern Bregasland is in the middle of its autumn flood and there's no dry ground in sight.

They march out into open terrain, with nothing but a few bedraggled trees for cover. It's hard to listen over the noise of hundreds of boots on flooded grassland, but scanning the horizon Isaella sees a grey-black line, dark against the white clouds. The enemy are here.

The Imperials push forward, muttering imprecations against Marcher mud and the rapid soaking their feet are getting. They change places as they move, the narrow column widening into a mass, with the shields towards the outside and the pole-arms in front. Their goal is a hidden depression in the landscape, where the reeds are a little thicker and the water a little deeper, ringed by knee-high stones. It is a regio, and buried in its centre is a fallen star. The orcs are close enough to see their faces when the magicians take up their mana and step inside.

Isaella has no time to watch the ritual. She knows more-or-less what it's about, how it's supposed to turn the marshes against the invaders, make them into hostile ground for anyone not of Marcher stock, but Spring magic still makes her skin crawl, and there are six hundred Jotun bearing down on them.

They are rapidly surrounded, when the Jotun crash into the shield wall and find it doesn't break. The Imperials make rings around the magicians, shields and billhooks and pikes, archers and mages and physicks, and one hard core of Highborn in the centre, blocking arrows from the magicians with their own plate-armoured bodies. Isaella keeps to the second line when she can, stabbing between shields with her spear. Jotun toes make excellent targets, if you can trust the Highborn in front to guard your head.

The ritual goes off – it must have done, surely, or the magicians would not be snatching up their weapons again – and the prickly mass of Imperials starts inching through the flooded meadow towards the Gate. The Jotun press hard at their retreating side, trying to push them into running and exposing their backs to the sword. The defence grows ragged. Isaella sees Nicovar go down, tripped by a broken pike, and twists her body through the line to reach him and pull him back behind the shields. She takes a club to the shoulder and another to the back before she's safe and reclaiming her spear from a baffled Marcher physick. She waves away his attentions. They're only a hundred yards from the Gate. Her hurts can wait.

James comes to find her while she's sitting on a field hospital bench, straddling it so she can lean forward on her elbows when she gets dizzy. She looks up at him from under her eyelashes. He's very tall from this angle, his lip bitten red with worry.

"You shouldn't have done that."

Isaella sits up to make room for him. "Which part?"

"That's the second time you've done something reckless to fetch Nicovar back."

"He keeps falling over." Isaella tries to shrug and regrets it. James squeezes her arm.

"Your collar-bone again?"

"No, it's a rib this time."

"You can't keep doing this."

Isaella meets his eyes and takes a deep, painful breath. "I'm a warrior."

"So am I." James looks away. "We need you alive."

"Not as much as you need an Empress."

"There are other – Empress Miriam would not be a disaster. Empress Inga. We can find other candidates, we don't have to choose between you and him. Did you even stop to choose? Before you threw yourself under the swords for him? Why does he matter so much?"

Isaella searches for answers. She's never told James about that first meeting, the moment of shock like tripping on a root. He is a Marcher, he doesn't understand the Great Dance, would smile it away as superstition. He watches her, his eyes dark and very serious.

In the end, it's James who speaks first. He half-shrugs, half-smiles. "Okay."

"I never promised you anything. But if I had, I'd have kept it. I'm not involved with Nicovar." The words burst out of her all wrong, too much like a confession.

"I know that." James says quietly. "He's just the most important thing to you. He always has been."

"James."

He shakes his head. "It's not just you. If you hadn't gone over the cliff for him – if you'd come back alone – I wouldn't have forgiven you."

"So why is there a problem?"

"We both deserve better than second best." James presses his forehead to hers, a long and wordless farewell. When he straightens up his hair brushes the canvas, a halo of black curls. Isaella longs to sink her fingers into it again. She grips her knees instead, curls forward around her broken rib.

"You rest," James says. "I'll move your things to the Navarri camp."

CHAPTER FIFTEEN – WINTER 199

The war in Liathaven is short and brutal. The Jotun have had enough of the Vallorn forcing them to creep around the edges of the forest, and the timber trade does not delight them. They want farms. The orcs stream north into Bregasland and die in their hundreds. The waters of the Marches are awake and every ditch a barrier. The Imperial armies sweep through Liathaven, and retake it.

Nicovar follows their progress from the library of Ankarien. The Heliopticon has not been still all winter, the specialised ushabti who watch the lights taking down endless messages in their precise, uninflected script, and making the mirrors dance to send them onwards. With practice, a human can read the flashes just as well as the ushabti can, and call out the words as they come in. Nicovar lacks the skill. He sifts through the little slips of paper instead, piecing together the days.

Overhead, the Wanderer burns red among the icy stars.

He travels to Anvil with more than habitual care. His spire have spent the season conspiring and they bring with them a new tent for a meeting room, the canvas dyed a painstakingly even burgundy, to stand out against the plain white of their camp. They leave behind one of the children who has grown big enough to be exhausting with his toddling, and persuade an army-bound sixteen-year-old to come and be messenger for them, bribing her with the promise she'll meet the egregore. They have new socks, and new warm underrobes, fluffy wool hiding beneath their silks. Ankarien is going prepared.

They reach Anvil in the chilly mid-morning. Setting up camp takes most of the day, the sleeping tents and the meeting room and the big Spire tent for the mess table and the smaller storage one and the firepit with its sloping awning. Nicovar finally changes into his Archmage regalia at sunset, and climbs the hill to Navarr.

At first the camp seems deserted. Nicovar roams around and finds the Striding banners he expects to see, but scarcely any people, until a massed cheer from the woods enlightens him. He picks his way along the woodland paths, avoiding the trees by lantern-light and glowstone, but he's not used to navigating through woods and the crowd breaks up and flows around him before he finds the clearing. He turns instead and follows them back to the open field.

Isaella has already returned to her tent, crouching down to pass hot soup to someone huddled in the blankets inside. They speak softly, Isaella's clear voice and an unfamiliar woman with the accent of Liathaven, weary and resigned.

Nicovar watches the candlelight blossom over her face, sleek as an otter, the sprig of red leaves tattooed on her temple, and thinks she looks nothing like the Warmage.

Isaella doesn't stand to acknowledge him until she's good and ready. "She has a headache," she says, defensive.

"It's none of my business," Nicovar says, shrugging a little. He works on keeping his face politely blank.

Isaella steps in close. Her hand is tense upon her knife. "What do you want?"

The familiar tension thrums between them. Nicovar knows she could kill him, almost wants to kill him, and his heart pounds with excitement. He is not carrying a weapon. A taut burn scar gleams on her left cheek, its edges sharp as a blade.

"We're allies," he says quietly. "Remember?"

Isaella relaxes just a fraction.

"What do you want?"

"We're having a meeting. Late, I'm afraid – there's no time between Senate and Conclave. It'll be midnight by the time we can start. But we need to plan. When's your election?"

"Tomorrow. Six in the evening. We have some time to work for that. I might not get it."

"You have rivals?"

"Of course. I'm the best qualified but they can appeal to Liathaven heritage, I'm Serenese by birth. We can discuss this at the meeting – what do you need me to do now?"

"Come to the meeting. We need to discuss military strategy. And I was going to ask if you knew where James was camped, but now I think you probably don't."

Isaella hisses through bared teeth, almost a snarl. "Fuck off."

Nicovar bows to her and sets off down the hill again.

The new tent glows warm with lightstones, but there's a frost coming on. Nicovar is abjectly grateful for his new socks, after a Conclave meeting that dragged on for hours, over sorcery accusations in Varushka and possible deals with the City of

Locks and an attempt to overthrow the Dean of the Lyceum which involved two mediocre research magicians being extremely pedantic about the principle of dominion for fifteen minutes, until finally one of them ran out of mana and everyone stopped asking questions in hope that the other would stop talking. Nicovar has been standing on cold ground all evening and he's anxious to rest his legs.

James beats him to the Ankarien camp by half a step. There's only one bench free in the meeting room and they sit down cautiously at opposite ends of it, politely distant, until Cressida saunters in and says "Scooch over," so there's nothing to be done but sit with their legs almost touching. James looks uncertainly at Nicovar, and then at his own feet, and finally he pulls a blanket from the pile of cushions beside him and spreads it over their knees, with Cressida under one end for courtesy's sake. Nicovar thinks about kicking off his boots, but that seems a little too pushy. He tucks the blanket around his legs instead and whispers, "I feel warmer already. Did you bring any of the ginger stuff?"

"You hate the ginger stuff," James whispers back, "I brought licorice cordial," and hands Nicovar a hip-flask, slightly heated by his body. It doesn't burn like the ginger, but that's the best Nicovar can say for it. He takes a second sip anyway.

"Lucrezia can't make it," Cress says once she's settled. "There are Heralds on the field looking for autumn mages and she has to go and impress them."

"Alright, then we won't wait," says Archimedes. "I have two items of business, then we'll go round the circle. If that's okay with you, Nicovar? Alright. First, the empire retook Liathaven, but the fighting is very close in Bregasland and the Grendel have stepped up their raiding against Urizen. There's a proposal before the Senate to rebuild the Barabbine Fleet. I'm against, but I want our collective wisdom on the question. Second, Isaella is standing for the Senate tomorrow. Who has contacts in Navarr?

Navarri elections are simplicity refined to art. Nicovar watches from the edge of the clearing and recognises with a swell of admiration how the shape of Conclave elections and Senate votes have been drawn from this ancient practice. He had never realised that something so straightforward had any origin but itself.

The candidates stand in front of their electorate. Observers cluster at the sides, keeping themselves separate by the native magic of the Navarri, reading patterns in how everyone steps. There are no questions, no debates. They give their brief speeches, and the people move. Everything in the open, everyone known.

Isaella's primary opponent is a fierce changeling woman missing an antler tip. She speaks passionately of her love for Liathaven, how she has fought for it all her life. After her comes a grey librarian, who says only that he stands aside in favour of Isaella. A third is brash and ignorant and she insults the crowd with every word she speaks; their distaste is plain on their faces. Isaella goes last and Nicovar can't help wondering if that was strategy, to leave her words freshest in the mind. Her speech is short but thorough: she knows the Senate and the Senators well enough to work with them from the start; she has fought in Liathaven since the invasion began; Liathaven has been retaken and what it needs now is roads, resettlement, and resources to rebuild the beacon towers.

When the voters line up before their candidates, Isaella wins thirty-five to twenty.

She comes to Nicovar in the shadow of the trees, grinning. "Hello, Archmage."

Nicovar bows. "Senator."

"Yes, I am."

"Congratulations. May your career be long and fruitful."

"Oh, I intend that it shall."

Nicovar says, very solemnly, "And may I count on your vote, Senator?"

"Not if you're a little shit like you were yesterday, no."

"I'm sorry."

"No, you're not."

"I am. It's just I'm so happy for you I can't help smiling."

Isaella grins wider, and then huffs. "You're Urizeni. You can always help smiling, you're not sorry, and you owe me a drink."

"So I do. Now?"

"That sounds – no, I have to go to work now. And then to the Senate, and then you have Conclave. I'll see Archimedes in the Senate, I know. Will you make sure Cress and Lucrezia know?"

"Of course." Nicovar bows again, before offering his hand to shake. "I really am happy for you."

Isaella takes his hand in both of hers. "I know. Go to work, Archmage. I'll see you later."

CHAPTER SIXTEEN – SPRING 200

The arithmetic of Throne elections is simple. At least two-thirds of the Senate must vote for the candidate; at least one-third of the Synod must decline to veto the result. The Synod won't veto Nicovar, not unless he does something astonishingly stupid between now and then. He's a virtuous citizen and an Archmage. They only need to persuade twenty Senators and the throne will be theirs.

They have five.

Archimedes was the first. Isaella makes a second. The twins and General Giuseppe have brought them Johanna of Holberg, while Isaac of Necropolis would vote for anyone to keep Miriam out of the office. Military strategy has become the popular distinction between them and Tessa will be theirs if they can only hang onto Bregasland long enough to have an election.

Cressida has started keeping a list. These will vote for Nicovar, those others for Miriam, two of the Varushkans for the Varushkan with no real chance. Most, undecided.

"I've been working on the Dawnish," she says as Isaella settles in for the Friday meeting. "Two at least are leaning towards you, but they won't commit until you publicly announce your candidacy."

Nicovar cocks his head. "I already did that," he points out mildly. "That's what we're doing here."

"Well, I suppose, in a sense, but you weren't very dramatic about it."

"Ah. You mean in the tournament square."

"A declaration could move us along," Isaella says, leaning forward on her knees. "We've been working on the Senators, but we don't have to do it all ourselves. The nations will push their own Senators to vote one way or the other, as soon as they know there's a contest underway. People don't like not having a Throne."

"Alright. I don't see a downside. It'll draw Miriam out of the woodwork, but I don't think it'll be any surprise to the Senate, will it?"

Isaella shakes her head. "The Senate in general? No. One or two of the newer Senators might be out of touch, but you two are the only serious candidates under discussion. Sofia Kovach wants to appoint her sister, but no-one else does."

"Can we switch her over?"

"I doubt it. She'll be voting for Silviya no matter how hopeless."

"Then we won't worry about her. Concentrate on Dawn and the Brass Coast for now. We need to get some momentum going – if we can pull in those two, we'll have a significant following."

Giuseppe looks around from his quiet conversation with Johanna. "The Freeborn? Let me have a word with them. I've negotiated with Freeborn before, I'm used to how they write contracts."

"Take a Senator to introduce you," Cressida says. "Archimedes, if he's willing. No offence, Johanna, but I'm working on a cross-national presentation."

Johanna waves a heavily ringed hand and turns her shoulders a little further towards Giuseppe. Cressida shrugs.

"So, that leaves you working on the Dawnish, Nic. How are you going to impress them?"

The answer turns out to be with warfare. Nicovar stands up in the tournament square on Saturday afternoon, while the knights are resting after a quest to the Barrens, and speaks in his clearest voice. He's not wearing his Archmage regalia, because he is not here as the Archmage. The sleeves of his robe are bound close to his arms with gleaming leather mage armour, a deep and bloody red. His rod hangs ready at his hip. Isaella watches, ready to mingle when he's done talking and nudge her friends here towards his candidacy, and understands the warrior-king he is showing them.

The speech is short and direct. She has a feeling he's written it like a Conclave speech, like the one-minute proposals she used to hear James rehearsing in whispers when he couldn't sleep. Nicovar doesn't hedge his words.

"People of Dawn! I am Nicovar of Urizen! I have no noble house, yet I have proven my worth. I have risen to become Archmage and led the Empire's magicians in the Conclave. Now I set myself against the highest challenge in the Empire, to lead it as Empress. I seek the Throne. I do not ask for your support, for I have not proven myself to you. Urizen will fight with Dawn in battle tomorrow. Let me fight with you, and I will show you who I am!"

A half-armoured knight beats sword against shield, her silver blazon gleaming in the sunlight, griffin wings outstretched. "It is a bold quest! I have no Senate vote, but I will fight with you!" She grins across the grassy square, caught up in the moment. "Come and show us your courage!"

Isaella rubs her bruised elbow, swollen and stiff from a badly caught Jotun club that morning, and silently promises vengeance if the Dawnish don't bring Nicovar home alive.

A Navarri senator has certain responsibilities, to her nation and her people. In the springtime, these responsibilities include judging a baking contest (first prize went to the cider carrot cake, with the honey biscuits coming in second and an honourable mention for the apple pie presented by the two six-year-olds) and bringing enthusiasm to the noisy sunset parade around the camps. Between the cake and the parade, however, Isaella is required to hunt for magicians.

The Hunt changes every year, rotating through the patchwork traditions of each territory. Last year Isaella spent the afternoon with a pocket full of ribbons, pinning them onto passing vates as stealthily as she could. The most decorated magician at parade time was slung beneath a pole and carried in the parade like a slaughtered deer. This year, the theme is greyhounds.

Six vates have volunteered to be the prey. They are gathered under the eaves of the wood, tossing their heads to make the long ears of their masks shake. From the absence of several faces in the crowd, Isaella guesses that other magicians are waiting around Anvil to take over as the hares. They are armed with daggers and light wooden bucklers, and whatever turn of speed they can find.

Isaella is ready with her spear. She turns it in her hands, feeling her elbow protest the movement. The hunt in her childhood steading was always done with sword-length wooden rods and the magicians had an hour's headstart to reach Lookout Hill and fortify it with brushwood. Those foggy mornings were the best times of the year. But the sun today is bright and the trees make a dappled green shade, and she can leap a guy-line as nimbly as any magician on the run.

She hops up onto a wide log, scraped clean of bark for use as a bench. The hunters ignore her until she blows on the ridiculous outsized whistle one of the vates handed her earlier. With effort and a mental squint, she can hear the resemblance to a shrill canine howl.

"Remember the rules!" she shouts to the watching crowd. "Anyone not wearing a hare mask is out of bounds! This year we're using real weapons, but that does *not* mean you can kill each other! No hitting anyone while they're down, this is play not warfare, and when you stab someone you get them a physick! Your goal is to collect the hare masks. Anyone who makes it back here with a stolen mask gets – what do they get, Bryn? Fame and glory, okay. You get fame, glory, and a bottle of cherry wine if you can present Bryn with a hare mask before sunset. After six o'clock, the vates get the wine! Let's hunt!"

She blows the whistle again. The vates dash out across the field, splitting up to make the chase harder. Isaella grins as she races after them. Spring has come to the Empire.

In the dusty morning, with a pounding hangover, she waits by the Sentinel Gate. The distant sounds of battle filter through, and the chatter of a stream that doesn't run through Anvil. On this side of the gate there is quiet, a handful of physicks who are waiting to patch up the wounded who straggle back early, a game of catch going on in the open space where the armies muster, almost the only space in Anvil big enough to throw a ball.

A heavy sigh heralds James's arrival, settling in to lean against the same gatepost Isaella has chosen. She peers up at him through her headache. "Morning."

"Morning, Sal."

"How was Conclave?"

James groans.

Nothing more seems to be forthcoming. Isaella gives it a moment before she says "So…?"

"Don't ask. Really, don't, it's stupid and annoying and *technical*. The Conclave loves its procedural arguments. Nicovar had a great time," he adds, at just the right moment to make Isaella dissolve into giggles. "How was the Senate?"

"We approved the Faraden trade embassy."

"Really? But they're heretics, I thought that was a sure failure."

"Everyone we can possibly trade with is a heretic. I don't regard it as a meaningful argument. If they decide they want to reciprocate we've – not agreed, not exactly, yet, but the general feeling is we'll offer them a spot in one of the Highguard ports. There's no shortage of good religion there."

"Well, that's true," James says, looking uncomfortable, "but I wouldn't want my householders – Here they come."

The returning army is soaked in blood. Isaella's stomach twists uncomfortably at the mud-smeared bandages half of them seem to be sporting. It must have been a rough battle. Varushka piles through the gate in a tangle of exhausted fighters and the wounded propped up between their friends. Isaella doesn't see any bodies, only dozens of injuries. Perhaps no worse than rough, and some of that blood is from orcish veins.

The Dawnish stagger home like drunks from a brawl, still smiling. The knight with the eagle blazon is hopping with one arm around her sister's shoulder, keeping all the weight off that leg. Isaella lets her get clear of the press before she tugs at James's sleeve and goes over.

"You look in a mess," she says. "Did we win?"

"Thoroughly," the knight says in deep satisfaction, still balanced on one foot. "There are two Druj generals dead in that valley. You're Nicky's friend, aren't you?"

James snorts helplessly.

"I don't think he calls himself that," Isaella says, "but please, carry on, he'll hate it. Have you seen him recently?"

"He's around here somewhere. He did pretty good. Dodged an arrow in the first five minutes and kept it up from there."

Isaella presses her hands together in solemn prayer. "Thank you so much. I've been trying to teach him to duck for years."

CHAPTER SEVENTEEN – SUMMER 200

The Senate has its building, walled in stone and floored in good flat timber. The Conclave has the Hall of Worlds, eternally shifting with the moods of the Realms. The Synod has a tent.

It's a large tent, but that's the best that can be said for it. It's poorly lit, a few lightstones hung from the central pole struggling to chase away the gloom, and the grass underfoot must be an icy morass in the winter. In today's summer warmth it's easy to find relief in the cave-like Synod hall. Or it would be, if Nicovar wasn't here for one of the least-used of the Synod powers.

He strolls over to General Miriam, here waiting just as he is. She nods at him stiffly, her hand twitching in the way that means a lowlander suppressing the habit of shaking hands. Nicovar bows nearly as shallowly.

"Pleasure to see you here, General."

"Archmage," Miriam echoes. "Did you know this was coming?"

"I'm as surprised as you are. Do you know, the civil servant couldn't tell me the last time they called for an inquisition?"

Miriam raises a grey eyebrow. "You asked?"

"I'm curious about these things. The Constitution implies some things about the Synod that the Empire in practice doesn't reflect."

"The Synod is a secondary body," Miriam says dismissively. "It's not intended to rule us. It only functions as a restraint."

Nicovar tilts his head, carefully puzzled. "Are you a constitutional scholar?"

"I'm a General. A very successful one. And you, I hear, are a moderately competent mage with a Navarri babysitter."

"I'll tell her you said that. She'll be tickled."

"You see? You can't stand on your own feet. Stop this nonsense, magician, you must know you're not fit to wear the crown."

"I don't know that," Nicovar says calmly. "I don't think you believe that either. It's a very obvious tactic, General, trying to damage your opponent's morale when you don't have the strength to defeat them. I'm not going to give up and go home. You're going to have to fight me, Miriam. Out in the open, in front of the Senate. How many votes do you have so far?"

She has eight, Nicovar knows. He has eleven. It could go either way, if they voted tomorrow.

Miriam stares flatly at him. She's very good at this, projecting her personal strength. Nicovar acknowledges to himself that she is older than him, and more experienced, and taller. He breathes deeply through his nose.

"Did you know," he says slowly, "that the Synod only calls an Inquisition when they think their target won't talk to them otherwise? I know I would have come on a friendly invitation. I'm shocked that a Highborn would refuse."

"They didn't ask. No doubt they expected a magician to wriggle out of it."

"Oh," Nicovar says, "this is a Lineage thing, isn't it? You don't want a draughir emperor."

"This isn't a campaign against you. Don't flatter yourself. I'm running because I would make a better Empress than anyone else available. Not to stop you. You never figured in my calculations."

"I hope I do now."

It's disappointing that a tent doesn't have any doors. Nicovar would rather like a door to creak open and put a clean end to the conversation. Instead, he holds Miriam's gaze for a few seconds, and then bows to her again and turns away.

Eventually, ten minutes after the inquisition was legally supposed to start, Nicovar spots a little circle of people lurking outside the tent, apparently trying to organise themselves. He interrupts them, as cheerfully as he can. "Good evening, friends. Are you here to inquisit me?"

"I -" The Varushkan woman in front looks flustered, turning to look at her companions for help. "Are you Archmage Nicovar?"

"I am. It's an honour to be here. You're… Cardinal Duscha?"

"Gatekeeper."

"Gatekeeper. Of Pride."

"Well done, you know who we are," the Marcher behind her mutters.

Nicovar squints at him, as through the sun were in his eyes. "No, sorry, Tom, no idea who you are, and I've never been rascally drunk on your cider."

Tom grins. "Alright. Yeah, Duscha and Joshua are here for you, and me and Annette will talk to Miriam."

"Is it time yet?" Duscha asks anxiously.

"We're a little late."

"Then let's get started," Tom says, and points Nicovar back into the dim Synod tent.

He sits cross-legged on the grass, his hands resting on his knees. Duscha has brought a cushion, but even so Nicovar winces in sympathy, looking at how she shifts to ease her hips. Joshua, younger than either of them, just drops down to a sprawl.

"Try not to listen to the other conversation," he says. "We wanted to do this in private but the Synod tent is really the proper place for it. Now, this is an Inquisition, which means you have to be here, but I'm supposed to remind you that you don't technically have to talk to us or tell us the truth, you just legally have to be here for an hour."

"Please don't lie to us," Duscha adds. "The Synod has the right to veto any vote for an Empress. We're not afraid to use it."

Nicovar smiles. "I would hope not. No Imperial body should be afraid to use its own powers."

"Well – exactly. I'm glad you understand." Duscha folds her hands over her lap. "Now. Nicovar. Please tell us why you wish to be Emperor?"

He meets her eyes. "I want to help build the Empire. It's not finished yet, you see. It was founded on a great ambition, to bring all the humans of the world under its wings. To give them a virtuous Way to follow, like Tian bringing fire to the nations. We've grown since we were founded but the orcs on our borders keep human slaves, the Faraden are heretics, the Jarmish and Axou are out there just waiting to be called inside. We have a fight to get there, but we are not done yet. I want to be a part of that work. Archmage is an honour and I am grateful to the Conclave for giving me its trust. But I know I can do more, so I am asking the whole Empire to trust me the same way, and together, we can build to greater heights."

Joshua leans forward. "You wouldn't fix the borders? Miriam talks about – oh. Sorry. One candidate at a time. But you think we should have an expansionist policy."

"Absolutely." Nicovar tilts in to echo him. "Would you abandon Bregasland, because it's been invaded? What about the Barrens? Should we ask the Navarr to give up Liathaven, just because the work isn't done? That's the whole point. The work isn't done. If we fix the borders, we are giving up our reason to exist. We might as well be separate nations again."

They look appropriately horrified at that. It's a ridiculous exaggeration, but it gets the emotions going, so Nicovar refuses to feel guilty, though the shade of his logic tutor is shaking her head from the mountains.

He steps out an hour later into a dusty sunlight. James is somehow leaning on the tent, twining himself around a guy-rope to stay upright. There's an empty coffee cup in his hand. Nicovar takes it, letting their fingers brush together. He tips it upside down and pulls a face. James watches him through half-lidded eyes.

"It's too hot for inquisitions," he says. "I vote we blow it off and stick our heads in a barrel of water."

"That's a wonderful idea," Nicovar agrees.

"Isn't it technically illegal?"

"Not just technically. It's a religious crime to skip an inquisition. Although – you know, I don't think the law says *anything* about taking a bucket of water to an inquisition and sticking your head in it?"

"That's it, then. I'm doing that."

"Alright," Nicovar says. "I'll fetch the bucket."

James groans. It takes him a minute to untangle himself from the rope and get his feet back under him. Nicovar watches how he moves and how the skin gleams where his shirt isn't laced quite closed at the neck, and says, "Don't sleep alone tonight."

James stares. He blows out a startled breath. "Are – are you – with you?"

"Yes." Nicovar grins. "I don't mean, find someone random to spend it with. I mean the other thing."

"Huh." James blinks. "I have to do an inquisition. How am I meant to concentrate on that now?"

"You're the Warmage. I have faith that you can handle one meeting."

"Your faith is entirely misplaced," James says dolefully. "Please fetch me an even larger bucket. I need to drown my urges before they ask me questions."

Nicovar waves the empty cup at him instead. "Need another of these? That much I can probably manage, if they don't call you in too fast."

"No, any more and I'll be twitchy." James stretches, tipping his face towards the sky. "Oh – you need to go and find Giuseppe, he's worked out a deal with the Freeborn but I've no idea what the terms are. It's got conditional clauses for if you don't stand, or if you want to break the deal, or if they do – I don't remember any of it, ask Giuseppe."

Nicovar salutes him with the coffee cup. "Yes, sir, at once, sir."

He can see, as he spins on his heels, James wearing an expression like a startled goldfish. Nicovar grins to himself, and goes to further his campaign.

CHAPTER EIGHTEEN – AUTUMN 200

Isaella finds out half an hour after the summit starts, when she stops by the Senate to check the evening's business.

Motion: To elect a Throne

Proposed by: Hahnmark

Seconded by: Casinea

Her stomach knots. Shit, they're not ready for this. They have fourteen votes so far, and they need twenty to win. Miriam will -

Miriam needs twenty votes just as they do, and she can't get them if all of Nicovar's supporters hold true.

Her boots churn up the Anvil mud as she hurried to the Urizen camp. The Ankarien camp is only half built, their luggage still out in the open, heaped in an unsteady pile on the groundsheet of a tent they haven't raised yet. Archimedes is in a huddle with one of his spire-mates, their robes embroidered with matching white scrollwork. The shorter figure turns to Isaella as she approaches the camp and nods respectfully. "Senator."

Their face is familiar, but not quite as Isaella remembers, with a newly shortened haircut. "Oh – Lucia?"

"Lucius, now."

"Lucius. Thank you, that's good to know. You've heard about the Senate motion?"

"We have," Archimedes agrees. "Nicovar is talking to the Civil Service to confirm his candidacy. You'll second him if we need a formal nomination?"

"Yes, of course. Do you have the prediction list to hand?"

Archimedes shakes his head, gesturing at the pile of baggage. "The board is over there, somewhere. I haven't made the time to dig it out. I don't believe we have the votes to succeed but all we need to do is hold the line. Will your Navarri colleagues vote with you?"

"I'm not sure." Isaella chews a dry spot on her lip. "Blodwen is of the opinion we don't need an Empress at all, yet. Possibly ever. She's – I don't know. She thinks the Empress is a figurehead and it would be – dishonest, to vote for one who didn't light her up with emotion"

Lucius shakes his head. "You won't change that in an hour."

"Go to Dawn," Archimedes says, "work on Roland. You won't change his vote but if you can get him preaching to Isolt, she'll turn our way just to spite him."

"I'm going. I'll see you at eight."

Sir Isolt is in the tournament square, teaching two youngsters in her House livery to use their shields against a greatsword. The shields are too large for them, sitting awkwardly on adolescent arms, the straps not buckled properly. Sir Roland is leaning on one of the wooden posts that mark the perimeter, watching them.

"Good evening, Sir Roland," Isaella calls to him. "How was your season?"

He takes a moment to look her way, pretending to be surprised to see her. "Senator Isaella! Always a pleasure to have you gracing our camp. My season was very successful, thank you. We raided the Barrens and killed a score of sneaking Druj."

Navarri fight like the Druj, Isaella doesn't say. She inclines her head instead. "Well fought, sir knight. We have an election this evening, did you see?"

"A motion to elect a Throne," Roland recites solemnly. "The greatest of our duties. And you've come to argue for Nicovar, again."

"I think he's the best candidate."

"You're bedding him, Isaella. Or – well – perhaps not bedding, I don't know how you people manage – marriage, and so forth – but you look sweetly at him. It clouds your judgement."

"Surely I am not hearing a Dawnish knight argue against love as a guiding force?"

"Of course not! Never said any such thing. But is it love that moves you? Or only baser urges?"

"My people don't consider them base," Isaella says, stung. "Apart from who I look sweetly on, what's your argument? Make your case against him and I'll hear it."

"I don't need a case against him. He's obviously unfit. Between an Urizeni scholar who's never seen battle and an experienced General, there can't be any contest."

Isolt looks like a fox whose ears are pricking. She says something to her young students and they turn to whacking at each other's shields, wooden swords bouncing off the painted covers. Her stance behind Roland speaks volumes, the greatsword still balanced on her shoulder, as though she would like to swing at him. "That's not entirely fair, Roland."

"Oh, not you too, sister?"

"I haven't been your sister for eight years," Isolt says, acid edging her voice. "I'm only saying, Nicovar has seen combat."

Roland waves a hand. "Skirmishes out of Anvil. Not real warfare. We need an Empress who knows how to *lead*."

Isolt moves her sword an inch forward, an inch back. She huffs in annoyance. "He's Archmage, Roland. How is that not leadership?"

"Well, would you trust a magician with an army? It's all very well to have him heading up the Conclave, but it doesn't translate. All he knows is how to count mana crystals. No, we'll have a Highborn Empress by midnight, you mark my words."

"Throne-*elect*," Isolt mutters. "Excuse me, Isaella, but I promised to teach my cousins how to guard their heads. I'll see you in the Senate."

"Of course. Sir Roland, a pleasure as always."

In the narrow lanes of the League camp, it takes Isaella long minutes to find the d'Holberg carta. She ducks into the dark tent and smacks her head on an unlit lantern. "Sorry!"

"Three," one of the twins says from a pile of sheepskin rugs. Isaella squints through the gloom to see the coppery filigree of a mask. Lucrezia, then. "If you're looking for Cressy, she's gone down to the Brass Coast. One of their Senators wants to argue over whether his contract obligations apply tonight. They *do*, but it does us no good to get the breach payment afterwards if he doesn't vote right."

Isaella drops to a crouch beside her. "You sound worried. Are we going to lose?"

"Probably," Lucrezia says, "at least, we'll hold enough votes to stop Miriam, so we can try again. It's not that. I'm not worried about *that*. It's the stupid Conclave. Someone's running for Archmage of Day, tonight."

"I didn't think it was due?"

"It's an Archmage election, they happen whenever someone gets up the courage to stand. Ordinarily I'd say Nic wasn't in any danger, but – *ugh*. Vultures. He's going to have to defend straight from the Throne election and we aren't prepared."

"What can I do?"

"Concentrate on the Senate," Lucrezia says without hesitation. "We *can* actually afford to lose Archmage, because I can throw Grandmaster over and keep him in an Imperial post. We can't afford to let Miriam win. Don't get distracted. *I'm* distracted but let me do the Conclave work. Who've you spoken to?"

"Archimedes, briefly, and then I caught Roland and Isolt both and got him at his most boorish, so with luck she'll be one of ours."

"Good. That's one for each of us. Virtues, I hate doing this in a hurry."

"We'll be fine," Isaella tells her. "We'll keep the Throne empty for another season and you'll finesse the Conclave. Stop panicking. I'm going to lurk around the Senate until it goes into session and catch people as they come in." She kisses the top of Lucrezia's head, between her horns, and barely dodges the lantern as she straightens up.

The Senate is crowded at eight o'clock sharp. By the time the bell rings, all the Senators but one are on the floor, and that one is ten miles out of Anvil with a broken cart-wheel.

Speaker Marianne is standing in front of the throne, which has been pushed right to the back of the dais to make room. Her voice hardly carries over the chattering crowd in the public gallery, until Tessa of Bregasland takes an empty tankard from one of the onlookers and bangs it against the railing.

"Thank you, Bregasland. Listen, please, citizens, I know we're all excited about the election, but we're having it last, because we have regular business to attend to. Anyone causing a disturbance will be asked to leave the gallery. If you're bored, please just go. Alright. Senators, thank your for arriving so promptly. Let's get started."

The regular business passes quickly. After that election motion went up on the wall, few Senators were interested in raising anything else. They work their way through the administrative motions without serious debate, and then the Conscience stands forth to speak on the only subject that really matters.

"Senators, Citizens. It is my duty and privilege to be the voice of the Way of Virtue in this assembly. I do not often urge the Senate to make its choice one way or another, but only bring your attention to the teachings of the Way, as each new season demands. Today I am breaking that habit. We have a motion before us to elect an Empress. The Imperial Throne has stood empty since Barabbas and his fleet were lost. We have gone on without an Empress and you may say we have managed well enough. The Empire was built that way. The Constitution gives us time to deliberate on who shall lead us. But an Empire must, in the end, have an Empress. We must choose someone. Now is not the time to resign ourselves to an interregnum. We have had two years to deliberate, and now, two candidates stand before us ‑"

"Three," someone says loudly from the crowd, no doubt a Varushkan taking the insult they've been offered, but the Conscience half-smiles and goes on with his speech.

"Two candidates stand before us who have held Imperial titles, who have served the Empire as their positions demand, and each of them is a sound candidate. You may vote for either of them without folly. I will not tell you which to choose, Senators, but I will say this: you should choose one of them."

Marianne clears her throat. "Thank you, Conscience, for your guidance. I have reviewed the Senate rules, and there is no provision for nominees to the Throne to address the Senate. Since the Senate has made no invitation to those citizens, they will not be called upon to speak. The motion before us is to elect a Throne, and I will allow debate on the merits of that motion now. Hahnmark."

The senator for Hahnmark is a thin, nervous-looking man, with a pink scar running through his beard. "Fellow Senators, we have been debating this motion in one form or another for two years, mainly outside this chamber. We have, as the Conscience reminds us, two very convincing candidates, and a third with the courage to present herself. I, as most of you know, favour Miriam of Highguard. I believe she would make a fine Empress and her plan to shore up our borders before we expand again is wise. I will be retiring from the Senate tomorrow. I would like my last act here to be the election of a strong Throne."

"Necropolis," Marianne says, choosing from the Senators with hands raised to speak.

"It must not be Miriam," Isaac says at once. "I agree that we should have a Throne. But this is not the only chance we will have to elect one! Vote for Nicovar – vote for *Silviya*, if you like – but vote against the motion before you give Miriam any power."

"Please confine your comments to the motion itself, and not the merits of the candidates, Senators," and so the debate goes on, with arguments for this side and that, unconvincingly disguised as discussion of whether the throne itself should remain empty.

Marianne lets the Senate talk for twenty minutes, and then holds off on nominating the next speaker, until the hands go down and the Senators watch her in tense silence.

"Three candidates have presented themselves to me in respect of this motion." A little satisfied mutter runs through the gallery, where some Varushkans are taking it as a victory that the Speaker is acknowledging their nominee. "Those candidates are Silviya of Varushka, Nicovar of Urizen and Miriam of Highguard. I invite the candidates to cross the Senate floor."

Isaella's heart beats painfully at the sight of them, all straight-backed and serious, though Silviya's face is pale with shock – it can't have been easy, to have heard herself dismissed over and over, and realise she never had a chance. But she crosses to the dais with the others and stands with her arms folded, her chin raised in defiance of fate.

Marianne points them towards places at the edge of the dais. Silviya on the right, nearest to the crowded gallery, Nicovar on the left, and Miriam proud in the centre, her hood raised.

"As there are three candidates, we will do this Navarri-fashion," Marianne says to the assembled Senate. "Senators will form a line before their chosen candidates. I will announce the totals, at which time any Senator who chooses may change their vote. We will continue with this until no Senator wishes to move, or until one candidate reaches twenty votes. Arturo, please stand to the side."

The Conscience smiles and steps clear, up to the corner of the dais, where he can't be mistaken for a vote. Marianne watches him, letting the moment draw out before she starts the voting.

When the crowd in the gallery are finally silent, barely breathing through the tension in the air, Marianne speaks.

"Senators, the motion before you is to elect a Throne. Votes for No will stand on the far left, by the wall. Votes for Yes will divide amongst the candidates. Senators, make your votes."

Isaella is not the first in Nicovar's line. That honour goes to Johanna, and then Isolt strides up, with a sour glance over her shoulder at Roland, smiling happily in Miriam's line. Two senators from the Marches. Isaella joins the line, counting in her head. Three for Silviya, all Varushkans. Thirteen for Miriam. Twelve for Nicovar.

Marianne tallies them off aloud. Before she can tell them to move again, the senators for Karsk and Meikarova are crossing the floor to Nicovar's line. Isaella hides a smile. No great love for Silviya, then, except from her sister, glaring at her compatriots from her stubborn solitary place.

One. Thirteen. Fourteen. Something untwists in Isaella's belly. They won't lose this tonight.

The remaining Marcher chews on her lip and crosses to Nicovar's line. Isaac is whispering urgently to the senator for Bastion, who is barely looking at him past the edge of her hood. Marianne counts again.

One, twelve, fifteen.

"Oh, fuck it," Hahnmark says. "Sorry, Miriam."

He crosses into Nicovar's line. Bastion follows him, and Sarvos and Temeschwar together, and Isaella is counting bodies faster than Marianne can speak, and then Therunin says quietly "Follow the river," and comes over with Blodwen of Hercynia on her heels.

"Would anyone else like to change their vote?" Marianne gives them a chance, a few seconds, before she speaks again. "The votes stand at one for Silviya of Varushka. Six, for Miriam of

Highguard, and twenty-one for Nicovar of Urizen. The motion passes."

"I intend to seek the veto!" shouts a Navarri from the gallery, jagged warpaint streaked across her face.

"Thank you," Marianne says, nodding to her, unperturbed. "The Synod will require time to deliberate the motion to veto. If the veto is not upheld, we will have a coronation. Until that time, we remain in interregnum. Nicovar of Urizen is the Throne-Elect as chosen by the Senate. That concludes tonight's business. Thank you."

The silence hangs for a moment, as senate and gallery work out what just happened, and then the cheering begins. Isaella threads through the suddenly-crowded floor to find James, leaning on the gallery railing, and drag him down into a hug.

He looks dazed. "Did we just win?"

"We just won," Isaella says. "We just *won!*"

There are parts of the Empire that are built for parades. They have broad paved roads overlooked by balconies and long shallow hills so the spectacle can be seen a mile away. Anvil has nothing but tents and its roads are grass and thick clinging mud.

For a Navarr like Isaella, nothing could seem more natural.

Nicovar became the Throne at three minutes past noon, when the votes from the Synod were counted. The veto failed to pass by a margin of eighty percent. So now, in the bright afternoon with the clouds so white overhead they could be marble, they are having a coronation.

The Civil Service does not arrange for these very often. But that's alright; few citizens have careers long enough to witness two. They make it up as they go along and Nicovar nods his head and does not quite stifle his grin, when Isaella catches his eye. He was the Archmage of Day until last night, when the attempted coup proved unnecessary and the position passed on amid congratulations. Isaella rescued a dazed James after the Conclave was finished and took him to Navarr to drink.

So he's not been the Archmage for most of a day, and he's been the Empress for three hours, but they start the parade in the regio anyway. Nicovar strips off his regalia piece by piece – the staff, the belt, the heavy enamelled chain – and hands them to the stocky Varushkan who holds the title now. She takes them solemnly, bowing over the gleaming bundle before she steps back.

From the regio to the Senate is only a short distance. The crowd is a dozen bodies deep on either side but the civil servants have rigged up string and bunting to keep the way clear. Nicovar walks that road alone, the magicians watching from the regio, the senators waiting ahead. The crown is glittering in Marianne's hands.

Isaella did not propose the motion, and so the speech is not hers to make. That honour goes to the greying Senator for Hahnmark. He would have preferred Miriam, but he steps forward to meet Nicovar with a delighted crinkle in his eyes. "Are you Nicovar of Ankarien?"

"I am." Nicovar pitches his voice to match the senator, loud enough for the crowd to hear.

"By the agreement of the Senate and the Imperial Synod, you have been called to wear the crown. Do you accept this burden willingly?"

"I do."

"We have called you here, believing in your ability to lead us. We have placed our greatest trust in you, and in return we ask for all you have. Will you do your best to lead us? Will you guide the Empire in peace and in war, in virtue and magic, for as long as the fates allow? Will you heed the advice of those whose understanding is greater than your own? Will you count every citizen of the Empire as your own kin? It has been said that a magician's tools are the will and word, and you have proven yourself in their use. Will you turn them now to nothing but the Empire's good?"

"One at a time, Hahnmark." Nicovar smiles, a deliberate Urizeni smile that doesn't conceal his happiness. "But yes. Yes, to all of it. I will, I will, I will."

The senator takes the crown and raises it for the crowd to see. They are cheering so loud even Isaella, standing beside him, cannot hear what Hahnmark says as he lowers it to Nicovar's head.

They take the parade all around Anvil's camps, after that, and the Empire rejoices in its Throne.

PART TWO:
DANGER FROM WITHIN

CHAPTER NINETEEN – WINTER 200

Nicovar's first meeting with the Assembly of Nine takes place in a questionably waterproof Synod tent, its roof sagging alarmingly under the weight of rain. The wind has been blowing steadily for three days and by now there is a sad little heap of rope and broken wood beside the entrance, the remains of deceased guy-lines too sodden to burn. Nicovar picks up one of the snapped pegs and pries a clump of mud and wet straw from the sole of his boot.

"There's no point," someone says in a thick Marcher accent. Cardinal Tom Brewer, sweating under a waxed hood. "You'll only grow new ones as soon as you step outside."

"At present I'm an inch taller than I belong," Nicovar answers, balancing on his newly lightened foot to work on the other. "I prefer not to start my reign by lying about my height."

"Very wise," Tom agrees. Nicovar doesn't miss the warning – *wise*, from a Cardinal, is not a synonym for *clever*, or even *prudent*, and arguably doesn't apply to the cleaning of boots at all. Lying, however, is certainly a concern of that virtue, and not to be done lightly. He drops his broken tent-peg back on the pile and sighs at the smears of mud on his hands.

"I understand why the Constitution forbids us to build on Anvil. And as Throne, I am of course bound to uphold that stricture. But I do wish our founders had left us some way to have a decent pavement around here."

"There's a sentiment that unites us all." Rosalind is somehow undamaged by the weather, wearing the raindrops in her hair like jewels, her fine green cloak as striking as any armour. "We'd best not try it just yet, Emperor. Constitutional changes need a firm foundation."

"And a lack of a firm foundation is exactly the problem," Nicovar agrees. "Do we sit on the grass, or stand?"

"Stand usually," Tom says. "Annalies has a folding chair she brings. Oh, here she is – here, Anna, let me set that up for you. Who else are we expecting?"

"Markus never comes," Annalies says breathily, settling her walking stick between her knees. "And Katja is still queuing up for the Civil Service, there's been some problem with her raiding party not being properly registered. I just spoke to her in line and she thinks it'll be an hour yet."

"I'm here, I'm here," someone says from the entrance, trying to shake the mud off her boots, "am I late? Oh, Nicovar, I'm sorry, I don't think we've met, I was only elected last summit – I'm Kesia of Samson's Guard, Cardinal of Courage." She grabs Nicovar's hand and shakes it.

"A pleasure to meet you," Nicovar says, putting his hands firmly behind his back against any further attempts to make contact. Kesia's eyes are a vivid green, and her collar is laced snugly all the way to her throat – she's a briar, and trying to hide it. "But you're not late. I don't think we're all here yet, are we?"

"We are now," Tom says, and Nicovar turns to see a Navarr and another Highborn, both with their hoods up, talking in whispers as they come in. "Evening, Cara, and Solomon. It's bloody cold so let's get started – that is, if the Emperor agrees?"

"Let's not start that," Nicovar says. "You've been chairing during the Interregnum? Then keep chairing now. I only have one vote here just like the rest of you."

"At least you're not wearing the silly hat," Cara says, putting her hood back carefully over her antlers. "Alright, we're here. Let's get this over with before the whole tent comes down."

Being the Emperor seems mainly to mean going to meetings. Nicovar misses the start of Senate, from being occupied with the Assembly of Nine, which means he's late for the Military Council as well. He steps into the tent to the turning of every head. Most of the stares are hostile.

"I haven't come to take over," he says calmly, warming his fingers on the cup of coffee he stole a moment to buy. "There's a whole line of citizens at Ankarien camp who want a word with me. But I'll need a military briefing and my usual advisor isn't here this summit. Could someone stand in for Giuseppe tomorrow and give me the summary?"

Long silence follows, and then "I'll be here all morning if you want to see the map," says Gwyneth, Isaella's old general, her joints too stiff to join the fighting nowadays. Nicovar bows to her.

"Then I'll see you here after the fighters go through the gate. Good evening, Generals."

Lucius meets him at the camp entrance. "Don't go in there," he says hurriedly, "there's a dozen of them waiting for you. Archimedes is handling it. We need to build some barriers around you or you'll never get anything done."

"I need an office," Nicovar agrees, "and someone to manage my appointments and send people away if it's not my problem to solve."

"Are you going to Conclave tonight?"

Nicovar shakes his head, scattering drops of rain from his hood. "No, they don't need me, and I was there all Saturday session last time sorting out the Archmage thing. I plan to leave them alone this time to get used to the idea of a Throne again – James will pass on anything urgent."

"Good. Because I think you should go to the League camp. The d'Holberg twins are holding court and I think you should remind their hangers-on that they're not actually the Empress."

"You don't like them."

"When have I? They're skilled at what they do. If you put yourself back in their web they'll be forced to acknowledge you, that's all. Have you spoken to James yet?"

"Not yet. He's around somewhere. Probably doing Conclave work."

Lucius looks at him strangely. "You should talk to him, Nicovar. You wrote six times this season."

"And I wrote to Isaella three, and Cressida four – what's your point?"

He doesn't get an answer to that. Only Lucius staring at him a moment longer, and saying, "Have you eaten? There's a delegation from Faraden waiting and you shouldn't face them on an empty stomach."

It's nearly two in the morning before Nicovar can seek out his bed. The Faraden wanted to preach heresy to him, in the hopes that he would build them a church in Sarvos – impossible, but they might get an embassy in Highguard, which is exactly what they don't want, too many priests around to disagree with them – but the reminder that Sarvos is mainly navigated by boat gave them pause. Apparently their horror of the sea extends to saltwater canals. And then after the Faraden came a pair of generals, very urgently concerned that he would appear at the Sentinel Gate to see the fighters off, who needed more reassurance than the "Yes, of course," and a bow he was hoping to give them. And then a half-religious dispute about sorcery and land holdings in the Marches – Nicovar never made it to the League camp.

The makeshift streets of Anvil are almost empty by the time he steps out of the meeting tent at last, into the damp wind. His robes flap about his shins as he walks. Nicovar's mind is spinning with a half dozen difficult problems, and he knows better than to lie down like this, his feet cold and his head too full to sleep. He turns the other way instead, and walks up the hill, as briskly as the mud will allow.

Most of Anvil is asleep, or laced snugly into tents, with only the soft sound of laughter and the glow beneath the canvas to give them away. Nicovar nods to the people he passes, an exhausted civil servant mopping out the privies, a pair of drunken Navarr who shout "Emperor!" and then hush themselves, remembering that people are sleeping. His feet take him through Dawn and the silent Varushkan camp, every tent closed against strangers. The fire is still burning outside the Marcher tavern and he stops there, to warm his hands, and recognises the lanky figure standing opposite.

"Nic," James says, softly, and stops. He turns his hands over above the fire. "We didn't see you tonight."

Nicovar stops the question that leaps to his tongue, the easy deflection into Conclave business. He says instead, "I know. I'm sorry."

James lifts one shoulder. "Probably not your fault."

"I missed you," Nicovar says, surprising himself. "Today. Tonight. All season."

"Well. You're too busy, now."

He reaches for James's hands, across the fire. Looks down at their twined fingers. "That's not true. Or – if it is, then I need you more. Not less."

"What can an Emperor need with me?"

"Don't," Nicovar says. "Don't do that. It's me, James. It's not some stranger. Don't leave me missing you, when we're both right here."

James makes a noise, not quite a laugh. "It's a lot to get used to, is all. You know they're already calling me *the Emperor's man*."

"Are you?"

"Of course I am. Have been for years."

Nicovar meets his dark eyes, solemn in the dim firelight. He bends a little, to kiss James's hand, and hears his soft intake of breath.

"Come to bed, dear heart," he says. "I'm sorry I left you waiting. Come inside and get warm."

James takes a deep breath. "Yes," he says. "Alright. Yes."

CHAPTER TWENTY – SPRING 201

Cara is the Cardinal of the Way, and Isaella likes her. They sit together on a hill outside Anvil, half a mile from the camp, on the eastward side where the traffic is lighter. They walked out here this morning, at an easy stroll so as not to spill the tea in their mugs, and finally found a rock to sit on and look out at the horizon.

"But you like him," Cara says, continuing a conversation from ten minutes ago.

"I don't know." Isaella taps her heel against the stone, thinking. "I don't *dislike* him. He's arrogant and presumptuous and he – he doesn't gossip, exactly, but he makes fun. Half the time I want to hug him and half I want to stab him and sometimes they're the same half."

"If you were ten years younger, I'd diagnose you with a crush," Cara observes dryly. "But you campaigned for him. That looks like more than attraction."

"It is more. I just don't know what kind of more. I do truly believe that he is meant to be where he is. And that I am meant somehow to be involved with that. It's like, every time I haven't seen him in a while, I get this little kick from the universe. Look, here's someone dangerous, you should help them!"

"You know what I'm going to tell you."

"I know. Follow the river."

"I can't tell you what he was to you before. Or will be in the next life. I can only tell you that right now, he is the Throne, and you are one of the people who put him there. The Dance does not run backwards. You must take the step that is in front of you. But you know, that's always the way. It's only more obvious to you now, because of the titles you both have. It would be just the same if you were ox farmers in Hercynia."

Isaella snorts. "Not such high stakes on which oxen to breed, are there?"

"But the same Dance, nonetheless. You have met the people you are meant to meet. What you do next is always up to you."

"I wish I knew whether we really were ox herders."

"You might find out tonight."

"Virtues, I hope not," Isaella says hastily, seizing the chance to change the subject. "Imagine someone coming back and saying they'd seen you, and you were up to your elbows in a cow."

There are certain rights and privileges due to the Throne, and amongst them is the first dose of True Liao to be prepared each season. This is no small thing: of all the liao produced in the Empire in three months, only five or six doses will mature into the most potent form. The ordinary liao will be drunk by priests in their thousands, to dedicate citizens or give testimonies or consecrate their churches. The few precious vials of the real thing will be brought to Anvil, for the granting of visions.

Isaella knows how the visions work. That, really, is the problem – too many late-night conversations with Cara, when she was serving as the guiding priest for Sir Isolt's vision last year. The True Liao doesn't, strictly speaking, cause visions. Strictly speaking, it kills you. The whole structure of the ceremony, the most sacred rite in the Imperial faith, is to anchor your soul in the present moment, so that after the liao has flung it into the Labyrinth and sent it to relive the choices it made in other lives, it will come back to the body it left. Without that ritual, it merely kills you. With it, the dying is temporary.

Nicovar is doing what any Throne is expected to do, if they haven't already had a vision as a candidate. He is using his dose on himself. Isaella agrees, and wouldn't dream of talking him out of it. She's excited, even, to hear what he brings back, who he used to be – secretly, to hear whether her own past life can be recognised among his memories.

She only wishes it wasn't going to kill him in the process.

His vision is first on the schedule, drawn up by the Civil Service with due concern for his status. There's hardly time for anything, between Isaella's responsibilities to attend the Standing and Nicovar's collection by a solemn Varushkan draughir even paler than he is, but Isaella finds a moment to stop in the Synod tent somehow.

"You're worried about me," Nicovar says.

"Of course I am."

"They haven't lost anyone in decades. You don't need to worry about me."

"No, but I'm *going* to. Anything could happen. You could come back cursed. You could lose your veil and get your face melted off. You could turn out to have been a traitor."

Nicovar blinks. "You're putting those three on the same level of consequence? I thought you liked my face."

"You don't think it would be a problem, for the Emperor to come back and say he'd betrayed the Empire?"

"I just think it would be easier to manage than having my face melted off. Which is also extremely unlikely. The Civil Service are good at this, Sal. And besides, if they lose me I think James will tie a rope to his ankle and dive in after me, and it would be very embarrassing to lose the Warmage as well, so they'll take good care of me. I have Tom to make sure I get home safe."

"He's stealing my job," Isaella says darkly, "I could have been your Guide."

"You'd need to be a priest."

"I know. But I don't have to like it. Oh, damn, that's the Senate bell, I have to go – if you die I will come with James, only I will be there to kick your ass, understand?"

"Yes, Senator," Nicovar says, almost convincing in his meekness, and clasps her hand before he lets her go.

Senate always runs short, this first session of the summit; Isaella is back in the Synod tent long before Nicovar returns. She finds James there, too tall for the enclosed space, restlessly rolling his staff in his hands. He looks at her, silent and tense-jawed.

"He's not back yet?"

James shakes his head. "You ever done it?"

"Never," Isaella says. "I heard Rhonwen talk about it – my old senator. But that was years ago. I wasn't involved. And Cara, but she can't tell me what she saw."

"What if he doesn't come back?"

"He will."

"You don't know that." James stabs the end of his staff into the grass. "Nobody knows that. He doesn't know it. He's just running in headlong, the way he does."

"It got him this far." Isaella rubs her arms. James's fear is infectious. She thinks of telling him that if Nicovar does die, they've all had practice at handling an interregnum lately, but it doesn't seem very comforting. Better to hold her tongue and watch James twisting grass up by its roots.

There's always noise in Anvil, along the main street by the Senate where the big meeting tents and the food stalls are all set up. Isaella only notices it getting louder when she hears Tom Brewer saying, "Not now, for pity's sake, he's just back from a vision, give him a minute before you start hassling him. Nothing's on fire, it can *wait*. No, you're not coming in here, piss off."

He shepherds Nicovar into the tent, his broad shoulders hunched. Nicovar is as calm and elegant as ever, except for the red flush high on his cheeks. He says quietly, "I'm fine, Tom, really," but he makes no argument when Tom closes the tent flap behind them to shut out the curious onlookers.

"You're back," James says, pressing his forehead to the tip of his staff, the only thing holding him up in his relief. "Welcome back."

"Of course I came back." Nicovar turns to put his back against the central pole and closes his eyes.

"What happened?"

"I died," he says, acidly. "And Tom died. And then a lot of other people died, and then I came back."

"He was a general of some kind." Tom has sat himself down, heedless of the damp grass beneath his trousers. "Or a battle captain, maybe, but I think a general. On a raid into Varushka."

"The cultists wouldn't give in," Nicovar says, without opening his eyes. "My troops were telling me we didn't have time to argue with them, that we had to get back before the gate closed, but if they didn't come with us something terrible – I don't know what would have happened. We just needed them to not be where they were, and they wouldn't go. I had a magician with me, she was very clear that if they didn't leave it would be a great help to our enemies."

"How do you know they were cultists?" James puts a hand on Nicovar's shoulder. Isaella can see how he wants to hold him, how only deference to Nicovar's nation – it would be like public nudity, to an Urizeni – is restraining him.

"They kept talking about a Sovereign," Tom answers for him. "Anyway, Nic's troops were hanging back nervous and didn't want to fight them – civilians, you see – and everyone was running around in a panic scared the Gate was going to close and leave them stranded. So he had to choose, then. They weren't going to go on their own, so..."

"So I had them all killed," Nicovar says, his voice flat. "It was a strategic decision. I couldn't leave them to empower their sovereign and they denied being Imperial citizens. I told my troops to kill them all, and lay the blame on me."

"And then we woke up." Tom tips his head back to look at the blank canvas above him, speckled with old mud. "Back in Anvil. Back in today. Make a moral out of *that*."

CHAPTER TWENTY-ONE – SUMMER 201

Cardinal Katja taps her fingernails against the head of her axe. "But what do you think is the *problem*, Nicovar?"

Nicovar rests his hand on the back of his neck, rubbing the tired muscles.

"He wants us to *do* things, Katja." Kesia has – Nicovar immediately regrets thinking the word – blossomed since her election, her enthusiasm sharpening into decisiveness. "At the moment we're not *doing* anything. We just let the Senate get on with it."

"What we do we do well," Katja grumbles. "You haven't been here long enough to understand."

"I understand that we have powers we haven't used in decades. Until the Throne campaigns the Synod hadn't used Inquisition for more than twenty years. I checked! It's in the Constitution for a reason. We are supposed to *use* it – That's what you're saying, isn't it?"

"Exactly, Cardinal. And not just Inquisition. I drew up a list of the Synod's powers and nearly half of them are out of use. When was the last time you revoked anyone?"

"Last year," Tom Brewer says. "We revoked Molly of Upwold."

Nicovar gestures his recognition. "You did. Almost unanimously, the Marcher assembly voted to revoke the Senator for Upwold. And why did you do that, Tom?"

"Age and infirmity, the usual reason. She wanted to retire."

"And that is my point. Our founders did not give the Synod the power to help Senators retire on their own schedule. It's all we ever use it for but it's not why we have it. It exists to remove the unvirtuous. Even if they're capable."

Rosalind leans back onto her hands, her cloth-of-gold tunic brilliant against the long grass. "Who is it you want us to revoke, then? Miriam?"

"He doesn't want us to revoke anyone," Kesia says, exasperated. "He doesn't even want us to revoke *someone*. He just wants us to remember that we *can*. Half of our powers are about chastising the unvirtuous and we don't use *any* of them. We don't inquisit, we don't condemn, we don't excommunicate. We barely even veto and that's the one thing everyone agrees we *should* do!"

"We raised a veto for the Throne election," Katja argues.

"Yes, but it didn't pass. I mean – think about the arguments over the fleet. We stayed out of that. I know I was only young but I *was* here and I saw how much people needed Synod guidance and we didn't give it to them. We left the Empire not knowing what the path of virtue even *was*. Even if we disagreed we should have made the arguments. We should have said, in public, here is the Courageous argument against, and, here is the Wise argument for, and – been more than just a vestigial government committee that hands out virtue funds and – and builds churches. A Cardinal is the equal of a Senator. Our only superior is the Throne and he is telling us, step up and do something." Kesia looks around the tent and turns suddenly embarrassed. "Okay, I'm done."

Katja frowns. "Solomon? You're here for Loyalty – these are condemnatory powers. Is it Loyal to use them?"

"You know I can't answer that," Solomon says, and rubs irritably at his eyes, swollen with pollen. "Should I condemn someone? It depends who they are. Should you? Who are you loyal to? The Empire is only the highest good if you believe it is. And this is a dangerously unitarian question. What does your Pride lead you to do?"

Silence falls for a moment after that pronouncement, until Annalies taps her walking stick against the grass. "Entertaining as it might be," she says, "to raise a Statement of Principle that the Synod should raise more Statements of Principle, there is not much use arguing about it. It will never be good to use our powers simply for the sake of using them. It will always go case by case. The Emperor says, let us be a little more forthcoming with our interventions. I take his point, but there is exactly nothing we can do about it here and now. Can we move on? There is the unrest in Faraden to consider."

Nicovar bows to her, a little awkwardly, from his seat on the grass. "I rest the question. Tom, remind us what's going on with the embassy?"

There is no easy solution to a religious dispute with a nation of heretics. Kesia and Annalies are arguing fervently over whether the recently built outpost in Faraden should be defended to the death or should yield, paving the way for conversions in the long term, when Isaella pokes her head through the flap of the tent.

She quirks an eyebrow in amusement, seeing most of them on the ground like children. "Forgive me, Cardinals, but I've come to kidnap Nicovar."

"Please, take him!" Kesia waves her arms, ushering Nicovar towards the exit. "He's all yours!"

"Not like that," Nicovar grumbles, but he stands up a little awkwardly, trying to avoid using the tent itself as leverage and risk pulling it down on top of them. He brushes the grass off his robes before he follows Isaella outside.

"Is there anything I should know about?"

Isaella shakes her head, her braids bouncing. "Nothing out of the ordinary. There may some difficulty over the Faraden embassy in Highguard, but you know about that."

"I do. I was planning on supporting a suspension of the work until our embassy in Faraden is no longer threatened – does that hold up?"

"That's good. You'll get easy votes for that. There's talk about accepting the Faraden workers as citizens if they want to convert, but no agreement on which nation should take them, so it will only be a handful if it happens at all."

"Could the Navarri take them?"

She chews the corner of her lip. "We could, but only on the same terms as we take Imperials. Easy to absorb them for a few seasons while they find out where they're going. They're foreigners, they have that going for them. Give them some kind of halfway status and I could find Stridings to take a couple of dozen wanderers. But I can't promise they'd be Navarri in the end."

"True. Well, it's a good option for the first few seasons, if we do get a rush. Good grief, are we that early?"

"No," Isaella says, "there's just nobody here." She slips away from his side to speak to someone in the public gallery, leaving Nicovar to claim his seat upon the throne.

Conclave is as crowded as ever, filled with magicians energised by the chance to have a meeting where their feet do not go numb. Nicovar can see more than one bottle being passed around. He makes his way over to the Arch as usual, letting Lucrezia crow and slap his arm, delighted to have the Throne in her Order. The new Archmage of Day is present, wearing her belt of office slung low on her hips, her head cocked to listen to Daniel of Rachel's Guard as he presses her urgently about scrying coordination. It is always scrying, with Daniel.

The first address after the counting is from the Dean of the Lyceum, soliciting for new rituals to be codified. Nicovar is listening to the suggestions with a smile he lets himself show, pleased by how successful the experimental magicians have been while he wasn't paying attention to them, when there's a shuffling by the door. He thinks nothing of it until the whispering crests around him like a wave.

"Emperor," someone says across the room, "Nicovar, you're needed at the gate. It's the Warmage."

He breaks all etiquette in his haste, crossing the circle to reach the door faster.

The Sentinel Gate is smoking and pulsing with a deep purple light. Nicovar arrives at a run, his robes flapping behind him as he follows his guide between the crowded tents. The knot of people opens up to meet him.

He drops to his knees beside the bleeding figure on the ground, a physick's hands working bloodily in her belly.

"Annie," he says, "Annie, what happened? Where's James?"

"We fucked up," Annie says. Her eyes are closed, the words rasping out, a broken whisper. "We fucked up bad. He's still there. He was fighting."

"No," Nicovar says. "No." He's on his feet, somehow, his hands raised to press against the Gate he knows will not yield for him. "James! James, it's closing, get back here!"

The smoke roils. A figure stumbles through, coughing, but it's one of the twins with a broken quarterstaff jagged in her hands, not James, and Nicovar peers through the shimmering portal, trying to find him. There is a twist in his guts like the physick's gripping hand. He can't see. There is something screaming in the grey mist beyond the Gate.

A space opens through the smoke and for a moment James is there, clear against the horizon, twisting to sink a knife into the chest of something too clawed to be human. His staff is gone, lost among the bodies at his feet. He turns at Nicovar's desperate shout, taking half a step towards him, and falls beneath a leaping weight, its wolf-teeth bared. He's lost against the dark ground, the bodies all around him. There is a snarling like the end of the world, and the smoke billows up.

"Please," Nicovar says, to James, to the closing portal, he doesn't know. "Please." His fingers twitch against the air, the symbols of constellations that cannot help him, drawn upon nothingness as solid as ice.

Howling in pain, James rolls through the smoke at Nicovar's feet. He shines in the gate-light, soaked in his own fresh blood.

Nicovar doesn't notice the portal finally closing, or the sobbing grief of the Marchers who count their dead. He is on his knees, clinging to James's hand, telling him to *look at me, say something, please*, until he looks past the bleeding wounds and realises that James can't breathe.

There's a physick kneeling beside him, somehow, already unrolling her tools. "Get his head," she says. "This will take surgery – Someone get me a light! You, hold his head. Tip his head back, like this, good, and keep his mouth open. If he coughs anything up, pull it out. Lantern over here! I'm going to drain his lungs, be ready for him to bite, okay?"

Nicovar cradles his head in one hand and lets James bite on the other, keeping his mouth open while he struggles for air. His eyes are wide in the darkness, the lantern lighting nothing but the blood on his skin. Somehow he raises one arm and clings to

Nicovar's shoulder, as the chirurgeon's knife dips into him. His fingers tighten.

"You're here," Nicovar says. "I'm here. You made it back. Just hold on. Hold on another minute." He curls forward, to press their foreheads together. "Breathe, love. I'm here. Just breathe."

CHAPTER TWENTY-TWO – AUTUMN 201

The old forge is loud with the hammering of rain. Isaella absently touches her fingers to the rusty horse-shoe hanging by the door, to honour the builders of Anvil, and looks around the room. James is easy to see, as tall as he is, but it takes her a moment to spot Nicovar hiding in the passageway by the back door.

She threads her way through the crowd to him. "You look nervous. Are you nervous, Emperor?"

"Of course I'm nervous." His voice cracks a little. "I have to do it shirtless. Did you know I have to do it shirtless?"

"You-" Isaella frowns at him. "Nic."

"There's a reason I'm not a sentinel!" Nicovar hisses. "Have you seen – you *have* seen James without his clothes on, I can't compete with that. OK, you're right, I know, it's not a competition, but this part is – *almost* a competition. I'm supposed to be very calm and in control and I'm not sure I can do that topless."

Isaella takes him by the shoulders. "Take a deep breath, Nicovar. First thing, you're performing for the Marchers. They will *like* it if you're not as poised as usual. It makes you seem more human to them. And second thing, put your overrobe back on over your skin, you dummy."

His eyes widen. "Can I do that?"

"Well, you're the Empress, I doubt they're going to pull you down from the barrel to strip you. Come on, friend. Take it off. You can't be late to get married."

James might not have warned Nicovar about the details, but he must have mentioned the barrel – Nicovar wore trousers this morning. He climbs quite comfortably onto the up-ended oak cask and stands there, his hands clasped loosely behind his back, black veins showing on his arms where his overrobe leaves them bare. Isaella has his sash folded through her belt for safekeeping.

Opposite him, on top of a second barrel, James is trying to find his balance. The floor isn't completely level and every time he moves the barrel tips a little, like a wobbly-legged table. He straightens up carefully, bracing his feet against the rim. There's a livid red scar on each side of his chest, between his bottom ribs, and a vicious ripping bite mark in his shoulder. Isaella notices the new scattering of white hairs on his belly with a flash of the old desire.

James is the head of his household, so the honour of starting the match falls to his coven leader. Annie climbs the rickety stairs towards the ruined second storey and leans out, shouting over the chatter of the crowd and the rain.

"Listen up, folks! We are here to witness James of Mournwold and Nicovar of – well, of the Empire, nowadays. Jimmy and Nic think that they'd like to be married, so we've come to give them a proper chance to change their minds. You won't have all been to Mournwold so I'll tell you how we do things there. Those are two good barrels of Marcher cider under their feet, and they're going to stand up there and speak the truth until they've got no more to say. Big or small, new or old, anything that stands in the way of loving, that's the truth you owe each other, so get talking, boys. James, you can go first. What's the matter with Nicovar?"

"I have to bend down to kiss him," James says seriously.

Nicovar raises an eyebrow. "His face is very scratchy in the mornings."

"All his good clothes are *white*." James spreads his hands, theatrically baffled, prompting Nicovar to point at him accusingly.

"He didn't tell me I would have to do this shirtless."

"He's not actually doing this shirtless."

That gets the first real laugh from the onlookers. Someone calls from the bar, "You want we should fix that?" and James says, "No," firmly enough to quell them into giggles.

"He keeps getting nearly killed," Nicovar says, serious again.

"Every time he goes to battle, he needs rescuing."

"He doesn't take politics seriously."

"He thinks about nothing else."

"He gets up at three o'clock every morning to piss."

"He is constantly sarcastic."

Nicovar looks genuinely hurt by that one, and Isaella worries. They must have talked about this in advance, surely?

"He treats me like I'm a child."

James straightens his spine. "He thinks he's the smartest person in every conversation."

"He thinks being Emperor makes a difference to whether I care for him."

"He skips Conclave meetings."

"He puts things into the Conclave agenda and doesn't tell me."

"He turns single incidents into a pattern."

"I only did that the once!"

The laughter of the crowd is infectious. Isaella is struggling to contain her giggles, listening to them bicker. James is wobbling on his barrel.

"He gave me the taller perch and I can't stand heights," he says, holding his arms wide for balance.

"He blames me for the vagaries of fate," Nicovar retorts, "I mean, what does he think I am? The Empress or something?"

James doubles over laughing. Between wheezes he gets out, "He is trying to kill me and none of you buggers is helping!"

"Disallowed!" Annie shouts merrily, "off topic!"

Nicovar clasps his hands, looking serene. "He is blaming me for his own decision to stand on a barrel."

"He flirts with me when I'm going into meetings on purpose to distract me."

"He confuses nerves for mockery," Nicovar says ruefully.

James shrugs. "He expects me to read his mind."

"He tracks mud into the blankets."

"Alright!" Annie interrupts, "alright! You're not going to solve this by yourselves. Make a space there, you rabble. Marriage is a community business. We're going to help them decide. Clear the floor between them! Time to take sides! No shoving, no interrupting, and change ends when you feel like." She ticks off the rules on her fingers as the crowd churns, citizens trying to make room for the game while keeping a good view for themselves. Isaella breaks the first rule at once, muscling her way to the front.

James folds his arms, squaring up. "He won't eat fruit if it's just a little bit bruised."

A loose knot of bodies immediately forms around his barrel, staring Nicovar down, mock-fierce.

"He puts *salt* in *porridge*," Nicovar answers, and gets his own little band of supporters. Isaella weighs up the charges and steps over to James. Nicovar's eyes flick over to her for a moment, betrayed.

James hums. "He's never once wondered if he was overreaching."

More people move over to him, though the Marchers in the crowd are holding other back now, trying to keep enough space for the players.

"He's underestimated me for years," Nicovar says. A muscled Marcher barks a laugh and changes sides, putting herself clearly in Nicovar's camp.

"He flirts so much in letters he forgets why he was writing them."

"He makes sad eyes at me instead of saying what he needs."

"He snores," James says simply, winning back everybody who changed sides and then some in a hail of delighted laughter.

"He's so handsome, and I'm not, and I worry he's just being nice." Nicovar's voice doesn't quite crack, but Isaella can hear the wobble starting. The crowd coos in sympathy.

James stares across their heads. "I'm *marrying* you, right now, and that's not enough proof for you?"

"Well, it's evidence," Nicovar concedes. Isaella is changing sides every time by now, following the rhythm of the Marchers in the game. "You do the most dangerous rituals on the books."

"You pretend to like my ginger cordial, but you don't pretend very well."

"You can't use chopsticks without getting food down your front."

"You once threw yourself off a cliff." That story must have spread wide; the crowd erupts in laughter again, and Isaella is slapped on the back by more than one hand, for her part in the rescue.

"Alright," Annie shouts over the merriment, "al*right*! There's only one way to settle this! Get them down off those pedestals!"

The players reach up to lift James and Nicovar down. James squeaks at the movement, wobbling on his feet. Nicovar somehow manages to look calm even as he's tilted off his barrel.

"We've heard all your grievances, boys, and there ain't no way to choose between you. So you'll just have to kiss, and make up."

James stumbles forward, taller than Nicovar and faster across the floor. Nicovar rests his hands on James's bare waist. He's blushing under his natural pallor.

James murmurs to him, "Are you nervous, lover?"

"No," Nicovar says, shaking his head a little. "You're all exhibitionists."

"OK," James agrees, and leans down to kiss him.

The sound of cheering drowns out anything else they might say. Isaella applauds with the rest, applauds until her palms hurt, while James and Nicovar hold each other, shining with happiness.

"Al*right*," Annie says at last, and the couple turn in their embrace. "If you haven't changed your minds yet, I guess you must be married. Put your clothes on, boys, and let's tap those kegs."

Nicovar's robe and James's shirt are resting on the bar, waiting for this moment, Many hands pass them forward. James swings easily into the ivory robe, made specially for this moment but even so a little narrow over the chest. He lets it hang open and reaches to hold Nicovar's overrobe for him, while he struggles into the unfamiliar shirt. James usually wears green, but this shirt is a rich brown, and Isaella loves him fierce and sharp, for thinking about it, what would look better on Nicovar and match his clothes best. The golden embroidery at the collar is all of apples and bees. James shakes out the overrobe solemnly, helps his husband back into it.

Isaella doesn't drink much that night, but she cries a little into Cara's shoulder, and lies awake in the morning watching the steady rain, claiming a headache.

CHAPTER TWENTY-THREE – WINTER 201

Nicovar hasn't been a regular at Conclave since his coronation last year, but he recognises the rhythm of the meetings. There's always a busy time at the beginning, before the conclave has officially started business, when the magicians are chasing down their contacts and firming up their plans, working the Net of the Heavens. Then the counting, the awkward shuffling of bodies as the Orders convene, all six of them trying to claim one of the four corners for their territory, the Grandmasters taking a census of the moving heads. It never starts exactly on time but Nicovar manages to be there promptly, though he's still working on his dinner even at nine o'clock, a bowl of long-cooled rice and curry balanced on his palm and cheap wooden chopsticks rough between his fingers.

"Empress!" Lucrezia throws her arms wide, theatrically delighted. "You came!"

Nicovar smiles back. "And I've missed you, Grandmaster. How does the Order stand?"

"We've picked up a half-dozen new members since you were last here. It turns out there's some advantages to being the Emperor's order. You *do* still have your Arcane Mark, don't you?"

"Of course."

"Oh, good! That gives us one more on the precedence count. We're not always bottom nowadays."

"We're not? Who did we overtake?"

"The Sevenfold Path. When Myra's Lance stopped attending they lost a lot of people. So, to catch you up, we're making a push on block voting at the moment, throwing our weight around to get ourselves noticed, but as you're the Throne I suppose you're an exception to that, if you don't make too much noise about it. Not that I can control how you vote, but it'll mess with our strategy if you make yourself *an Arch member splitting from the Order* and not *the Throne doing their own thing*, if you follow me?"

"Of course," Nicovar says, bemused. "I've always agreed broadly with your voting choices before, Lucrezia, I'm sure I will tonight as well."

"We'll see," she says, cheerful behind the glittering glass chips in her mask. "Don't be afraid to use your own speaking nomination, is what I'm saying. If I nominate you you're an Arch member, if you speak for yourself you're the Throne. Deal?"

"Yes, deal."

"Lovely. I'll tell Ruth our numbers. Be good."

Ruth has new boots, stern and plain and lined with white rabbit fur. Nicovar envies them a little.

"Good evening, citizens," she says, "let's not waste time. I know we'd all rather be around our campfires. Before we start, a reminder that we have the Throne with us tonight, and the Throne is counted as an order for the purposes of nominating speakers, and takes precedence. He does however only have one vote in any Declaration. Any questions on procedure?"

Heads are shaken around the hall.

"Then we'll start with addresses as usual."

Business ticks through quickly, whether from Ruth's encouragement or the cold it's difficult to say. Nicovar gives half his attention to the addresses, the usual round of updates on Realm politics and the research work at the Lyceum, and the rest to watching the crowd. He's dangerously out of touch; can feel the currents moving but not quite track them, too many unfamiliar faces and alliances he can't see. He can't regret it, the Senate and the Synod need all the time he can give them, but the loss of his Conclave stings.

"On to the declarations," Ruth says. "First nominee from every order and the Throne is free for declarations, subsequent nominations and time must be paid for. Our first declaration is from Daniel of Rachel's Guard, "This Conclave agrees that a fund of mana for strategic scrying should be formed from the Conclave vaults for immediate access by ritual magicians working for the Imperial good."

Daniel is a fidgety, balding man, who probably has a personality when he's at home and not focused on his magic, but Nicovar has never seen it. He speaks in a hoarse half-shout, "Friends of the Conclave, I come to you every season through the Archmagi to ask for mana for strategic scrying and it wastes time. We could be working on Friday evenings but we can only do that if we can front the mana ourselves and not all of our scrying covens have that kind of bank. I propose to set up a fund of mana to be drawn in advance and routinely supplied by the Conclave in a single efficient payout. We have been working diligently for the Empire for years and we should not be asked to take the risk of not being repaid for our mana."

Nicovar hides his wince. Up until then, the argument was fairly sound, if no more than half likely to pass. But the Conclave has this argument every year, about whether the mana in a magician's pockets belongs to her or to the Empire, and whether Imperial work should be refunded from Conclave funds, or counted as a donation – the principles shift back and forth, but the truth is that the Conclave can't afford to pay for every divination and empowerment, and the magicians who hold out for pay are always undercut by the ones willing to donate. Raising that argument here and now will kill Daniel's scrying fund stone dead.

"I'll take questions," Daniel says. "Yes, you there."

"Who's going to hold this fund?" asks one of the Golden Pyramid, focused immediately on the prospect of Daniel trying to enrich himself.

"Whoever the Conclave selects to be custodian." Daniel puffs his chest slightly, proud of his obvious integrity. "Next question. Yes, you there, in the hat-"

"One minute," Ruth says.

"Oh. Well, I – never mind, let's go to the Orders, I suppose."

"Nicovar, does the Throne wish to speak?"

Nicovar looks around. "I'll nominate the Dawnish in the hat who didn't get to ask her question."

It's a safe move, using his power to nominate to prove he isn't scared to participate, staying out of the discussion himself to avoid the bad blood the argument always ends with. He might have been bolder, chosen to use his power to sway that argument, but Nicovar is acutely aware of his uncertain footing. Better to make sure he comes out of tonight undamaged.

The Dawnish asks her sensible question, about how much mana this scrying fund would require, and gets her sensible answer that anything less than twenty mana would probably not save any time or effort, but the more the better, and Daniel has figures for scrying expenditure stretching back eight years for anyone who wants to see, although he is missing autumn and winter 195 due to an injury, for which he apologises.

But the second speaker seizes on his point about the risk magicians take of not being refunded and shakes it like a terrier with a rat. Magicians should donate their time and their mana, just as the warriors who go through the Sentinel Gate donate their time; they don't risk their lives the way the Imperial heroes do, so they should accept the risk to their finances; she makes her case well, but it's a familiar exchange, and sure enough Lucrezia nominates herself and makes the usual answering point that the Conclave magicians risk their lives in performing magic and dealing with Eternals, and their mana should not be taxed, when they already pay their coin to the coffers of the Senate.

Nicovar takes the chance to finish his cold dinner while the argument rages around him, and declines to nominate a second time. The Conclave votes the motion down.

The next declaration is the reason Nicovar came tonight. James nods to him across the open circle and unfolds himself from the floor, leaving his damp cloak on the grass.

"Evening, everyone," he says quietly.

There is a challenger for the post of Warmage. She is a Leaguish mercenary, wearing a velvet wolf mask pushed high on her forehead, carrying a steel-banded magician's rod at her hip. James has at least ten years on her, and the polish on his staff is from heavy use.

"It's time we had a change," the challenger begins. "You all know me, I'm Felicia de Sarvos, and I've been responsible for battlefield buffs for three seasons now. I'm well connected, but I'm also independent, and we all know we can't say that about James any more, much as we all love him. It's time for our good Warmage to retire, after long service that no-one denies has been – very dedicated. But the Military Council is in danger of forgetting that the Conclave is more than just James and Nicovar." She bares her teeth. "Vote for me, and I'll remind them"

James shrugs. "I won't claim to be independent of my husband, no. I will say that the independence of the Conclave is not in doubt. The task of the Warmage is to guide and advise the Generals on strategic magic, not just the small rituals of the battlefield. The Generals will take more than we can give them, every time. I know them, and they know me, and so they trust me when I say what we can do. It's because they know me that you don't get Generals knocking on your tents at midnight demanding rituals you don't have the mana to give them. They come through me. They know I'll tell them the truth about what can happen and what can't. That trust will have to be rebuilt. I'm sure you could do it, but we're at war. It's not the time to start over."

Nicovar can't speak on this – he knew he wouldn't be able to, not without strengthening Felicia's case. He says only, "I'm here to vote for James, but I won't preach to you about why. This is a decision for the Conclave. The Throne does not appoint the Warmage."

Felicia smiles fiercely, as if he'd just endorsed her candidacy. The Sevenfold Path grandmaster asks the usual useless question, about whether James's coven will still be willing to work major Winter rituals if James loses his position, to which James can't say anything but yes, and then it's Lucrezia's turn.

"I stand with Felicia," she announces, and the ground falls silently away from Nicovar's feet. "We need a change of guard. James has been the Warmage for ten years. How long does the average Archmage last? The Throne himself, when he stood for Archmage, said we are in danger of stagnating. I agree with him. I know James will always do his best to represent the Conclave but the Generals will see him as an extension of the Throne and we deserve better than to be Nicovar's pet committee. No offence."

"Some taken," Nicovar answers, acid eating his words.

"So I'm not saying James has ever done badly by us. But it's time for a change, and he can't be an independent voice in the council. The Celestial Arch supports Felicia."

Later, Nicovar will sit with James by a campfire in Navarr, their legs pressed close beneath Nicovar's cloak, sharing a cup of honeyed tea to soothe their wounded feelings. But for now, James has to stand and hear himself dismissed, and Nicovar can only watch, and know before the vote is called that this time they won't win. James loses the challenge twenty votes to thirty-five, three abstaining. Nicovar is the only one of the Arch to vote for him.

He looks over at Lucrezia in her sparkling filigree mask, and seethes.

CHAPTER TWENTY-FOUR – SPRING 202

The Sentinel Gate slides over Isaella's skin like the brush of feathered wings.

Anvil, as ever in the spring, is soft with mud. The ground beneath her feet hardly changes as she steps through into the Marcher borders, wet clay piled into ridges by the plough. The Navarr are the second to go through, after the Highborn shield-wall whose task is to hold the gate against all comers, and they can see at once this is good ground for them. The open fields are cut with drainage ditches, making nettle-filled traps for unwary enemies to be forced down into, and stretches of dark woodland where the Marchers harvest their timber. The scouts spread out into the countryside.

In the village, half a mile away across turnip greens and dark earth, the farmers are under the orcish whip. The Jotun take slaves just as the Empire does, and just as Imperials do they need to eat. The village has become a staging post as well as a supply depot and the Imperials are here to destroy its use to them, by conquest or by flame.

That is why the Marchers of Anvil will fight tomorrow instead, in the perpetually threatened hills of Segura, against orc bandits with barely a leader worth the name. Pest control. Better to let them vent their feelings on petty raiders than to send them here to fight their kin. The Highborn have been sent instead, unforgiving of treason even under duress, and the Navarri, more sympathetic, no less ruthless when the moment comes.

The fighters are almost silent. The sky is empty above them, the pale sunlight bright and bleaching, swallowing the sound of footsteps and jingling chainmail. A squad of Highborn drum swords against their shields, three short thudding beats, and go still again.

As the Varushkans filter through the Gate and take up their places, a loose band of fighters around the back of the Gate, a stronger anchor on each flank of the Highborn core, the first shouts go up in the village. Isaella feels her shoulders settle lower, relaxing into the familiar patterns of battle. Her spear is light and eager in her hands.

She hears the cheer from Anvil as if through glass, dimmed by the barrier of the Gate. Nicovar has come with his guard of Urizeni sentinels, to be joined at once by the Highborn, the Navarri, the Varushkans – no nation would give up the honour of defending the Throne when he marches to battle. They will advance forward soon, flattening the wet soil into roads by the weight of their boots, to hunt orcs across the greening fields. But first they see a little band of ragged refugees, hurrying with their heads down, as if the sky could hide them. They run towards the bristling army with the weariness of long hunger. The Imperial line reaches out to catch them.

Most are children, thin and dirty, the babies carried in teenage arms. Isaella reaches out to squeeze the shoulder of one girl who clenches her fists around empty air, looking back at her home, her need for a weapon obvious in the set of her jaw. She is young, growing with the spring, bare ankles showing between her socks and the unpicked hem of her trousers. She steps back reluctantly when Isaella pulls.

"You'll come back," Isaella tells her, quiet as the children themselves. "You will. Leave it to me for now. Go with the others."

The girls eyes are flat with anger. She shrugs Isaella's hand away. On her other side, Cara holds out a short axe.

She reaches for it and stops, not breathing. Cara waits.

"I promised my mam," she mutters at last, and turns towards the gate, where the Emperor bends to comfort the children, ghostly pale amongst the shadowed trees.

Cara pats Isaella on the shoulder, her axe already back in its loop. "Eyes on the ball, Sal."

At the edge of the village, beneath a wavering line of apple trees, orcs have begun to gather. They are still putting on their armour, still tightening the laces on their boots. Like a wolf pricking up its ears the Imperials watch, and whisper, and move.

The Jotun were not expecting to be attacked today. It's unusual for the Gate to open on a place like this, neither a fortress nor an army, no general in sight to take command. The equinox should have made no difference to the safety of this place. But here they are, streaming across the unguarded fields, and the Jotun are not ready. When Isaella reaches the apple trees the orcs are scattered underfoot, spitted already on Varushkan swords.

They turn along the edge of the village, aiming for the rough wooden barracks at the top of the main street, where the Jotun quarter their troops. Those are the main target, along with the bridge to the north, deeper into enemy territory. Most of Urizen has gone that way, with scouts and Varushkan heavies, expecting to find the bridge defended. Isaella stays with the main force and jabs her spear into a twitching orc as she passes. The Marchers peer out of their doors or close their shutters, closed-off and sullen. An Anvil rescue is too late and much too little, unable to rescue anyone except the children, and with no occupying force to leave behind in place of the Jotun they will kill. The villagers expect to be re-conquered within the month. Isaella can't blame them for their anger.

They meet the first real resistance just before the village opens out at the top. The orcs in the barracks have had enough warning to arm up and prepare – there's nothing like a real fortification, but they can bottle the Imperials up in the street instead of facing them on open ground. The Varushkans roll into the enemy shield-wall with a shout.

The street is too narrow. Isaella can hear the weapons biting into armour, can smell the blood they spill, but she's trapped behind a dozen other fighters, far away from the fighting. There are more orcs pouring out of the barracks, ready to defend their position in the village. In the back of her mind an hourglass is running. They've been here too long already. If the Jotun can hold them here for another forty minutes, they'll have to retreat back to the Gate or be caught here in the borderlands.

Others have made the same calculation. Gerwyn the archer is kneeling on the slope of a nearby roof with barely room to draw his bow, steadily cursing as he drives arrows into flesh. Isaella pushes over to him, leaping to catch a precarious grip on the thatch and pull herself up.

"We have to clear them out," she says.

Gerwyn lets another arrow fly. "Obviously." His quiver is half empty already.

"Can we flank them?"

"I – Good question."

They climb higher, their boots slipping on the matted straw roof. Gerwyn flattens himself to peer over the top. "Too many damn hedges. They're all hawthorn, you'll never get through."

"Wait," Isaella says, "there, through the orchard. There's a gate."

He looks at her sidelong. "Just don't burn the trees."

"Obviously," she agrees, and slips back down on her belly to collect the nearest fighters and get them moving.

It's not that the orcs see them coming. That's not the problem. The problem is that they have the high ground, and the ground around their barracks is trodden flat and toughened with straw, while Isaella's makeshift band have to slog through tangled orchard grass untouched since the pigs were slaughtered. They can't move fast enough to reach the battle before the orcs redeploy their forces. Some Jotun commander will be getting a promotion out of this; she marshals her troops as efficiently as any general, and the gate they thought was theirs spills grey-skinned enemies into the orchard to hunt them in return.

It's a deadly mess. Isaella tries but she can't keep her fighters together, inexperienced as they are. They split up into twos and threes, trying to chase down the Jotun, exposing their backs to every passing orc. Isaella puts her whistle in her mouth and keeps blowing, even as her hands are busy with her spear to keep the enemy swords away. A hammer blow to the hip almost cripples her. She staggers into a tree and stays there, bracing her back against the trunk. Her whistle falls from her lips. The orc with the hammer is still coming at her, beating down hard enough to smash her skull if she doesn't deflect every blow. If the fates are merciful her spear will hold up. She's using it like a staff now, purely defensive, and it was not build to be a shield. There's a rustle in the grass, a sound of breathing behind her. Someone coming up behind the tree. Isaella braces for the knife in the back.

A slender figure in pale robes darts past her and under the Jotun's guard. The orc freezes instantly, his chest barely moving with his breath. Isaella flips her spear around and drives the point into his throat.

Hot blood spatters her face and stains Nicovar's robes with a spray of red. He catches her as she wobbles, his arm around her waist.

"Hi," she says, absurdly.

"Hello." Nicovar pulls her in and hugs her. "Six hells, Isaella, don't die on me."

"I didn't."

Somewhere nearby there's shouting. A trio of Varushkans, fresh from killing their own targets, are whooping at Nicovar. He draws away, looking sheepish, one arm still supporting her. "Can you walk?"

Isaella tries it, and flinches. "No, but I can limp."

"Gate," Nicovar says firmly.

"Can you leave? What about the battle?"

"The battle already went to shit. We're retreating. I'm taking you back to the Gate."

He lets someone take the burden of her spear, and Gerwyn feed her a bitter twist of herbs to ease the pain, but when she finally staggers back through the Sentinel Gate it's with her arm still flung over the Emperor's shoulders, bringing her safely home.

CHAPTER TWENTY-FIVE – SUMMER 202

The carta's tent is one of the finest on the fields of Anvil. It stands a little apart from its neighbours, its guylines daintily unentangled with theirs, leaving it framed in narrow paths of trodden-down earth. There is a silk curtain billowing across the open entrance. The torches outside are clasped in a month's worth of woodcarving.

Nicovar stands beneath the extravagant bunting of satin and brocade, his feet planted in the grass. The urge to smooth down his robes stirs in his bones, awakened by the splendour of the tent. He ignores it. To his right, Cardinal Rosalind drums her fingers against her belt.

"Are you ready for this, Nicovar?"

Nicovar smiles at her. "Come on."

In the dim warmth of the Carta's audience chamber, Rosalind's rich embroidery seems at home. Nicovar has robes that would have suited the room, all deep burgundy and walnut brown. He has worn instead his old Ankarien clothes, pale ivory, the better to foreground himself. He has come, like Rosalind, bare-faced.

There is a large table stretched across the tent, its polished surface almost glowing. Lanterns hang from the rafters, unlit and unneeded in the sunlight filtering through the canvas. It gleams from fluted glasses and the curving cambion horns of the d'Holberg twins. Cressida sits upright in a heavy chair that clamours to be called a throne, her face naked. Lucrezia stands a little behind her, masked and gloved in black, resting one hand on her sister's shoulder.

Nicovar admires the staging intensely.

"Welcome, Emperor," Cressida says. "We are honoured by your visit."

Nicovar bows his greeting. "It has been too long, Cressida, Grandmaster."

"What's a title between friends?" Lucrezia gestures at the table. "Please, sit. Let's have a drink together."

"Let's," Rosalind agrees. She pulls a pale bottle of wine from some invisible pocket, as only a Dawnish can. Nicovar steps over the low bench on his side of the table.

"This is better chilled, but it's been cooling in a bath all morning." Rosalind picks up a corkscrew from the table and eases the cork from the bottle. It hisses with the promise of bubbles. The wine she pours is as pink and bright as quartz.

Nicovar sips from his delicate glass, letting the others follow his lead. "This is very good, Rosalind."

"Of course it is, it's from Grovesyard. They've grown the best grapes since before there was an Empire." Rosalind swings her legs over the bench and plants her elbows on the table. "Right then. You're here, he's here, we've all got a drink. Sort this out."

Cressida smiles over her glass. "I don't think I know what you mean."

"Really? Well, I'm not stupid, and you are feuding." She waves at them all, Nicovar and the twins and back. "Only, you're doing it wrong."

Lucrezia spins one of the empty chairs and drops into it, straddling the back. "Are you here as a Cardinal?"

"I'm always a Cardinal," Rosalind says dismissively. "And you must admit it *does* seem cowardly, avoiding each other like this. But more importantly you're just being dreadfully boring."

Cressida splutters with laughter. Lucrezia grins. "We've never been called that before. You should spend more evenings here, Rosalind."

"Why? Will you start talking to each other again if I do? Oh, I know I'm supposed to scold you for lack of virtue, but I really can't be bothered with it. No matter which side you take it makes for a very dull story, the rivals refusing to meet. How am I meant to turn this nonsense into a song?"

"You put her up to this," Cressida says, looking pointedly towards Nicovar instead of her accuser.

Nicovar spreads his hands. "The Dawnish Cardinal of Courage? You think I could tell her what to say?"

"And you've been cowardly too, Nicovar."

His wince is deliberate, but honest. "Yes. Rosalind talked me into this meeting as well. You'd have enjoyed that conversation."

"Did you bleed?" Lucrezia taps her wineglass with the curve of a silver ring, making it chime. "Anyway, do we have an agenda, or are we just here to kiss and make up?"

Rosalind lifts her glass in a toast. "Lucrezia, darling, we *all* have agendas."

When the laughter subsides, Nicovar reaches into his robe for a parchment scroll, its surface pearlescently white. "I had this, from a very silent herald, a week before the summit started. It's addressed to both of us."

Lucrezia leans forward to take it. "What kind of herald?"

"A merrow with golden scales."

"Kimus?" Lucrezia looks sharply up at him, the scroll half unrolled. She sets it down on the table to flatten it out. "We haven't heard from them in ages."

"They want to speak to us – you read it."

"Honoured Imperator of the Empire of the way, Bearer of the Legacy of the Unnamed Empress, He Who Wears The Crown; Grandmaster of the Path Celestial, Conductor of the Dancing Heavens, She Who Wear The Mask; Kimus, the Ever-Burning, the Flame with a Thousand Tongues, bids you greeting."

Rosalind pours herself more wine, to recover from the volley of titles. "What was wrong with your names?"

"It pleases Kimus to hold audience once more with the magi of the Empire, to enquire upon their understanding of that which is. The door will be opened at dusk on the day of the year's turning-"

"Midsummer," Cressida translates, exasperated.

"The year's turning, and those who are admitted shall be the chosen companions of the Crown and the Mask, whose thoughts are most pleasing to them. Seven magi shall be permitted into the hall of Kimus, besides the worthy persons here addressed, and in addition two mortals may take the mantle of servitor, to pass amongst the gathering as do the Radiant Eyes – I'm going to throw *sand* in those eyes, Nicovar. What does that all mean that couldn't be said as "Come to tea, bring some friends"? Ridiculous creature."

"It has no friends," Nicovar says mildly. "It loves only philosophy. Philosophy and spying."

"So is that seven or nine people going?"

"I think it's eleven. Two of us, nine magi, two other magicians who only get to watch."

"Rough deal for those two."

Cressida leans back in her chair. "For an audience with an Eternal? You could auction it off."

Lucrezia flaps a hand at her, pulling ink and paper from a drawer beneath the table. "So, we want interesting mysticists, from groups worth courting -" She bangs the ink-pot down and glares across the table at Rosalind. "Damn you."

Rosalind smiles. "I told you you were bad at feuding."

The chamber in which they first met Kimus was small and bare, too cramped for three to meet in by Nicovar's standards. This time it is an expanse of clouded glass that rings like marble underfoot, the walls fading into distant mist. The expressionless figure of the Eternal stands in what might be the centre, or might not be, its yellow veils rising in an unfelt wind. Shimmering glass spheres circle it, the thousand eyes of legend. Perhaps the lights overhead are eyes as well, moving in the same gentle tide, glowing in every colour of the sky.

The passage from the Hall of Worlds hardly ripples Nicovar's robes. He moves forward at once, to clear the way for the others following. Beside him, Lucrezia lifts her head to look at the moving stones. The yellow silk ribbons looped between her horns look grey and artificial in the Realm-light.

The mages lucky enough to be invited filter into the chamber behind them. Last of all comes a wordless merrow, her face warped by the strength of her lineage, patches of pale yellow mottling her skin. She made eye contact with each one of them, counting them, before she ushered them into this half-real place.

The floating eyes stop in their orbits, and rush towards their visitors.

Nicovar does not flinch. He remembers these oddly menacing orbs from the first time. Lucrezia does too, raising a hand as if inviting the eyes to land upon her palm. But the others gasp, or duck, or take a full step backwards in the case of poor nervous Daniel. One eye follows him like a glassy wasp, until Julia snags his sleeve and murmurs advice.

Nicovar pitches his voice to carry through the open space. "The Empire of the Way greets Kimus of the Thousand Eyes."

"You are welcome to my chamber, Nicovar, and you also, Lucrezia, Grandmaster of the Celestial Arch, and your companions. This chamber has been created for our use, to speak upon the nature of creation. Come, let us understand. In whom does Existence reside?"

Nicovar catches Julia's gentle sigh, and the start of a quiet lesson to the younger magicians on what Kimus, the arch-solipsist, is asking them. Daniel says, "No. No, that's not the right question, at all," and is immediately mobbed by three flying spheres, their voices sharp and shivery, demanding to know what he means.

Nicovar bows to the statue-still central figure out of courtesy, though the first resonant voice seemed to come from everywhere. Lucrezia elbows him.

"You should be right at home here, Nic, they're wearing robes like mountain people."

"Very old-fashioned robes," Nicovar disagrees.

"Ah yes, whereas you are at the cutting edge of fashion."

"I am, actually."

"Well – yes, but only because the Throne *defines* the fashion, and that's cheating."

"I'll bear that in mind. Come on, let's be interesting. If one of us is fake, which one is it?"

They argue unseriously for a while, bringing in parentage and age and which of them sounds more like a fairy-tale, before a large eye approaches them, its glass marbled through with pale blue streaks. "Emperor."

It feels absurd to bow to a little flying ball. Nicovar compromises on inclining his head.

"Grandmaster."

"Hi," Lucrezia says brightly. "Are you a Herald or a bit of an Eternal?"

The eye rotates on the spot. "That is an interesting question, Grandmaster. I am a part of Creation. All creation is a part of Kimus. Therefore, the only logical answer is that I am a part of an Eternal. If all things partake of the Eternal's dream, how shall we speak of Heralds and mortals as other than their wellspring?"

Lucrezia blinks behind her mask. Her mouth opens. "But then – I don't think *I'm* a part of Kimus."

"All things that are, are part of Kimus. All things that are not, but are conceived of, are dreamed by part of Kimus and part of Kimus themselves. All things that are not, are part of the great nothingness, which is conceived of, which is part of Kimus. Why should your thoughts prove it otherwise?"

"Forgive me, but that line of reasoning is utterly insane."

"Insanity is part of Kimus also." The glass ball sounds distinctly smug. "Do you not perceive yourself as part of a greater whole? Do you stand apart from your dreams?"

"But I still have *edges*. I stand apart from Nicovar."

"Far apart, lately."

"Shush, you. There are things that I am part of, but they don't subsume me. It's not like drops of water. It's metaphorical."

The ball begins to spin the other way. "Then you, Imperial Grandmaster, are not part of the Empire? You will stand beside the Emperor and reject your part in that whole?"

Later, long after darkness has fallen in the world outside, Nicovar stands alone between two circling specks of light. He is watching Daniel lying on the floor with his hands pressed against his eyes. "Why is he so upset?"

"We asked him if Paragons had become perfect and ceased to exist, like a fire that has burned out. He did not like the ending of fire being named its perfection. He was quite insistent. He drank of the waters of Day for refreshment. He is seeing many things."

"I'd appreciate it if you didn't drug my subjects."

"Then you may instruct them not to drink."

"I cannot be everywhere at once. Unlike you, I only have two eyes."

"That is unfortunate. What would you do with more?"

"I suspect I would become very confused."

"Yes. That is a mortal limitation. You cannot bear to know too much."

"I like to know as much as I can. Not as much as Daniel, perhaps. Will he be alright?"

"The visions will fade. Beyond that, I cannot say."

Nicovar clasps his hands behind his back. He would like to walk with the Eternal, but the floor of this chamber curves, and those who wander are turned around like drunkards. "How is your project progressing, to understand Creation?"

"I am questioning the apparent existence of Time."

Nicovar nods solemnly. "Of course. It would be silly to take it for granted."

"It is spoken of as a thing that passes, like the water in a river. But – if it is real at all, if it is causative, if the mind of that which is perceives it outside of the dreams of its smallest parts – what is the shape of the river? To what sea is it running down?"

"Argument from metaphor," Nicovar says, "there needn't be a sea at all."

"Perhaps you are climbing a ladder. Perhaps you are a leaf in the river and what passes is the bank of true reality. Would it make a difference? What are the contours of the riverbed?"

"Maybe it doesn't flow at all," Nicovar says, picking up the theme. "Maybe it's a rope pulling us up. Or it's a circle, or it's a spiral. How could we test that?"

"What happens to humans when they die?"

There is always some reason behind an Eternal's question, even one that seems to change the subject. Nicovar obligingly follows the thread, positing that the souls of the dead are moving outside of time, and their virtue determines their direction. "And then, the wider the angle, the less time appears to pass for those on the circle before they reappear, until finally their direction is outside the circle entirely, and they transcend."

"You should think on this, Emperor," the orb says. "You should think upon the nature of Time. You are the steersman for an Empire. How will you guide it, if you do not understand the river?"

Nicovar smiles. "Thank you, Kimus. I will consider these questions. Do you imply that our time together, whatever Time may be, is at an end?"

The ball bobs in the air. "It is midnight. The year is turning. You must return now to the mortal realm, or else remain."

"We'll go, thank you. Will you open the door for us?"

"You have only to walk away from me, and you will find it."

Daniel proves capable of walking if he keeps one hand on the back of Julia's chair. She glares at the ever-silent merrow who shepherds them towards the gate. Nicovar submits to Lucrezia's slap between his shoulder-blades.

"I thought that went pretty well!"

"I need coffee," Nicovar says. "Lots of coffee. That creature makes my head spin."

CHAPTER TWENTY-SIX – AUTUMN 202

Isaella draws her legs up beneath her, trying to sit comfortably without getting her boots on the fluffy sheepskin rug. Senator Isolt is playing with a child's toy, a magician's rod in miniature, spinning it back and forth in her hands. "Damn this mud," she says, nodding towards the sodden tournament square. "One fall and you're soaked to the bone."

Isaella grimaces in agreement. "The only firm ground in Navarr is in the wood and that won't hold up for long, not with all the traffic it gets. Did you see the motion Temeschwar put up this morning?"

"A proposal to lay roads and drainage around the Imperial Capital of Anvil, as befits a great Power," Isolt recites. "Honestly. As if nobody had ever thought of that before."

"She does have a point."

"But no follow-through. We can propose anything we like. The constitutional scholars will never let it through. If roads didn't count as buildings we'd have had them years ago."

"Maybe Trod magic would work," Isaella speculates. "Make the place re-green faster."

"You want to infuse Anvil with experimental Spring magic?"

"Mm, no. Let's not do that."

"What about the fleet? How are you going to vote on that?"

"I don't know."

Isolt raises both eyebrows. "You don't think we need a fleet?"

"I do think we need one. But it took us so long to build the first one, it took so much of our resources – we're only just getting the armies to where they could have been if we'd spent the budget on them instead. We have proposals for fortifications we can't support if we divert weirwood back towards the docks. And can any of the seafaring nations promise five thousand sailors? I know the Brass Coast will refuse to take it on."

"And the League won't have it either." Isolt sets the end of her plaything against a fold in the rug and rolls it between her fingers, twisting first one way then the other. "It would have to go to Highguard. They're the only ones who could sustain another army. But I think they could be persuaded. Of course, they might make Miriam the Admiral."

"I don't hate Miriam. I don't," Isaella insists, seeing that Isolt is about to disagree. "Just because she dislikes me doesn't mean I have to reciprocate. She's a fine General and I'm glad we can depend on her. If the Highborn senators think she's the best choice – I'm about to sound like a hypocrite."

"Why?"

"General Argent."

"Oh. Him." Isolt's lips twist in distaste. "What do we do about him?"

"You persuade your priests to pass the revocation."

Isolt hesitates.

"What?"

"It's not that," she says reluctantly. "The revocation is being handled. It's my dear once-upon-a-time brother."

"Roland?"

"Him. He's… He's got hold of a proxy note for Semmerholm. I've seen it, it's genuine."

"You don't sound convinced."

"It's pay-to-bearer. They've had such a mess with the floods up there, Earl Perille wasn't sure who she could send. I seriously doubt it was ever meant for Roland, but he's carrying it now and the Civil Service have accepted his claim. He's outraged that mere priests would dare to revoke an Earl."

"You're saying he'll try to re-select Argent."

Isolt nods. "And Maisie has to go along with it. You can't blame her, Argent is her head of house. She doesn't like him."

"But if he calls on house loyalty, Maisie will have to follow." Isaella leans back on her hands. "Okay. You're going to be overruled on Argent. What can we do about that?"

"I'm working on it." Isolt starts spinning her stick again. "But in the meantime, the fleet. How would you vote if the Highborn volunteered to handle recruitment?"

The wooden floor of the Senate does not drum under Isaella's boots, caked as they are with an inch of mud. The liquefied muck outside is dotted with lumps of compacted earth, left by Senators scraping their soles on the ramp. Even Nicovar looks grubby, perched upon his throne like a bird on a rain-soaked nest. The air is heavy with mist.

Isaella makes her rounds quickly. She arrived only minutes ahead of the bell, having made herself stop and eat before the session. Ten years ago she could skip meals with equanimity; nowadays she must have food and sleep or her wits will fray. Isolt nods to her across the room; Roland pointedly ignores her. Isaella spends her precious time with the Varushkans instead, trying to allay their fears that establishing the second fleet will leave their defences too thin.

Speaker Marianne, damp but not bedraggled, thumps her staff against the floor. "The Senate will come to order. No citizens on the Senate floor, please. That means you, Gatekeeper."

"Sorry, sorry, sorry," Anya says as she shuffles down the ramp.

"Thank you. The business of the Senate today begins with a proposal by Temeschwar, seconded by Segura, to pave the roads of Anvil and lay drains. I will remind you that motions like this are routinely rejected by the Constitutional Court and cannot go into effect. As such, I am using my privilege as Speaker to bypass debate upon the matter and we will proceed directly to the vote. Ayes to the left, nays to the right. Senators, please cast your votes now. Thank you. The motion is not carried. The next motion is a proposal by Reikos, seconded by Astolat, to create a new army in Highguard, said army to be a Fleet, after the pattern of the Barabbine Fleet." Marianne holds up a hand to stem the muttering. "This would require construction of the fleet itself and significant improvements to at least one port, and accordingly, supplies of weirwood and white granite would need to be found. The proposers have therefore put this forward as a non-budgeted item seeking Senate approval but no funding at this time. However, if this motion is carried, recruitment will begin and Highguard will not be able to establish any further armies until the fleet is either completed or disbanded. We will now hear debate on the motion."

Sir Isolt, for Astolat, is the first to speak. She talks of the obvious Virtue of reclaiming forgotten ambitions, the loss of Imperial stature in abandoning the project. Isaella admires the call to arms, but she is more convinced by Isaac of Necropolis and his arguments about defence.

"The Grendel come at the Empire from the sea, but so do corsairs and raiding bands of Jotun. As the Empire expands on land, it must also consider the sea as a vulnerable border..."

The debate flows back and forth, heated but polite. These are well-established arguments. They have been having them since Barabbas was lost. Isaella takes her turn, giving cautious support to the motion to rebuild. She has spoken to her brokers about the figures, and the docks could be improved without risking the northern forts, if the Bourse owners would give up their hoarding. There's some laughter at that from the public gallery, and some quietly vicious hissing.

Isaella stands to the left when the vote is called. A majority of her colleagues stand with her.

Marianne's staff sounds against the floorboards. "Motion carried."

"Vetoed." Nicovar's voice cuts through the room. "The Barabbine Fleet will not be rebuilt. I do not permit it." He sits upright in his throne, a blade drawn from its sheath. "My duty is to govern this Empire. My duty is to overrule this Senate, when it makes poor decisions. The fleet will not be rebuilt. It is a luxury we cannot afford. We face *one* maritime threat. That is the Grendel, and they are the least of all our enemies. Even Barabbas planned to sail north and come upon the Jotun from the coast. We have made that gamble once and lost. We will not throw more lives into the sea."

The speech hangs in the air, Nicovar's flat denial echoed by the stillness in his face. He waits, a pale spider alone in his web, to be sure no voice will rise against him.

"And since the Senate cannot be trusted to steward the Empire's armies, I will take one more step. By my right as the Throne, I hereby remove General Argent from his post. I will personally command the Hounds of Glory until such time as the Dawnish can select a more suitable candidate – one who does not sell the armour from his soldiers' backs. Speaker Marianne, please proceed with today's business."

Nicovar leans back. The spell and the silence break. Isaella pushes through the commotion to the public gallery, where James is leaning against the railing, folded over with his head on his arms.

Isaella reaches for his hand.

"I worked so hard for that," he says, muffled into his sleeve. "That fucking fleet. I spent years making that happen and he just -" James snaps his fingers. "Just like that. Half my career. Worthless."

"I know," Isaella says, remembering long hours in the Military Council, planning out whole campaigns that can't be fought without a navy. "I could punch him."

James groans. "Don't. Treason, probably."

"Did he warn you?"

"Did he warn me? Has Nic ever warned anyone? He didn't need me for his strategy. I thought it was happening."

Marianne's staff is pounding against the wood. "Order, please! The Senate will come to order! Quiet in the gallery!"

"I'm going," James says, lifting his face at last. His cheeks are flushed dark with anger.

"Wait-"

"Leave it, Sal."

He takes a step back and is gone, out of the gallery and into the grey mist beyond. Isaella longs to follow him. On the dais, Nicovar sits silent and steady on the carven throne, and

Marianne reads out the next motion. The Senate is resuming its business.

She does her duty. She stays.

CHAPTER TWENTY-SEVEN – WINTER 202

Miracle of miracles, the ground is solid underfoot. A wet autumn and a dry winter have produced a flourishing of grass, and some zealous Civil Service groundskeeper has stopped all traffic at the boundary. Even Trader's Row is substantially walkable.

Nicovar bounces on his heels in the Military Council tent. "Good evening, Senator."

Isolt half bows to him. "Good evening, Empress. How is the eastern front?"

"Not much changed. The Barrens is still caught up in Druj infighting. They aren't organised enough to bring more than raiding parties against us."

"Give it a month and that might change." Isolt hesitates. "Nicovar, I've had a lot of letters from the Hounds."

"They want their General back."

"Not – not exactly that. Most of them are glad to be rid of Argent and his profiteering. But they want a Dawnish leader for Dawnish swords. I'm sorry, but they do."

"And can you, their Senator, give them one?"

Isolt stiffens. "I'm *working* on it."

"I know. But until you have an answer someone has to command the Hounds, and constitutionally, it has to be me. I'm not doing this for fun."

"Can you give me your word that whatever candidate we choose, you will surrender the army to them?"

"No," Nicovar says, slowly, "no, I can't promise that. You are still balanced against Roland, and he is still a fool."

"I'm not going to choose another Argent, Nicovar."

"*You're* not."

Isolt stares at him for a long moment, but Nicovar is resolute. Her cloak catches the tent flap on the way out and sets the canvas flapping in the breeze, a hollow mimicry of applause.

Nicovar struggles with the generals' meeting. Military tactics do not come naturally to him and he is lacking the easy familiarity with the map that even the newer generals show. He is uncomfortable aware that his glory is borrowed.

Miriam stands opposite him, furious and bereft. She has not forgiven him, not for the fleet and not for the Throne. The strength of her anger breaks over Nicovar like the wind, heavy in its promise of thunder. She rules this room, with her plain woollen hood for a crown.

"Don't advance yet, Erik," she is saying to the general of the Green Shield. "Give it another season. It will take another army to invade Bregasland and win. Wait for the Wolves of War to reach you and do the whole job at once."

Erik rubs his stubbly beard. "We could establish a beachhead, for the League to shore up in the summer. The Jotun have been squatting in Western Scout too long already."

"If you hurry you'll be surrounded and cut all to pieces."

"Who by? They're all in the Marches."

"Liathaven is *ours*," young Raelyn says, her emphatic sibilance a habit caught from her naga wife, with Gwyneth grey and glowering at her back for contrast. "It isn't Jotun territory. It is *home*. We deserve to have it reclaimed, not leave our greenest gardens to rot under orcish boots. And the same goes for the Marchers."

Miriam is dismissive. "I'm not suggesting we should abandon Western Scout. Only that we should think twice before we invade a Vallorn."

"Invade a Vallorn?" Erik's hand drops from his face, stopped mid-fidget in his surprise. "We're not going to do that. There's plenty of room between the border and the Vallorn's heart. We know the Jotun are using Liathaven for resupply. Why should we let them?"

Nicovar clears his throat. "Drive for the beachhead, Erik."

Erik's eyes widen. He looks between them, Nicovar's cool poise and Miriam's glare. "Oh," he says. "Oh. Didn't expect *that* to happen." He chews his lip for a moment. "Alright then, Emperor, I'll – well, I'm glad you agree with me. We'll strike west at once."

Miriam is too careful to snarl in public. "Then the Wolves of War had better move quickly to reach you. Yes, Benvolio? Good. Let's talk about the Thule."

When the council finally agrees to its tactics on each of their several fronts and the expeditions through the Gate that will best support them, the sky outside is beginning to clear. Nicovar looks up at the patchy stars with displeasure. Beautiful they may be but the view is much better from the towers of his spire, and clear skies promise a cold night. The grass is a chilly dampness clinging around his ankles.

Senate has long since started without him. Nicovar passes it with barely a glance at the crowd massed below his throne. He heads for Ankarien's camp, which has grown a shell since his Archmage days, the symbolic fence of sticks and bunting replaced with woven willow panels well braced against the press of leaning bodies, and noise-making bells hung on the inside edge in case it ever does go over. Visitors are more welcome than ever, but they must pass through the gatehouse tent first, to give their Throne a chance to breathe.

Nicovar drops onto a cushioned bench beside his long-legged husband. James pats him on the knee, wordlessly, and passes him a bowl of no longer steaming rice.

"I love you," Nicovar says involuntarily.

"How was Council? Did you give away the farm?"

Nicovar shakes his head, hunting in his robe for his chopsticks. "I upset Miriam very much but I mostly stayed out of it. I told Erik to advance instead of hold on the Liathaven lines, but he wanted to do that anyway. It bought me some goodwill."

"Erik?"

"Tall, gingery, scrawny with a short beard-"

"Oh, him." James stretches his legs out in front of the bench. "Yes, he needs more confidence in his convictions. It always took a nudge for him to disagree with Miriam."

"They don't like her, do they?"

"Of course not. She lost the Throne campaign and now she acts like she's Queen of the Armies. They take her advice, usually, but they resent her for it. There's no such thing as a Chief General. She's been told that to her face more than once."

"Oh, I'm sure that went down well."

"You should set up an Assembly of Nine meeting. The army power isn't used much. I know Katja is worried about precedent."

"I'm not planning on using it willy-nilly."

"Well, Katja doesn't know that. She thinks you're after personal fame and that's why you vetoed the new fleet."

Nicovar leans sideways, bumping James with his shoulder. They've talked about this, in long dark hours and heartfelt letters. He still owes James some grovelling.

"Alright. I'll arrange something. What's the time? Shouldn't you be at Conclave?"

"Fuck Conclave. I don't care. Nobody's going to notice if I'm gone."

"No, I think you should go. We both should. Otherwise Lucrezia will set up more dominoes to knock down without us."

"Remember when Conclave used to be fun?"

"I remember. You were already Warmage by then, old man."

"And you were thinner. Okay then, come on. We'll have missed the counting as it is. We should go if we're going."

Inside the Hall of Worlds they are shielded from the sinking temperatures by the simple press of bodies. Nicovar's instinct to seek space has been dulled by years of Conclave meetings, crowded in like this on all sides. He stands a row or two back from the front, present, but not dominating the room. He watches Ruth, the civil servant, riding herd on them. She looks pinched with the cold, or else not well.

The rasp in her voice confirms his suspicions. "Alright, alright. That's the last of the addresses. *No*, citizen, you cannot add to the agenda now. Conclave is already in session. Bring it to me tomorrow. Declaration of Principle from Jo Shepherd, "This Conclave agrees that the position of Warmage is intended to provide the Military Council with sound magical advice, not to act as a mouthpiece for that body in the Conclave." The proposer will have one minute to speak."

Shepherd is unusually willowy for a Marcher, her long straight hair drawn into a Navarr-style plait. She stands hand on hip, filling out the space her shoulders don't take up.

"Yes, it's political," she says to a grumbler on a straw-stuffed cushion, "of course it's political. If y'don't like politics go back t'your campfire. Friends, we all remember why James lost his position, but Warmage Felicia isn't doing any good. Whatever the generals want, she tells them they can have. The magical defence of the Empire is *our* watch. What do the generals know about scrying magnitudes? What do they know about mana funds? Felicia is telling them they can have everything in our vaults. Well, we need that mana. If we burn it all on the war there's nothing left for research, nothing for the economy, nothing for dealing with Eternals. The Warmage is failing. She should be our messenger to the generals and they think she's the commander of us."

"That's not true." The Warmage stamps forward, faintly absurd in her gilt-scrolled armour, the only one here in such warlike finery. "That's *not* true."

But this is contrary to protocol, and the Conclave which has no legal rules of order clings ferociously to its principles; Felicia is drowned by scores of voices calling for her mana before they will hear her, and she retreats in dismay.

Nicovar has the right of first nomination. He uses it on himself.

"Jo is right," he says bluntly. "We can argue about whether the Warmage is doing her job. I can tell you she isn't. I can tell you she did not attend council today, and she takes her orders from the handful of generals who own her loyalty. But when I was Archmage, I would have directed you back to the wording of the Declaration, and I will do the same now. It *is* the duty of the Warmage to advise the Military Council. It is *not* their role to carry orders to the Conclave, which is senior in constitutional standing. The Conclave makes law. The Generals do not. Any Warmage who presumes to command the Conclave is out of bounds, and that is all the Declaration says. If Felicia objects, she condemns herself."

For the second time tonight, the weight of his still-new office sways a room. Nicovar watches in secret delight as the Orders, one by one, concede his argument. Only Lucrezia tries to hold out, arguing that to condemn their Warmage will weaken them in the eyes of the Empire. She has nothing but indignant denial when asked if that forms a confession. Jo has been too clever in her wording.

There are more abstentions than usual. Nicovar takes note of that, a limitation on how far his voice can carry them. The declaration still passes handily, and Jo Shepherd nods to him across the circle, confident of her new standing in his court.

James leans down to mutter in his ear, "I don't want the job back. I did my time."

"That's fine," Nicovar whispers back, "we'll give it to Jo and you can be a Grandmaster."

His husband grumbles and straightens up, looking politely towards the next speaker. Nicovar smiles to himself. The Conclave is a living thing, and it is answering again to his hand upon the reins.

CHAPTER TWENTY-EIGHT – SPRING 203

Isaella feels livelier than she has in years. Liathaven was under an enchantment this season, magic running through every river and rainstorm, sustaining the Empire's soldiers as they rooted out the Jotun from their last hiding places. It helped the Jotun too, of course, and turned the green spring into a deadly hide-and-seek between the trees. The forest is surging with life.

She travels back to Anvil with a merry heart. She could walk this route blindfold, the long trade road across the width of the Empire. It curves south around the great bay to Casinea and little unlovely Anvil, the two stone monuments and one ruined forge, with the tents billowing white along makeshift lanes.

She trots up the ramp into the Senate building, the floorboards swept clear of their seasonal load of leaf litter, the sheep chased away from the sheltering walls and the familiar canvas roof stretched over the space. Senate will not be in session for another hour yet. The children know it and take advantage of the chance to play, before they are ordered out again. A pair of toddlers are sitting in the throne.

Isaella bows to them. "Good evening, Citizens."

"We're not citizens yet," the girl says scornfully. Isaella looks again and corrects her estimate of their ages; she's small, her limbs are short, but she has elaborate embroidery on the yoke of her blouse of a kind nobody bothers with for a fast-growing four-year-old, and sharply pointed eyeliner.

"How long do you have to go?"

"Two years," the boy says, his broad nose a perfect match for his sister's.

"One and a half," she corrects him sternly, and to Isaella, "Mama won't let me take the tests early. She says I'll get myself killed."

"Are you going to be a warrior?"

"Not *all* the time. I'm going to be a fur trader like my aunt. But if anything comes to my vale I'm going to shoot it and stab it until it's *dead*. I'm *very* hard to hit."

Isaella grins. "I used to be a soldier with the Black Thorns."

The girls jumps to her feet. "You're a Navarr, aren't you? Can you show me a knife trick?"

By the time Marianne arrives, there is a nasty bruise on Isaella's thigh, from Sveta's wooden dagger stabbing at her femoral artery. Marianne has had a new livery tunic made to better fit the gradual middle-aged widening of her waist. It clashes with her Imperial sash just as badly as the old one.

"This is the Emperor's throne," she says reprovingly, "you shouldn't play in it."

The boy sticks out his tongue and jumps down, running noisily across the floor with Sveta in swift pursuit, her knife and her voice both raised.

Marianne shakes her head. "I never behaved like that when I was a child."

"No grown-up ever did." Isaella pats the arm of the throne. "They haven't hurt it. The Empire will survive."

"Hm. Don't encourage them, Liathaven."

Senate is over with quickly. Nicovar misses it again, busy with the Military Council; Isaella makes a mental note to mention it to him. There will be new Senators tomorrow and they will feel slighted if he doesn't attend at least once this summit. For now she needs to track down Cara and ask about the rumours of a Peace cult springing up in Therunin.

"It's not exactly a cult," Cara tells her, "because it doesn't seem to have a leader. The converts we've been seeing are all claiming to have had spontaneous revelations."

"But of a false virtue. That's a cult."

"Are we sure it's false? I'm sorry, I shouldn't say that to you – that's a Synod thought experiment. No, really, don't look at me like that – I've just come from an Assembly of the Way meeting and it was all we talked about. There are no Paragons of Peace, so Peace is not a real virtue, that's what it boils down to."

"Don't frighten me like that, Cara."

"Sorry. Anyway! My accidentally sounding like a heretic aside, we *do* have a Peace problem in Therunin. We can do some good there with a Synod motion, to get some orthodox preaching into the region, but we think there's a malign spiritual presence there as well. Want to join the exorcism party?"

The right alignment of the Sentinel Gate doesn't roll around until Saturday afternoon, after half of Anvil has marched upon the overbold Thule rebuilding their broken fortress and come back daubed in orcish blood. The Navarri expedition is constrained to eight souls by the lesser strength of the conjunction, and it makes a mercy of the wait – they need all of that time to agree on the guest list. Isaella goes, with her senatorial authority backed up with a barbed spear, and Cara for the religious weight of a Cardinal. Cara can't perform an exorcism, though, so along with two fighters – just in case – they have a cadre of Vigilance priests, their faces blazing with matching red warpaint.

Under other circumstances, the Weedkiller vigilance sect would be an obviously bad choice of diplomat. They are the most abrasive group of priests on the Anvil field, spending their liao recklessly to pull down magical auras, even well-known enchantments that generations of vates have ruled as harmless. Nobody is more likely to spoil a pleasant conversation. But they have twice the exorcism strength of any other Navarri group, and the congenial Highguard team can't come on this expedition; the Gate won't let anyone through except Navarr.

A helpful magician opens the portal without fuss, her gestures wide and confident, framing runes with her blood-smeared fingertips. Under her touch the Gate is calm, yielding to distance with barely a ripple. She waves to the gathered party and goes off whistling to find some shade.

Cara steps through first. Therunin is the home of her childhood and her gait shifts too fluidly to be conscious, adjusting to the ground conditions as she passes the Gate. The green pasture of Anvil looks dull next to the wetland moss.

Following her, Isaella goes ankle-deep in a sinkhole.

Cara laughs at the splash. "Who fell in? Watch your feet, everyone! Duck-weed isn't for walking on!"

Isaella shakes foliage off her boot and tries to step where Cara does after that.

At first, they're lost. They could find their way back to the Gate easily enough, and in long-inhabited Therunin they are not scared of getting trapped; the walk back to Anvil would be long, but follow any trod in this territory and they'd find a wayhouse by midnight. But getting home is not their only concern, and the Weedkillers are muttering about vates leading them wrong when a gigantic dragonfly zips between the trees.

Isaella smiles at the youngest exorcist's flinch. She's seen bigger bugs than this, bred in these swamps and trained to return to the wrist like hawks. In the summer they are shipped to Seren for flying displays, along with crates of fist-sized flies for them to hunt. Others are bred to be message carriers, or especially aggressive, for those steadings plagued by stinging wasps. But this arm-length creature is one of the common green kind kept as pets, hardly changed from its wild cousins.

They follow their accidental guide along the bank of a tiny stream, no different to any other in this wet forest, until it opens into a clearing. The water soaks into the mossy floor and disappears. Tents and hammocks dot the treeline. Above the seep, balanced on stilts, is the makeshift Temple of Peace.

From outside, nothing is obvious. There's an echo of a presence, like the last high lingering of a bell when the note has died away. It's only when Isaella climbs inside that the full effect reaches her, settling over her shoulders like a heavy shawl. It is the feeling of leaning back into a padded chair, the feeling three breaths before sleep. It seduces.

The noise of voices beneath her reminds Isaella to move away from the ladder. It is set into a corner pillar, continuing up to the woven roof to let the climber step off it on the level. Easier on the joints than suspending it from an open hole, and this whole room is built for ease. It may be tied together with vines, and those vines may be sprouting new green leaves from their knots, but the floor has been tiled with thick cotton mats and the circled benches have been given sturdy backs, more comfortable than anything in poor tired Anvil.

Someone is sleeping in an untidy heap in the far corner, their limbs tangled into the folds of a soft blanket. They don't stir until Cara, stepping nimbly backwards off the ladder, says "Hey! Hey, Grandma, wake up!"

The face that emerges from the pile doesn't quite justify the greeting. Her hair is pale enough not to give away, in the dim light filtering through the straw ceiling, how much is blonde and how much grey. Her tattoos still have a sharpness that speaks more of forty years than sixty. She yawns slow and wide, showing her teeth like a waking cat. "Are you pilgrims to the shrine?"

"We're visitors," Cara says. "Are you the Guide here?"

"I'm one of them. Sit down, friends, it's a place for resting."

One of the Weedkillers hisses over his tongue. "Did you *make* it?"

The guide tilts her head. "It's not the work of human hands. It is a sign of virtue. A miracle."

"It is a *false* virtue," he snaps, stepping forward with his hand upon his knife, until Cara's arm swings up across his chest.

"That's enough, Dafydd. Why don't you and yours go back downstairs? There's work to be done."

He bares his teeth at her before he leaves.

"Your friend seems very angry," the Peace follower observes.

"I don't think he likes your shrine. I don't like it much, either."

"*She* does. You ought to be more like her. Ready to hear what the universe is saying."

"She – Isaella! Isaella, you plank, snap out of it. You've gone all gooey-eyed."

Isaella sighs wistfully. The blanket this place offers is so *nice*. She could sink into it and take the weight off her feet, like going barefoot into the stream-soaked moss below. But Cara is right and she came here to work, so Isaella takes a breath and concentrates. The relaxing pressure snaps away from her mind the moment she conceives of it as a restraint.

"We should introduce ourselves," she says. "I'm Isaella, I'm a Senator, and this is Cara Tarrylong, Cardinal of the Way."

Their host wrinkles her nose. "I'm Dana Heartease. We didn't ask for any Cardinals."

Cheerful as ever, Cara says, "That's alright. I'm interested in your Virtue. We were discussing it all day yesterday, how we could prove that you were right."

"Your friends outside are trying to desecrate the shrine. But maybe they're not your friends? Sit, don't worry. They won't be able to destroy the miracle. Let's take some time. Sit, sit."

Isaella recalls, from moments ago, the feeling that no argument could be worth the effort it took, compared to a restful acceptance of what was. She sits beside the guide, to keep her in her soothing shrine, and helps Cara wring her dry of secrets.

CHAPTER TWENTY-NINE – SUMMER 203

Midsummer dawns bright and sticky-hot, untouched by breezes. Nicovar thinks longingly of his study in Ankarien, with its granite flagstone floors, covered with rugs in the cold mountain winters but in weather like this unhidden and allowed to cool bare feet and draw down the heat from the air. Here in Anvil, the only shade is inside airless tents that trap the warmth under canvas. The children lie down in the narrow shadows, knife-sharp against the grass, and whisper gossip from camp to camp.

The Senate is not much cooler than anywhere else, but it feels easier to breathe in here, the space airier than a tent and out of the sun. Nicovar is holding court. Lucius has taken over his throne, with permission, and sits hunched over to use one broad arm as a desk. Nicovar perches on the edge of the dais next to him. There is not exactly a queue, but those who want to speak to him take turns, and politely point out when someone else has been waiting longer.

"Emperor," a sunburnt Marcher says. Lucius looks up at him and points silently down at the step. "I – oh. Oh, sorry, I thought – Emperor." He addresses Nicovar this time, scrubbing his sweaty palms on his shirt. Nicovar takes pity on his nerves and reaches up to shake his hand.

"Speak, citizen. What's troubling you?"

"It's Bregasland, Emperor. It's been under Jotun rule for too long now. My youngest girl hasn't ever seen it. It's not right. It's not right for Marcher blood. It might do for other nations, I can't say, but we're people of the land and it's not right for us to live anywhere else. So what I've come to ask is, how much longer before we can go home?"

Nicovar nods. "You're right. It's been longer than anyone would have wanted. We're doing our best, citizen, and I know that's small comfort when you're waiting to go home. The Green Shield have crossed the border and established a foothold this last season and we have three other armies backing them up. I can't promise you it'll be this season or next, but Bregasland is the most important fight now. In the meantime – there's a project being set up by the Oak and Staff, you'll find them in the Marcher camp, to bring apple seeds and Marcher soil to the refugees in the League. The Senate will be approving funding for it this evening. Speak to them. Tell them your youngest needs to plant an apple tree."

The Marcher hesitates, unsatisfied by what Nicovar knows is an inadequate answer to a soul's yearning to go home, but he nods and says "I'll do that," so it will have to do.

Next is a group of new citizens, fresh from their adulthood tests, who want to see the Senate and didn't expect to find the Emperor there. They stare in silent awe until the quickest of them puts up her grey hood and bows to him, suddenly a formal Highborn adult instead of a nervous teenager, and says, "If you need our services, Sieur, you have only to call for us."

"Thank you," Nicovar says. He squints at her insignia. "You're from the Beacon Guard chapter, on the Reikos border?"

"That's right, Sieur. We patrol the edge of the Forest of Peytaht."

"I remember a magician from Beacon Guard, when I first came to Anvil. She was a very strong speechmaker."

"Hannah. I'll tell her you remembered her, Sieur. She'll be very proud. Thank you for your time, Sieur."

Lucius watches them go. "She'll do well, once she loses the verbal tics."

"She's sixteen. Give her time, my friend. What time is it? Oh, Isaella, welcome – is that a bacon sandwich? Are you giving me a bacon sandwich? Did you just bring me lunch?"

"She's right on time," Lucius says, smug. "Eat your sandwich, Emperor. Thank you, Sal."

"I serve the Empire," Isaella says, straight-faced, and goes to sit on the gallery railing and chat with the strays at the edge of the court, who have no real business but are happy to find a Senator at a loose end. Nicovar tries not to get grease on his robe.

There's a steady trickle of visitors all afternoon. Lucius changes which side he's leaning on, trying to avoid cramp. "We should formalise this," he says in a lull between supplicants. "It works better than doing it in Ankarien."

"It does," Nicovar agrees, "but have you noticed how many we've been referring to the Civil Service?"

Lucius looks at the ceiling, counting in his head. "At least a third," he says eventually, "and most of those were routine queries, or agenda items. We've had five issues for Ruth of Highguard alone."

"And she's always a nightmare to find in the mornings. We could invite the key civil servants to join us here, do you think?"

"It might make it very crowded, if we have their queues as well as ours."

"But we already do, only they're queuing up for – Felicia!" Nicovar interrupts himself, startled. "Warmage, good to see you."

She ducks her head. "Empress. Can we talk?"

"Of course."

"Privately?"

Nicovar tries not to frown. He'd have been cautious about a request like that, from a known enemy, long before he was crowned. "It's honestly harder to eavesdrop on us here than in a tent. Why don't you sit, Felicia? What's troubling you?"

She looks around, perhaps trying to catch someone's eye for moral support, but Lucius is quietly ignoring her. He does that, when he disapproves of someone. So Felicia has no-one to defend her, and rather than argue she sinks to the floor, awkwardly cross-legged. She'd be more comfortable on the edge of the step, on the level with Nicovar. He takes note of that gesture.

"I wanted to talk to you about the Military Council."

"Of course, Warmage."

"Well, not exactly the Council – I'm sorry, I know I insulted you when I stood for election but Lucrezia said it would be the best way to get votes and -" She takes a deep breath, her eyes closing. When they open again her face is calm. "There's a reckoning coming. That's what I wanted to tell you. There are too many people who've lost out because you won."

"Who are you working for, Felicia?"

"The Empire, of course."

"It's not Lucrezia. She got you the job, but that was a slap at me. She's not invested in your career."

Felicia nods, wry. "She told me that at the time. It was the Conclave election she was interested in. Since then I've been on my own. Except for the Generals, but I tell them what they can't have, I really do, and they just keep asking for it. And it's – I've been – I think I owe James an apology."

"Why's that?"

"Because I came here, and I saw him getting things done, and I thought, well, that doesn't look so hard. I could do that. But it's like acting, isn't it? It only looks easy when you're good at it." Bitterness creeps into her voice, a prickly edge to every word.

Nicovar looks at her. "Warmage."

"Yes, Empress?"

"*Warmage*." He leans forward. "No-one's taken the title off you yet."

Felicia breathes in deep. "I think," she says, "I think that's because the eyes of the mighty have been turned elsewhere."

"Doesn't matter." Nicovar sits back, shrugging. "You're the Warmage. You hold a high Imperial office. You *are* one of the mighty."

"So – what do I do with it?"

"You said a reckoning is coming?"

"It is."

He smiles. "So, pick a side."

"You're not serious."

"Aren't I?" Nicovar looks past her, at James and Isaella sitting with their backs to the wall, legs sticking out in front of them, poring over Isaella's budget figures. He tries to frame his thoughts. "How can I put this? When I sought the throne, I did it because I thought I could make the Empire better. And what makes the Empire better is that we strive. We make war on every border, to make ourselves greater. We challenge the edges of knowledge. We dig up the weapons of the past, and if they cut us, we will learn to master them. If I took the throne, and every Senator and General fell in line behind me, I would have made the Empire smaller. We are the sum of all our citizens. We compete amongst ourselves, and whoever wins, we are all the greater. So take up your mantle, Warmage. Make some bright youngster at the back of the Conclave think your title is worth the work."

"I don't know how." Felicia is grim with frustration.

"Warmage, you are in too deep to tell me you cannot swim."

She looks at him through her eyelashes, terribly young suddenly, and her head bowed with responsibility. "You're not exactly helping, Empress. I was trying to warn you about something."

"And you did. You told me that Miriam is planning something. It is Miriam, isn't it?"

"I – I didn't say that. I am speaking only of – general concerns."

Nicovar smiles. "See? You do know how to swim."

CHAPTER THIRTY – AUTUMN 203

Isaella rubs her forehead. "Sorry, say that again. Taking down the Peace aura is *illegal*?"

"Yep." Cara lifts her hands in an exaggerated shrug. "Don't blame me, I don't make the laws."

"I know, I know."

"That's your job."

Isaella stares at her, while Cara's grin widens.

"Sorry. It's not one of yours, actually, it's a Barabbas-era law. Imperial citizens are forbidden from removing any miraculous spiritual effects upon places or objects."

"Why not people?"

"I suppose the Senate thought if you didn't want things on your soul that was up to you. But I checked with the civil service and in the opinion of the magistrates, miraculous is the same as spontaneous and the law makes no distinction between true and false virtues – so exorcising that aura in Therunin is illegal, since our friends in Highguard so helpfully proved it was natural when they went to visit. If they'd just knocked it down we'd never have known they shouldn't."

"That is *bullshit*. Cara, come on. It's sitting there turning our citizens into potatoes and we can't remove it? I'll talk to Marianne. If there isn't a loophole she can help me draft a repeal motion."

"You'll need True Liao to pull it down anyway-"

"I can get that. That's not a problem. What's the punishment if we don't get the law changed first? A fine? We could just do it and pay up afterwards-"

"Legal excommunication,"Cara snaps. "Which someone is sure to follow up with the real thing. You have enemies, Sal. You can't just run around breaking laws."

"I *make* the laws," Isaella grumbles, but she settles back onto the bench and picks up her tea. "Alright, alright. So give me the gossip. Has Isolt found the nerve to speak to Felicia yet?"

Autumn has started hot all over the Empire. Isaella walked here mainly in short trousers, letting her knees get tanned on the broad clear roads, with her tough nettle-kickers rolled up on top of her pack in case of need. The war has moved on from Liathaven into the fens of Bregasland, with a civilian army of Marchers following close behind, re-occupying their land as fast as the soldiers can take it. Isaella has been a peacetime Senator for once, and spent her time on fortification supplies and the minor social disputes any nation gives rise to. She has it easier than her peers in handling those – no Marcher would accept a judgement that the feuding families should pack up their lives and walk in opposite directions. For the Navarri, it's dramatic, but at least it's on the table.

She drenches her tunic on Saturday morning and wears it wet to the Gate. The assembled crowd is smaller than usual and there's a pang of guilt in that thought, for the armour she isn't wearing and the spear that sleeps in her tent. But her often-broken collarbone has been troubling her lately and her hopeful visit to the field hospital last night only confirmed her physick's diagnosis: no fighting and gentle exercises, for another season at least, if she wants to hold a weapon in five years.

So the fighters muster without her, and Isaella has only come to see them off. The early morning mist has already burned away. Even the trees are still rustling green around the Gate, not yet surrendering to autumn. There will finally be an attempt to select a Dawnish general this afternoon, now that Roland has been trapped in a gambling debt and his surrender called in as payment. But for now, the Throne still commands a Dawnish army, and so Nicovar is out amongst the fighters. The soldiers of the Hounds of Glory resent him, but the Dawnish who come to Anvil have learned to take a kind of perverse pride in the situation – their Senators and General may be disgraced, but Dawn has a claim to the Empress no other nation can boast. He has become one of theirs. They have begun to love him for it.

Isaella smiles at him through the crowd, his familiar colours reversed to a red robe with an ivory sash, and steps into the muddle of her own people. Here it is all brown and green and leather, tattoos on bare arms and brands on faces. She taps fists with the archer Gerwyn, whose bow and scowl have grown heavier every year. She hugs Cara and ruffles the hair she cut short in frustration with the heat, fluffy as a baby chick. Cara mock-growls and wriggles free.

"Don't die," Isaella warns.

"Sal, *honey*. When have I ever died yet?"

Isaella looks at her until she laughs and flaps her hand. "True Liao or it didn't happen. We'll be back by lunchtime, Mother. Put the kettle on."

"Kill some Jotun for me."

After the battle, they count their dead. They carry Navarri bodies to the corpse glade, Dawnish to the carts to be taken home. Nicovar holds his court through the afternoon, his sallow face made paler by a smear of orcish blood. James spends a strangely long time in conversation with Isolt, before the senatorial tournament where he cheers every victory with diplomatic equality, the Consort nearly as good a witness as the Throne. Isaella is on her feet most of the day trying to drum up votes for her repeal motion. The Senate is concerned about flip-flopping on the laws, and blighted with the usual ahistorical perspective, as if a law passed before they came to Anvil was as ancient as the Empire. The motion they end up with is so convoluted Isaella has to refer it to the civil service to check if it's even grammatical. She has meetings and arguments and adulthood tests to observe, until at last in the velvety midnight she hears voices from the Senate floor.

She turns up the ramp into the familiar tented room, its floorboards warmed by the light of glowstones. There are often people in here late at night, taking advantage of the dry space. Nicovar is usually in his own camp by now, making time for his husband, but tonight James is sprawled sideways on the throne and Nicovar is squaring up with a Dawnish noble, hefting a borrowed sword.

Isaella finds an empty patch of wall to lean against and settles in to watch.

"Now, remember," Nicovar is saying, "no killing me."

The noble grins. "But killing *blows*, right, Empress? This is a real fight? We've got physicks waiting all ready for you."

Nicovar looks around for an answer. The Dawnish who form most of his audience smirk back.

"Alright," he says, "we'll do this your way. No holds barred. On three?"

"Three," his opponent answers, lifting her own sword. "Two. One!"

They meet in a ringing of steel. Nicovar is no great swordsman, his movements betraying his preference for a magician's rod. He can defend, but in attacking he forgets to use the point. Isaella critiques his style even as her heart is pounding. People die in Dawnish duels. James is twisted at the waist, watching the fight intently with his legs still hooked over the arm of the throne.

Nicovar backs away. The Dawnish follows, still grinning. Her blade flashes towards his head, a wide distracting flourish to occupy Nicovar's sword, while her fist swings into his ribs. He staggers. She lets him open the distance, her eyes on his chest. They are not armoured for this and any twitch might telegraph his next attack.

He steps sideways, turning as he goes. On this smooth floor neither of them needs to watch their feet. The Dawnish, impatient, cuts towards his legs, a heavy blow he barely deflects. She tries to repeat it but Nicovar dodges and his blade slides across her forearm as she moves. The blood drips from her skin.

She bares her teeth. Nicovar is driven back by her answering flurry, her sword moving almost too quick to follow and Nicovar struggling just to guard himself. Even wounded, she is stronger, and he's tiring fast. Isaella's hand itches for her knife. Navarri do not care for honourable duels.

Nicovar has spotted a weakness at last, an opening on the noble's off-hand where she is used to a shield to block with. He is trying to jab into that gap but the Dawnish attack doesn't let up. They are moving in a circle, Nicovar always backing up, on the defensive. She leaps at him, sword swinging down towards his head, and the blades scream when they meet, grinding down towards Nicovar's face.

He grins, very suddenly. He move sideways, slippery as a fish, his blade sliding out of contact, and drives the point into her thigh.

The Dawnish falls to her knees. Nicovar dances away at once, his body a long sleek line, drawing down to the blood on his sword. Isaella's stomach kicks.

"Citizen?" Nicovar is holding his position, waiting for the Dawnish to rise on a leg he has plainly crippled.

She tosses her head, flyaway hairs clinging to the sweat on her face. "I yield, Empress. Well fought! You sneaky fuck!"

He joins with the laughter from her companions. "Then as the victor of this fight, I claim the right to determine who shall command the Hounds of Glory, and it's you. You can have the job. I give it to you with all the troubles it may bring."

"That's fair," she says. "I can't argue with that. Can I get this leg stitched up now?"

Nicovar hands his sword back to one of the watching crowd and helps his opponent stagger to a physick. Isaella has seen wounds like that before – has taken them before – and she's sure the new General will be fine. She'll ache for months, but she won't be limping next summit, if the physick knows their herbs.

She pushes off the wall. James is tipped back so far now his head is almost upside down.

"And I thought Urizeni were mad," he says cheerfully.

"Oh, they are. All of them. The Dawnish are just more boisterous about it."

"You should fight him," James says, peering up at her. "He's used up his enchantment now. I promise you'll win."

The Dawnish and her friends are trooping noisily down the ramp, one on each side to support her. The room seems darker without them, more welcoming.

"You can't promise that," Isaella says, reasonably. "Not unless you plan to help."

James sits up. He looks at her, at the muscles of her arms. He looks at Nicovar.

"Hey, Nic," he says, and stands. His staff is leaning against the back of the chair. It lifts easily into his hands. "Nicky. Think fast."

Nicovar turns towards them. His eyes narrow. He pulls the rod from his belt.

Isaella draws her knife.

They are silent at first, caught up in the tension. James holds his staff in balance, striking out with each end to pin Nicovar against the wall. Isaella darts into the space he makes. She keeps her strikes to taps, the flat of her blade against his arm, his belly. Nicovar's rod smacks her forearm without half his strength behind it. She lets the blow turn her anyway. He blocks James's next swing and Isaella sets her knife to his throat.

Nicovar lifts his chin. He's panting, his eyes crinkled in a smile. His gaze flicks to James.

Isaella follows his glance. James has pulled back to turn the staff in his hands. He frowns slightly.

"Sal," he says, "think fast."

The two of them together, against her single knife, drive her easily across the room. She manages to tap James on the knuckles and he hisses, aware of how that would end if she had used the edge. But the room is only so large, and her reach is less than theirs, and seconds later she is pressed against the gallery railing, her knife hand trapped and the staff tapping lightly against her shins.

She looks at Nicovar. He looks at James. For a moment they are still fighting, ready to switch again and drive James into surrender together, but instead Nicovar leans in close, and kisses her.

Isaella lets her eyes close, just for a moment. Nicovar is not so brash as he once was, not so insistent. He tilts his head to fit their mouths together. His weapon lifts away from her arm.

"Hey," James says, his voice rumbling. "Hey, Nic. Don't be greedy. Share."

His broad hand cups Isaella's cheek as Nicovar lets her go. She smiles up at him, at the heat in his dark eyes. She kisses him too.

CHAPTER THIRTY-ONE – WINTER 203

For the first time in a year, Nicovar spends his season at
Ankarien spire, and not on the road with an army of rowdy
Dawnish. He feels better for it. Rested. No wonder the army
power hasn't often been used. He is home for the harvest
festival, which they hold privately, nobody invited but Ankarien
and a handful of Urizeni friends who aren't there to see the
Throne. A month later, before the storms turn against them, they
host a religious meeting, for all those who are interested to
discuss the Peace problems. Isaella comes to defend Navarri
piety and share his bed. He knows, when he reaches Anvil, he'll
find his husband in her tent. His spire-mates know it too, and
crinkle their eyes at him in amusement.

Even the mud of Anvil doesn't spoil his mood. He has good
boots well broken in and a robe cut short for the weather.
Unliving ushabti servants packed their baggage, but here on the
lowlands human hands must do the work, and Nicovar spends an
hour with fencing posts and a mallet before someone tracks him
down to start talking politics. Lucius, bringing over the woven
panels, takes the mallet off him.

"Alright," Nicovar says, resigned, "I'm all yours, Kesia. What's the problem?"

"Can we walk and talk, Nic?"

"Yes, of course." Nicovar lets her lead the way. Her head is bare, but there's a hoods-up kind of feeling in the air, a sense that this conversation is business. Kesia is on duty.

"It's Miriam," she says bluntly. "You know there's a problem with Miriam, right?"

"I know she doesn't like me very much."

"Then you're much stupider than I thought you were. Miriam *hates* you, Nicovar. With an almost religious fervour. It's become a point of principle with her to hate you."

He looks at her sideways. "I was being diplomatic. Yes, I know how Miriam feels about me. I think the whole Hounds of Glory thing made it worse."

"*Much* worse. She could try to ignore you when you were in the Senate. The Military Council was hers and the rest was yours and Miriam could *almost* be content with that, and then you walked in and she couldn't do anything about it. You know if they don't like a general, they can shut them out or stop them getting re-selected or hell, even come to the national assembly and start agitating but you can't revoke a Throne and you can't take the army off them either. It was *clumsy*, taking it on yourself. You should have used a Favour."

Nicovar stops mid-stride. He stares at her.

"What?"

"You're right. I should have used a Favour."

Kesia hastily backtracks. "Oh, don't get me wrong. I mean, it was a *great* way to point out that actually you *are* the Throne and people had better take you into account. It did that really well. It's just the Miriam thing – And really it's not even her Council. She just clung to it because she'd lost the bigger prize."

"There's no such thing as a Head General."

"Exactly, exactly. So you didn't actually do *wrong*. Just that now we have a bigger Miriam problem. And it *is* a *problem*, and you need to stop ignoring it."

"What do you suggest? As far as I can see, she hasn't done anything illegal, ever. She hasn't misused her office. She doesn't seem to be unvirtuous – I know there's always the loyalty debate but the virtue doesn't require her to be loyal to me. If she's loyal to what she's loyal to, that's the virtue. She has ambition, she has bundles of pride, she's not unvigilant or foolish or a spendthrift – I really don't think there's grounds to revoke her."

Kesia sighs, her head bobbing. "And you really *can't* take her army away. That would make it a lot worse."

"Right. So, I agree, I have a Miriam problem, because one of my most influential generals hates me and I can't direct military strategy without her fighting me. But it's not a problem I can solve with legal powers."

"Are you suggesting illegal ones, Empress?" Kesia grins and hops onto a bedraggled clump of grass, avoiding a puddle. "I'm joking. Please don't do illegal things. I would *hate* having to condemn you for them. I'm just saying. Put it top of your list. Do some strategising. And then do *something*. I will condemn you for cowardice if I have to."

The main business of the Senate that evening, besides budgets and approving new statues, is a proposal to amend the law on destruction of miracles. Isaella is the proposer, and Nicovar has to work harder than before to keep his face calm while she's speaking.

"Friends, colleagues, this proposal won't be news to most of you. I've been working on it for a couple of seasons and I know I've had conversations with a lot of you to try and formulate something we can agree on. The impetus here is that we have a spontaneous and very powerful Peace aura in Therunin. It's been there for a very long time but only now has a church been built around it and too many of our citizens are being led astray. I'm not a priest, but I know there are seven Virtues, and I know a false virtue shouldn't be left where it is to corrupt our people. We would have taken it down already but there's a law requiring miracles to be preserved.

I'm not asking you to just repeal that law. I understand there are reasons to protect miraculous effects. But this one needs to go, so the law isn't adequate. What we're proposing today has safeguards. It allows miraculous effects to be dispelled only with the agreement of the nation's senators, and only if they're aligned to a false virtue. If you pass this, we can get rid of that effect in Therunin by the end of the summit and the Synod can root out the heresy."

The Senate is politely silent through Isaella's speech. There's muttering when she finishes, from the public gallery and from the floor. Nicovar takes note of the stubborn set of some faces, the senators who will be committed votes against. There's only a handful of them.

"I support this proposal," the senator from Segura says first. "Get in there and take the aura down. We've fucked about for long enough."

"Agreed," chimes in Necropolis, before Marianne can shush him.

"Question for the proposer," Sarvos says, once he's been properly invited to speak, "will you actually be able to take this effect down?"

"I have a team of exorcists just raring to go," Isaella answers.

"But – forgive me, I'm sure you've considered this – I've seen the scrying results from the Highborn who went to look at it and it won't be as easy as that. This is a very entrenched effect. I'm sure your exorcists are very enthusiastic, but you're not going to succeed unless you go with True Liao. No offence to the senator from Liathaven, of course, but I didn't see your name on the Gatekeepers' list? Can you afford to buy a dose at auction?"

Anger curls in Nicovar's chest. He keeps still. Isaella, on the floor beneath his throne, puts her hands on her hips.

"What a good question, Sarvos. Thank you so much for bringing it up." She turns away from him. "Nicovar. Can I have some True Liao?"

The twist in his ribs opens out into startled, delighted pride. Nicovar reaches into his robes and pulls out the little glass vial the Civil Service hands him, every season, to use as he sees fit. He tosses it to Isaella. She plucks it neatly from the air.

"Thank you. Sarvos, any more objections?"

He splutters and retreats. The proposal passes easily. Nicovar waits until he's back in Ankarien to laugh.

Isaella doesn't come back from the Sentinel Gate until nearly midnight. She fought that morning alongside Navarr, and spent most of the afternoon pulling together the expedition team and a second political delegation, a diplomatic group to visit the Faraden embassy they didn't know they needed until a letter came that morning. The Faraden are finally willing to consider allowing trods on their territory. Nobody in the Empire would speak against it, but it has to be the Navarr who persuade their foreign allies that it's safe. Faraden has refused so far, worried that the trod network would let the Sentinel Gate reach into their land, and that the enchantment was a precursor to invasion. It's taken years of peaceful embassy building for them to even consider it. So it's no surprise if Isaella didn't stop to rest after the battle.

She trudges into Ankarien's camp and falls onto a bench. "I'm not here," she says. "If anyone asks, I'm not here. You never saw me. I'm a ghost."

"Okay," Nicovar agrees. "Are you cold?"

"I am wet to the knees and I hate it."

James wordlessly reaches down for the kettle and sets it back on the fire. He rubs Isaella's back, between her shoulder-blades, when she leans to warm her hands above the coals. "Did you take the aura down?"

"We kicked ass. Not literally, they're Peace cultists, kicking ass isn't really their thing. But we gave them a good hard desecration. It is *so* creepy doing that while they're just staring at you. I was expecting shouting."

"Didn't they react when the exorcism went off?"

Isaella straightens up. "Sort of? They'd been soaking in it a long time. But no, they didn't want to fight. I guess they're sincere. Sincere cultists. Somehow that's worse than rabble-rousers."

"I am not a theologian," Nicovar says, "but I'm pretty sure we did the right thing."

"Yeah. Yeah, we did, though. Thanks for the liao."

Here, around a campfire with the two of them, he lets himself grin. "That was smooth, Sal. That was a really smart gamble."

"Asking you for things is not a gamble, dear."

CHAPTER THIRTY-TWO – SPRING 204

Isaella is drifting in a warm haze of cherry brandy. The food has been collected for Welcoming tomorrow, the Navarri won't be fighting until Sunday, and she can afford to court a hangover. The d'Holberg tent has been fixed up with a brazier and the smouldering coals make the place as cosy as her own cabin. It doesn't hurt that the twins can afford layers of rugs, or that they keep the good alcohol coming around.

"The point – lemme sit up, I can't see you – the point, Isolt, is that you have to decide something. You can't just wait for it to go away."

"But it *might* go away."

"She's not just going to stop being a Leaguer, though."

Isolt turns an empty bottle on the table. "And I'm not going to stop being Dawnish. So what do I do?"

"You could stop being Dawnish."

"I just said I can't."

"No, but I mean, it's an option you have. That you could consider. And she could become Dawnish, right? Anyone can do a Test of Mettle?"

"The First Empress did," Cressida chimes in. "On a horse. So if she was a horse-"

"Right! So Felicia could just test into Dawn and then you could marry her."

Isolt looks glum. "Test of Mettle. And then Test of Ardour. And she'd have to give up her old family – it's just, it's a lot of ask of her, you know?"

"But if she loves you-"

"I don't know if she does, though! How do you tell with foreigners?"

"She's not a foreigner," Isaella says pedantically, "she's a – a – an Imperial cross-national. Like the Throne and the Consort. They're not the same-"

"And *you*," Cressida says, "let's not forget *you* in that example-"

"Shut up, Cress, that's not even the point – what was that?"

"Don't change the subject-"

Isolt sits up straight. "No, I heard it too. Is someone having a duel?"

"It's very late if they are. What was it? I didn't hear it. Is it swords?"

"No," Isaella says, "it was – I don't know, maybe it was just someone coughing."

"That was not a cough," Isolt says, very definite. "We should go and check."

Isaella needs Cressida's hand to get back to her feet. She fumbles with the tent flap, trying not to trip over the guy lines.

Isolt is ahead of them, a little way up the hill, searching for the source of the noise.

Isaella spots the shape in the grass just as Isolt drops to a crouch beside it. She shakes the figure, rolls them partway over.

"No!" Isolt is back on her feet. She draws her sword. It shakes in her hand, the moonlight shattering along the blade. "Show yourself! Coward! I will find you, I will fucking find you, stand and face me! Where are you? *Who did this?*"

Isaella staggers up to her. The body in the grass, wet blood gleaming on his chest, is Sir Roland. Isaella draws a deep breath and shouts for a physick.

Cressida is already here and reaching for her surgeons tools. "Go look after Isolt," she says brusquely. "You can't help me here. Go on."

In the darkness, through the fog of alcohol, Isaella can't see her at first. She finds Isolt in the shadow of a tent, sword up, her teeth bared.

"I'll kill them," she says. "I'll fucking kill them."

"Isolt-"

"If anyone was going to kill him it was going to be *me*. He was my brother, Isaella! Don't tell me to be calm! He was my brother and he's been *murdered!*"

There are people already racing up the hill. Isaella recognises the tabards of the militia, the lanky figure of Sally the magistrate alongside them. They break around the scene like water, looking past the death for any sign of fugitives. Behind them, hurrying to catch up, comes Sveta, embroidery blood-dark on the collar of her white blouse.

"I saw them," she says, panting. "Isaella. Isaella, *listen* to me, I saw them."

Still unbalanced and half-sick with drink, Isaella sits Sveta down beneath the bright lights of a trader's stall. She buys a coffee for herself, and a bacon roll. Sveta devours it, teenager-hungry.

"It wasn't a fight," she says with her mouth full. "I mean obviously it was a fight *eventually* but that's not how it started. There were two of them besides Roland and I think one was Highborn. She didn't have her hood up but her ears were all ragged at the top."

"Unveiled," Isaella says.

"Yeah. Like her ear-tips were cut off. Which is creepy, I just want to say. Who cuts off their ears? It's too weird."

"The fight, Sveta?"

"Sorry. Yeah. They were just talking. I wasn't listening because I didn't think anything was wrong. I was just going home."

Isaella swallows a mouthful of coffee. It fights her, feeling sharp and solid in her throat. "Why were you out so late?"

"I was watching the new play! It's really good. You should go see it. It's really romantic." Sveta rips another huge bite from her roll. "Sorry. I mean, I was on my way back from that, so I was in the League camp, and I was just passing the alley where those people and the knight were. What's his name?"

"Roland," Isaella says, the reminder sobering her up as much as the coffee. "His name was Sir Roland."

"Roland. He was talking to those people and he didn't look interested? I mean, he looked worried. It looked like they were trying to get him to do something and he didn't want to. And he didn't have his sword on but his hand was doing that thing where he was feeling for it anyway, and then he turned to walk away from them, and that's when the other one stabbed him."

"The other one? You mean not the Highborn?"

"The Highborn didn't stab him. She just stepped back and then she ran off towards the trees. The one with the knife went between the tents. I tried to follow but I couldn't see where they went so I went running for the Watch. I knew Sally would be outside the tavern. She's always there in the evenings."

"It was a good thought. Did you stop to check on Roland?"

Sveta stops with the roll halfway to her mouth. Her eyes go wide. "I didn't – I'm so sorry! I didn't think – is he okay? He's a knight, he can handle it, right?"

Isaella puts an arm around her. "Sveta. Honey, listen to me. This is important, alright? I need you to listen. Roland is not going to be okay. Roland died from the knife wound. And it's really important that you know that isn't your fault. It's not, at all, and I need you to understand that."

"I didn't stop for him," Sveta says, shock drawing pale across her face. "I should have called a physick."

"Next time you'll do that. But we heard the fight and we were there within a minute and Roland had already gone. So I think that the knife was poisoned, and even if you had stood and shouted for a physick, he would still have died."

Sveta nods. She puts the rest of her bacon roll on the table and rubs her hands together. "I think it was a little bit my fault," she says, her voice small. "Because I didn't do that. And you might have been on time, if I'd shouted."

"Or you might have died as well." Isaella hugs her closer. "You didn't stab him, sweetheart. You didn't poison him. We're lucky you were there at all, or we wouldn't know what happened. You didn't do the absolute perfect thing, but you ran for the Watch. That was a smart reaction."

"Okay." Sveta leans into her. "It was a really good play, though. Before that happened."

Isaella rubs her arm. "We should get you home to your parents. I think."

"It's just Mama," Sveta says. "And Auntie. But she only comes sometimes. Not this time. She wasn't feeling well."

"Alright, then let's get you back to Mama and let her know you're safe. It's been a while since the play ended and I don't want her to be worried."

Isaella walks Sveta home to the Varushkan camp. It's well past midnight and no surprise that the Varushkans don't invite her in; she hands Sveta over to be fussed at by her relieved family and walks back up to the League alone. Isolt is still there, weeping into Cressida's shoulder. The body has been taken away.

"There were two of them," Isaella says, too exhausted for preambles. "One Highborn changeling with severed ear-tips and another that Sveta couldn't identify. They tried to talk him into something, he refused, they reacted."

Isolt snuffles. She lifts her head away from Cressida's cloak, arms still wrapped around her. "I want to kill them. I don't want to wait for the magistrates. I want to kill them."

"And I wouldn't blame you for it. But we have to find them first. And we have to find out what they wanted from Roland. We have to make sure this doesn't happen again."

CHAPTER THIRTY-THREE – SUMMER 204

There is another body, on the first day of midsummer. Nicovar crouches in the tall grass beyond the Highguard camp, examining the symbol on the corpse's cheek.

"That's Navarri warpaint," he says quietly.

"I can see that," James agrees, "but I don't think any Navarr did this. It's not showy enough."

"Not showy *enough*?"

"If the Navarr wanted to make an example of this fellow, they wouldn't leave him here with a cryptic bit of face paint. He'd be strung up outside the Senate with a note pinned to his chest. Besides, warpaint means something to them. You can ask Sal but I don't think they'd use it for this. This smells like a set-up."

Nicovar nods. He tilts the face of the dead man, looking into his eyes. Deep, deep gold, framed by silver maze-lines. A cambion. "So who does that leave?"

"Well. Everyone else at Anvil. You can get warpaint at three different traders that I know of and I don't even buy the stuff.

Anyone could have bought a pot. But if I were the militia, I'd be looking at Highguard."

Nicovar glances at him sidelong, unwilling to voice his doubts. James, recognising his look, shrugs. "We've got a Highborn assassin who was seen last season, and now a Highborn magician is found dead outside of Highguard – it's not much of a leap to say Highguard is involved."

"I just wish I knew what the symbol meant," Nicovar says. "Red wings, outstretched. It doesn't match anything obvious. How can we stop them if we don't know what they want?"

James stands up, his hands on his knees for balance. He doesn't answer the question, and Nicovar doesn't expect him to. They've learned to understand each other's rhetoric. He asks instead, "What are you going to say to the Senate?"

"Oh, hells. I'm going to have to say something. I don't want to tell people to be wary, that can't come from me. The Throne has to be a beacon."

"You could say you're sure we'll catch them. Or something about pulling together. Something inspiring."

Nicovar stands up and brushes the clinging grass seed from the hem of his robe. "Inspiring, of course. I'll just pull a sign of Paragonhood out of my shirt. That's easy. One inspiration, coming right up."

"I have faith in you, Empress." James pats him on the shoulder.

Before the Senate convenes there have been two more deaths.

Nicovar arrives late, sweeping up the ramp and through the assembled crowd to take his seat. The public gallery is packed, citizens leaning over the railing and standing up on the benches to see. The audience overflows onto the grass outside. Murder in Anvil is rare. Four in three months is unheard of. There is a crawling dread in the air, as if Death lurked behind every shoulder, her daggers already drawn.

Marianne looks at him, ready for a moment to insist on proceeding as normal, and then lowers her sheaf of papers. "Empress. Will you speak before we begin?"

"This is not normal," Nicovar says, pitching his voice to carry. The chatter of the crowd gradually dies away. "This is not normal. This is not acceptable. The citizens of the Empire should be safe, here of all places. So hear me when I say this: the Red Wing murders are an act of treason. We have lost a Senator, a prominent magister, and two priests of Loyalty. This is not a personal feud. It is a campaign against the Empire and I will not stand for it. It will be stopped."

Marianne gives him a moment, a space where he could take questions, but Nicovar waits still and silent for the session to begin. He can't face questions from his citizens just now. He doesn't have any answers to give them.

Highguard and Navarr fight the next morning in the hills above Skarsind. Old arthritic Gwyneth is found dead in the Military Council's tent, her blood finger-painted over the map. A red bird hovers over Anvil. Nicovar calls an emergency meeting.

He lets Isaella pace, her spear ready in her hand. "She was *my* General," Isaella snarls. "This is *targeted.* Matthias was James's ally in the Rod and Shield. Roland was Isolt's brother. The Gatekeeper of Loyalty was putting James forward. This is about *us*."

"Obviously," Cressida says. She's standing with her arms folded, a black velvet ribbon carefully coiled around one horn. Without Lucrezia's mask, the lines around her eyes are obvious. "It's always about *you*. No, I'm sorry, that's not helpful – Yes, this is targeted, but it's at Nicovar and his supporters. It's got fuck all to do with your sex life."

Isaella's shoulders tense, the spear coming alive in her hands. She holds Cressida's eyes for a long moment. "That's what I meant."

"Right. Sorry." Cressida half-turns, breaking the tension. "Archimedes, any thoughts?"

Archimedes shifts on his cushion. "This has never happened," he says heavily. "We did not expect this, when we supported you, Nicovar. We did not expect murder in Anvil because you rose to prominence. I did not bargain for this on my conscience."

"You didn't do it," Nicovar says.

"Obviously."

"And neither did I. This isn't our fault. It's not something you could have avoided by supporting Miriam-"

The name sticks in Nicovar's throat. He looks around the tent, at the tense unhappiness of his allies, and says slowly, "Do we have any reason to think this *isn't* Miriam's doing?"

Isaella rolls her spear between her hands, the barbed head catching the light. "Say the word."

"Don't kill her," Archimedes answers. He levers himself up from his seat. "It's probably Miriam. We've been warned about her before. Apparently, that's come to a head. How long since you last spoke to her, Nicovar?"

Nicovar looks away. "A long time," he admits. "I haven't confronted her."

"Confronted – You haven't brought her *in*. We told you when you first started this – when you cut *us* out. You cannot do this alone. You could not campaign and you cannot rule on your own. If you could not talk to her you should have found someone who could."

The flush is rising to Nicovar's cheeks. He can feel it burning, as the shame thickens his tongue. He swallows to control it. Archimedes is watching him, unyielding.

"You're right, Arbiter," he says eventually. "I have failed in my duty."

Cressida interrupts, with her usual impatience for other people's business, "That's all very well, but what are we going to do about it? All of us who campaigned for you, we're obvious targets."

"You less so, perhaps," Archimedes says, the same deliberate rebuke in his tone. Nicovar can see it passing beneath Cressida's attention. A lifetime of lowlander shouting has blunted her perceptions.

"Because we've been pursuing our own ambitions since? They just killed Gwyneth and all she ever did was be a damn good general and take Isaella as an aide. I don't think a little squabbling over the Warmage is going to protect us – James. Where have you been?"

James pauses with the tent-flap held open. His eyes narrow for a minute, before he turns away from Cressida and speaks to the others. "It's still the solstice, technically. We could cast Whispers next summit and try for Gwyneth."

"She won't come," Isaella says, quick and definite.

"You can't know that until we try."

"No, you told me – you told me, years ago, when you were planning to cast for Barabbas, that the soul won't come if it's reluctant, if it's already moved on from that life."

James nods. "Right."

"Well, Gwyneth has been ready to go for a while. She's been talking about taking the Long Walk, like Empress Teleri. Like the Winterfolk do. If we wait three months – no, I know, I know we have to – but give her three months and I don't think she's coming back."

"She might be born by then," Cressida adds.

James glares at her. "Nobody gets born that fast. Not even Exemplars and Gwyneth was fine, but she wasn't one. Nic, I'm just saying, it's an option. It's something we could do."

"Archimedes," Nicovar says, "you understand Winter better than I do. Can you two do some planning? Work out what we might learn?"

"Who killed her would be a good start."

"Who – wait. Sal, your witness, the girl who saw Roland killed. Would she recognise the assassin? How old is she?"

Isaella lifts her head, the prospect of something to do immediately calming her. "She's not young. She's just small. Fifteen, maybe sixteen by now? She's nearly of age."

"So she could identify that first killer."

"Not the killer. She didn't see who did the stabbing. But she saw who else was there – the changeling with the missing ear-tips."

Cressida shudders, the usual reaction to that Highborn practice from anyone with horns. She reaches up to adjust a mask that isn't there. "You're talking about a *child*."

"And I'll try not to put her in danger. Help us, or go, Cress."

"Don't be stupid, of course I'm staying. Look, you can't have an identity parade of Highborn women, I'll – I'll help you figure something out. You can show Sveta how to be sneaky. It'll be fun."

"Then do that," Nicovar says. "Even knowing her chapter would be something to go on. James, if you can front the mana or get it from the Conclave, then we should try Whispers, because at least it looks like we're doing something. I'm going to have a swarm of senators around my ears when I step outside and there's no time for anything concrete. The summit's nearly over."

"There's at least an hour left. I don't need an hour to kill someone." Isaella's spear is still ready in her hands. Nicovar reaches out to squeeze her shoulder.

"Not today," he tells her. "Not yet. That time may come."

Isaella sighs. "Promise you won't have the party without me?"

CHAPTER THIRTY-FOUR – AUTUMN 204

Isaella goes down to a crossbow bolt in the dark.

She fought this morning alongside Dawn and the Marches, navigating the battlefield by the colours of the tabards around her. She took a solid blow to the knee from a nail-studded cudgel, almost taking her legs out from under her, and the bruising has stiffened the joint nearly to immobility. She couldn't run down the hill towards the tavern lights, even if the crossbow hadn't knocked her to the ground.

She can feel the bolt between the ribs in her back. There's an awful feeling when she tries to breathe, as if the metal point was pressed against her lungs and sawing into them with each movement. Even if she could reach, she wouldn't dare pull the shaft out of the wound.

There is a choice she has to make. It is starkly clear before her. She can play dead, now, lie as still and quiet as she can and hope the assassin does not follow up with a knife across her throat. Or she can struggle and scream and hope that help finds her before this bolt can do its work – and that the assassin does not silence her with a knife across her throat.

Reluctantly, feeling as if her thoughts were setting into amber, although it's only been three breaths since the spike drove into her back, Isaella fumbles with the things around her neck. Not the silk cord, which is a favour she carries from Isolt; not the tooled leather strip, which is a purely decorative thing; it must be here, somewhere, and finally her sweat-slicked fingers slide across a fine metal chain and she drags the whistle up out of her tunic, he muscles trembling with the strain.

The first attempt to sound it makes black spots dance in her vision. It was not made to be used with a punctured lung. But it is all she has, and she cannot run or scream. The whistle will have to keep her alive somehow.

On the second try, she makes a high thin wailing, rattling around the trapped steel ball. Again, she tells herself, do it again, Isaella, or you'll be blowing whistles in the Labyrinth. Blow the damned whistle. You're not done with this life yet.

She passes out before the rescuers can reach her. She does not feel the hands lifting her, or the unmerciful hands of the physick wrenching out the bolt. They work by lantern-light, swearing all the while under their breath, until finally Isaella opens her eyes again and sees the bobbing lights around her, half of the League turned out to search for a murderer.

She sits in the d'Holberg tent, propped up on a rolled sheepskin while Cressida fusses over her wound.

"These are messy fucking stitches, Sal."

"I'm sorry, I'll ask for the embroidery upgrade next time – *ow*, ow, please don't touch that, it's very bad – *ow*-"

"Don't get fucking *shot*. You reckless *asshole*. What were you doing out there on your own?"

"Coming to see *you*."

Cressida scoffs, picking at another stitch. "I'm not worth it, darling. You can get cherry wine anywhere. I'm clearly cursed, what with Isolt and now you – no, hold still, let me get this -"

The tent flap is pushed wide and Isaella turns automatically to see – Cressida, dressed in the same fine doublet as the Cressida behind her, an expression of shock on her familiar bare face – and then she swears and ducks away, and Isaella remembers that the twins are identical, with only Lucrezia's mask to tell them apart most of the time. She must have left it off in the confusion. She fumbles with her belt pouch for a moment, finally turning back with a mask of golden filigree pressed against her skin, still looping the ribbons around her horns.

"The *hell*, Isaella?"

Isaella buries her face in the sheepskin. "I tripped and fell on a crossbow bolt."

"Is that what all the fuss is about outside?"

"I don't know, I'm *inside* – ow, ow, please leave it alone, Cress, I'm fine."

"You are not fine," Cressida says firmly, unless it was Lucrezia saying it from behind her. "I'm trying to get the wool out so you won't get infected. You're not meant to wear cloaks on the inside of your skin. Oh, what *now*?"

The door flap is pushed open again, this time by a smaller figure in a bright red cloak. Sveta takes two steps into the tent and claps her hands over her mouth. "Oh sh – *shoot*!"

"Someone did," Cressida says, and Isaella deeply regrets trying to laugh. "She's alright, friend. They missed anything important. Must have hit her in the brain."

"I will cut you in your sleep," Isaella says. "I'm fine, Sveta."

"You too?"

"Me – what do you mean?"

Sveta lowers her hands, still clasping them tightly together, her knuckles going white. "James. No no no, he's fine, he's fine, they didn't hit him – they tried to shoot him through a tent and they missed – but they sort of hit the lantern and set the tent on fire and I was coming to tell you – what *happened*?"

Cressida's hand squeezes Isaella's shoulder, on the good side, a silent promise of support. "Someone tried to kill her. Probably the same people who tried to kill James. With a crossbow, in the dark."

"Did you see them?"

Isaella shakes her head. "They got me in the back. I didn't see anything but grass in my face."

She hears Sveta take a deep breath. "I'm sixteen next season."

"You're a baby," Lucrezia says from across the tent, "you can't fight them all."

"I can *find* them. Let me help? Please? I'm the only one who's seen anything so far. I know I could recognise that changeling again. I'd just have to keep looking around Highguard until she showed up."

"We'll talk about it." Cress starts pulling Isaella's damaged tunic back down over the bandages. "No, don't make those big eyes at me. We will talk about it in the morning and you will help us find the people responsible. We were going to ask you for help anyway."

Sveta nods, still wide-eyed but reassured. "Okay. Okay, do you want me to do anything tonight? I could run messages?"

"Just point us towards James and Nicovar, please."

The big meeting room in Ankarien has been pressed into service once again. Nicovar is pacing, the colour rising high in his sallow cheeks. James rises as they struggle through the door, Isaella half carried over Cressida's shoulders and being poked with sharp horns whenever she looks around.

Nicovar hisses at the sight of her, angry as a cat between his bared teeth. "Tell me you saw them."

"I wish I could, Nic."

"Tell me something good. Please."

"She's not dead," Cressida says, her cheerful tone almost sounding natural. "That's very good news."

Isaella lets James settle her beside him on a cushion. It's bigger than she remembers the cushions in this room, and then she sees a familiar figure shifting to a bench instead and smiles at her Senate colleague. "Thanks, Archimedes."

"Any time you get shot, you deserve a cushion. Don't take that as recommendation."

"It's a nice cushion, but it's not worth the price."

Nicovar turns to glare over her head, at something far distant from the sun-faded canvas. "How many militia do we have this summit?"

"It's two per nation," James answers. His voice is soft, soothing. "Eighteen. But some will be off duty and too drunk to get back on."

"We need more. We need to get them out on patrol. Why is anyone roaming Anvil with a loaded crossbow and not being stopped for questioning?"

"It's dark out there."

Isaella lets her head tip onto James's shoulder. "Has he been doing this for long?"

"Since they had a go at me," James says, resigned. "Best to just let him get it out."

Cressida and Lucrezia look at each other, and shake their identical heads. "We're going back to the League. See you all in the morning. Someone's got to keep the peace out there."

Nicovar nods at them stiffly and resumes his pacing. Archimedes rises from his perch, the bench creaking beneath him. "I'll hold the fort here. You three – We'll strategise tomorrow. For now, don't leave Ankarien, and don't spend too long in the open spaces. I'm going to ask Lucius to find you hot tea, and I'm going to ask James to make sure all of you drink it."

James wraps one arm around Isaella, pulling her closer. "I'll do my best. This one won't be a problem. It's your Nic who's the troublemaker."

Archimedes smiles and leaves them alone. The glowstones set around the eaves throw Nicovar's shadow onto every wall, a dim and distorted thing, impossible for any archer to target. His shoulder are hunched. Twice he tries to speak, and shakes his head.

Eventually, when Isaella's joints have started to ache viciously, he drops onto a bench and puts his face in his hands. "I'm going to kill them. Somehow. I'm going to make it legal, and then I'm going to see them dead. What happened? How did they find you?"

"My knee hurts," Isaella says, and bursts into tears.

CHAPTER THIRTY-FIVE – WINTER 204

"No," Nicovar says. "I refuse."

"Nic-"

"I will *not* have a bodyguard. This is Anvil. If the Emperor, in the capital of the Empire, does not dare to walk amongst his own citizens, we have ceased to be what we are. I will not concede this of all places to a heretic with a grudge."

"We thought you'd say that," James says quietly. They are sitting, the three of them, in Nicovar's tent, in the gold of a winter sunset. "But for once, believe us, it's not the Emperor we're worried about.

Isaella draws her knee up, clasping her hands around it. "Roland, in the spring. Gwyneth in the summer, both of us in the autumn. They've been marching the attacks closer in to you. We don't want to lose you. We've talked about this."

"Now *you're* plotting against me?"

His lovers say "Nicovar," almost in unison, and he sighs. "You're right, I'm sorry. I can't be part of every conversation. It's just – I was angry they were killing my citizens, I was angry they were targeting my allies, but then they threatened you. And now I am furious, and I will not give them anything that looks like a victory."

"If they kill you, it will be a real victory." James shifts closer, their knees brushing together. "Miriam – if she's still – she needs an interregnum. I don't think she's got a real chance to take the Throne, if she kills you. But I think she thinks she does."

"Who would it go to, if I died?"

"James," Isaella says. "No, don't look at me like that. I'm not a newcomer confused about succession. If the Senate had to choose someone tomorrow, it would be James."

Nicovar looks at her for a long moment, and then at James. The last light of sunset filtering through the canvas makes him almost gilded, a warm glow clinging to his skin and bringing out the laughter in his eyes. The silver threading his beard only makes him seem fatherly. "They love you."

"They do," James agrees. "More so since I became just the Consort. I'm a figurehead, even more than you are. I can support you, but all the controversial things are still your doing. I just kiss the babies and witness the tournaments. They all know me."

Isaella nods. "If they had to choose tomorrow, nobody would get revoked for voting for James."

"Speaking of which." Nicovar leans back on his hands. "We're going to revoke Miriam this evening. The Assembly of Nine."

"Can you do that?"

"Mm. If we have a greater majority. For instance, if we invite the civil service to the Assembly meeting, and do it there and then. Then it takes effect immediately."

James gnaws on his lip. "You're going to miss the Military Council?"

"Probably, yes."

"They'll make her the field marshal for tomorrow, you know."

"Not if we interrupt them."

Isaella bares her teeth, delighted. "This should be fun."

The Assembly of Nine has met every summit on Friday evening, regular as clockwork, since Nicovar took the throne. The faces in the damp Synod tent have changed through the years, Markus replaced by Pia, Annalies by Joshua, but the meetings have always been the same. The same disagreements coming around, the same compromises to support this principle, disburse those funds. More than anyone else, the Cardinals have felt themselves to be Nicovar's equals.

Today Cara of the Way and Solomon of Loyalty are sitting cross-legged on the grass together, Cara's cloak spread out beneath them both, speaking in urgent whispers. Kesia of Courage strides over to Nicovar as he enters, with the same bounce in her step that has always revealed her lineage, even before the bark climbed up her cheek. "I got your letter, Nicovar."

"I'm glad you did. What's your opinion?"

"Unquestionably heresy. And almost a confession, if you think about it. Why write about the virtue of murder if you're not planning to commit some?"

"Exactly. Which is why, as soon as Elvira gets here to record it, I'm proposing that we revoke Miriam."

Kesia nods at once. "We'll have primacy. Of course, that's going to provoke her."

"No more so than passing it tomorrow. And as you've explained to me, she's been sufficiently provoked already."

"I *didn't* get your letter," Solomon calls over, from his seat on the ground. "Give me the summary now?"

"Did you read Miriam's pamphlet about removing the unvirtuous from society so they can't hold the others back?"

"Oh, *that*. It's nonsense. Highguard are *very* offended she used our name to defend it."

"Well, then."

Solomon tilts his head back, looking at the canvas roof. Cara watches him in turn. "Is that the only reason, Nicovar?"

Nicovar sits down in front of him, gesturing Kesia to follow suit. Pia stops checking her notebook and comes to join their circle. "I still think Miriam is virtuous. As I've been saying all along, her personal actions seem virtuous to me. That hasn't changed. And as I've been saying, and Kesia has been saying, our task as the Assembly of Nine is not just to judge the virtue of individual citizens."

"We're guarding the Empire," Solomon finishes the thought. "That's the rub, isn't it? If we revoke Miriam, who is a clearly virtuous individual, because she is spreading heresy and ought not to have an Imperial title to lend it weight, are we diminishing her worth as an example of how to live? How do those actions balance out? I have some personal loyalty to her, as you know but – there are rumours, and rumblings, in Highguard, that I find very disturbing. Nothing concrete, but enough to make me very concerned about my nation's future. And for Miriam to be a good example is no help if she is actively leading people astray."

"Exactly," Kesia says, "exactly that. I've heard the same rumours. We should talk about that, I think the National Assembly needs to do something about it and I could use your help with the wording."

Solomon nods. "Of course. Whenever you need me. Are we quorate now, for this? If we're in agreement I want to get it done."

"Not yet," Cara says. "And – I'm going to vote for this, because I think we need to act, but I want to say, I think we're taking very drastic action over a pamphlet. I've read that pamphlet, and nowhere does she say it's settled doctrine. It's presented as something to consider and – I don't know. She's engaging with the doctrines, I think sincerely, and we are cracking down hard on that. It's not a great precedent."

Pia leans in. "If she wants to talk about theology, she can come to the Virtue meetings. You don't put out heretical pamphlets and say you're just thinking aloud. We have places to do that safely, without leading others astray."

"I suppose." Cara sighs. "Like I said, I'm voting in favour. I just want us to think about the consequences."

The Military Council is in full swing when the Cardinals enter the tent. Someone, predictably, says "Hey, you can't–" and is drowned out by three voices in concert saying, "Right of Witness."

The Generals fall silent as they approach the map. A priest or two might come to witness the meeting, but for the Assembly of Nine to arrive in force, six of the Cardinals and the Throne alongside them, that is something new.

Miriam stands up from behind the map table. "Say your piece, Empress."

Nicovar doesn't answer her. Elvira clears her throat instead, her civil service sash gleaming purple in the lamplight. "Miriam of Levi's Stand. The Cardinal of Loyalty has raised a declaration of revocation against you, to be judged by the Assembly of Nine.

The Assembly of Nine have come to me with primacy and therefore this judgement has passed immediately. You are hereby revoked of your position as General of the Silent Tide."

The silence is a vast and breathing thing. Around the map, more than one hand is creeping towards a sword.

Wordless, Miriam reaches into her belt and pulls out the field-marshal's rod. She sets it down on the table, the iron bands cracking sharply against varnished wood. She reaches up and pulls her hood back with both hands, letting them brush against her hair in a Highborn gesture of contempt. In the shadows between the Generals, she seems suddenly very tall. Nicovar meets her gaze.

"Until next time we meet, then, Empress."

He bows to her, the shallow bow one gives to an enemy. Miriam's smile matches him perfectly. She sweeps past him without a word to the Council she is leaving.

Nicovar is still eating his breakfast when word comes that half the Highborn camp has emptied overnight. He is still finishing his coffee when the word becomes Sveta, running at full tilt, shouting for him to come and see the Senate at once.

There is a clamouring crowd around the entrance. As they approach Isolt pushes her way out and races up the hill towards Dawn, not seeing them in her haste. Nicovar is prepared to put his Conclave skills to good use and thread his way between the massed bodies, but someone shouts "The Emperor!" and the crowd parts before him, every face turned his way. They make space for him to read the notice nailed to the wall, between the dusty flyers for plays and fortune tellers. A red bird soars above it, thick paint dripping from its wings.

It is printed in spiky black capitals, a little smudged from being stacked while the ink was wet. Nicovar scans the first few words and his veins prickle with ice. He will not read this aloud.

It is entitled "A MATTER OF PRINCIPLE".

"We, the Faithful of Highguard, hereby declare that Emperor Nicovar is the head of a corrupt Senate; that the Council of Nine has betrayed the Way of Virtue; that the Imperial Conclave has abandoned its duty of protection; that the Military Council has recklessly pursued a course of unsustainable conquest; that the Bourse has neglected to serve the needs of the people.

When the Empire was first created, these five powers were woven together into a single body, empowered by Virtue as the bone and blood of a human vessel are empowered by the soul. When one part of the body rebels, we look to a physick to correct it. When one part of the Empire is corrupted, the other four may work to bring it back into the faith. But when all are corrupted together, then the soul must flee.

As the Highborn of old carried the light of Virtue across the sea, so must we now tend the flame alone. We dare not remain within an Empire so damaged by evil rule. Our chance of transcendence lies in the single-minded pursuit of Virtue. Our hope for the world is that Virtue may be spread. We must depart from the Empire and become our own nation once more.

Pilgrims of the True Virtues will always be welcome in the chapters of Highguard. We will open our doors to any Highborn who wishes to join us. Those of other nations shall be our most honoured guests, until they choose to depart, or else to take the oath and cowl and join us in our great work. There will be no violence on our borders, unless it be brought by others. The Empire has fallen from Virtue; yet it remains our heritage and our future and we will not make war against it.

Be it known that we take no pleasure from this act. We mourn the wholeness of the Empire-that-was. We strive to maintain true religion and teach it to the Imperial lands, as our forefathers did before the First Empress reigned. We seek only our own preservation, and the purity of the citizens in our care.

May Virtue guide us all."

Beneath the text, eleven symbols are printed, the crests of each great chapter of Reikos, and under them the signature of Miriam of Highguard.

CHAPTER THIRTY-SIX – SPRING 205

There is a hole in the Highguard camp as desolate as a grave.

Around it, the familiar banners go up, the chapters of Casinea and Necropolis. At its edge stands one lonely bell tent hung with bunting in several liveries, where three nervous Highborn stand biting their nails, a tiny delegation of loyalists. But where Reikos should lift its colours to the wind, where Rachel's Guard should open its bar and Levi's Stand should spill into the road, there is only a green spread of grass. Reikos has not come; Miriam has not come, to raise her voice against Nicovar. They have chosen their own place for a summit, their own empty field on a wind-swept hill, and sent formal invitation to the Empire to attend.

Isaella eyes the empty space warily. Nobody seems eager to cross it, instead skirting the edges, as though to avoid admitting that the hole is there. She would ask a Vate, if this were a Navarri camp, to give an opinion on whether that pattern should be allowed to continue – whether it was better to keep moving as if Reikos were present, to acknowledge their place in the Empire, or to cross the space and thus deny the seceding rebels the right to control their camp. But this is Highguard, so although she will ask the vates anyway, and they will discuss it with vigour amongst themselves, the Highborn will not care for their opinion.

For now, Isaella takes her cue from the locals and makes her way around the edge of the space, to speak with the Reikos ambassadors.

"Greetings, friends."

The least nervous of them adjusts her tunic self-consciously. "Senator. Good to see you again."

Isaella squints at her. She doesn't recognise the uniform these three are wearing, stark black and white embroidered with rearing horses, but the speaker's blonde hair is familiar. "You're from Rachel's Guard, aren't you? The brewer?"

The woman nods. "Adina. And this is Ruth, from my chapter, and Ezra of Lazarus – sorry, of the Silent Tide."

"Honoured to meet you," Ezra says. His voice is husky, as though he has been shouting and only recently stopped. "My old chapter has broken their creed. I won't return to them."

"Highguard colours," Isaella says, realising it even as she speaks. "You're wearing Highguard colours."

Adina smiles wryly. "We could hardly wear our own, could we? Officially, I'm on a visit to my father, and Ruth is my bodyguard in hostile Imperial territory. Though my Exarch isn't a fool and I'm sure she knows where I've gone – but she's a traitor and a rebel, so she'll probably be executed in the end."

Ezra reaches over and squeezes Adina's shoulder, wordless in his support. Isaella lets the bitter prediction go. Time enough for that when the Empire is united again.

"So then, unofficially, how many in Reikos feel as you do?"

The Highborn share an uncertain glance. "It's hard to say exactly," Adina says. "We can't really take a census. But – *most* of Rachel's Guard are unsure about it. They're following orders for now, but if Jael said we were coming back into the fold, they'd follow her there too."

"It's not a popular rebellion," Ezra agrees, his voice rasping. "The Silent Tide is stationed here in Casinea, along the border, and we all want to go home and shake our chapters into seeing sense. We've got hundreds of people camping with us who wouldn't stay outside the Empire."

Isaella nods sharply. "So, it's the rebellion it seemed to be. Led from the top, not a popular uprising. Good."

"How is that *good*?"

"Because it means we can reclaim Reikos," she says, matter-of-fact, and watches understanding straighten their spines. "This is an unprecedented situation. I don't want to mislead you about what happens next, because I'm not sure myself. For now, Reikos is still part of the Empire, so far as the Empire is concerned. Is your Senator planning to attend?"

The Senator for Reikos is not in attendance. Of the eight Reikos citizens present, five are part of the little self-appointed embassy. Two are Synod priests, here to talk doctrine with a stated intention of staying out of politics, and one is a merchant who sailed back into harbour to find his nation in pieces.

The Senate convenes shortly after sunset with a full public gallery and the Emperor present. Isaella sees James jammed into a corner of the gallery, doing his best to keep order. On this of all days, the Civil Service should not be tempted to take the session private.

Nicovar sets his rod sideways, across the broad arms of the throne, and leans on it. He nods to the Speaker. "You'd better start us off. We have a lot to discuss."

"Senators," Marianne says, "at the request of the Throne, regular business will take place *after* the status of Reikos has been dealt with. As you will all be aware, during the Winter Summit of the two-hundred-and-fourth year of the Empire, a faction within Highguard declared its intention to withdraw from the Empire and form a new independent nation in the territory of Reikos. Communication from Reikos has been limited in the three months since. The Civil Service has been expelled. The Senate budget is therefore reduced by the unpaid taxes from Reikos, and there have been no new citizens or army recruits from that territory. As far as we are aware, the chapters of Reikos have continued to patrol the border with the Barrens and to deal with intrusions, but unless they allow the Silent Tide to enter, there will be no strong defence against invasion. This is the first meeting of the Senate since the withdrawal began and the Senate must therefore decide: is Reikos a part of the Empire, and if not, what status do the former citizens of Highguard possess?"

The debate is long and painful. Isaella stakes out her position early and works to hold it. Reikos is not an independent power; Reikos is an Imperial territory, subject to Imperial law, and it cannot sever itself from the rest of Highguard. A nation might withdraw from the Empire, that would make philosophical sense, and be a question the Empire would have to take seriously. A mere territory cannot.

The opposing view is one of contempt. Reikos wishes to go; well then, let them go and be barbarians, and when the Druj cross their borders and wipe them out, the Empire will pick up the pieces.

They argue for almost an hour. The public gallery empties and fills again, as the watchers grow tired and seek their dinners. Nicovar keeps them on track with an attention he's rarely paid to the flow of debate, his usual aloofness abandoned, instead trying to summarise each argument and keep them moving into agreement.

Isaella has to soften her approach, in the end, nudged by her infuriating lover into following his strategy. Reikos could leave

Highguard, if it was properly handled, with the Highborn senators and synod priests all in agreement. But since it has made no such petition, the Empire is not obliged to accept its withdrawal.

Nicovar blinks at her once, slowly, like an affectionate cat, and moves on to the fractious Freeborn and Marchers, who are half inclined to let Reikos go its way and become a tenth Imperial nation, although Reikos has made no effort to rejoin the Empire on any terms and was very clear, in its declaration, that it considered itself still Highborn. But the romance of revolution must be given its space, and the visions allowed to pass in their own time.

Eventually, Nicovar sits back in his throne and sets his hands on the arms. "Senators, thank you for your thoughts, and your patience. Speaker, will you take down a motion, if I reel it off?"

Marianne shrugs. "If you like, Empress."

"Thank you. And I'll ask for a second once it's written. Senate motion, Spring 204 YE, proposed by the Throne: "The Empire does not accept the withdrawal of the chapters of Reikos from the nation of Highguard or the wider Empire. Citizens of the Empire within Reikos are considered still to be citizens of the Empire and are free to leave it as before. Imperial Law applies in full to the territory of Reikos and the citizens who reside there. The chapters of Reikos shall have until the summer solstice of 205 YE to allow the Civil Service to resume their duties unhindered and to permit the free movement of all Imperial citizens. If they do not do so, the Senate will pursue a military solution to their lawbreaking." Is there a second for that motion as written?"

"I'll do it," says tall Elina, "I'm happy with that wording."

"Thank you, Kallavesa. Then when you're ready, Speaker?"

Marianne leans over her chair a moment longer, writing the motion down. Her hands are steady despite the weight of the moment. She turns back to the Senate. "Does anyone need me to read this again?"

Isaella joins in the low chorus of denial.

"Then we'll proceed straight to the voting. This motion has been thoroughly debated and I don't think we need another round. Under the circumstances, if we have more abstentions than decisive votes, I will allow a repeat motion to be raised tomorrow. Ayes to the left, No's to the right, abstentions move to the back. Senators, make your votes."

The crowd can count faster than Marianne. They start applauding the motion even before it passes.

CHAPTER THIRTY-SEVEN – SUMMER 205

A messenger from Reikos arrives with the summer. She runs through Anvil without a word, her eyes fixed on the Senate tower. She is shirtless and sweating under her tabard, but her hood is still raised, a guard against temptation. Highborn are still a common sight around Anvil, the secessionists barely a quarter of the nation. Even so, the crowd on Trader's Lane clear out of her way.

Nicovar watches her coming out of the sunset. Senate ran short, today, and he is waiting on the dusty ground by the time the Highborn reaches him. No doubt she intended to arrive while they were in session, lingered just outside Anvil for the perfect moment. He can see a flicker of frustration in her eyes as she comes to a stop before him, her dramatic interruption spoiled. He bows deeper to her than he ever has to Miriam. The messenger's lips twitch.

She salutes, her fist pressed over her heart. "I am sent with a message for the Empire of the Way."

"Then you may leave it with me," Nicovar says, keeping his voice calm. "I sit upon that throne."

"You are Nicovar of Ankarien?"

"I am."

"I bring you greetings from Miriam of Highguard."

Nicovar smiles. "I'm glad to see they come in writing this time, and not as a knife in the dark."

"Of course not," the messenger says, and that surely wasn't part of her script. She pulls herself together. "The chapters of Reikos decline to allow your Civil Service entry to our nation. We do not acknowledge any right to collect taxes from us, or to take our soldiers for your armies. We do not seek war, but we – We do not offer our surrender."

She licks her lips. Nicovar can see how tense she is, and not from running into camp. This woman is not certain she will leave Anvil alive.

Fury wells up in his chest. One of his own people, subject to his Throne, afraid she will be murdered for speaking to him.

"Who has water for my friend here?" he says. "Will you come into camp and rest? No? Then step into the Senate with me. Come out of the sun. There'll be plenty of witnesses if anything happens."

The messenger adjusts the hood over her sweat-spiked hair. There's an eagle embroidered on her tabard, with its scarlet wings outstretched. Nicovar hates the sight of it.

"Come," he says again, and raises his arm towards the Senate floor, gesturing for her to go first. He will not expose his back to this one's blade.

Just to remind her of where she is, he climbs the dais to the throne. He lets the messenger stand for a moment, straight-backed with her bare shoulders tense, before he holds out a hand for her burden.

The scroll is fresh crisp paper, kept pristine by the scroll-case slung across her back. Nicovar unties the ribbon and spreads it on his lap. Better typesetting on this than their articles of secession in the winter; they've had more time to prepare it. He scans it quickly. Not much more than the messenger already said to him, only more flowery. Reikos rejects the Empire's claim to authority, reiterates that it is not at war, and promises to defend itself if the Empire invades. There is no signature, only the same eagle blazon pressed into a wax seal.

Nicovar rolls the scroll back up.

The messenger fidgets, shifting her weight. "Is there a response?"

"Patience, citizen," he says.

"I am *not* a citizen," she starts, offended, but Nicovar isn't looking at her. He's looking over her shoulder at the little cluster of adolescents who have arrived, with perfect timing, to be sworn in.

He stays seated, though normally he would get up to greet them. This time, he needs the theatrics of formality. There are three youngsters today, all freshly washed and persuaded into clean outfits by the head of the Anvil Academy. They might be less willing if he was their teacher all year, but they see him only at summits and he gives them adventures. For Uncle Jaromir, the children of Anvil would do anything.

Not children much longer. Jaromir steps forward, his chest puffed out with pride. "Emperor Nicovar, may I present to you the newest citizens of the Empire?"

"Come forward," Nicovar says. "Let me look at you. What are your names?"

"Robert," mumbles the Dawnish lad. He's the tallest in the room by several inches, with a bass voice to match, and if he spoke up they'd probably hear him all the way back in Dawn.

"Yeofolk or nobility, Robert?"

He's trying to be solemn, but the grin breaks through anyway. "I'm getting my test tonight."

"Good. We can always use more knights. And Sveta, of course, I've met before. I thought we'd see you here last season."

Sveta crosses her arms. The embroidery on her blouse is so thick she looks like she's wearing pauldrons of white thread. "Auntie wouldn't let me until she could come and watch." She turns to glare over her shoulder at the Varushkan woman still coming up the ramp, her heavy boots sounding against the wood, and turns back with an innocent and unconvincing smile.

"And you, friend?"

"Gisela."

Nothing more seems to be forthcoming from the merrow, but Nicovar can see from her clothes and the sturdy black notebook hung from her belt that she's Leaguish, and probably heading straight into a reckoner's guild.

He nods to Jaromir. "This is a good day, teacher. We have a witness from Reikos."

"*Holy* Reikos," the Highborn mutters. The whole room turns to stare at her, children and Nicovar and stray senators alike. Jaromir is the only one with sense enough to press onward.

"That's good to hear, Empress. All the Empire should recognise these new citizens."

"Will you vouch for them, Jaromir?"

Jaromir beams. "I will, Empress! These three have passed the tests that the Civil Service set for them, in arms, in virtue and in law. They are all fit to be citizens of the Empire, accepted by their egregores and ready to join their nations in full. Will you recognise their claim?"

"I will, and gladly so. Be welcome to the Empire, citizens. May you walk in Virtue and make her proud."

It's a small litany, but the crowd behind the new citizens bursts into applause anyway, friends and family and some just passing by, stepping in to watch the simplest moment of happiness this building ever sees. Nicovar presses his hands together and bows in his seat. The youngsters bow back, none of them very well, but all happy to echo the Throne this once.

"Thank you, Jaromir," he says. "Bring us more, next time. We need every good hand we can get. And now, our friend from Reikos. Do you have a name? We have a lot to discuss before you leave us."

"Nicovar," Sveta says.

"I am only here to carry messages," the Highborn says. "I am not a witness to this."

"Nicovar!"

He hates to break the tension, but Sveta is at his side and almost tugging on his robes with eagerness. He turns to her, intending to send her away, but though Sveta is still smiling happily she leans up and murmurs, "Get her to show you her ears. I *recognise* her."

Nicovar smiles back. "Thank you, I will. But your family are waiting for you. You shouldn't keep them waiting."

He looks back at the Highborn. "So, no name? Has Holy Reikos abandoned the use of them?"

"Of course not." Messenger or not, this one wasn't chosen for her tact. "But I am not here *personally.* You don't need to know my name."

"Of course, I understand. You're afraid to have it recorded, in case history judges you unkindly. Anyone would feel the same in your position."

Her back can't get any straighter. Nicovar shrugs at her, non-committal. "But if you're not here to negotiate, you really should take that hood down and have a rest. We won't send you back until you've eaten and had some water, you know. We can be very annoyingly persistent about these things."

The messenger rolls her eyes. She flings her hood back and folds her arms, almost exactly like Sveta sulking over her delayed ceremony. "My name is Tabitha. I will accept your hospitality while you draft your reply."

No longer shadowed by her hood, the pale scarring on the tops of her ears is obvious, an ugly jagged line where a point once rose. It looks like she did it herself. No neat surgeon's cut; this was done to hurt, and to remind. Across the room, Sveta widens her eyes and nods. She reaches towards the knife strapped across her back, apparently ready to attack at once. Her aunt steps between them before Sveta can move. She speaks in an urgent whisper, too quiet for Nicovar to hear, but whatever she says cools Sveta's fire. The moment for violence passes.

Nicovar smiles at the assassin, and memorises her face.

CHAPTER THIRTY-EIGHT – AUTUMN 205

Autumn blows in on a cold wind. The ground at Anvil is wet from sudden rainstorms, sweeping across the country like a giant's paintbrush. It was a dry summer and the rain hasn't had time to settle in; there's damp underfoot, but not yet mud.

Isaella stands in the Ankarien camp, one foot up on a bench as she laces her boot. "Don't be silly, James. I'll be fine."

"You've never fought Imperials," James says. "None of us have. And these are Highborn."

"You think Navarr can't handle Highborn? We're not afraid of our monochrome friends."

His hand is warm on her shoulder. "I think the Navarr are not best suited to breaking a shield-wall."

Isaella finishes her laces and sits, patting the bench next to her. James settles down, their legs pressed together. "I would have said we should go to the other battle," she agrees. "Our generals tell me that was the original plan, until someone ran the numbers. There just aren't enough Winterfolk here. Varushka has to go to Varushka, because they're the only ones who know the terrain. Highguard has to go with them, because they can't be asked to fight against their own nation. It wouldn't be fair."

"And I have to go to break the fort," James says, resigned.

"Exactly. So that's the bill-blocks accounted for, and if Navarr went to Varushka as well it would leave all the small nations to face Highguard, and the Winterfolk can tackle a shield wall but they can't do the whole job by themselves. We're needed for this one."

James leans over, his head on her shoulder. "I hate this," he says. "I hate fighting our own. We have to, I know, but – it's not right. I don't want us to do this."

"The armies didn't meet serious resistance," Isaella says, as quiet as he is. "Maybe we won't, either."

"The armies went in at a crawl and lost too many people to assassins. Watch out for Unconquered, Sal. They'll be more dangerous to you than the cataphracts."

Isaella kisses him before she goes to the Gate.

The Army of the Citadel has made an opening for them. Ordinarily, a single territory like Reikos shouldn't take long to conquer. An army can cross whole nations in a season if they're unopposed. But this isn't all-out war, and can't be. This is more like surgery. The Urizeni soldiers have moved in slowly, the scalpel to isolate the chapters from each other and throttle their supply lines, avoiding bloodshed whenever they can. The Imperial scribes have written down every Reikos casualty as carefully as their own.

Isaella hardly notices the moment of passage through the Gate. They are less than fifty miles from where they began, near the northern border with Broceliande. The same grey clouds are racing overhead.

She settles her spear into her grip. From here, they must already be vigilant. James's point about the Unconquered was well made; in this terrain, a Highborn in brown leather might easily be mistaken for a Navarr slipping out of the trees. The cataphracts are more obvious, a cluster of soldiers down in the broad valley, black tabards belted tightly over polished steel plate. They will raise their shields, when the Imperials get close, and lock them together like a wall. The spears will be needed for that.

It's a slow battle. For nearly half an hour, the forces manoeuvre around each other, the Imperials – she hates to exclude the Highborn from that word, but there's no better way to put it – the Imperials trying to squeeze the separatists into a more vulnerable line, against the sturdy sheep-fence that blocks the far slopes. The Reikos soldiers, for their part, are pushing towards the Gate, trying to separate the Imperials from their way home.

The first blow is struck by a separatist. Later, Isaella will remember that, as a talisman against dreams. The first blow is struck by a young woman with a long plume fixed to her helmet, in imitation of the horse-hair trophies of ancient warriors, before the Empire's birth. She lifts her shield against a grim-faced Urizeni sentinel, stalking close to keep their flank from folding away, and he comes one step closer than she likes, and her sword rings against steel chain.

The field dissolves into war. Isaella is moving with the rest of Navarr, spears in the front, archers behind, to pierce that shield-wall in three places and make the separatists struggle to keep together. Navarr are not trained for the front lines. She sees too many of her people go down, spitted on Highborn swords, their spears too short to do the work of bill-hooks. The physicks will never get to them in time.

She drives her spear into a Highborn shoulder anyway. This is not a time to be distracted. One in the shoulder, to make her lower her shield, and then drive the butt into her chest to make her stagger backwards, and then defend against the sword from her left while the Navarr on her right works to widen the gap. Step to the side, keep the rolling mass of Navarri moving, their strength in movement as the Highborn strive to hold their place.

There is a banner in the centre of this group. Whether there's also a commander there, she can't be sure; she thinks not, from how the fighters are moving, a little uncoordinated, with more than one sergeant to shout at them. But the banner rises from their ranks all the same, the scarlet eagle on the black field, the symbol of Holy Reikos. The title makes every priest in Anvil frown. And the Navarr know the value of symbols, and their destruction. They have plans for that banner. All Isaella has to do is keep fighting until she reaches it.

It is an ugly battle. When the Imperials finally leave, almost late enough for the Gate to close on them although they never left sight of it; when they leave, there are Highborn scattered across the valley. One sad little clump is a squad of Unconquered arrogant enough to come out of their trees into a Navarri flank, not realising that flank was an ambush. Most of the rest are cataphracts, going cold inside their armoured shells.

But it is not only Highborn lying dead. The Imperials take the time to gather their fallen, as the gate hisses and smokes behind them. They could leave them here, as they have on so many battlefields before, but there is too much grief already in this fight. Bad enough to leave the Reikos soldiers here to rot.

They carry two Dawnish knights back with them, their bright tabards the only thing to distinguish them from cataphracts. One Urizeni magician, a woman in pale blue that Isaella recognises from years of scrying for the military. Five Winterfolk, carried in the arms of their people.

And seventeen dead Navarri.

She has no time to seek out her lovers. There are dead Navarri to be prepared for the corpse glade, and three were Thornborn like her, part of the loose family of wanderers who have no home but the army. Isaella carries one of them back, feeling the blood soaking her tunic from Gerwyn's ruined chest. His bandoleer is empty of bandages and herbs, everything used up and wasted. His bow is still here, slung sideways across his chest once his quiver was empty, and she carefully unstrings it and draws it away. It's a good bow, short enough to use amongst the trees, for someone with archer's shoulders. They'll make good use of it, and his boots, and the work-softened harness of leather that held all his supplies.

She strips the body methodically of all but his clothes, the ones too bloodied and torn to be salvaged. She washes Gerwyn's face, skirting around the warpaint striping his nose, cleaning off the blood and the dust. Around her, a dozen Navarri are doing their same for their friends, for their families. There is a sturdy changeling lying in the grass nearby, the blood oozing from a broken antler, and Isaella keeps her eyes on Gerwyn and her work until finally someone names the changeling as Gwyn, and she can relax knowing that Cara is alive, somewhere, and not fallen in treacherous Reikos.

When Gerwyn is ready, his dignity restored though he frowns even in death, Isaella sits back on her heels. The warm hand on her back is too familiar to startle her. She leans into James's side.

He kisses her hair. "What needs doing, Sal?"

"We need a fire," she says, too tired to refuse his help.

"To burn them?"

"No, no. There's a corpse glade, a mile along the Trod. We always put the Anvil heroes there. We need the fire for the living."

"Alright."

He holds her for a long minute, before he rises to look for firewood. Isaella runs her fingers over Gerwyn's bow. The paint along the spine is bright in the dappled shade.

She does not speak any promises of vengeance. Navarri do not say such things, not unless they mean them. Reikos is not to be wiped out. Reikos is to be brought home, and this is just a skirmish, a minor battle in a minor war, and the Navarr were careless. But she sits with Gerwyn for a long time, recalling his steady presence in battle, his scowl whenever she needed his herbs, and when she goes to speak to her nation she is not ashamed of the tear tracks through her warpaint.

CHAPTER THIRTY-NINE – WINTER 205

Nicovar is standing on the border of his Empire.

It is important to do it this way. There are no forms for this, no established precedent, but the instinct for ritual runs deep. The Throne must come, with full panoply and escort, and demand that the rebels surrender. It would not be proper otherwise.

Today, the border of the Empire stretches all the way around Reikos, to Broceliande in the north and the Barrens in the east. It runs along the familiar lines on the map. Only here is there a difference, a little circle that is not Imperial, around the walled chapter of Levi's Stand.

The other chapters have surrendered, one by one. Some came easily, glad to be admitted back to the Empire that is their heritage. Some fought to a bloody and bitter end. At Rachel's Guard, the Imperials raised their banners and saw the Exarch stand alone before her gates, the last defender of a lost cause. At Maria's Keep, they found only corpses inside the walls.

There is no hope left for the secession. Levi's Stand will be the end of it.

So Nicovar is here, marching through the Sentinel Gate to a green hill scattered with snow. He has brought the banners of the Empire that hang on the walls of the Senate, nine bright symbols for nine nations and the golden horse flying above them all. He has the warriors of Dawn and Highguard, shining in their heavy plate, and the gate-breaking magicians of the Marches. Representatives, too, of all the rest, sworn to mercenary banners so the Gate would let them through, so that every nation should be here at the Empire's edge today.

Levi's Stand is an ancient place. The great walls have been built up and up, and over time the earth has been raised against their sides until now the whole fortress is ringed by a steep grassy hill, the better to keep siege engines away. Nicovar has visited, and seen the massive gates, the archery screen that tops the walls, a lacy veil of stone. When the Highborn first took Reikos from barbarian orcs, they built this place to defend it.

To his left, in a cluster of magicians, James is spinning his staff in his hands. Nicovar refuses the pinch of worry in his chest. James has brought down a dozen forts over the years. He knows how to duck. And he is needed here, for the gates of Levi's Stand are supported by towers and tunnels, a dark maze where the defenders lie in wait. The attackers cannot go through that killing ground. They must bring the gatehouse down.

Slowly, shields raised, the Imperials advance towards the walls. The magicians fall in behind the line, carrying their crystals and masks. They can't work their ritual until the right moment, or James – always James, the fastest and least powerful, least necessary to the casting – will be killed by the backlash before he can deliver the curse.

As they approach, the gates swing open. For one wild moment Nicovar thinks that the Highborn are mounted, have reached into the forgotten past and brought forth *horses.* Another breath and he sees the archery platforms for what they are, painted wood built inside the gatehouse tunnel, making use of the height that once accommodated riders. Between those menacing pillars the defenders stand ready.

Nicovar recognises Miriam in the front line. She is taller than the others, even without the plumed helmet of a cataphract. Her shield is painted like the rest with a scarlet eagle. It screams defiance across every breastplate.

He knew she would come. There are forms to be observed.

The Imperials stop a hundred yards before the walls. They wait in unaccustomed silence, listening to the banners in the wind and the jingle of mail. Every sword is drawn, and still they wait.

Nicovar steps out in front. It's a gamble, exposing himself to every archer on the walls, but he knows his enemy. Miriam's war is lost, but her ambitions have not dimmed. She will take this one chance to meet him as an equal.

He can hear muttering behind him as a little honour guard ventures through the gate. *Wait,* he thinks, but he can't communicate it without breaking the spell. He has to stand here with his feet going numb, with the banner of the Empire flying behind him, and let Miriam approach.

The cataphracts stop ten feet away. Nicovar holds his ground but the rhythm of the thing has caught them both up, now, and Miriam doesn't hesitate to come forward to meet him. She stands at arm's reach, fearless, her hand curled gently around the hilt of her sword.

"You should have let us go," she says.

"I left it to the Senate," Nicovar answers her. "It's not the first time they've decided against you."

"The Senate is full of cowards, and you're the worst of them. How long did you avoid me, and now you come here with an army at your back?"

"Don't sell yourself short. You didn't do this for my attention."

Miriam lifts her head. "No, I didn't. I did this for all the reasons I told you. You are the head of a corrupted Empire. You have led it into the dirt. I couldn't save the nations, so I did what I could. I led my own people back to the Way."

"Lead them again," Nicovar says quietly. "You know this war is lost. Today, tomorrow, next month – you can drag it out, if you're lucky, but you can't win. The Empire will retake this land. Holy Reikos is dead, but the people don't have to be."

"We'll fight."

"You have refugees in there, Miriam. You have *children*. We know you can't feed them all. How long until the well runs dry? How many will die when the gatehouse falls?"

"We'll fight," Miriam says again, a bleak courage layering her voice, the expectation of grief. "We have never been conquered and we will not be now. You'll have to kill us all. Or you could let us be. This doesn't have to end like this. One chapter, Nicovar. One among hundreds. What harm could it do?"

Nicovar shakes his head. "If we let you go, we lose magical dominion over Reikos. I'm sorry. We need this patch of ground. But there is another way."

"What are you suggesting?"

"We don't imprison our citizens. We won't keep you here against your will. Surrender now and I can promise you safe passage to the border or the ports, whichever you'd prefer, and you can go. You can be the holy remnant wherever you like. Just not here."

The colour is high in Miriam's cheeks. "How dare you? We built this Empire. We founded the Way, and you want us to *leave*? So you can pick over the corpse with the rest of the vultures? I am the Patrician of Reikos. You can leave, or you can fight. We will stand our ground."

Nicovar lets his shoulders drop. "Please, Miriam. Don't make others die for your hubris."

"The word is *pride*, Empress, and my people understand it."

She turns to walk away. Nicovar lets her go. He doesn't shout, doesn't raise a hand to his weapon. Miriam is barely out of reach when she seems to trip over nothing and falls, the breath punching out of her, a green-fletched arrow in her unarmoured neck.

Nicovar keeps his place as the line surges forward around him. The shields go up, as the archers on the fortress walls start shooting. Four cataphracts came for an honour guard; they charge into the shield wall and are cut down at once.

He crouches behind the raised shields. There is a war-painted changeling suddenly beside him, though only a handful of Navarr are here, and she must have worked her way forward alone just to take that shot. She drags at the still-twitching corpse. "You need a sword, Empress?"

"No," he says. "I use a rod."

"Alright, then. Just the shield. Hold this a minute."

He feels absurd, huddled behind the line with arrows bouncing off shields three feet from his head, clutching a pot of white paint. The Navarr works quickly, painting something onto Miriam's shield with a rag. She takes the pot and pushes the shield into his arms. "Show them all that and then let's fight," she says briskly, and scrambles along the line looking for a better vantage point.

Nicovar fits the shield onto his arm. The surprise is fading, replaced by the tense urgency of battle. Of course a Navarr would do that, when Miriam did not surrender; of course. He's heard a dozen stories of the same thing. Of course they wouldn't risk him giving her an honourable warning.

He doesn't usually fight with a shield, but the Navarr was right about the symbolism. There is a broad white streak painted across the Reikos eagle. Nicovar turns towards his forces, trusting the line in front to keep arrows off his back, and raises the shield like another banner.

The Imperials roar. The Gate is behind them, stone more ancient than the fortress walls, awaiting their return. There are three solid columns of warriors, with the physicks stalking between the lines, the magicians waiting with crackling mana in their pockets. He can see James circling with his coven, weaving the threads that will tear the gatehouse down. Ten minutes, to get the front line close enough for him.

Nicovar raises his weapon to fight.

PART THREE:
THE BOUNDS OF HISTORY

CHAPTER FORTY – SPRING 206

Spring comes in a riot of bluebells. Nicovar picks his way through the Navarri woods, on the gentle slope above Anvil's famous meadow. If he stepped out from the shadow of the trees, he could look down towards the crumbling walls of the ancient forge, and see the white canvas of the Senate and the brooding stones of the Gate. Here beneath the leaves he might be in any tarry in the Empire, with low tents pitched between the branches wherever the space is large enough, tiny paths trodden through the flowers to every door.

He could be anywhere in the Empire, except that he knows every face. Has sung around the fire on warm evenings when the bugs were biting; has slept under canvas in these woods, a quarter-mile and a world away from his place in Ankarien camp. He spots Isaella outside a faded green tent and finds his way towards her, along a path so narrow his robe brushes against the bluebells on either side.

"Morning, Cara," he says, "Good to see you again."

Cara pats the ground next to her, inviting him to sit. "Isaella tells me you've got a mad idea."

"Did she indeed?"

"I did," Isaella says, deadpan. "I put it in exactly those words."

"Nice to know you have such confidence in me. It's not really a mad idea, Cara, it's just a way of organising ourselves better."

Cara passes him a bowl of crumbly flapjack pieces. "We seem to organise ourselves quite well, that's the thing. The way Isaella put it, and sorry if I've misunderstood, is that you want to have a central civil service point where everyone has to go? But we already have a synod tent and it works fine. I'm not keen on fighting with the Conclave every time we need to vote on something."

Nicovar nods. "If it helps, I'm planning on it being a *big* tent. It'll have to be, because as you say, everyone will be doing their business at once. The point is, you'd always be able to find a civil servant. How much of your life have you wasted chasing Elvira all over camp?"

Cara cocks her head, her antlers exaggerating the movement. "At least an hour every summit," she admits. "Every day, some years. Depends how much voting there is."

"And I've had the same with Marianne," Isaella says. "She does her best but I've missed deadlines for raising motions because I'm ready, but I just can't find her in time."

Nicovar spreads his hands. "It's the same in the Conclave. I don't want to sound infantilising, this isn't because I think we can't handle it. I think we're wasting time that we could spend on our actual jobs. We're here for a reason and playing hide-and-seek with the civil service isn't it. "

"But we've all got our own chambers. That's what worries me about this idea. If we were just asking the civil service to bring more staff to Anvil, so they could always have someone on duty in the Synod, and the Conclave and the Senate, that would be one thing. But you're asking us to centralise all those individual bodies. The Constitution sets us up as separate powers. It opens the door to intimidation, if the Senators can stand there watching us vote to revoke them."

Isaella takes another piece of flapjack. "They could do that already."

"Well, no, because they'd have to follow Elvira all around camp. Nobody spends four hours doing that. But sitting in a nice dry command tent where they can catch the whole Assembly one by one – it affects our independence. I don't like that."

Nicovar leans forward on his elbows. "What would change your mind?"

Lucrezia, polishing her rings before Conclave, has similar concerns.

"Why not post a board in the Hall of Worlds, darling? That would make more sense."

Nicovar sits on the edge of the carta's long table. "Two reasons. One, I don't want every Herald who wanders in to have access to the agenda before it's finalised, or they'll rip things off the board and it'll be chaos. And two, it's not only magicians with the right to raise declarations."

"Should be, honestly." Lucrezia considers a polished blue band and tries it on a different finger. "I know it's not, but since they can't argue for them anyway it would force them to find a magician to speak for them and they'd have much better luck getting anything passed. But that's not really the point. Nicovar, have you thought what this would do to the politics?"

"Of course I have."

"Have you really? Finding Ruth is part of the challenge. If you can't track down one civil servant who stays near her camp, why should we listen to your ideas? It keeps all the bright young things from thinking they know everything. I don't want to deal with six newcomers every summit raising motions we've already dismissed. It would be a mess."

"Like I said, I've thought about the politics. The Conclave has been going stale since before I started here and our traditional ways of doing things are partly why. Because the old guard has a stranglehold on the agenda."

"*You're* the old guard," Lucrezia says, glaring at him through her mask. "And you're going grey."

Nicovar lets his tone sharpen to match hers. "It's an unconstitutional barrier. A new attendee is a full member of the Conclave and has the right to raise items for the agenda. Making them jump through hoops to figure out which civil servant they need and how to find her is not part of the law. They don't have to have that knowledge. They just need to be magicians."

"Oh, Nicky." Lucrezia sits down beside him. "Always the idealist. It's not about principles. Philosophy is nice when you're drunk, but we're dealing with reality here. You're trying to up-end our whole way of government, but you won't admit how much it would change. I won't vote for that."

"Technically -"

"Technically the Senate, yes, I know. Technically, I know the law as well as you do. Look, you can probably push this through, but if you want me to give the Arch a free vote on the thing, you make me a deal, right now."

Nicovar turns sideways to look at her. "Go on?"

"You leave the Orders out of it. You can have your noticeboard somewhere on the field and you can even make Ruth stand beside it to take declarations, but I want it understood that's Conclave business *only*. Nothing binding within the Orders. No official meetings, no requirement to announce candidacies, no –

no voting policies getting posted there. You let the Orders keep running themselves."

Nicovar hums. "Technically – sorry – elections are Conclave business. I'm with you on the candidacies but I think we're going to have an elections schedule posted and it'll include the timings for Grandmaster votes."

"Fine," Lucrezia says stiffly. "Elections can go on the board. But no campaigning. That's Order business and I won't have it publicised."

"I can sign up to that." Nicovar nods. "Alright. When I speak for the proposal, I'll make that clear."

"And I'll let the Order vote their consciences and not whip the block." Lucrezia works a glittering gold band around the curve of her horn. "You used to be such a nice, biddable boy. What changed?"

"Thanks, Lucrezia. I like you too."

James ambushes him at the regio. "Nope, you're not going in there. Come with me. Come on."

"Help, help, I'm being kidnapped." Nicovar lets himself be turned on the spot. "Where are we going?"

"Did you eat yet?"

"I had lunch," Nicovar says. "At – about three o'clock. So, recently! I'm fine, honest!"

James shakes his head. "Nope. We talked about this, Nic. New rules. You have to eat three meals every day. If I let you go in the Hall of Worlds you won't come out again before Conclave."

"You ought to put me in disguise, or someone will find me and we still won't get to eat." Nicovar takes his hand. "I did have several cups of tea with the Cardinals earlier. So I am well hydrated, at least."

James bumps his shoulder affectionately. "Did you get your votes for the hub?"

"We're not calling it that. It makes Anvil sound like a windmill."

"Whatever you say, Empress. Did you?"

Nicovar sighs. "I'm not sure. We might get – I don't know. The civil service has some discretion over how they perform their duties. They could, if they wanted to, change to a centralised location for themselves. But I don't think they want to, so we're doing this."

"And if we vote it down..."

"Then they'd be going against our directly expressed wishes as the duly elected, selected and dissected rulers of the Empire. Which, traditionally, they do not do."

"Well, I think you've got the Conclave. Lucrezia is still kicking up a fuss, but she's just afraid of anyone else being able to find Ruth. For the rest of us, it would be lovely. And I'm not afraid to say that if she starts pontificating."

Nicovar nods. "I'm going to have to leave it to you. Senate clashes again and I expect they'll be fractious after the Reikos mess. I need to keep an eye on them tonight."

"Leave it with me," James says, reassuring. "Oh look, a stall selling jacket potatoes. Yes?"

"Yes," Nicovar says, and smiles up at him. "Love you, James."

"Love you, Nic."

CHAPTER FORTY-ONE – SUMMER 206

There has been a change in Trader's Row. Isaella comes up to it from the regio, her paperwork flapping in the dusty wind. She's late onto the field this season and had to stand in line to register her attendance with the civil service. And the civil service were more harassed than usual, and overstretched, and now she turns the corner to see why.

The new tent is enormous. The wooden walls of the Senate standing opposite are half the height of its striped roof. The Navarri make tents like this, to hold the great Standings that a territory must have sometimes, and for celebrations in bad weather. They do not usually dye the canvas in bright red and white. The traders have had to make a second line to accommodate it and now there are two Rows, one on each side, to catch the citizens spilling out from the big top. Isaella ducks through the nearest entrance and blinks in the sudden darkness.

"You need to get some glowstones up on that pole, Adam," she says to a nearby civil servant. His sash, usually pristine, is streaked with grass-stains.

"I know," he says, "I know. And a clock, we need to get one of those, or we'll be forever arguing with you lot about whether the deadlines have passed. Did your boyfriend know how much *work* this would be?"

Isaella grins. "I'm afraid he did. He might even apologise, if you shout at him."

"Will he mean it?"

"Now you're asking too much."

"Then I shan't ask. Shouldn't you be in the Senate already?"

"It's not that late, is it? Is it? Oh, damn, it is, goodbye, thank you!"

Luckily, the new hub is directly across from the Senate. She arrives thirty seconds late, enough for Marianne to raise an eyebrow at her, but in time for the start of business.

"First on today's agenda," Marianne says, so familiar with the forms she doesn't need the notes in her hand, "the new Civil Service tent has been procured as per the requests made by several Imperial bodies last summit. All Senate business will be conducted in the Senate as before. Motions should be raised using the same paperwork and signed off by the Senate civil servants. The only difference is that you can now find us across the road in the Civil Service tent instead of out amongst the camps. Second, and this is just for information as we are already at war with them, and have been since the Empire was founded, but the Civil Service can confirm that the Druj are once again massing on the border with Holberg. The Senate may wish to bear that in mind when allocating the budget."

Soft laughter answers her. Marianne's eyes crinkle. "Now, we'll proceed to regular order. Holberg proposes a new fortification in Reikos, to be built on the former site of Levi's Stand. Necropolis seconds. Senator, say your piece."

"I'll hand over to Reikos for this."

"Um, hi." The new Senator for Reikos is vaguely familiar and Isaella hunts through her memory for blonde hair braided against the skull, until she manages to place her as Adina. "I'm from Rachel's Guard – I'm one of the ones who surrendered." She stares defensively at the public gallery until the muttering subsides. "Anyway, I didn't want to raise this myself, because Reikos shouldn't really be asking for new fortifications right now, but we do actually need this one. Levi's Stand was a major part of our western defences – most of our patrols were resupplied from there, or at one step remove – and we're struggling to maintain a border guard without it. We're proposing to put it on the same site because it still has its foundations and most of the walls, so it would cost less than building something from scratch nearby, but I do want to say – Levi's Stand, as a chapter, has been dissolved and the new fort would not be run by the same people, it would be a whole new chapter. The same place, but not the *same place*. Yeah."

Marianne gives her a moment to elaborate further before she opens up the debate. Several senators have their hands raised to speak. "Holberg, you first, then Astolat."

The proposal passes, but barely. Isaella works her way over to Adina as the session is closing. "Come and get coffee, Reikos."

Adina spins around in surprise. "I – what – sorry, I'm still not used to that."

"Give it time. But really, let's get you out of here before anyone tries rehashing that argument."

"Oh. Okay, that makes sense." Adina follows her out of the Senate, still looking nervously around. "Did I do alright? That was my first Senate speech."

"You did fine. Honestly."

"You couldn't tell?"

"Well – no, I could tell. You were very nervous. But you'll get over that. In six months, it won't bother you anymore."

There is, predictably, a line for the coffee stall. They settle in to wait behind a knot of Freeborn haggling over where to drink tonight.

Adina puts her hood back with a sigh. "I didn't want to be Senator, you know. I just got given the job because we're so short of people."

"Reikos does look smaller than it used to."

"It is. Rachel's Guard had twice as many people before the secession, people who would come to Anvil, I mean, and it's the same for everyone. And Levi's Stand has been completely broken up. Some of them lived and have come with other chapters but only about three. So they were short of options, and they gave it to me and now I'm – I am captain of the doghouse."

"Mm. That's why I wanted to talk to you. We need to change that narrative."

"But it's real though, isn't it? I mean – we seceded. That happened. A lot of people died."

Isaella shrugs. "It did, and they did, but it's not on you. Miriam holds the blame for that, and the exarchs who listened to her."

"But we followed, too." Adina's shoulders slump. "If it had been Navarr – and I'm not just beating myself up here, this is true – if it had been Navarr, it would never have happened, because even if someone had got all the Brands in Therunin to agree, the Navarri wouldn't have gone along with it. But we're Highborn, so we do what we're told, and we killed our own. And now everyone knows that's all it takes. One general with a grudge."

"Alright," Isaella says. "Black coffee, please, with cinnamon syrup. Adina, you can tell me how bad your nation is, but is that really what you want people to think?"

"It's what they *do* think."

"It's not what I think. I remember most of your nation *not* seceding. Even some Reikos chapters were right with us in that last battle." She takes her coffee with a quiet thanks to the merchant. "But even if they think that – they're the same people who think the Navarri will betray them, because we betray our enemies."

"Oh." Adina goes quiet while she adds sugar to her tea. "Because of what happened to Miriam, you mean."

"Every few years we give them another reminder. I give it twelve hours before someone proposes sending the Navarr into Holberg, because if we fight like Druj we should go against them."

"I was surprised. I mean, I shouldn't have been, I know how Navarr fight, but I guess..."

"You thought we'd be more honourable in a civil war."

"Did you know it was going to happen?" Adina finally looks up from her drink, her eyes wide in the dusk.

"I didn't know the archer," Isaella says quietly. "I didn't know what she was planning. But yes, I was expecting someone to do it."

"I don't think I follow," Adina says, despairing. "Why's it the same? You didn't do anything wrong, not really, and we definitely did."

"Because the people who are offended will stay offended. You can't apologise enough for them. If you're ashamed, you just convince them they were right about you. You have to act like you still belong."

"Okay. Okay. I think I get it." Adina turns downhill automatically, towards the Highguard camp, and Isaella follows her lead. There are worse ideas than making some friends in Highguard today.

"So," Isaella says, "what are you going to do with your Senate motion?"

"What?"

"Your Senate motion. You got Holberg to raise the fortification for you today, so you still have yours left."

Adina's eyes go even wider. "Oh, Virtues. I have no idea. I don't know how to do this job! Isaella, help me, I don't know *anything*. I'm a brewer! That's what I do!"

"Okay." Isaella puts an arm around her shoulders. "First, breathe. You need to breathe. Second, drink your tea. And third, the only politics I know is the conniving bastard kind, so I'm going to ask you to do something for me."

"Of course," Adina says, trusting. "What do you need?"

"I'm looking for a changeling who might have survived the war."

CHAPTER FORTY-TWO – AUTUMN 206

On a mercifully dry autumn equinox, Nicovar is sitting on a table in the Hub. The smell of the dye is still seeping from the canvas, the table is in reality one of the huge crates used to store the big tent between uses, but the system is working. The Civil Service, reluctant at first, have adopted the idea as if it had been their own, and taken the name he argued against just to rub it in. Attendance and off-Anvil property rights are still handled in the row of battered awnings outside of the summit proper, but for anything that requires Anvil staff, citizens are being sent here. There's a growing heap of cushions in one corner for the civil servants to use as an office.

Three of the new information boards have fallen on their faces already today and one of them has been part-eaten by rats in storage, but Nicovar is ignoring that along with the name.

It's early morning, too early for the Hub to really be open. Nicovar is here with an untidy sweet pastry, flaking its crumbs into his lap as he eats. Ankarien are hungover this morning and he can't wait for the cooking fire to heat back up. There's a battle to be fought soon.

He brushes the crumbs onto the floor and steps out of his quiet moment, into the gathering bustle in the Senate. Last summit they tried to centralise in the Hub, but the Civil Service immediately kicked them out; the Senate is the nearest place and so the support magicians have gathered here, under the watchful eye of the Warmage. She has the kind of mental list he used to keep, of covens and ritual strengths and targets, but hers is concentrated on the enchantments that keep a fighter on her feet, or break an enemy's line.

She nods to him as he comes up the ramp. "Empress, Are you fighting today?"

"I am."

"Are you in a banner?"

"No, Ankarien doesn't – Don't rework your numbers for me, I can see you doing it. I didn't come looking for enchantment. Only to talk strategy, when you've a moment."

Before the secession, Felicia would have dropped everything to make time. Now, having survived that awful time without losing her office, she has a new confidence. The works she is doing comes first. Nicovar perches on the arm of his throne to wait for her.

"Alright," Felicia says, after two groups of warriors have been lined up for the Navarri magician who is working through rounds of a simple enchantment with apparently endless mana supplies, "I've got a minute now. The Urizeni sort themselves out and the Winterfolk will come in a rush at the last minute."

"This seems to have caught on very quickly. You weren't doing this last year, this kind of organisation."

"No. Well, I was, but I was working the pairings out in advance and telling people which camps to go to. This saves me a good hour of tracking magicians down in the dark. It's better."

Nicovar nods. "I wanted to ask about the battle tomorrow."

"Against the Thule?"

"Mm. We'll need to cast the pillar ritual three times almost simultaneously and we can't know how far apart those pillars are until we get there. Do you have three covens for it?"

Felicia pulls a face. "You really screwed me over, sending Urizen to Holberg. I know most of you don't do Autumn but I could have used Ankarien."

"Sorry about that. Though we're not as strong in Autumn as we used to be, some people have stopped coming. But tell me honestly, can you do it, or do you need a miracle? We have time. We have a full day. We can work a miracle if you need one."

"I think I can do without the miracle. I just need a couple of Archmages to glue covens together, and luckily two of those are in the League."

"That's right, the new Summermage is in your carta. Congratulations."

"Thank you." Felicia looks rightfully proud – building the connections to hold two Conclave posts in a single coven is no small feat.

"And how are things with Isolt?"

Felicia looks straight at him, trying to keep her face blank, but unpracticed at it. A smile tugs at her lips. "Things are fine, thank you."

Nicovar smiles back. "Okay, okay, I won't pry. But can you do me a favour?"

"Of course."

"Add me to your scrying list."

She shakes her head. "Can't do that. I need Ankarien to cast Master Strategist."

"No, I know that – Ankarien will still be doing that. But organising that many people, plus a general, plus me, hasn't been working, and they can reach the magnitude without me. Lucius and I are forming our own smaller coven for scrying rituals. Those are easier to organise and his apprentice is willing to join with us. We can do both the Eyes rituals with full mastery."

"Hmm." Felicia is staring over his shoulder, her eyes unfocused as she calculates.

"Only ourselves, though, no covenstone, so we can only do two rituals a day for now."

"Does that include today? I know you're battling, but I want to get a look at Spiral and we had to leave it off the list-"

"Yes, we can do Spiral today. Both ways?"

"If you have the mana for it, yes."

"We can fund ourselves for this summit. I'll let you know about next time."

She nods. "In advance, please. Funding is easier if we get it all at once."

"I remember. I'll give you enough warning. Thank you, Warmage. I haven't cast a ritual for the Empire in a year, and I hate feeling useless."

It seems like a normal battle at first. The Imperials have come to rescue a group of stranded civilians from the path of the Druj army. They're being harassed by a forward unit, only two hundred orcs, but that's enough to put an unfortified village in danger. The Anvil heroes intend to wipe it out, and perhaps demoralise the Druj slave soldiers who follow after.

For nearly an hour the battle goes on, a stubborn knot of orcs holding the road between drainage ditches that make flanking them difficult. The Imperials make themselves a crossing and create a second line at the back, pinning the Druj forces in place. The civilians have armed themselves, those who can, and come up to join in the battle. Most of them are unpracticed, but any adult citizen has been taught to use a weapon. Their numbers help.

Until there is an unexpected screaming from within the civilian forces, and a collapse of their front line.

Nicovar is caught up in the Urizen ranks, working in concert with the sentinels. He knows some basic combat magic, and a rod to the skull is just as good as a sword. The screaming breaks him out of his focus – he barely guards himself against an orcish spear – and he starts working his way back from the line. He needs to get eyes on whatever is happening with the Leaguers.

It takes him more than a minute to get clear of the fighting. Over on the other side, where the civilians should be bunched up to hold their place, there is an inward-turning chaos. A dozen people are bleeding out into the grass.

Nicovar grabs the nearest shoulder. "What happened?"

"They just turned on us! They're traitors!" The Leaguer is wild-eyed with fury. "They just started *killing* us!"

"Leave it with me. We need you to hold the line, friend. The Druj are still coming."

"Who the fuck are you?"

Nicovar straightens up. "I'm the Empress," he says, matter-of-fact.

"Oh, shit."

"I'll figure this out, I promise, I will fix it, but I need you to get your friends and keep fighting. Alright?" He turns the man by his shoulder. "Are you hearing me? Fight *them*. I know you can get your friends to pull together. I will fix this, but we have to keep fighting."

His new friend nods. A deep breath, a sigh, and he's stepping forwards towards the struggling front line and shouting to the Leaguers around him to focus.

That will do for a start. Nicovar moves towards the centre of the mess. The fighting has worn itself down to wariness, civilians brandishing swords at each other, guarded and frightened.

Nicovar raises his voice. "The Druj! The Druj are coming!"

He can see a Wintermark captain on the other side, doing much the same work. They get the line rebuilt, as much as they can, but a full third of the civilians are just standing around. Thank the Fates it's a road battle and the Druj can't move to chase them.

"Okay," he says at last, to a woman examining the fresh corpses. "Tell me what happened here."

"Traitors," he says later, resting in Ankarien's meeting tent. "That's what happened with the villagers. I just don't understand how they could have got there."

James settles a blanket over his cloak. He's folded up on a pile of rugs, almost round despite his long legs. "Don't they live there?"

"Not the traitors. Nobody recognised them. They were dressed like Leaguers and there have been people moving in towards Holberg for months, trying to get clear of danger, so nobody was suspicious. But they must have been working with the Druj."

"Nobody works *with* the Druj," Isaella says, "Only *for* them. They keep a lot of slaves."

"Mm. But I'm worried about the orcish labourers in Holberg. We can't afford an uprising."

"You mean *our* slaves? I'd be worried about that, too. If they hear humans are turning to the Druj side it'll only encourage them."

"I don't understand why any human would."

"Maybe they didn't," James says. "I mean, if nobody knew them – Maybe they weren't traitors. Not Imperials at all. Maybe they were just Druj."

Isaella grins. "If they can't beat us, they'll out-breed us?"

"Maybe. Either way, if they've used that tactic once they'll use it again. It's going to be an ugly war."

"They always are."

They're spread out in the meeting room, but only the three of them are left now, and Isaella takes advantage of the space to move to a cushion next to James. She sits cross-legged, looking suddenly nervous. "Speaking of breeding."

James blinks. He sits up.

"I'm not, yet," Isaella says, hastily. "But I'd like us to talk about it. I always thought, one day, I'd settle down and that's when I'd think about it. And I seem to have settled here."

Nicovar lowers himself to the floor alongside them. "I never thought about it," he says.

"I did. But I stopped, when I married Nic, no offense."

"None taken, I *would* find it difficult to conceive."

"Well, exactly." James shuffles forward. "Is it – I mean, do you – How does it work, among Navarri? Do we need to, I don't know, formally marry you? Nic, what do you think?"

Nicovar takes a moment. There's an excited tingle along his spine, the kind he gets when any new ambition is proposed. "I have questions," he says. "I have concerns, even. But they all seem to be logistical. I'm not opposed to the idea."

"The way it works in Navarr, I don't have to – I could find a willing Navarri to sire a baby for me and then walk separate ways, and that would be fine. But I never wanted to be a solo parent."

James reaches for her hand. "You don't have to be," he says quietly. "You don't have to do it alone. We won't make you do it alone."

CHAPTER FORTY-THREE – WINTER 206

Anvil mud is a familiar enemy. Isaella knows it, how it will cake on the sides of her boots and weigh her down all summit, how the ridges will show her where it's solid enough to walk. It makes everything she does more exhausting, on a day when she's already fighting the cold. She must have grown soft since she left the army.

Today she is in good company. Every soul at Anvil is struggling through this same mud, waiting for the bitter evening that will, as one small mercy in the dark, freeze the ground and let them walk on top of it. Sveta has climbed a tree near the Sentinel Gate, to watch the fighters marching back. Isaella heads over to her, trying not to slip.

"Usually people watch them going *out*, my friend."

Sveta swings her feet. "I know that. I'm not watching for the parade."

"Why are you watching, then?"

"Highguard was fighting today."

Isaella drags her cloak tighter around her shoulders, trying to interpret that. "You're looking for Tabitha?"

"I think I've found her. I'm not *sure*," she adds hurriedly, "not for certain, but I think I have. Or maybe her sister? There's a merrow who looks very familiar, and I know there are ways to do that, magically. So I'm watching Highguard battles to see if she moves how I think she will. Or if her friend with the knife is there."

"Thank you," Isaella says, considering that. "I've asked Senator Adina to keep an eye out, but I don't think she will."

"Coward," Sveta says, scornful. "She's scared of losing her job."

"She's scared of doing it, as well. It's not easy, being the Reikos senator right now. She's trying to keep the peace."

"Well, *I* don't care about the peace. Did you know Jo Shepherd is going to be voted down tonight?"

Isaella blinks at her. "Who?"

Sveta looks down and grins. "The Rod and Shield Grandmaster. Don't you talk to the Consort? He's running for it."

"No, I knew that, I just didn't – why are you so sure about Jo Shepherd?"

"She's not very good at being Grandmaster. I don't know about the meetings, I can't get into those – they really should hold Conclave on the field – but she doesn't know what to do when people argue with her. And they're the battle magicians. They argue all the time. So they're all fed up and either James or Sarai will get it. I don't know which yet."

"Do you think you could affect it?"

"What?"

Isaella leans on her own tree. "I mean, if I wanted to put pressure on that election, I could. Even though the Conclave isn't my business, I'd know who to start talking to."

"Well, everyone knows about you and James-"

"It's not a secret. That's not my point. I'm asking – I'm realising how much you listen. How much you notice. I'm asking, is that all you want to do, or are you running for something?"

"Senator," Sveta says, decisively. "I'm not a magician and I don't want to be a priest. I could be a General, maybe, but I'd rather be Senator. It's going to take me a few years, though, I need to learn tact."

"You-" Isaella laughs.

"I do! Auntie says it all the time. That's why I'm watching. I need to see how it's done."

"I see you have one Senator on side already."

Sveta grins. "I'm counting on you."

Isaella, like Sveta, is barred from the Conclave chamber. It's not a legal barrier, the kind that keeps her out of private auctions. It's just that the votes are held in the Hall of Worlds, and she can't reach it without a magician's skill or a trinket more expensive than she can justify. So instead, as the Rod and Shield straggle into the eye-bending void between the regio stones, she watches the scrying rituals.

Felicia is managing them all, deftly keeping track of which covens have gone and which are waiting to work. Nicovar explained to her once why the regio mattered, but half of it was algebra and the other half magical theory; it didn't sink in. What she knows is that the regio helps them work.

"Hi," Nicovar says from behind her.

She glances over her shoulder to smile at him.

"What are you thinking?" he asks.

"That they don't even look like they're using different weapons."

"Sorry? Run that by me again?"

Isaella shrugs. "I've never really stopped to watch before. They're all doing the same ritual, I know that, because Felicia keeps confirming the name of it. But it's not like fighting with a spear, versus fighting with a rod. Those look different but you can see the goal is the same. But this? One minute they're using mirrors and the next it's a puppet show. I don't get it."

"I'll tell you a deep magical secret," Nicovar says, "nobody gets it. Even scholars of comparative magic have a way that *they* perform rituals. I couldn't do Marcher dramaturgy if you paid me."

"That's the puppet shows?"

"That's the puppet shows. What time is it?"

"Nearly time for Senate. I was hoping James would come out victorious before then. Are you going to watch?"

"I'm going to do a ritual, if there's time before Senate. Where's Felicia? Sorry, Isaella, I'll see you in the Senate. Felicia, I need to interrupt your list -"

Nicovar's ritual is not the same scrying magic Felicia has been marshalling all afternoon. He starts with a silver bowl of water, held up by an expressionless youngster from his spire, and he and Lucius weave strange patterns of starlight into the air. The water begins to glow, gradually, reflecting absent moonlight.

"Leviathan," Nicovar says at last, "by crystal and silver, I claim the right of knowledge. I cast myself into the depths of your ocean. I have come to listen to your voice in the deeps. I have come to ask you *why*."

"Speak your question," Lucius responds, "and Leviathan will hear you."

"I have come to ask you this: Why are there traitors in the lands of Holberg, where there were none before this invasion?"

Lucius nods sharply, whether in assent or approval Isaella can't tell. The stones around them are deep black in the gathering dusk, the faint mage-light casting impossible shadows. The inside of the circle is wrong, subtly, an underwater distortion. Isaella thinks her legs are shivering from weariness, until the rumbling gathers into a voice.

"Hmmm. A good question. A good question, indeed, for an Emperor. Why are there traitors in the lands of Holberg? Why are there traitors now? But it is difficult, Emperor, to answer your questions when you bring them to me upside down. There are no traitors in Holberg. A traitor must be turned. Those who oppose you in Holberg have always been your enemies. I see only Druj there."

Nicovar turns on the spot, as if trying to pinpoint the voice. "You mean they're spies."

"They are slaves, Emperor. You keep them yourselves, you should know what they are. The Druj took many prisoners, the last time they invaded. A slave is ruled by fear, not loyalty. Fear is a powerful force."

James fades into existence from the dark surface of a regio stone. He's grinning, ready to celebrate, until he feels the earth groaning underfoot and swallows his laughter. He steps quickly over to Isaella and whispers, "Leviathan?"

Isaella nods. "He asked about the traitors in Holberg."

"Ahh." James nods sharply and stands with her to watch. She finds his hand and squeezes it, a silent congratulations.

"Not all slaves," Leviathan is saying, in that bone-shaking bass voice. "Yours might not be. But the Druj are fierce against rebellion. They are not sure enough of your victory to disobey their orders."

"So we can't turn them to our side?"

A humming, underfoot and in the breastbone. "I do not see the future, Emperor. You might do many things."

"What would you recommend?"

"One question was your promise, and one answer you have had. You should speak to the others, for that one. It is not in my domain to answer it."

Nicovar nods. "Of course. Thank you for your – insight."

"It was a good question." The voice sounds almost wistful. "Speak to me again, Emperor. It is good for you to understand."

Isaella knows Nic's face. That little twitch around the eyes is a smile, escaping his Urizeni calm. "I'll come with good questions, if I come."

Lucius has his hand outstretched over the silver bowl. He waits for Nicovar's nod before he touches the water, spinning its surface and scattering the eerie light. The ground shivers for a moment longer, and goes silent.

"Did we learn anything, there?"

"No," his apprentice says. "That is – perhaps. We didn't *know* they were spies before. We only suspected they might be."

Nicovar rubs his eyes. "We didn't learn how to find them. We're just going to keep losing civilians until we figure it out. Damn that philosophical thing, I needed information, not musings about slave loyalty."

"Well, it didn't cost us much," Lucius says. "We did some diplomacy. We learned one thing. I can tell you something else for free."

"What?"

"Your husband is standing over there grinning like a new Grandmaster."

CHAPTER FORTY-FOUR – SPRING 207

Lucrezia stands in the Conclave circle, shaking with anger. The dim light of the glowstones shivers on her glittering mask, on the gems embroidered into her doublet. Her shirt is yellow silk, gleaming through the slits in her sleeves. Every face is turned towards her.

"This is unconscionable," she says. "No, I will not surrender my time – There is no question to be asked here. This is an outrage. Holberg is an Imperial territory, occupied by Imperials. It is a major population centre. Do you realise how many people live in the city of Holberg? This is not empty farmland! You are proposing to unleash *plague* upon our city. I will not stand for it!"

"You don't have to," Felicia mutters.

Lucrezia whirls on her. "Don't get too comfortable, Warmage. I've toppled that position before. If you collect this gambit, if you cast this ritual, I will see you cursed. I will *ruin* you if you do this thing. Holberg is not a place on a map. It is real, it is living-"

"One minute," Ruth says clearly. Lucrezia holds out a mana crystal, buying herself more time.

"I have not forgotten about -" Felicia says, but Lucrezia snaps "This is still my time," and the Warmage falls silent.

Lucrezia turns back to the room. "I know there's been no vote on this. I know the Conclave cannot forbid this. *I* forbid this. Me! Because those who should defend it will make my city into a sacrifice. When Reikos rebelled, they took every precaution to save Highborn lives, but Holberg? They will throw us on the pyre. If you fund this, you are my enemy. If you cast this, I will come for you. Understand? Good."

In the silence that follows, Ruth looks towards Nicovar, next in the order of precedence. "Any further comments from the Throne?"

Nicovar steps between the seated magicians in the front row, into the circle. He drops a crystal into Ruth's hand as he goes. Lucrezia has not yielded the space. She stands, arms folded, glaring at him.

"I respect the feelings of my colleague," he says. "None of us could happily contemplate Rivers Run Red cast upon our homes. But this is not being done out of spite. It is done with grief. We do not wish for Holberg to suffer. This is a surgeon inducing a fever. The Druj are digging in for the summer. If we want to end this quickly, we need this ritual. The Grandmaster may curse me – it's legal – but I stand with the Warmage and her strategy."

The room mutters around them. Beneath her mask, Lucrezia's eyes are red with tears.

Ruth asks, "Are you finished, Empress? Then are there any further comments from the Rod and Shield?"

James is standing near the back, scrubbing at his beard with one hand. "Does anyone from my order wish to speak?"

A Highborn in a red hood raises her hand, and James nods to her.

"I'm from Reikos," she says, bluntly. "My chapter seceded. And if you'd cast Rivers Run Red on us, it would have been fair. You would've had the right. It's on the books for a reason. If we didn't think it should be used, we could have interdicted it any time. Grandmaster, if it was my home in danger, would you be making these threats?"

Lucrezia's breath heaves. "No," she snaps. "My loyalty is to Holberg, I will not be ashamed of it-"

"My time, Grandmaster. Then, like Nicovar said, I appreciate your feelings. I understand. But we should still do this, because strategically, it's still needed."

Ruth makes a little tally on her notebook, keeping track of the orders. "The Golden Pyramid passed. Any further comments from the Shuttered Lantern?"

"I'll nominate the Warmage, again."

Felicia steps forward. Nicovar eases back, to give her space – Lucrezia still hasn't moved, making herself the opposition to every speaker, but the circle is only so big.

"Yes. People are going to die. Imperial citizens are going to die. Do you know why? Because the Druj invaded us. This gambit – I'll remind you again, we don't need the Conclave's permission for this, we're just asking for funding – was agreed with the Military Council yesterday. They asked me what they could have and I advised them to do this. We're using other strategic rituals on the armies to minimise our own casualties. This isn't reckless. It's hard, it's ugly, but it's necessary."

"Unfettered Mind and Sevenfold Path have already passed. Celestial Arch?"

"I mean it about the cursing," Lucrezia says, quieter now, to make them all listen. "I mean it, that when you choose this, you are my enemy. Every single one of you. You are poisoning my home. I will do the same to yours. For every stone that falls, you will pay. This is a reckoning written in blood."

Ruth shuffles her papers. "Threats are not illegal, citizens," she says mildly. "Anything further from the Throne?"

Nicovar looks at Lucrezia for a long moment, a figure in black velvet, furious and alone in the Conclave circle. "Let's proceed to the voting," he says at last. "The arguments have been made."

"Rod and Shield?"

"Anyone? No? Then let's vote."

"Shuttered Lantern?"

"Warmage, anything to add? We'll pass, Ruth."

Ruth checks it off on her list and looks over to Lucrezia. "Celestial Arch, if you have the mana?"

Lucrezia lifts her chin. "Vote."

They get one minute to discuss the gambit amongst their Orders, before the Grandmasters are asked to pledge their funds. Lucrezia is still holding the space, a silent counterpart to the Warmage in her gilded mage-armour. No need for discussion. They all know how the Celestial Arch will decide.

Ruth readies her pen and runs through the orders, unmoved by the rhetoric, sounding almost bored. The Throne has no mana funds, but Nicovar doesn't need them. The gambit is comparatively small, and the Rod and Shield stand stubbornly with James as he pledges twice the usual share for his order. The others follow his lead, and the Celestial Arch are never asked for their pledge. There's nothing left for them to give.

Nicovar lingers in the Hall of Worlds afterwards, not wanting to step out into the dark and Lucrezia's accusing anger. Easier to let her go back to the League, first, and plot with her sister how to get their revenge.

The Warmage is gnawing on her thumbnail. She looks at him when he wanders over. "Are we doing right, Empress?"

"We got the gambit passed, so the Conclave thinks we are. I think we are. What do you think?"

"I think a lot of people are going to die in Holberg."

"You knew that yesterday."

"I didn't know it quite so clearly. That's not really what has me worried. Lucrezia and Cressida make bad enemies."

"That's also why they make good allies."

"Do they?" Felicia looks at him sideways. "You do know Cressida's a magician, don't you?"

"She's – Is she, then? I wondered. I've never caught them out."

Felicia nods. "They both have night pouches and I've seen Cressida working hers. That's not a magical item. That's a spell. So they're both magicians, and they're pretending not to be. What else might they be hiding?"

"A pair of cambion Autumn mages?" Nicovar taps his fingers against his arm. "Almost anything. Not that I ever thought – You're right. That could be useful to know, when they go all out against us."

"You think that as well, then. That they're going to."

"I would be astonished if they didn't follow through on those threats. That was the most sincere I've ever seen Lucrezia be. I think we touched a nerve."

"Holberg is her home."

"It's not just that."

Felicia thinks about it. "No. Not just that. They're frightened they're losing power. James wasn't supposed to get back into the Conclave. They didn't bargain for that."

"What else are they afraid of?"

"Are you trying to find weak spots?"

Nicovar shrugs. "Of course. We might need them."

"Me, then," Felicia says. "They're worried about me. That's ironic, I know. But I'm like James, I didn't follow the path they planned for me. I think I was supposed to be temporary. I know I was supposed to fall in love with one of their carta. She pursued me all year. They just weren't counting on Isolt."

"Dawnish can be very compelling," Nicovar agrees. "I've tussled with a few in my time. Thank you, by the way. For speaking for that gambit yourself."

Felicia nods. "I could have asked the Summermage. But Antonio's a sweetheart, he really is, and he's brilliant at all the posturing and flattery, but he doesn't do well with this kind of thing. The internal conflict, and the hard choices. He likes things to be clear."

"We need people like him."

"To keep people like us on the level."

"Amongst other things." Nicovar smiles bitterly. "Spies in Holberg and enemies at Anvil. It's going to be an interesting year, Warmage."

CHAPTER FORTY-FIVE – SUMMER 207

Isaella is running through the woods towards the screaming. The sun is still high, the summit barely started, brambles snatching at her ankles as she goes. It's coming from deeper into the trees, beyond the bare-earth tracks.

These woods are well kept but the trees are leafy with summer. Isaella can't see anything until she gets close, and by then the noise has resolved into words, into someone shouting frantically for a physick. Three people are on the floor, one in the dark colours of Highguard, all of them bleeding. Isaella drops to her knees and shakes the nearest casualty by the shoulder. He is a Navarri vate with a feathered serpent tattooed across his cheek. His face is wet with blood.

"What happened?" she demands. "What were you doing?"

This is a magician's injury, familiar from years of bad news around campfires. It happens when they overreach, or misstep in their rituals. Bleeding from the eyes.

"I don't know," the magician gasps out. "I don't know, I didn't – it just *snapped* – please, get help -"

"I'm here," Cressida says briskly, jogging up behind Isaella. There's a dark crack spiralling along one of her horns, an old injury gradually splitting it in two, that Isaella can't remember seeing before. She lets Cress takes over with her surgeon's kit, pulling out a bundle of bandages and salve, and Isaella moves on to the fallen Highborn.

Ice drops into her belly when she pulls back the dark hood. She knows this face. Half-transformed into a merrow, with gills peeling open on her neck, but her ears are still raggedly scarred. Tabitha.

Isaella is no physick. She can't do anything for an injury except put pressure on it, and that won't help here. Not with the narrow fletching of a crossbow bolt still half-buried in Tabitha's back. She can only call to the Navarri running up with bandages tucked into their bandoleers, and say, "Save her life. We need to execute her later."

She stands over the scene, watchful, as Cressida patches up the magicians and the crossbow bolt is noisily extracted from the struggling assassin. There is no sign of the archer, but it's been more than a minute since the screaming began. Anvil's woods are only so wide. They'll be back in camp by now, pretending they didn't hear anything. Whoever they are, they've done Isaella a favour.

A suspicion begins to tickle in the back of her mind.

Tabitha is put back together, enough to keep her from dying from either the injury or the botched ritual effects, though both are likely to scar. The ritualists are helped to their feet, blood still staining their faces but no lasting harm done. One of the Archmagi has arrived, looming between the trees with her arms crossed, to demand answers from them. Isaella leaves the magicians to it. If they did anything illegal, she'll hear about it later. For now she has a magistrate to see.

Sally is just coming on duty down at the Hub. She looks up from a stack of mismatched papers – posters to be stuck up around camp, reminding the more fractious citizens of what the right to exclude someone from camp actually entails – and her face falls. "Senator. What are you doing to this Highborn?"

"Bringing her to you," Isaella says briskly. "I would like to bring evidence against this citizen for involvement in murder."

Sally straightens up. "Right. Citizen, what's your name?"

"Sara," Tabitha says, her half-transformed face contorting around the word. "Of the Granite Pillar."

"Tabitha," Isaella responds, "of Miriam's inner circle."

"I'll remind you, Senator, that the only formal *crime* committed by Miriam of Highguard was tax evasion. I can certainly impose a fine on this citizen if she participated in that, but nothing worse. The secession was not illegal, and you know that."

"I said murder, not seceding. This is one of the assassins."

Tabitha's head turns sharply. She bares her teeth. "That's a lie."

"Enough," Sally says sharply. "You've brought this to me, now let me handle it. Senator, you've got an hour to bring me your evidence. Citizen, I'm sorry, but we're going to hold you for that time while we sort this out. If you've got friends in Highguard who can confirm your identity, let me know. And can we get this enchantment removed? It's confusing matters. Are there any magicians in here?"

Isaella allows herself ten seconds to breathe. She watches Sally turn away from her papers, looking for a magician, looking for a runner. She watches a scowling Navarr let go of Tabitha's arms and stand, arms folded, waiting for her to run. Then she turns on her heel and heads back into the bright sunlight, looking for Sveta.

She finds her in the public gallery, standing on one of the benches. Sveta makes her eyes go wide at the sight of her, looking between Isaella and the Senate floor, already in session without her. Isaella shrugs and beckons, insistent, until Sveta hops down and follows her back outside.

"Why are you *late*," Sveta demands, "you're meant to be *in there*, that's your job!"

"Something came up. I need you to come and talk to the magistrates."

"To the what? Why? What's happened?"

"You haven't heard -" Isaella frowns. Sveta is looking at her still wide-eyed, the picture of innocence. That nagging suspicion grows. "Someone tracked down Tabitha and shot her during a ritual. I need you to come and explain what your saw when Roland was murdered."

Sveta nods enthusiastically. "Of course, I can do that. It's so lucky that someone found her!"

"Mm. Isn't it?"

Sally is tall, and Sveta is not. They compromise by sitting on the cushions the Civil Service use for their office, letting Ruth the Conclave mistress mutter to herself and find a table to lean on. Sally sets a sheaf of rough paper on her knee. "Alright. You're an Imperial citizen?"

"I am now," Sveta says cheerfully. "Roland's murder happened before my test."

"So an Imperial child at the time. That's fine. Could you tell me, please, what you saw on the night of Sir Roland's murder, and why you believe this woman is the assassin?"

Sveta makes a good story of it. She sits up straight, her voice hushed, and leans so much on the atmosphere of a moonlit night and a green field that Sally has to chivvy her along. The murder itself happened quickly – an unarmed victim, and a practiced assassin with a poisoned knife – but Sveta gives enough detail to be sure that she really could recognise Tabitha.

Sally rubs at her forehead. "That's more or less what Isaella told me at the time. You got that from her, Isaella? Okay. So you didn't speak to her or know her name."

"She ran a message for Miriam," Isaella explains, "Nicovar got her name when she arrived. It might not have been her real name, but she wasn't dressed up as a merrow that time. She looked like herself."

"Scarred ears," Sveta says, and flicks at her own undamaged ones.

"There are a lot of Highborn with scarred ears. You saw her from a distance, in the dark – I'll accept she's the woman who ran the message, there are many witnesses to that, but I don't know if I can take your word that she's also involved in the murders. And, you said yourself, she did not wield the knife."

Sveta looks stunned. "You're letting her *go*? You can't do that!"

"I *can*, young citizen. In fact, I must. I cannot execute an Imperial citizen who denies all involvement with a crime for which there is only one witness, and which in any case she was only an accessory to. The most I can do is impose a fine, which I will, for tax evasion. Involvement in the murders I have to rule is unproven. I'm sorry."

"But-"

"Come back when you have more evidence and we'll try again."

Sveta stands up. "You don't believe me," she says. "You think I'm stupid. I hate you. I hate you!"

Sally watches her run out into the dusk. She sighs. "Isaella, I wish your witness was more reliable."

"So do I," Isaella says. She stands up to follow. "Do you need me, Magistrate?"

"Not unless you can tell me something that will convince me."

"You'll forgive me for saying it, but I wish that archer had had better aim."

Sveta has climbed into her usual tree, up by the Sentinel Gate. There's a group of Freeborn gathering to go on an expedition, but Sveta isn't watching them. She's kicking her heels against the bark and glaring at Isaella as she approaches.

"Sally's being stupid," she says, once Isaella is within reach.

"Is she?"

"It's Tabitha, and she did it, and you *know* she did! Why isn't that enough? She's supposed to be dead!"

Isaella leans against the tree, facing out across the field. "In Navarr, we have a saying."

"Is it, *Always shoot from hiding*?"

"That's a different saying. This one is, *Actions have consequences*. When you choose to act then you choose the consequences, whatever they are. Whether it goes to your plan or not. If someone shoots an assassin mid-ritual and doesn't kill them, then the consequences will follow."

"I didn't shoot her," Sveta says sullenly.

"I didn't ask. If I knew you had, there would be consequences I'd rather avoid."

Disbelief from the branches above her. "Would you turn me in?"

"We live in an Empire that depends upon laws. If you want to be a Senator, you need to think about that. We are here, in Anvil, to make and change the laws. We can't be exempt from them. If you could get away with murder just by coming here, why should you think that the law matters in Liathaven?"

Sveta kicks the tree again. "Laws are just rules. We make them up."

"Of course we do. That's why we have to keep them. If the Empire does not have laws, it will fall apart. We are too different from each other. The Empire is – it's a net, holding us together. We can't cut holes in it."

"But it's not *fair*. She tried to kill you, she deserves to die."

"Justice is not a virtue-"

"Neither is obedience." Sveta clambers to a lower perch. "Do you want to know what I saw? Lucrezia and Cressida don't look alike."

Isaella blinks. "Pardon?"

"They're using the same magic that Tabitha was. To pretend. And they always dress exactly the same. Why do they need to *stay* identical?" She looks sideways at Isaella, smiling with teenage spite. "You should probably ask them about that."

Isaella struggles for a moment, certain she hasn't persuaded Sveta of anything, and gives up. "Okay. I'm going to the League-"

"Thought you might."

"Don't get into any more trouble tonight. Please."

She's only steps away when she hears Sveta dropping to the ground. "Wait! Isaella, wait! When's the baby due?"

"What?" Isaella turns slowly. "How do you know about that?"

"You're showing," Sveta says, scornful, "and James's coven leader is knitting baby clothes. I'm not *stupid*, you know."

CHAPTER FORTY-SIX – AUTUMN 207

The Hall of Worlds is dark this evening. Half the glow-stones have burned out, damaged on their journey from the workshops of Urizen, and the remaining light throws shadows over Lucrezia's face.

She is masked, just as she always has been whenever Nicovar has seen her. She is dressed in a black doublet, yellow silk spilling through its opened sleeves, matching the clothes of her twin who waits in Anvil. But there are new gilt bands around her left horn, pinning the two pieces together, and beneath them the crack is still growing towards the root.

Cressida, outside, does not have a crack in hers.

"I must congratulate you," Nicovar says, "on a lie well told."

Lucrezia smiles, her eyes still cold beneath her lacy mask. "I'm sure I don't know what you mean."

"Oh, it's a compliment, Grandmaster. I appreciate the skill involved. You had us all fooled for *years*. I don't think anyone knew for sure what you were pulling off."

Lucrezia lifts her head. "We weren't pulling anything off."

Nicovar gestures at her split horn.

"A war wound," she says. "One I happen to dislike. So I found some night magicians and I had it changed. For cosmetic reasons. You understand, I'm sure. You wouldn't keep a disfigurement if you didn't have to. And all of this metal is much less elegant."

"I can see the strain it's having on you." Nicovar turns at a breath of air from the wavering portal, but it seems to be only the breeze.

"Yes, it's quite heavy."

He smiles, almost to himself. "Not that. Wearing one name, all of the time. It's weighing on you."

"Oh, dear." Lucrezia's voice has turned smooth, a barely-sheathed weapon. "I do hope you're not suggesting anything untoward? I am an Imperial Grandmaster. It would be awfully illegal to send my sister to use my official powers."

"And you would never break the law," Nicovar agrees.

"Of course not. Not unless it bought me an advantage. What you're suggesting would be a very risky scam, and how would we benefit from it?"

Nicovar shrugs. "A pair of Autumn magicians? From the League? You might do it for the joy of the plotting. But now, well. Kimus might still like you, but I don't think your Order are quite as convinced."

Lucrezia hisses under her breath. "Don't you dare. The Celestial Arch is mine."

"Of course it is," he says mildly. "I am merely an ordinary member. I have no particular sway over my colleagues."

"I will see you burn."

"Mm. You said that in the spring, you know. And how is Holberg doing nowadays?"

Her eyes are fire in the dim light. "Fuck you, Nicovar. *Fuck* you." She spins on her heels, striding towards the other portal with a quick stamping fury. Nicovar stares at her back.

"You're forgetting the audience-"

"I am fucking off without it. Talk to the statue by yourself." Her hands are swift through the air, an odd series of linked gestures, drawing runes in the empty doorway. It shivers into cold wind before she vanishes.

"Hm," Nicovar says finally, to the empty room. "That was interesting."

He feels the door opening behind him and turns back to it, to the solemn merrow in yellow robes who stares at him unblinking, her face moulded like ridged clay into a fish's mouth. Nicovar bows to her. "I am here to speak with Kimus, by invitation."

The merrow stares for almost half a minute. Nicovar resists the urge to speak words into the silence. If he opens the subject of Lucrezia, the herald will certainly let him talk; if he says nothing, he may not have to make excuses.

Just as his own eyes are starting to itch in sympathy, the merrow blinks once, and beckons him forward.

The chamber of the Eternal changes every time he visits. The only constant is the figure draped in veils that stands, silent and unmoving, blindfold on its pedestal, and the crowd of circling eyes. Today the Eternal seems distant, shrouded in waves of mist. The glowing spheres light up the air around them and cloak Nicovar in a matching haze of colours. He walks towards the figure, but it hangs ever distant before him, though the floor is solid underfoot.

One eye drops to meet his gaze, a sparkling thing of bright blue and gold. "Do you come alone, Emperor? I invited a pair."

So much for that plan. Nicovar spreads his hands in apology. "Lucrezia is indisposed, and cannot join us tonight."

There is a tiny chiming noise, somehow resigned. "No matter. When the Emperor comes, the thoughts of the Empire must speak through him. Else what is the Empire for? Have you considered since last time we spoke?"

Nicovar stops walking. "Remind me, great one? We spoke of several things in our last conversation. Which is it that interests you?"

"On the question of time," the little sphere says impatiently. "We were speaking of the question of Time. On whether it exists, and what it is, and how it might be navigated. Surely you have given some thought to that?"

"Of course I have," he lies. "I am very taken with the question of direction, and how souls might have more directions of movement than embodied persons. Tell me, how does Time look to you, when it passes? Is it different here than on the mortal plane?"

For almost an hour, Nicovar walks and talks with the hovering glass spheres that make up Kimus. Sometimes there is only one, speaking with a single voice. Sometimes a chorus of eyes orbit his head, singing their single thoughts, or else disagreeing with each other in a way that is confusing enough for Nicovar to hear; what it must be like to argue with oneself that way, he can't fathom. He makes little progress on the question of Time. They agree that it must affect the dead soul differently from the living, and that the past must have some effect upon the future, for all values of those terms, but it is all common sense rephrased. The marble floor is hard, and Nicovar's feet ache.

"You are a brilliant mind," Kimus says, drawing itself back into the first glittering orb. "The limits of mortal thought are not the chains you believe them to be. They cannot be. You are an Emperor."

"You are kind, Kimus, but that is a title I hold. It is not a change to my nature."

"Is it not? Are you the same man who first stepped into my Realm, and spoke with me on the boundaries of the Self? Are you unshaped by your past when even Time must yield to it? A bold claim, Emperor."

"Bolder, perhaps, than I intend. I must think about that for a while."

"You should. I would like to speak of that next time we meet. But it grows late in your world, and our time – our Time – draws to its close. You will find the door behind you."

"Goodnight, great one," Nicovar says, but his voice falls suddenly flat, as if the mists and marble had turned into void. The light is drawing further from him, the motionless figure in its centre retreating, silent, towards an invisible horizon.

Nicovar swallows a sigh of irritation, and steps backwards. For all his walking, the door catches him at once.

Outside in Anvil it is full darkness, pierced by glow-stones and the white brilliance of the moon. Nicovar steps out between the regio stones and immediately longs for a cloak. The grass beneath his feet is frost-hard and glittering to match the stars. It crunches under his boots.

The fires of Anvil make a map as familiar as the constellations. Nicovar doesn't need a light to navigate back to his camp. He goes briskly, as much to avoid conversation as to keep his muscles warm. This is unseasonable weather, but the veterans of Anvil bring their good cloaks no matter what the auguries say, and will happily keep him standing while he shivers in his thin robes. He is coming into Urizen when he hears footsteps racing behind him.

He has just enough time to worry about assassins before a blizzard of light sweeps him away.

Nicovar floats. Somewhere, far distant, far too small to care about, he can hear the shouting, and feel the grass prickling icy against his hands. He understands, in a rush of exhilaration, that that shouting and that cold are happening *now*, that that is *now* and what happens in it is the first moment of freedom in the world and the last one of certainty and the universe opens before him like the coiling paths of the Labyrinth. He can see it laid out, the shape of Creation. He can see the endless loops of Time overlaid, each shaped by what came before, each pinched and twisted by the choices of the past, each point repeating its effect on every turn and turn of time and the souls that weave through the world are shaped by Time as they try to shape it and Nicovar can *see* how the memories they hold are their chains, binding the future to ancient mistakes.

He sees it, so clear in the moment, a perfect spinning pattern, and the secret locked inside of how all his subjects can be released from their prisons, and he knows what he has to do.

CHAPTER FORTY-SEVEN – WINTER 207

Isaella is sitting up in the early dawn light, feeding the baby. She was born with soft brown skin, lighter than her mother but by no means as pale as Nicovar's draughir colouring. Privately Isaella thinks she belongs to James, but they won't be sure of that unless she grows up tall. It hardly matters anyway. There are no siblings out there for Kat to avoid marrying.

James named her that. Ekatarin, her full name is, in a quiet acknowledgement that she is not entirely of Marcher blood. But she became Kat on her second morning and Kat she will stay, until she's old enough to choose. With three nations in her parentage, she certainly has the right. Isaella will take her out on the trods when she's bigger. Children take to change easier than adults and she shouldn't cry for home too much. But for now, the baby lives in Mournwold, the youngest member of James's boisterous household, and Isaella is staying with them both. They bought a new cart, well padded, and took the journey to Anvil gently.

She strokes Kat's little head, murmuring soothing nonsense at her. Nicovar rouses at the noise and rolls over in his blankets, reaching for something out of dream.

"It's alright," Isaella says, quietly so as not to startle anyone. "We're at Anvil."

Nic stares at her, blank. His eyes haven't focused in the mornings since the winter. It takes him a long time to recognise her, and then a smile curves his lips, unguarded as his smiles have never been. "Hello, Kat."

Isaella smiles back. "Come over here, lover. It's chilly on my own."

He's been more biddable since the curse hit him last summit. Usually, she would expect sarcasm, some flippant comment to pretend his daughter wasn't his favourite thing in the world. But he is always half-distracted now and so Nicovar crawls over without argument, bringing a sleep-warmed blanket to spread around both their shoulders and slinging an arm around Isaella's waist. "Hello," he says again, taking the baby's tiny hand. "Is it breakfast time?"

"I hope so," Isaella says, "I'm so hungry from feeding this one. When James wakes up we can send him for porridge."

"I like porridge," Nicovar says. He doesn't sound entirely certain.

The curse is called All the World in a Grain of Sand. Isaella had never heard of it before it was used last summit. It's a magicians curse, tailored to serve their interests. Nothing has happened to Nicovar's body, or the resources he controls. Instead it took his mind and swept him up into a vision he can't describe, and snatched it away again. He is trying to reclaim that moment of understanding; that is why his eyes don't focus, and he doesn't remember clearly. Half his mind is always reaching for it.

It makes her furious, how little the curse really does. Nicovar can't work magic as well as he should, that's all. He can still manage if Lucius leads the ritual. It costs them more mana and they can't reach the same heights, but he can still do it. He can read and write and make his way through life. It's just a constant nagging daydream that pulls him away, and she hates it.

Isaella wrote three times to Sally the magistrate, and every time the answer was the same. There is no law against curses.

"You're stewing," Nicovar says, resting his cheek on her shoulder. "Don't do that."

Isaella settles Kat in her other arm and tucks herself back into her tunic. "Sorry."

"Mm. Don't do that either. I like it when you get mad about me. But you're making yourself upset." His arm tightens around her waist. "I really am fine."

"You were dreaming about time again."

"I always dream about time. It doesn't bother me. And you know, this will wear off."

"In nine months. I could make Kat all over again in that time." Isaella sighs, leaning into his side. "Should we wake James up?"

Nicovar shrugs, a little awkwardly from being pressed close to her. "Maybe. Should we go back to bed?"

"Maybe."

Isaella has taken a leaf out of Nicovar's book and set herself up in the Senate. She's easily found here, by anyone who needs her and the Empress when he loses track of his world. It's not ideal, leaving the Navarr camp for most of the summit, but her nation understand the circumstances. It's winter, and her chair here is padded and out of the wind. They make do.

"Liathaven," Felicia says, "there you are. Listen, we've got a problem."

Isaella leans her head back against the wall. "Alright," she says, wearily, "I'm listening. What's the problem we have?"

"It's the Empress."

"It's always the Empress, Warmage. You'll have to be more specific."

"He's put in a declaration – look, I know you don't follow the Conclave much, but this makes no sense. I mean, it's gibberish, and it runs almost a whole page. He can't put this in."

"Will it do any harm?"

"Lots." Felicia perches on the arm of the throne, still too polite to sit in it properly. Isaella smiles at that. "It won't do any harm in itself, because it doesn't make any sense and that means it won't get passed. Honestly, I don't think it'll even get a proper debate, because I can't work out what it's trying to say, except I think he's asking us to rule on the nature of time? But my point is, the Empress putting in nonsense declarations does a great deal of harm to *him*."

Isaella draws her cloak closer around her shoulders. "Makes him look more insane than he has to."

"Exactly. I know he is, a little, but the less it shows now the easier to convince people it's worn off on time."

"Alright. I understand the problem. What do you need me to do?"

"The thing is – where's the baby?"

"With James."

"Right, sorry. The thing is, it has to be Nicovar that withdraws the declaration. I mean, it has to be, because Ruth won't let anyone else do it on his behalf. It's part of the rules of order. So, I need you to talk him out of it."

Isaella rubs her forehead. "Strategy? Please?"

Felicia looks awkward. "I was sort of hoping he'd do it just because you asked."

"Ordinarily, maybe. Right now, he might, or he might spend an hour trying to convince me he's sincere."

"Then we need to distract him. Like – sorry, this is a horrible analogy – like giving a toddler a new toy so you can take the helmet away from them."

"Lovely," Isaella grumbles. "Not inaccurate, but so very nice to think about. He's got Order elections today, surely you can do something with that? Persuade him to keep his declaration until next time, so he can talk the new Grandmaster into it?"

The Warmage brightens. "That might work. Yeah, that might work. I'll go try that. I don't even know who the new GM is going to *be,* so I doubt Nicovar does either."

She nods to Sveta on her way down the ramp, and Isaella sits up straight to accept a cup of coffee.

"You know," Sveta says, "mostly he doesn't say anything at Senate. You could just park him in here and tell him to listen."

"I can't tell the Empress what to do," Isaella says reprovingly.

"Uh *huh.* Sure. Still though, if you're worried about the Conclave, he can't go to both."

"I thought I'd send him to the Military Council," Isaella says, just to see Sveta's look of horror. "I'm sure he's got some wonderful ideas for Holberg."

"You can't be serious. Please, don't be serious, I will honestly throw up if you're serious."

"No, I'm not serious. If we can extract him from the Hall of Worlds after his order election, we can have a family outing to the Senate. Kat ought to see it in action."

"She's like three weeks old," Sveta says sceptically. "Can she even see properly yet?"

"Six weeks. She can definitely see by now. She laughs at Nicovar when he's talking nonsense. That makes her old enough to get involved."

Sveta hops up into the throne, entirely unselfconscious despite its solemnity. "That baby is going to get started before I do. Do you suppose she's going to like girls?"

"I – what?"

"Will she like girls?"

"I understood the question, I just don't like where it's going."

"Well, you and James and Nicovar make such a good team." Sveta grins, and Isaella realises she's being paid back for the crack about Holberg. "I thought I could be Empress and have her for Consort. Don't you think we'd look pretty together? Ooh, or I could be Warmage and she can be Archmage, that's a partnership proven to work. There are so many possibilities!"

Isaella disentangles her arm from her cloak, not trusting herself to answer, and takes a sip of her coffee.

CHAPTER FORTY-EIGHT – SPRING 208

Nicovar rubs his forehead. "I'm sorry. Can we go over it again?"

"There's a Druj spymaster called Kern," James says, patient although they've been through this litany three times. "She's responsible for the traitors we thought we had in Holberg. You remember them, you were in the first battle when they posed as Leaguer farmers."

"I – think so. Yes."

"Okay. She's been active in the Barrens for years but we thought she was only dealing with scouts. Now we know she's using human slaves to infiltrate and directly caused a lot of civilian casualties, and she's currently in Holberg territory, so we can use the Gate to reach her. Does that make sense?"

Nicovar nods. "Kern," he says. "Kern. Druj spymaster in Holberg. Kern. This would be easier if I didn't have to give a speech, Jimmy."

"You could let the generals handle it-"

"No, no, I'm going so I'll say something. About Kern, who is a Druj spymaster and keeps sending – fuck – slaves against us?"

"Right. Dressed in stolen uniforms, mostly."

"Spies. Okay. Sun's coming up already."

James looks stern. "Don't think about that. There's time for thinking about time later. Right now we're thinking about tactics."

"Right."

The spread of ground before the Sentinel Gate is almost bare this year. Winter was hard and dry, and the torn-up grass from last year's summits hasn't had time to regrow. The sparse green shoots are lost under a sea of Imperial boots.

Nicovar is up at the front, nearest to the gate with the rest of Urizen. The Marchers will come through behind, and the Brass Coast and the League, but Urizen will be leading the charge. It's meant to be an honour, but Nicovar knows they'll be holding the gate while others press forward to hunt the enemy. It makes sense, for a smaller nation. It makes sense when the Empress is half-drowned by a curse.

The egregores go through their rituals, opening the arched portal to a grey morning far from Holberg's walls, on the very edge of Imperial territory. This is a mission of vengeance as much as strategy. Kern has done too much damage to be allowed to try again and her death will be another blow to end this brutal war. And she would try again, as surely as she has tried before, and the egregores would go through their rituals as they have for long centuries and every turn of the stars would bring them back to where they stand with the carven Wanderer leering down-

Nicovar shakes his head sharply. Tactics, he tells himself. He can feel James standing behind his shoulder, ready to distract him from his thoughts. He straightens himself and watches for the shimmering veil of the gate to appear.

As it whispers into view, he steps forward alone. "Heroes of Anvil," he calls out, in the loudest voice he can manage and still sound calm, "The Empire is grateful for your willingness to fight. I know your Generals have told you why we are here. We are hunting a Druj spymaster, who has sent many enemies against us, dressed as if they were us. We have lost many lives to her tricks. She must not try again. We will find her, and we will stop her today."

He closes his mouth, certain that if he keeps talking, he will make himself a spectacle, and strides back to his pace among the sentinels of Urizen. The waiting force doesn't cheer, but they stamp their feet and drum their swords against their shields and that's good enough for today. Nicovar goes forward with the rest, stepping through the portal and into a cold wind.

Battles never make very much sense. Nicovar is clinging to that comforting thought as the chaos shifts around him. He knows where the Gate is, close to the Urizen forces and looming half-spectral at their backs, the image of a stone arch that stands a hundred miles away. He knows where James is, always behind his shoulder, watching to be sure that Nicovar does not go wandering. Beyond that, it's hard to be sure. His attention span doesn't stretch from one minute to the next.

There are little clumps of both forces intermingled at the front line, he can understand that much. The Marchers have condensed themselves into sections, hedgehog-prickly, funnelling the orcs between them and the points of their long bill-hooks. The League forces are waiting for them behind the Marcher line. It looks like slow going – it must be, surely, with a formation like that cutting down the front lines to points of heavy fighting – and the Brass Coast are having trouble on the left flank. The Urizeni are pinning down the right, with the Gate as an anchor, but Nicovar's weapon is quiet in his hand. The orcs haven't seen him, or they don't care.

He forgets, until it happens, that Kern is a spymaster and known for using slaves. Orcish slaves are rarely brought to Anvil and the Empire does not keep human ones, and so he forgets that the Druj make no distinction. They couldn't have made it all the way to Anvil, but in the confusion of the Imperials passing the gate and forming their lines, they must have stolen into the League forces; there is a wild commotion on the near end of the line and suddenly the Urizeni are facing a grim-faced troop of human fighters, dressed as League mercenaries, striking towards Nicovar.

He is not a soldier, but he has practiced with his magician's rod for years, week in and week out, to keep his body fit and be ready for moments like this. His body settles into a fighting stance without needing instructions. The sentinels on either side are armed with swords and stand poised to defend him.

The hand on Nicovar's shoulder makes him flinch. "Step back," James says, a low rumble in his ear, and Nicovar hisses through his teeth. "No," James insists, "you're better behind the lines, we need your spells," and that make something yield inside him. He takes two steps backwards, letting James push forward to take his place, his staff raised to strike.

The interlopers are already falling on them. The real Leaguers, still holding the line, have no bodies to spare for flanking. They are trying to plug a gap with too few swords. The Urizeni must do this part alone. It's bloody fighting, neither side heavily armoured, hacking at each other with short weapons. Nicovar paralyses two of their attackers for the others to cut up, darting through gaps to reach them and releasing his spells against enemies preoccupied by sharper swords. Dirty tricks, but he has never held to ideals of honourable combat. Leave that for the Dawnish and the Summer realm. Here in battle, he prefers to win.

Kern does not enter the fight until it's almost lost. She has been holding back, directing her troops from the rear just as Nicovar is – or as he appears to, if no-one looks too hard at James and the tense calculation in his eyes. The Imperials are nearly at full strength, no more than two or three lying dead, although many fighters have cycled towards the rear to have white bandages packed between the sections of their armour. The orcs have died and died on their swords.

Retreat might be smarter. Would be smarter, would restart the cycle and Kern could build up her forces and lick her wounds and come back with renewed hatred to follow the same pattern Druj spymasters have followed for generations and the walls of Holberg would turn like a millstone and crush another army under their feet -

Retreat might be more strategic, but Druj do not look kindly on defeated generals and Kern will not be welcomed back to the Barrens now. Her only chance is to strike forward and meet either Nicovar, or a heroic death to please her ancestors. The Marchers abandon their formations and close around her, a bloodstained fist.

The battle ends abruptly, with no signal on the orcish side. They only stop, all at once, and turn to run, and Nicovar cannot quite see what takes their spirit. But he knows what retreat looks like, and knows these fleeing enemies will not rally again. The Imperials chase them down the broad valley, but they quickly vanish into the trees and they have not brought Navarr along for woodland scouting; the surviving orcs make their escape. Nicovar straps his magician's rod back to his belt and bumps his shoulder against James. "How did it go?"

James looks down at him, his gaze steady. "We did alright. A handful of dead on our side. A hundred or more, on the other. And you saw us kill Kern."

"Oh," Nicovar says. "Is that why they ran?"

James sighs, very quietly, and kisses Nicovar on the top of his head. "Let's go home, love. Back to Anvil, anyway. We've got to get through Conclave yet today."

CHAPTER FORTY-NINE – SUMMER 208

A dry winter means a dusty summer. Isaella ought to be used to this by now, but after a morning's hard battle in the Therunin swamps, driving the last lingering orcs back into the Barrens, she's longing for rain to settle the Anvil ground. It would churn up into mud immediately, but at least they'd be able to breathe.

Sveta seems unbothered by it, or by the summer pollen that makes misery for half the citizens in camp. Her blouse is a brilliant white unstained by the endless dust. Isaella makes a note to ask Sveta's mother how she manages that without fading the red embroidery on all their clothes. Bleaching, done the ordinary way, is ruinous to green Navarri dyes.

But however it's managed, Sveta looks comfortable despite the dry heat, and Isaella is wearing her jerkin over bare arms and doing her best to keep everyone in the shade. Kat is seven months old and restlessly unhappy with all these strangers. For now she's dragging herself across the grass in pursuit of the rag doll she has learned to throw. Guessing when anyone is minded to return it is still a little beyond her.

Sveta rolls on her back, folding her arms behind her head. "But, Felicia," she says, continuing a conversation thy were having this morning. "Can we count on her?"

"I think so," Isaella says. "Yes, I think so. She would have stood with the d'Holbergs early on, after they got her into her position-"

"I wish I'd been here to see that, I missed so *much* waiting to grow up-"

"Everyone starts somewhere. And Felicia started on the d'Holberg side, but that changed during the feuding afterwards. You never saw it, but the twins were close allies during the interregnum. It was only afterwards it started to go wrong."

"Nicovar was rude to them, wasn't he?"

Isaella nudges Sveta with her foot. "Of course not. He got into *that* habit later on. No, he just forgot about them, when they expected to be close advisors. Too many moving parts to keep track of. So they worked up a little coup in the Conclave and Felicia got her position out of it."

"I know this part. I'm just not sure why, when that's how she started, you trust her now."

"Things changed during the secession. I mean, it wasn't easy, being Warmage during the secession. She was responsible for rituals on armies that were fighting against our own. It took a lot of balancing work. And there were two or three attempts to unseat her, and she came through it, but I think the twins – they pulled the trick off once and got control of the Conclave, more or less, so why not twice? Then her carta took the Summer staff without d'Holberg help and since then things have been – very cool, between those parts of the League."

Sveta nods, tilting her head to watch Isaella sideways. "And then Rivers Run Red."

"And then that. I'm astonished they didn't curse her, too."

"They couldn't persuade the Highborn to do more than one target, is my guess. Although – there's a Night curse I would have tried if I were them."

"*Someone* scared the Night covens off from working with the d'Holbergs."

"So they did." Sveta stretches, very pleased with herself. "Do you think they'll ever catch the archer?"

"They found the crossbow in the woods the next morning. Stolen, from a Navarr who swears blind they didn't shoot anyone."

"Well, they would say that, wouldn't they?"

Isaella sighs. "They're a Navarr. If they make an oath to tell me the truth, then I trust them to keep it. I'm not their enemy and if I were, they wouldn't have sworn to me. *Whoever* that archer is, they should count themselves lucky-"

"Heads up."

Isaella glances around at Sveta's warning and sees Cressida strolling towards them, her hands loosely tucked into her belt. Her clothes are no less fine than when her sister was Grandmaster, but the loss of position shows in the tilt of her horns, the set of her shoulders. Cress and Lucrezia are scrabbling at a cliff-edge, and the mask on Cressida's belt is a snarling leopard. There is a dark crack just visible in the spiral of one horn.

Sveta sits up, glancing at Isaella. She doesn't say anything, instead busying herself with Kat's rag doll, to keep the baby occupied. Isaella takes her cue and turns towards Cress. She leans back on her hands. "Afternoon, Cressida."

Cress makes a show of squinting through the bright sun. "Is that you, Sal?"

"It is."

"Made it through one more battle alive, huh?"

"Come and sit down, my friend. We have water."

Cressida drops onto the grass. "Oh, thank goodness. Water would be lovely."

That seems unfeigned, but either way, Isaella wouldn't withdraw the offer once made. She passes over a waterskin, half-full and unappetisingly warm from sitting out in the weather. Cress pulls a face at the leathery taste. "Isaella, darling, I have a problem."

"You should see a physick for that," Isaella responds automatically.

"Oh, not that. I've got a cream for that. No, my problem is your husband and his husband."

"Technically, none of us are – Well, not in League terms – It doesn't matter. I know who you mean. Which of them is bothering you?"

"Well, it seems that our dear Consort is helping the Empress with duties that really ought to pertain to the Throne."

Sveta, playing with the baby, tilts her head. Isaella pauses before she answers. "In other Imperial positions, exercising the power of the position without holding it would certainly be an issue.

And I've heard some of the accusations that went around about you. Not that I believe them, of course. I'm sure you and Lucrezia have never switched. But with the Throne, there's the favour power to think about."

"But does he have a favour? Unless it's written down, with a witness from outside the Throne's circle, I'd say that doesn't hold water." Cress leans forward on her knees. "You see my point, Sal. With the Empress indisposed, it would be easy for an unscrupulous consort to take advantage."

"Oh, very easy," Isaella says, trying to conceal how her heart is thumping with anger. "But very difficult to prove, don't you think? Any Empress is entitled to have advisors. James has never sat in Nicovar's place."

"Only whispered in his ear. And such a good opportunity to whisper, in the Throne's own bed, with that nasty curse still working. I wonder if we will get our Nicovar back as he was before? I wonder, did James have a hand in that casting? Permanent proxy for the Throne is a place with some wonderful advantages, and history will always blame Nicovar."

Isaella stares at her. She can hear her pulse roaring in her ears, and Sveta murmuring, "Shush now, shush now" to the cooing baby. Her hand itches for the dagger in her belt.

"I think," she says at last, "that only a very stupid person would suggest that. And only an exceptionally stupid person would expect the people to believe it."

"Really?" Cressida shrugs and leans back, tipping her head up towards the sky. "In my experience, an explanation is always more satisfying than a mystery."

"Not when the explanation is absurd."

"So what do you suggest, dear Sally? Who brought doom on the draughir?"

"We all know the answer to that, Cressida. It was the Highborn Day coven and they have sworn not to reveal who paid them and I am satisfied with that answer. They will answer in the Labyrinth for the virtue of their actions. And two of them have been cursed in return and I do not get involved in magicians' rivalries." She smiles, or at least, bares her teeth. "I leave that to my husband the Grandmaster."

Cressida's eyes narrow. "The Senate might have something to say about that, if they were asked. To be both Grandmaster and Consort could be a conflict of interest. Two Imperial positions at once."

"Consort isn't an Imperial position by the meaning of the Constitution," Sveta interrupts, her voice dripping with scorn. Cressida looks over to her, a diplomatic smile slipping back into place.

"But the Senate could define it as one, youngster. That's my point. The situation can always change. And for that matter, curses can always be re-cast, so perhaps we should all start planning for the long haul? Will Nicovar try to keep his position, if he can't perform his duties for another year?"

Isaella forces her hands to stay on the ground, unthreatening. "The Empress will do as he sees fit. As he is doing today – or didn't you notice him at the regio? The curse doesn't prevent him from scrying. Or from battle, or attending Senate. The Throne's powers are being exercised by the Throne. No amount of advice changes that."

Cressida's eyes glitter like the fangs of the mask she carries. "Of course not, Sally darling. Of course not. I'm only speculating."

CHAPTER FIFTY – AUTUMN 208

On a rainy morning in September, Nicovar wakes up.

He stares at the canvas above his head for a long minute,
listening to the rain falling. It sounds sharper than usual, clearer,
each pattering drop making a different sound. He can hear the
soft trickling where the water runs down the seams to the
soaking ground. He listens, and he notices there is no particular
pattern to how the raindrops fall, and suddenly he realises he's
been listening for three minutes together and he hasn't wandered
into his own thoughts once.

"Oh," he says, under his breath, and hears it in the new quietness
of his mind. "Oh."

He sits up straight. The blankets resist him, gathering at his
waist, and he looks to the side and sees James stirring from
sleep, curled up to fit himself into the tent's length. There's
damp at the end of the blankets where his feet have pushed them
into the canvas.

He blinks up at Nicovar, already working one hand out of the
bedroll. It's been habit for a year now to soothe him when he
wakes.

"It's me," Nicovar says. "It's over. I *missed* you."

James props himself up on his elbow, and his smile goes wide.

Isaella is back in her old tent for the summit, up the hill with the rest of Navarr. Nicovar trots up there as soon as the day begins, with a much-needed cup of coffee in his hand. There's so much work to do now, he can hardly spare the time for anyone. But he will, for Isaella, and for little perfect Kat gnawing miserably on a wooden beetle.

"Poor baby," he says, crouching down to pick her up. "Growing teeth is hard work." Kat burbles at him, and hits him with her beetle.

Isaella eyes him critically. She's half-dressed, sat on a bench outside despite the drizzle, with her boots unlaced. "You're very chipper this morning, Nic."

He smiles at her, longer and wider than he intends, and the spark lights in her face. "You're back."

"I'm back."

Isaella hugs him so tightly that Kat complains, squashed between their bodies. "Never *ever* do that to me again," she says, her voice muffled in the shoulder of his robes. "Never."

Nicovar nods against her braids. "I didn't die," he says, by way of mitigating the offence.

"If you'd died I would have killed you."

"I know."

"I never want to hear about time again, understand?"

He draws back. "Well. About that."

"No. Nic. You can't be serious. You're supposed to be back to normal."

"I am. I promise, I'm perfectly sane. But I think I really did understand something."

Isaella takes Kat out of his arms. "Will you do me a favour?"

"Of course."

"Are you going to battle this morning?"

"I – No," he says, thinking it through. "I'll see them off, but I have so much to catch up with, I can't spare the time for it."

"Alright. So make the time for me, instead, and sit down with the rest of the Day magicians and talk about what you think you've understood. Just – talk it through with them. Figure out if it's just the curse talking. Please?"

Nicovar smooths a stray braid back behind Isaella's ear. "I will," he says. "I will, I promise. Today, and no later. Dear heart, I'm so sorry for making you worry all this time. Come to breakfast? You and Kat? It's been so long since the three of us could really talk."

"Alright," she says softly, and Nicovar realises with a pang how much he's worried her, all over again. He glances around for witnesses, catches himself, and resolves not to care. He is back to his right mind, and he is going to kiss his lover now.

"I'm perfectly sane," he says later, to the handful of magicians who have been trying to understand his ramblings for a year. "I realise that doesn't mean very much coming from the victim, but you have Titus to reassure you."

"You're not *cursed,*" Titus says pedantically. "I can't certify you as *sane*. You'd need a specialised physick for that."

Nicovar shrugs. "Close enough. I'm not cursed, and it was only the curse making me irrational. What I have now is the accidental benefits."

"There are no benefits to-"

"You can't use Day magic to teach someone an untruth," Nicovar interrupts. "You all know that. It is fundamentally a realm of truth."

"But not necessarily of understanding. You're not an Eternal. You might have misinterpreted what you saw." Felicia is sitting cross-legged, using her cloak as a cushion. "So, now you can keep a train of thought together, tell us what you're thinking. We'll work through it together. If it doesn't make sense, wouldn't you rather know?"

Nicovar nods. "Of course I would. Thank you. So let's figure this out."

This is what Nicovar saw:

Time is not a river. It is not an ever-flowing stream, carrying the past away beyond retrieval. It is not a ladder, to be climbed into a fixed future, or a tapestry to be woven from the million threads of our lives.

Time moves in an endless spiral, and each turn is shaped by the one that came before. Our souls, passing through the Labyrinth, stitch the layers of time into each other like the wadding in a quilt. We are born new, and we do not know ourselves, but we carry all the turnings of history in our souls.

We do not know ourselves, and that is a blessing. To remember our past lives is to be bound by them. Shaped, over and over, by mistakes of the ancient past, as paint will split along an old crack. The True Liao grants us knowledge, but it harms the one who takes it, for the memory regained will stunt their growth.

The records of history, the stories and the archives that we are so eager to write, all of them are hindrances to our transcendence.

What we remember, we are condemned to retrace. Time overlays its own coils, the strands piling up ever higher, and each one echoes the one beneath. We are the instruments that shape it. We confine ourselves with every book we write.

The Empire was founded to bring human souls to Virtue, and to do that, it must free them from the past.

Felicia stares at him open-mouthed when he has finished explaining. Nicovar shrugs and leans back against the tent-pole.

"I haven't quite perfected the explanation yet," he says, into the breathless silence. "It needs refining. But that's the basic shape of it. Ha. Shape."

"It's astounding," Titus says. "It may also be lunatic. I'm not sure."

"I wasn't sure myself. But I've had a long time to think about it – the revelation only lasts for a moment, you know. That was over within ten minutes. All the rest of the year I've been trying to work out what it all meant, and I couldn't explain it properly."

"Mm. I'm not sure you've explained it properly now. It's the memory part that I'm not sure about. Time as a spiral seems logically coherent, but human souls as the mechanism?"

Nicovar nods. "Nothing else travels through time as we do. We know that the orcs don't have souls like ours, we know that animals don't. The Labyrinth, I think, is the name we give to the space *within* Time's spiral. In the centre. The aim of a soul – on some level we're not conscious of – is to steer outside of the spiral and escape it entirely. Virtue helps us pull away from whatever force sucks us into the centre. Which, I think, is possibly the urge to repeat ourselves, but that's for the priests to discuss. I'm confining myself to the shape of the world."

Titus is drawing shapes in the air, trying to translate Nicovar's words into thought. "So, the transcending soul moves at a tangent, instead of a chord?"

"Exactly!" Nicovar snaps his fingers, delighted with the new phrasing.

"It's plausible. I don't know how to test it. Does the Synod have a theory of Time?"

"No. I checked."

"So this isn't heresy – You know, the Navarri have a belief that we meet the same people, life after life, and live out the same relationships. They call it the Great Dance."

Nicovar nods. "They do. And the Dawnish believe something similar, about love repeating in each reincarnation. It's not official doctrine, but I truly believe there is something in it. I think we shape the world with our actions, and our actions are shaped by expectation. I think we are in a cage of our own making."

Felicia takes a deep breath. "You're the Empress."

"Yes?" He blinks at her. "Sorry, I don't follow."

"If you're right, and you're saying that the Empire needs to change its whole approach to recorded history – You're the Empress, Nicovar. What are you going to do?"

CHAPTER FIFTY-ONE – WINTER 208

Nicovar is pacing across the Senate floor. Isaella watches him, how his whole self is poised to strike. It's late on a Friday, after all the business of the summit is finished for the day, and in the winter midnight his breath steams white when he speaks. There is dragon-fire behind his words.

"We are not here to debate the purpose of the Empire. It is written in the constitution, it was proclaimed by the First Empress. We were founded to further the transcendence of humanity. I have found a way to do that and as the Empress, I *must* pursue it."

"You go too far, Nicovar."

"No, I don't, Archimedes. I do as I must." Nicovar's expression barely softens as he meets his mentor's eyes. "I am a child of Urizen. I was raised in your spire. You know I do not delight in the loss of knowledge, but we have made a mistake. We must change our thinking. We have to destroy what holds us back."

Archimedes shakes his head. "You are wrong, my friend. This will not save our souls, and what we lose, we will never get back."

"That's the point – Sorry, Nicovar."

"No, go ahead."

Isolt looks towards Archimedes and the crowd of dissenters around him. "If we could undo it, it wouldn't be worth doing. It's not enough to take our own children out of the cage. We have to prevent it from being rebuilt."

"Our children?"

"We all know too much." She shrugs, bitterness creeping into her voice. "How many of us here have had past-life visions? Seven, eight? Nicovar's had one. He's not going anywhere. So do it for yourselves, because on the next turn around, I don't want to be caught in the same trap I am now."

"It is too much to ask," Archimedes repeats. "We have been recording our history since before the Empire began. It is generations of work, it is the vocation of whole spires and chapters. You cannot just cry, "Halt!" and expect to be heard. No matter if your philosophy is right, your will alone is not enough for the task."

Nicovar's smile is gentle. "I know that, old friend. You've taught me that lesson well. That is why I have come to you – to all of you. The Throne can do many things but this is beyond me. I am asking you to go to war, senators. I am asking you to take it that seriously."

"We're taking it seriously," Isolt answers, and a dozen heads nod in agreement.

Adina raises her hand. "Liathaven? What about you?"

"I stand with the Empress," Isaella says, automatically. She hesitates over her next words. "I'm not much of one for speeches. But Nicovar used to be Archmage of Day. This sort of thing is in his realm. So if he says this is necessary, I'm willing to trust him."

"No reservations?"

"Just that we have to do it carefully. To preserve what we understand about virtue, and magic, and the vallorn – But the everyday names and places, we can survive without. The Highborn already do that, writing down what we need to know and leaving out what might mislead us."

"That's not entirely – okay, close enough. But the Urizen won't like it."

"We don't," Archimedes says, his deep voice rumbling. "We don't like it, and we won't vote for it."

There are restrictions on Synod voting, Isaella knows. The priests have to be given time to consider their verdict. So it's not really a surprise, when Cara comes to find her the next day with a slip of paper in her hand.

She settles on the wooden bench next to Isaella, around the big firepit where she's holding court, taking her nation's opinions on a proposed new bridge.

"This is a copy," Cara says. "The original is with the Civil Service. But I wanted you to know that it's passed."

She hands over the paper, a neat paragraph written out on the back of Civil Service stationery, with "Statement of Principle – PASSED" across the top.

Isaella takes it. "Nicovar will be pleased," she says lightly, "he's always wanted the Synod to take more initiative."

She reads the statement carefully. Synod declarations like this don't have the force of laws, but they're important nonetheless. The populace pays close attention to how the Synod votes. This one is painfully predictable: the Assembly of the Way does not support the Emperor in his beliefs on the nature of Time, and cannot support any action to suppress or reverse the recording of history.

Isaella folds the paper and hands it back. "I thought you might say that."

"You should have counted on it. Are you really going to support this, Sal? You have to know it's mad."

"It fits with the Dance," Isaella says quietly. "You remember I told you once that when I first set eyes on Nicovar, I knew he was important to me? That I didn't know whether I should love or hate him, but I was certain he would matter?"

"I remember."

"And now I think this is why. I wondered if it was the secession, but – any Throne could have faced that problem. Any Throne could have fixed it. Getting a revelation from a curse from insulting a political rival, and using it to change our whole approach to history, that could only be Nicovar. Anyone else would have doubted themselves, at some point along this road."

Cara nods. "You're right. But you also told me you thought he was dangerous and I agree. If he doesn't get his new laws – and he won't – I don't know if he'll accept that defeat. I don't know if Nicovar knows when to stop."

On Sunday, Navarr and the Marches fight together. The fields of Varushka are frozen solid this time of year, their furrows outlined in wind-blown snow. The armies are at the border, holding guard against the endless threat of the orcs, and so this creature crouching in a ruined tower is for the heroes of Anvil to deal with.

The first enemies they meet are long dead. Their armour rattles over frozen bones and joints that barely hang together. Still, they move, and their swords are sharp. A wave of unnatural dread rolls across the battlefield before them. Isaella steels her will and pushes onwards, towards the tower walls.

A shout goes up from the Marcher line. Isaella looks over, expecting to see James racing forward to pull the tower gates down, but instead sees the coven being clapped on the back. She grins along with them; the gates are already open and the magicians can pull out their weapons and fight. James is spinning his staff in his hands, already looking for some skulls to crack. The Highborn, with their heavy shields, are circling the ruin. There will be no stray monsters escaping to terrorise the locals.

They meet resistance at the walls. The gate may be open, but it is still guarded, by more half-skeletal warriors and a pack of clawed creatures, their fur spattered in blood. The Imperials take the creatures three or four against one, stabbing at their backs when they turn to attack. It takes time, and more than one fighter is saved by the physicks, but when the last of the monsters falls they can turn their attention to the tower and spread out inside the stone walls.

She meets James on the top of the battlements, his grin wild as he knocks an undead soldier into open space. For a moment he draws back, ready to swing at her head as she climbs the crumbling stairs, but she meets his strike with her spear and it is barely a love-tap by the time it connects.

He throws an arm around her shoulders. One tight hug, one brief kiss, and they turn together to face the next wave of monsters.

At the end of the summit, there is a meeting in Ankarien camp. Isaella finds herself a seat in the meeting tent, on the same benches and cushions they've been using since before Nicovar was crowned. Archimedes is perched upright on his cushion, waiting.

It's a crowded room today. There are senators here, but also generals, the Warmage and Summermage and magicians Isaella doesn't recognise, all with the same tension around their eyes. Everyone understands the situation. Nicovar raised his proposals in the Senate, and they did not pass. He raised them in the Conclave and they did not pass. Three Assemblies of the Synod have spoken out against his plans. This plan might die before it starts.

Except that one of the generals here is Septima of the Army of the Citadel, and she is bowing to Nicovar's orders.

"I can't require you to do anything," he says. "But as General, you have complete authority over where your army goes, and you're already on the southern border. You could make a start."

Septima rolls her shoulders, letting her armour settle onto them. "It's a lot to ask of the troops, Empress. They all have homes to go back to. This isn't like fighting in Highguard."

"I know that. And I appreciate the warning. I know this will be hard. But we have to do it, General. What is the point of the Empire otherwise?"

"None at all," Kasia agrees. She is Cardinal again for this year, after a time as Gatekeeper, and the responsibility is weighing on her. "I don't like it, no Highborn could after the secession, but Nicovar is right. *If* he's right, then we have to do it, for the sake of our souls, and if he's wrong – it's just facts and figures. We can live without those. We have to take the chance that he's correct."

Archimedes rises heavily to his feet. "Are you resolved to do this, Empress?" His hands are clasped loosely behind him, stern and formal.

Nicovar meets his eyes. "I am, Arbiter."

"If you turn the armies upon Ankarien, we will not surrender. We will guard our home, and our libraries, with every power we have."

"That is your right," Nicovar says. "You are the Arbiter of the spire, I cannot make you ignore your conscience. But – But Ankarien is my home. It always has been. Please, old friend. Do not make me break those doors. Do not make me kill those sentinels. I love Ankarien, but right now that library is the greatest weight around the ankles of an Empire I have sworn to serve. Please, Archimedes. Please. Help me."

Archimedes takes one slow breath. "I cannot help you," he says. "I will not surrender Ankarien. If you lead an army against it, you will have to go through me."

CHAPTER FIFTY-TWO – SPRING 209

Nicovar sits on his throne, his daughter in his lap.

The archives of Urizen are burning. Parchment scrolls from before the Empire, paper books from the presses of the League, research notes and letters from the dead; all of it has gone to the flames. He wanted to be careful, at first, to take Isaella's advice and winnow out what could not be kept from what ought to be spared. But the Senate would not back him, and the Synod condemned his proposals. There was nothing left to do but fight.

Archimedes died on the steps of Ankarien's great library. His body is ash and dust, along with the work he was trying to save.

Nicovar is here ahead of time, for a Senate meeting he knows will be difficult. General Septima asked him to met her here, and how many reasons could there be for that? He has Kat as much for himself, to keep him from rash choices, as to let her mother go to her re-election unencumbered.

Septima's robes are pale blue and shine like moonlight in the dusk. She bows to him, short and formal. "Empress Nicovar."

"General Septima. You asked for an audience."

"I did, Empress. At the winter summit, you asked me to lead the Army of the Citadel against our own people, to destroy the libraries of Urizen. I have done that for three months. I can do it no longer."

There is a murmuring from the public gallery, where the crowd is already gathering, and from the senators assembling on the floor.

Nicovar nods. "Thank you for your candour, General."

"I accepted this task because I was convinced of your sincerity, and that we ought to try your plan if there was any chance it might lead us to virtue. But I have killed many citizens of Urizen. I cannot believe it is virtuous to slay our own."

"It cannot be virtuous to let the libraries stand, when their removal would free us from so much."

Septima blinks hard. Tears, perhaps, threatening to shatter her poise. "That may be true, but even if it is, the Empire has stood for hundreds of years. This project does not have to be done this month, this year. We could do it the gradual way. We could persuade. I will not raise the sword again on my own folk."

Kat is a warm weight on Nicovar's thighs, a breathing anchor. He keeps his expression calm. "Thank you for your service to the Empire, General. For the time being, I will command the Army of the Citadel myself."

She bows. "As you wish. I thought that might be the case."

"I don't question your loyalty. I will not seek your revocation. After this is over, you can have your army back."

"Thank you, Empress, but I don't believe that will be necessary." Her smile is bleak. "I intend to defend my spire, and if I die doing it, perhaps that will be a measure of atonement. Goodnight, Nicovar, and may you come to your senses."

The senators filter into the chamber. Some wear expressions of grim tension, under Highborn hoods or Leaguish masks or on their own bare skin. Others are fierce with pride. Nicovar can see, watching them, how many of the Senate will stand with him if pushed – a third, at most. Isolt, leaning over the railing to speak with Felicia and Sveta in the public gallery, will follow him. Adina is one of the grim ones, her grief unconcealed, but she will still hold true. All three of the Varushkan senators, one of the Winterfolk, none of Urizen. Archimedes has been replaced by Lucius, and Lucius meets his eyes across the floor and does not bow. Nicovar knows, without trying it, that he is not welcome in Ankarien's camp.

Marianne wakes the glow-stones on her arrival, almost exactly on the hour. She steps up to her place beside him. "Thank you for attending, Nicovar. Is the baby staying?"

"Ekatarin," he says. "I mean, yes, she is."

"Alright then. Let's get started."

"Wait a moment? The Navarri aren't here."

"Then they're late," Marianne says, raising one eyebrow. "Isaella at least should know to be on time. The last I checked – and I've had reason to review – the powers of the Throne did not include delaying the Senate-"

Four figures in practical green and brown stride up the ramp, one stopping to lean her bow against the wall. Nicovar's eyes play tricks on him for a moment, turning that bow into a spear, that stranger into Isaella. But the Navarr comes forward and there's no denying the strange tattoos on her face, her short hair, her grey eyes so unlike Isaella's clear brown.

"Emperor," she says. "Speaker. I am Teleri Turning Mountain, the new senator for Liathaven."

Nicovar grips the arm of his throne until his fingers ache. He keeps the snarl out of his face. "Welcome to the Senate."

"Thank you. You should know, Nicovar, that Isaella lost because she stood with you, and I will not."

"It's so kind of you to tell me."

"I just – I thought it might help with your calculations – I think we're a little late, Speaker, I apologise."

Marianne straightens her shoulders. "That's quite alright, Liathaven. And now, let's get started."

Since the Hub was created, the Synod tent sees less use. The priests do most of their coordinating in the larger space next door, with the civil service convenient to record their votes. The old tent is only kept for a meeting space.

The Assembly of Nine has been meeting in this same place since Nicovar was elected, with the same familiar footprints on the roof. Some careless civil servant made them years ago, walking on the canvas before they raised it, and no amount of rain has washed them out. Nicovar settles himself on the shaded grass.

"I came," he says. "Did you really think I wouldn't?"

Lazarus, Cardinal of Wisdom since Tom retired, leans back against the tent-pole. "Right now, Nicovar, none of us knows what you're going to do. Explain Ankarien, please."

Nicovar makes a sound he can't quite justify as a laugh. "Just Ankarien? You're not worried about the rest?"

"Ankarien is the worst. If you can justify that, the rest will follow. If you can't..."

"You know why I did it. I told you exactly what I was going to do and I told you why. If nothing else, it should prove to you that I'm sincere."

Solomon leans forward to touch his arm. "It's alright, Nic. Some of us are with you."

"Solomon!"

"That's enough, Lazarus. He did tell us, all along, exactly what he was doing. Stop trying to lean on his feelings. They're not going to change your mind."

"They might, if they made any sense. Give me a good reason we shouldn't revoke you, Nicovar."

This time, Nicovar manages laughter. "You can't, Cardinal. Haven't you checked the Constitution recently? It takes the General Assembly to unseat me. I respect your anger, but I question your arithmetic. You don't have the votes."

Cara tips her head back and groans at the muddy ceiling. "Damn you."

"Am I wrong?"

"No, you're not wrong. The General Assembly is divided and won't revoke you without clear guidance from us, and *we* are divided. At my best guess, you've got another season's grace and even then we need to talk Solomon around, and probably Kasia as well."

"And that's why I love the Navarr." Nicovar is fighting it, but the smile is winning out. He's giddy with victory. "Who else would tell me when I'd beaten them?"

"Like you beat Archimedes?"

"That's *enough*, Lazarus."

"No, it's a fair question. Unkindly phrased, but I'll answer the good Cardinal's concerns. I sent the army against Ankarien for the same reason I sent it into Urizen at all: to destroy the libraries of history which are preventing Imperial citizens from achieving their greatest virtue and transcending. I judge it a matter of urgency and I will not wait for the worthies of the Synod to debate what is plainly clear to me. There is no wisdom in delay."

Lazarus flicks his hood a little further forward. Cara huddles in on herself. "Just this once, Nicovar. Just this once. Couldn't you have tried to listen?"

In the crowded Hall of Worlds, Nicovar can feel every gaze turned towards him. All through the counting, through Ruth's familiar announcements and the handful of minor addresses, his skin prickles with the weight of their stares. There's no room to sit, so he stands with his Order and keeps his hands loosely clasped behind him, to keep from fidgeting.

"Antonio, Archmage of Summer," Ruth says. "Speaking on the subject of the destruction of the libraries."

The Summermage is a heavy man, and the ranks of magicians have to shift to let him through. He puts a handful of glittering mana into Ruth's hand before he starts speaking, and she counts it and nods to him.

He tucks his thumbs into his wide belt of office. "Alright," he says. "Alright. To make things clear before we start, my carta formally supports the efforts of the Emperor and I stand with them. This is a discussion, not a battle. I know the Emperor is here somewhere – right, there, thank you – but we heard from you last season, and I assume your position is unchanged?"

"It is," Nicovar says above the heads of the crowd.

"Then if he'll permit it, I'd like to call upon Grandmaster James."

James looks up with surprise. He reaches for his staff instinctively, but it's leaning against the back wall, out of reach. He steps forward instead, between those of his Order who have managed to sit themselves in the front row. "I'll answer what I can, Tonio."

"How bad is the damage to Urizen?"

James rubs his thumb against his lips. "It's bad," he answers. "The army met resistance at basically every spire. Some places it was symbolic, just guarding the books, and they yielded when they were beaten. Some – Some spires have been destroyed. The Great Library at Ankarien is gone."

Angry muttering follows that confirmation. Nicovar catches Archimedes' name amongst the whispers.

Antonio raises a hand from his place in the circle. "My time, please? Thank you. James, I know it's been a point of contention before, but this time, I'm asking you as the Imperial Consort."

Nicovar's pulse thunders in his ears, but James seems unruffled. He only squares his shoulders and says, "Go on?"

"Nicovar is doing something that we may never – already, can never entirely recover from. If this is a mistake, we will never be able to undo it. So knowing that, and knowing his intentions, do you still support him in this?"

"I trust my husband," James says. "But more than that, I trust the Throne. I trust the man who was Archmage of Day, to be the judge of what he has found in that realm. I trust the Emperor to put the Empire first, above me, above Ankarien. Above his own legacy, because the work will not be finished if he is remembered for it. Yes, I support him. I have not seen his visions, I couldn't have written his philosophy. But I stand with Nicovar."

CHAPTER FIFTY-THREE – SUMMER 209

Nicovar runs his fingers across the map. Here is the northern border of Urizen, pressed up against Highguard, where the next stage of the burnings must take place. Spiral is already grey with ashes, from the spring campaign, the soldiers under his command breaking open every spire for the knowledge held caged within. Spiral, and most of Redoubt, and this morning he has bullied the generals into sending a force from Anvil to pacify the Druj on the border. That will free one of the Varushkan armies to join the inward march.

He traces the lines of the rivers. First, Highguard, marching into Casinea along that open trade route and taking in the chapters with the great archives. Then they must skirt the edge of the vallorn in Broceliande and come to the walls of Holberg – but no enemy has ever taken those walls and Nicovar will not try his own forces against that fortress. That must be done with politics, to get the League senators on board, and perhaps their priests. He will talk his way through the unbreachable gates. So to Holberg, but not to attack; down the river instead and towards Miaren. He knows the Navarri soul. They are hoarding books in their forests.

The tokens on the borders have lost their interest for him. Druj and Jotun and Thule, putting their toes across the line to see how fast they can lose them. The Empire has turned them all back a dozen times. This is a new battle, the one they fight with themselves, and Nicovar's blood is singing for the challenge.

From a distant corner of the field he hears the shouting from the Sentinel Gate, the sounds of a victorious return. He is more interested in the long march from Dawn to the Marches, and whether he can spare any armies – persuade any generals – from the western border to turn their soldiers inward for the work.

The Military Council's tent is a heavy green canvas, casting a dim shadow even in the bright midsummer. Nicovar knows when someone comes in by the flash of light through the opening. He doesn't look up until the flap is closed again, to keep his vision clear.

Isaella is still bloodied from the battle. There is dust clinging to her braids, kicked up by heavy boots on the dry border soil. Her dark arms are bare beneath her jerkin. There is a spear in her hand, held at first like a walking stick, but as the tent flap drops behind her she lifts it. Her stance drops to a hunting stalk. The spear's barbed point comes down.

Nicovar's heart kicks. "Oh, my dear," he says, and reaches for the magician's rod in his belt. "You took your time."

Her eyes are dark on his. As he steps away from the map they circle each other, half a turn before her spear lashes out, and he catches it on the length of his weapon, guarding his head. Another strike, another block. Nicovar aims for her shoulder, on the bad side where the old breaks are, and misses by a whisper and the twist of her spine.

Their breathing is heavy in the silent room. Nicovar revels in the chance to match himself against her. He manages a blow to her wrist, sharpened by magic; she knocks the butt of her spear into his knee and he staggers into the table, turning to raise his guard again. Isaella steps too close, turns her spear in a way her weakened wrist cannot quite sustain, and now Nicovar has a moment of leverage and his arms are spread wide, and her spear is flying off into the grass.

He grins. He takes a breath to speak, and only then notices the knife under his ribs.

Isaella doesn't blink as she holds him there, spitted on a blade she has always carried. He brings one hand up to her face, his fingers already numbing from the shock. Dust, in her flying braids.

"I know," she says. "I know. We'll do better next time around."

She pulls the knife away. The heat of the wound spreads through his chest. The world spins.

Nicovar closes his eyes.

Isaella watches the blood spread over the map. It pools in the spaces between the tiles, a stained-glass tracery in brightest red. She sets the bare knife on Nicovar's chest, where the linen is ruined and torn. She leaves her spear on the ground where it fell.

She steps back from him, and waits until she is sure.

There is a whistle hung around her neck, carried by long habit. When the body is pale, beyond the reach of any physick, she lifts it with a hand that does not shake, and blows the alarm.

This tent is pitched on the main street of Anvil, only yards away from the Hub. The militia are the first through the door, with Sally the magistrate close on their heels. They freeze at the sight of the corpse.

Isaella lifts her chin. "The Empress has been murdered."

Sally pushes between her militia. "I see that," she says, and her voice trembles for both of them. "Who killed him?"

"I did."

"Isaella." Sally meets her eyes, her fingers tapping against her sword-hilt. "Am I to understand that you are confessing to the murder of Emperor Nicovar?"

Momentum carried her from battle to this last fight, but it has already faded down to shakiness. Isaella has nothing left for rhetoric. She only nods her head. "I am."

Sally turns her head to the militia. "Lawrence, please ask someone from Ankarien to come and see this. Don't make a big noise. I just want an Urizeni here before we move the body."

"Lucius would be best," Isaella says. "They were close, before all this."

Lawrence sheaths his axe and shakes his head, sorrowful. "I'll get him."

"Isaella, we're going to go next door into the Synod tent, and I'll hold you there for now. Ordinarily – Ordinarily, I would take your oath that you would not try to leave Anvil, and I would give you a militia guard and send you to put your affairs in order. Under the circumstances..." Her gaze slides over to Nicovar, lying in his blood over the map table. "We have had one extra-judicial execution today. I do not want a second. So we'll keep you under watch until it's over. You understand, if you do not seek clemency, the punishment for murder is death."

"I understand. May I have visitors?"

Sally looks relieved. "Yes, of course. When Lawrence gets back I'll send him to find Cara. Unless you'd prefer some other priest?"

This part takes courage. Isaella breathes in deep and finds it. "I'm not going to seek clemency."

"You – Isaella, if you do not there will be nothing I can do. The law requires your execution. But I will be minded to listen to any priest who speaks on your behalf."

"I understand. And I appreciate your willingness. But I don't need a priest today."

She is hustled into the Synod tent, with militia in front and behind. There is already a crowd watching, standing in Trader's Row trying to crane their necks and see what's happening in the military tent. They mutter about the blood spattered over Isaella's arms. One breaks away towards her home camp, looking over her shoulder, trying not to miss anything. The rumours will start soon.

Isaella sits down cross-legged with her back against the pole. Sally looks down at her. She's blinking hard, more than the dust can justify. "So, visitors. You can refuse any of them you like. You have an hour to plead for clemency, after which I will formally sentence you. If there's anyone you need to see, you can ask Lawrence to find them. I expect the news will get out very quickly." She looks at the guards. "I don't want her mobbed, no public spectacle. We'll do this decently. And it's summer, someone get her something to drink. Isaella, I have to put things in order. I'll see you in an hour."

The tent flap closes behind her, and Isaella is alone in the cool white shade.

The first to come is Cara, as Sally promised. She stumps through the door still armoured from the battle, ducking her head to keep her antlers from catching on the canvas. "What the hell, Isaella?"

Isaella shrugs, lifting her hands wide. "What else was there to do?"

"I could name half a dozen things. But really, pick your virtue. Courage, wisdom, vigilance – loyalty – I could make a case for any of those. Vigilance or Wisdom would be best-"

"Didn't Sally tell you?"

Cara glares at her. "She did, and I'm not taking that idiocy seriously. Of course we're pleading for clemency. You did what someone should have done before he sent the armies in, and maybe it should have been you, but it's done now. So all that's left is damage control."

"I've thought about this, Cara. I *can't* plead clemency. I don't want to die, but I have to. It's the only way to avoid starting a trend."

"A trend." Cara's voice goes flat. "You know I can't plead for you unless you agree."

"I know. So give me a hug, if you can bear it. I've had my final battle, love. I'm just waiting to bleed out."

Sveta's entrance is a whirlwind of grief. "I hate you. I hate you so much, I'm so mad you right now!"

"I know."

"How could you *do* this?"

Isaella blinks. "What happened to "he needs to be stopped"?"

"Not that, I don't care about *that*, I mean getting yourself – You shouldn't have done it! When you need someone killed you come to *me!*"

Isaella reaches up to her. Sveta drops to her knees, her chest heaving, hands scrabbling for a grip on the shoulders of Isaella's leather jerkin. Isaella wraps her up in a hug.

"I would never," she says, muffled by Sveta's blouse. "I couldn't. I would have had to turn us both in."

"You could just take the clemency. You don't have to die this way."

"I do." Isaella draws back to smooth Sveta's hair back from her face. "You remember what I told you, about actions having consequences? This is what I meant. I chose my actions. These are the consequences."

"But-"

"If I don't, then history will show it is possible to murder the Throne and get away with it. It doesn't matter what he was doing. Nobody can kill the Throne and live. I can't stick around and be a hero to half the Empire. That's not the kind of hero they need. How can the next Throne do their job, knowing that I might just come along and kill that one too? I have to follow this through. Otherwise, I've done more harm than good."

Sveta shakes her head. There are tears smudging her eyeliner. "That's not true. That can't be true. Clemency – Clemency is *in* the laws. It's in the constitution. It's not breaking any rules to use it."

"It's not against the law. But it wouldn't be right."

Sveta flings her arms around Isaella's neck, and weeps silently into her shoulder.

Isaella is exhausted when Sally returns. She ought to stand, but instead she tips her head back against the tent-pole and looks up at her.

"Several priests have come to me to offer clemency," Sally says. "Are you determined not to accept?"

"Yes, I am."

"Then as the magistrate you confessed to, I am obliged to sentence you to death. In view of the public nature of your crime, we will hold the execution an hour before sunset, to allow the people of the Empire to see it carried out. Until then, I'm going to ask you to stay here. I think if I let you go, you'll either be murdered, or someone will fight the militia trying to rescue you. Do you have any strong feelings on who carries out the sentence?"

Isaella shakes her head. "No, none."

"Then I'll ask for a volunteer from the militia. Anything you need in the meantime, ask your guards. I'll make sure you get a meal. And I shouldn't say this, but I'm glad someone did it."

Kat is eighteen months old and well into the toddling stage. She comes through the tent flap when James opens it for her and stumbles straight over to Isaella. "Mama!"

Isaella gathers her up. She strokes her curly head and listens to her baby babbling, tells her that mama doesn't have any fruit to give her right now. Kat has a straw poppet at her belt and a ragdoll puppy that must be played with.

She puts her chubby hand on Isaella's cheek. "Sad?"

"No, baby lamb. Mama's just tired. There was a battle this morning. Do you want to go and have lunch now?"

Kat shakes her head, firm as only a toddler can be. Isaella ruffles her short hair. "Still, sweetheart, I think you have to go play somewhere else now. Mama needs to have a talk with your dad, okay? Give me a hug and then you can go back to camp? There we go. Hi, baby. Be good for your mama."

She hands her daughter into James' arms, and he steps out for a moment, speaking quietly to someone – Annie, probably – and passing Kat off for a while.

When he comes back, he sits down next to Isaella.

Long moments pass before James speaks. He has to take several breaths before the words will form. "You could have told me."

Isaella looks at her knees. "Would it really have been better? To have your last night with him, knowing what I was planning in the morning?"

He shakes his head. "I don't know. What do I tell Kat, Sal? What on earth do I tell her about you? About him?"

"The truth, I guess. Some version of it. It's not like you can keep it a secret. You can – you can make me the villain. If it's easier."

"I don't want to make either of you that." James shuffles closer and puts an arm around Isaella's shoulders. She leans into him, tears blurring her eyes. "You always said, when you met him, you wanted to fight him."

Isaella nods against his shirt.

"He felt the same. It's -" He breathes for a moment, his warm chest rising under Isaella's cheek. "I don't know if I'll ever forgive you, for making me lose both of you."

"I have to-"

"I know that. I know."

He is still holding her when Sally returns. She waits for him to dry his eyes, to straighten his damp shirt and step out into the golden light. Isaella can't bear to watch him go.

"It's time, citizen."

Isaella's knees crack as she stands. Her wrist is bruised, her leg aches where an orc smashed her with a mace in the battle earlier, but she's whole. She can walk to the Gate.

"There's a crowd," Sally says, "along the road and at the Gate. I'd appreciate it if you didn't rabble-rouse, but legally, I can't stop you from speaking. I could chain you for the journey, but if you give me your word -"

"Of course, you have it. I'm not trying to avoid this."

"Then we'll do this the easy way. Come with me, please."

Sally was not overstating things. All of Anvil seems to have turned out to watch. They line Trader's Row, a whispering mass with their drinks and dinners in hand. There is a silent wall of bodies along the edge of Urizen's camp, and a knot of magicians at the regio, the nations mingled together to mourn the loss of a great mage. The road passes between Highguard and Wintermark, but Isaella couldn't have guessed from the crowd. Everyone is here. She sees every Striding at Anvil turned out to watch her go.

Two hooded priests step into the road. Sally raises her hand and stops the little procession. "Let them do it," she says quietly to her militia, and they relax back from their defensive stances.

Isaella takes three steps forward. It is Solomon and Kasia, the cardinals of Loyalty and Courage. Solomon has a copper bowl of water in his hands.

"You know it's too late to save me," Isaella says.

"We know." Kasia shakes her head. "Friend Isaella, your journey is coming to an end. All that you have done, all that you have been, is behind you now. You pass into the Labyrinth of Ages, and whatever may lie beyond it. If you live again, we will see you again; if you pass beyond life, we will honour your memory. Wash off the dust of the road, and leave behind all that is not Virtue."

"You know I'm not Highborn, right?"

"Just wash your hands and face," Solomon mutters, trying to be stern. He holds the bowl steady and Isaella tries not to splash him, cleaning the dried blood from her hands and wrists. She cups her hands to lift the water to her face.

Kesia sets both hands on her shoulders. "Virtue guide you, my friend."

She kisses Isaella's forehead, and they step back from the road.

It is only a short way from there to the top of the slope where the Sentinel Gate stands, its grey stone warmed by the lowering sun. Isaella turns to look back towards Anvil. She can see faces in the crowd, of magician and priest, of the warriors she has fought alongside. Navarr takes up one edge of the circle. Two familiar figures anchor the other wing, one masked, one bare-faced, with golden bands around their spiralling horns. She cannot look for James. She could not bear to know if he was here.

"It's time," Sally says again. She gestures Isaella forward, into the centre, almost under the arch of the Gate. Lawrence is there, running his fingers restlessly over the haft of his axe.

"I'll be quick," he says gruffly.

Isaella smiles. "That's kind of you."

She looks back over the canvas roofs of Anvil, at the senate bell-tower standing proud in the light. She looks at her own hands, damp and still bloody under the fingernails. Her tongue is silent in her mouth. She lowers herself to her knees, and bows her head.

The axe falls.

LOOK OUT FOR THE NEXT EXCITING
NOVEL FROM THE PEN OF BENEDICT
VON KEIN,

EKATERIN

A TALE OF LOVE AND LOSS IN
MARIIKA'S EMPIRE

PROVENANCE

I am told by a historian of my acquaintance that their most
beloved documents can all be clearly dated from within the text.
I will therefore note that Nicovar reigned from 200 YE (Year of
Empire) to 209 YE, and this work was composed and published
in 382 YE, during the reign of Lisabetta Giacomi von Holberg.
It is my sincere belief that Nicovar and Isaella did live; that
Nicovar became first the Archmage of Day and then the Throne;
that in the last year of his reign he conducted a campaign of
destruction against the great archives of the Empire, including
the library at his home of Ankarien; and that he was murdered by
the Navarri warrior Isaella, who refused clemency and was
executed. Nicovar has since become known as "the Mad", and
Isaella as a shining example of courage, loyalty and vigilance.
For the sake of my friend the historian, I must admit that most of
the rest of the book is fiction.

GLOSSARY

This book was originally written and published within the Empire of the Way, on the Bay of Casinea. In light of its wider circulation, this edition has been supplied with a glossary, to aid the curious foreigner.

The Chalice: One of the constellations understood within the Empire and invoked in magic. The law of the Chalice is "Things come together". A constellation *inverted* may be used to represent its opposite.

The Empire: A united body of ten nations around the Bay of Catazar, governed from Anvil. At the time of Nicovar, the Imperial Orcs had not yet been freed from slavery and the Empire comprised only the nine human nations: the Brass Coast (home of the Freeborn), the Marches, Wintermark, Navarr, the League, Varushka, Dawn, Highguard and Urizen. It is bordered by orcs on all sides: the Jotun in the west, the Thule in the north, the Druj in the east, and the seafaring Grendel to the south. It has trading partners in the nearby human nations of Faraden and the Iron Confederacy.

The Throne: The leader of the Empire in politics, religion and magic. Colloquially, the Throne is referred to as "the Empress". A male Empress is sometimes called an Emperor.

Egregores: Little known outside the Empire, Egregores are distillations of the national spirit. They are responsible for keeping each nation true to its own character and heritage. Anyone wishing to join an Imperial nation (including children seeking adult citizenship) must be found acceptable by the Egregore.

The Way of Virtue: The religion of the Empire and the reason for its founding. A soul which has reached sufficient prowess in one of the Virtues in life may transcend the Labyrinth of Ages (the place inhabited by the dead) and escape the cycle of reincarnation. This basic understanding is shared in several parts of the world, with variations in the lists of virtues. The True Virtues accepted by the Empire are Courage, Vigilance, Wisdom, Pride, Prosperity, Loyalty and Ambition.

True Liao: Consumption of liao enables a priest to perform religious ceremonies such as exorcism. True Liao is a rare refined form of liao which can be used either to grant visions of a person's past lives, or in the creation and removal of permanent spiritual auras.

Paragons and **Exemplars:** Outstanding examples of virtuous living. Paragons are those believed to have transcended. Exemplars are those of lesser stature who are held worthy of emulation.

The Great Dance: The Navarri belief that human souls will seek each other out in each new incarnation and re-enact or continue their relationships from previous lives.

The Realms of Magic: The six realms are a basic fact of magic known throughout the world. Each realm has a consistent nature and empowers similar rituals throughout the world but there is limited agreement on their names; for the sake of clarity the realms are described within this book by their common Imperial names of Spring, Summer, Autumn, Winter, Day and Night.

Eternals: The most powerful magical denizens of the Realms.

Heralds: Subordinate magical creatures, capable of entering the human world.

Lineage: The name given in the Imperial language to the inborn effects of the magical realms upon a human body. Each realm grants different physical characteristics and accompanying mental changes, which may be subtle.
Briar: Touched by Spring, with characteristics of a tree. Lively and vigorous.

Changeling: Touched by Summer. Most have pointed ears, many have antlers or colourful markings on their skin. Bold and fierce.
Cambion: Touched by Autumn. Most have curved goat-like horns, some have golden eyes or maze-like metallic patterns on their skin. Cunning and manipulative.
Draughir: Touched by Winter, with a corpse-like pallor to the skin and sometimes visible black veins. Ruthless and protective.
Merrow: Touched by Day. Almost all have gills, some also have fish-like scales, webbed fingers, or barbels around the mouth. Calm and cerebral.
Naga: Touched by Night. Almost all have snake-like scales upon the face, some also have unusual eyes or a tendency towards sibilance. Passionate and secretive.

Particular Rituals: Several magical rituals are mentioned within this book which may not be familiar to persons outside the Empire. I have summarised them here for convenience.
Rivers Run Red: Spring ritual dramatically increasing the likelihood of infection and disease in a targeted territory, increasing casualties on both sides of any conflict.
Inevitable Collapse into Ruin: Winter ritual to damage or destroy a fortified structure.
All the World in a Grain of Sand: Day curse which exposes the target to a momentary vision of reality as a whole. The vision rapidly fades and the target is unable to recapture or articulate the meaning of what they have seen. The curse lasts for one year and effectively robs the target of their magical mastery.
Eyes of the Sun and Moon / Eye of the High Places: Day rituals revealing the placement of armies and the magical effects in place upon a territory. Used heavily in military scrying.
Clarity of the Master Strategist: Day ritual targeting the general of an army to embue them with tactical brilliance for one season.
Swim Leviathan's Depths: Day ritual summoning the Eternal called Leviathan, whose domain is causation, to answer a single question beginning with "Why".
Twilight Masquerade: Night ritual to change the appearance, including lineage, of a target for one season.

Printed in Great Britain
by Amazon